EMINENCE

DANIELLE KNEUSEL

Contents

To my family, who never made
me feel like perfection was the only option.

"Perfection is achieved, not when there is nothing more to add, but when there is nothing left to take away."

—Antoine de Saint-Exupéry

PROLOGUE

The sky was bright and sunny, feathery clouds floating through the expanse of pristine blue. A gentle wind graced the square, rustling slowly through the gathered crowd. The day was beautiful, lovely—perfect, if you could ignore the screaming.

The crowd shifted uncomfortably at the sound, peering curiously at the single-file line that stretched across the stone platform. It was a neat and orderly line, usually filled with only the quietest of tears and soft murmurs of regret. And yet ... a sharp shrieking noise rang out near the end of the line, cutting sharply into the relative peace of the day. Parents drew their kids closer into their arms, shielding them as the woman thrashed. She appeared rabid, almost feral as she fought against the arms that grasped her, terrible cries escaping through heaving sobs.

"No!" She repeated the word again and again, horrified eyes fixed on a point in the distance. "It can't end this way, it can't..."

Her words trailed off suddenly, as if she had simply forgotten what she meant to say.

"Now you shall go forward peacefully into the Beyond, so you may serve your purpose for Atvas." The booming announcement was eerie as it echoed across the square. The Sovereign bowed his head to the line splayed in front of him, arms open wide. A golden crown lay upon his head, gleaming in the sunlight. "May you live in the beauty of perfection."

The people in line robotically echoed his words back, none daring to look directly at him. None, that is, except for one. The woman continued to screech, long strands of hair whipping across the faces of the guards surrounding her as she turned suddenly. Eyes of dark brown widened, landing on a new target, and her screams cut off suddenly. She had turned not towards the crowd that stared, but rather away from them. She looked toward the backmost area of the stage, where a young girl stood. The girl couldn't have been older than ten, and yet she stood with perfect posture despite the fear filling her green eyes. She flinched imperceptibly as the woman jerked toward her.

"Please," the woman rasped, voice raw from screaming, "don't let them take me!"

The girl merely stared as the woman was dragged away. The crowd didn't notice the girl's quickening breath, or the marks her fingernails left as they dug into the flesh of her palms, or the way she hid her quivering hands behind her back. They noticed only the woman, weeping desperately as the train pulled away, face white as a ghost as she yelled one last time.

"Remember me. Remember us all."

I will, the girl thought silently. *I will remember you.*

1

— · —

Once Upon a Time

My mother once told me that long ago, it was believed that true perfection was unattainable. She sat me down between my lessons and told me of a place of acceptance and hope—a place, she said, where everyone was considered perfect in their own way.

That place was long gone.

Eyes met eyes in the mirror as I stared at my reflection, warped slightly by the moisture exuded from my breath. My voice ricocheted eerily off the ceramic walls, strong and poised as it should be.

"My name is Willow Aldridge, and I am perfect."

The woman who told me stories had become almost as imaginary as the places she'd told me of—a point made all too clear as she stormed into my washroom. The fog quickly receded as a cold gust of clarity streamed in through the open door, and the image in front of me grew sharper.

"Good morning, Mother." My sigh was barely contained as I turned to face the inevitable lecture.

"I see you're not prepared." The disappointed tone of her voice was mirrored on her face, a look so common nowadays that I sometimes wondered if the mother I once knew was merely a dream. "I should hope you understand how important today is, Willow. Today marks the beginning of the Pathway to Perfection—and that shall change every-thing."

She would know. It was a well-known fact that my mother had just barely lost the final round of the competition. One mistake, and her future had changed from Sovereign to Sovereign's wife.

"It is crucial that you pay attention today. It is, after all, your last day in the discipline of Charisma. It'd behoove you to treat it well."

A wave of nausea rose in my chest at her words, a desperate protest against the change. I forced it back down. It was about time that I moved on; I'd been studying Charisma since I turned eight, when all children chose their discipline of focus.

"I understand, Mother." After all, I did. I knew better than anyone how important it was to make a good impression, to go into the Pathway with elegance and grace.

The Pathway to Perfection. It was an ironic name, really—a pleasant cover for the brutal competition it truly was. Dozens of students would participate, originating from any of the five disciplines. The rules to enter were simple: a participant must be seventeen years of age, and they must obtain a Sponsor. This could be any older member of society, so long as they were of a high status. For me, this was my father, the Sovereign himself, but for many, this was not so easy to find. For the next two months, the participants would be examined in all five disciplines—Service, Charisma, Aesthetics, Intellect, and Legality—before competing in one final assessment that would integrate all five.

No doubt, the competition would be taxing and difficult, but the rewards were too tempting to pass up. Achieve any of the ten spots in Court, and I would be slated for a life of wealth, a life of influence and power. Win the number one spot, and I would rule Atvas, as my father had been before me, and his father before him. Win, and make my parents proud. Yet if I lost, if I failed to place in the top ten...

The thought raced through my head ceaselessly, taunting me as I moved through my morning routine. It wasn't until an hour and a half later that I found peace, sitting with my knees tucked to my chest on the ground of the garden. My heart slowed the moment the earthy scent of dirt flooded my system, though I couldn't release the anxiety still pumping through my veins. It was a constant in my life, and the sensation had only intensified in the past few weeks. With talk of the Pathway looming over each lesson and every dinner, it was hard to feel anything other than dread.

"Don't tell me you're pondering the Pathway already." The deep voice sounded from behind me, irritation concealing a layer of what might have been underlying anxiety. "You do know we're not actually getting scored today, right?"

I turned, taking in the figure that strode towards me, tall and classy with a cool sort of stride that I could only hope to one day master. I took the steady hand Auden extended, pulling myself to my feet from the ground.

I hadn't heard him approach—thinking too deeply to notice, as usual. Dirt fell from my skirt, and I brushed it off with a frown. That was the problem with sitting on the ground of the gardens, I supposed, but I didn't mind. The peace and serenity of the leaves that surrounded us, of the cool breeze rustling through the bushes that bore them ... yes, that was worth a little dirt. Sometimes I would sit in the gardens for hours, imagining it as green and blooming as the literature described. A fool's dream, of course; nature had lost its vibrance long ago, back when the Olden World fell into ruin. Some bio-attack or another, when science overtook nature at last. Not that I knew much about that. Perhaps I would, had I studied Intellect. Another fool's dream.

Sometimes I wished I had the luxury of being foolish.

"You know, there's a bench for a reason," Auden murmured, tracking my hands as I brushed the dirt from my fine clothing. I glanced at the bench in question, an uncomfortable mesh of wire and stone that I avoided at all costs. Besides the obvious discomfort, it made me feel … disconnected, as if I were on the outside looking in. I already felt that way far too often. I knew I couldn't say this to Auden, though; he could never understand.

"What's the point of visiting the gardens if you're not willing to get a little messy?" I said instead as we wove carefully through the Palace grounds, moving steadily towards the main road.

"I'm not sure there's much of a point to visiting the gardens at all." His voice was joking, yet I knew he meant it. Auden was a true discipline of Charisma, dutifully practical to whatever end. He always had been, from the day we first met as young children. Poised, pragmatic, perfect—that's who Auden was.

That's who I should be, too.

"It's pretty." It was an oversimplification of what the gardens were to me, of the way they made me feel.

"It's a lump of brown plants."

I didn't bother replying to that. It was true that the gardens were nearly all faded, decayed beyond recognition, and yet … I couldn't help but find them breathtaking. Sometimes, I'd spot a green leaf, as vibrant and beautiful as I had ever dreamed. It reminded me of the way the world once was, in the stories from so long ago.

"Perhaps you should have studied Service," Auden laughed as I scowled back at him. "Then you'd have plenty of opportunities to play in the dirt."

"Oh, because you can see me slaving away in the kitchens?" I challenged, raising a brow. I knew he was joking, but it grated on me nonetheless. Those in Service were so far from the future I hoped to obtain, so far below the status of the Court, that it was hard to see it as anything but an insult. The Court was comprised of the top ten members of each Pathway to Perfection, and the discipline of Service... Well, it was defined by serving others. They couldn't be more different.

Not that Service had ever been an option for me, anyways. I was to study Charisma; that much I had always known. Everyone knew that disciplines of Charisma won the Pathway more often than any other discipline.

"Perhaps you should learn some Service." My words were sharp, and yet I couldn't convince myself to soften them. I had never quite grasped the silver tongue of Charisma—not in the way Auden had. "You'll need it if you hope to do well in the Pathway."

"There you go again with the Pathway," he sighed. "I'm already sick of it, and it hasn't even begun."

"The Pathway determines our future," I pointed out, irritation still evident in my tone. "It's the most important thing we'll ever do."

Auden laughed, a sharp sound that felt more like an expression of pain than mirth. "Oh, I know. It's all my father talks about these days."

I cringed at the dark undertone in his voice, annoyance begrudgingly fading. It was no secret that Auden's father was intense at best, a disgruntled man who had missed the opportunity to become Sovereign by only a year. Despite him placing first in his own Pathway, a new Sovereign was only chosen once every eighteen years—which, unfortunately for Ruben

Bonavich, happened to be a year before his competition. He'd never gotten past it, bitter and unsatisfied. Despite being made my father's closest advisor and earning himself a small fortune, he never forgot his dream of having a Bonavich on the throne. And so, he'd had Auden.

Despite all assurances that it was a mere coincidence, the timing of Auden's birth was no accident. Another thing we had in common; we were both bred for the Pathway, every detail of our lives carefully cultivated for the Sovereignty. We were destined to be rivals, two Sovereigns forged for one throne. As much as my mother pushed me towards perfection, Ruben pushed Auden harder. I could see it in even now in his posture, in the clenching of his jaw, in the furrow of his brow.

"Only two months more," I reminded him, offering what I hoped was an encouraging smile. I never was very good at comforting people, always unsure of what to say—yet another reason to doubt my placement in Charisma. Auden smiled back anyway, a fake sort of smile that was clearly for my own benefit, but I appreciated it nonetheless. I was lucky to have him, not only as a friend and rival but also as my whole future. For at the end of these two months, when the Pathway was completed, we'd be married.

I knew that people used to choose their own partners, back in the Olden Days. It was an inefficient practice that led only to messy divorce and divided families, and one that was ended decades ago. In Atvas, citizens were paired at age eighteen according to scores. For those not going through the Pathway, this was merely the member of the opposite gender closest in P-score. For myself and the other Pathway participants, it would be determined by rank. Seeing as Auden and I were almost certainly going to be the top two placements, our marriage was more than likely. It was practically inevitable. Friend, rival, betrothed—we were so much to each other, Auden and me.

The scores were a tradition borrowed from the academics of Olden North America, in which a score quantified their success in academia. Of course, that was back when everyone sought to achieve only mediocracy in all subjects. They would study aspects of all the disciplines, as if they could hone them all at once. Luckily, we knew better. Perfection could be reached only through society as a whole, and those select few who were able to perfect all five disciplines. Those like me. Now, our P-scores ranged from 0.0 to 5.0, based entirely on our performance in our area of discipline.

A soft sigh left my lips as we neared the buildings where lessons were held. They leered down at us, impressive compared to their run-down surroundings. When the first citizens of Atvas had arrived, the entire city had been practically rubble. It had been an *exhibit*, where the Oldens had come to admire the ways of tradition. Why they bothered to admire what they themselves had destroyed, I didn't know. It had taken years to rebuild the city, a process still well underway. Some areas had been restored to their former glory—the Palace and the school building in-cluded—while others remained the rubble the Oldens had so adored.

We passed through the arched passageways, stopping in the large courtyard. It was packed, its stone benches crammed with students. Many even sat on the ground, splayed out on the cracked stone as if it were a luxurious settee. While we weren't mandated to sit within our disciplines, most did. It was with them that we spent the most time, made the most connections, and had the most in common.

It took only a glance to tell which discipline was which. Around the edges of the yard sat the Intellect students, talking quietly amongst themselves with books open on their laps. They drew no attention to themselves, yet still I couldn't look away. Legality was crowded around two tables, a tight-knit unit as usual. They always seemed to be discussing something serious, though no one could guess what with how secretive Legality students were. Service, of course, was spread across the back, rowdy voices contributing to the fray. I saw a dark haired boy shove his friend lightly, who in turn retaliated with a good-hearted punch to his shoulder. What they had to be so abhorrently enthusiastic about at this time of the morning, I couldn't begin to imagine.

Aesthetics, unsurprisingly, was monopolizing a cluster of benches near the center of the yard. A few of them had spread blankets on the ground, all wide smiles and soft giggles. Many, Auden included, looked down on Aesthetics for their softness. It certainly seemed a silly field, concerned mainly with arts and beauty, and I had to admit I had little interest in it myself. Despite my love for my gardens, I could never handle the delicate intricacies of Aesthetics. Yet I knew there was power in it all the same. My mother herself was originally in the Aesthetics discipline, and she'd managed to earn the second spot in her own Pathway to Perfection.

"Beauty is a weapon," she'd once told me, back in the days when I knew little about this world. "Learn to use it correctly, and you'll be practically unstoppable."

But there were many different weapons to wield in this world—the trick was learning how to balance them all at once.

Auden and I wove through the crowd to the front row, where the Charisma students sat. It appeared that a hearty debate was occurring, as was so often the case in the discipline of Charisma. They bored me to no end. We already debated enough in classes, and I saw no particular reason to do so outside as well. Besides, all that rhetoric and abrasive tone irritated me, the way that the smallest change in words could cost you the argument altogether.

Not that I would ever say that aloud.

I tried not to let my eyes drift to where the Intellect students sat, surely discussing the wonders of our universe. Intellect discussions were always about the material itself, rather than the way you presented the information. Quiet, respectful discussion about fascinating material—now *that* I could get into.

"Oh, please tell me we're discussing the fallacies of the Olden individualistic tendencies," Auden quipped, sliding into an empty seat. The girl next to him, Lina Portley, glared, giving me the distinct impression that she had been saving the seat for another. She didn't dare reprimand him, though; smart, considering it was the day of the Sponsor Ball. After tonight, the Sponsors would be set and would not change, but until then, they could withdraw at any moment. To anger Auden or me, with our parents being so influential... Well, it wouldn't do much good for her reputation.

"Feeling prepared for the Sponsor's Ball tonight?" The voice came from the other side of the girl, but I knew the source without even looking. I leaned forward anyway, turning towards the question. She didn't say my name, but she didn't need to; Emmaline always seemed to be focused on me, in some way or another. Sure enough, her blue eyes bored into me, bitterly sharp despite the soft smile that graced her delicate features.

"*Prepared*," she'd said. Not excited, nervous, or anxious. *Prepared*. Coming from another discipline, I may have taken it as a mistake, but not from Emmaline; she knew the power of a simple word as well as any Charisma. As well as I did.

"Of course," I said, keeping my voice light yet lofty. "It'd be hard not to, with the Service setting up my home already. The Palace, I mean."

Subtle yet overt, my words hit in just the way I knew they would, and she glanced away with a clenched jaw. Strange how words can do that. One simple reminder, and even the most stubborn of wills can be bent.

It wasn't as if I enjoyed the way her eyes flashed in jealousy, or the brief fear that crossed her face. It was a necessary exchange, out of self-preservation more than malice. It was as my father had always told me: "Relax for one moment, and off the ladder you will fall." Besides, Emmaline had always had a habit of going out of her way to demean me, subtly invalidating me at every opportunity. It was as if we were rivals in some sort of game, except she was the only one playing. I'd never much cared—her P-score was far below mine, so she'd never been much of a threat.

My thoughts were interrupted by a hush falling over the crowd, spreading rapidly as an older man crossed into the stage-like space in front of us. I recognized him vaguely: Councilman Mullerson, a member of the Court who had been selected for my father's small Council. The Court, comprised of the top ten participants in each Pathway to Perfection, was an elite group as it was. To be one of the four members selected for the Sovereign's Council was the highest honor and greatest prestige.

Murmurs began to spread through the crowd, many amazed by his presence. It was rare for Council members to speak at assemblies such as this, usually leaving it to lower-ranked officials. Even the Legality disciplines seemed awed, their normally guarded faces morphing into something like astonishment. It was strange to see such an expression on them; they were so intense and serious, I often wondered if they smiled at all. I knew it was part of their dogma—protectors of Atvas and all that—but honestly, it was boring.

"Children of Atvas!" Councilman Mullerson addressed us, voice ringing throughout the Courtyard despite his brittle appearance. "For many of you, today is a day like all others, unremarkable in every way. Yet for some, this marks the start of a new journey. Indeed, the moment you've anticipated has come at last." He paused for a moment, as if to create suspense. "For tonight marks the start of a very special event. For the first time in a quarter of a century, the Pathway to Perfection will result in a Sovereign! That's right, my children: the future of Atvas stands among you!"

Applause erupted around the courtyard—as if this were new information to any of us. I clapped all the same, face calm despite the many eyes upon me at his words.

"Any one of you may enter, from any discipline, so long as you obtain a Sponsor by the Sponsor Ball, held this evening at the Palace. As always, a Sponsor may only sponsor a single participant. This Sponsor must be above the age of eighteen and deemed worthy by the Sovereign's personal Council. Due to the special circumstances surrounding this year's competition, the Council has decided that a Sponsor must hold a P-score of 4.5 or higher."

Now, *that* was news. Usually, Sponsors only had to have a P-score of 3.5 or higher. Murmurs erupted across the space in a wave, shock and discontentment rising. It was hardly an unexpected reaction; many would be left with no Sponsor at the last minute. I glanced at Emmaline. She remained silent, every part of her relaxed in a way that suggested indifference—and yet the nails digging into her palm told a different story. With such little time left, many would be forced to withdraw from the competition. I could only hope she was included. I hid a smile as I glanced forward once more to where the man stood silently.

Councilman Mullerson hushed the crowd, continuing as though he hadn't just shattered the dreams of many. "Sponsors will be presented tonight, along with their candidate, at the Sponsor's Ball. Any who hope to compete must sign up and find a Sponsor before then, for afterward ... the annual Pathway to Perfection shall begin!"

A shudder raced through me at his words. *Eighteen years of work, eighteen years of pretending, all for one competition—and it starts tonight.*

2

THE FLAWED AND THE FREE

As with any event worth anticipating, each hour leading up to the Sponsor's Ball felt impossibly long. Lessons dragged on, boring despite the upbeat ambiance of our final day. Those not participating in the Pathway would continue attending classes, but that would be so few of us. Charisma was the most represented discipline in the Pathway each year, and this one was winding up to be no different.

I was halfway through my last class of the day, though I honestly couldn't recall a word uttered during it, when a knock sounded on the door.

"Come in," our instructor called, looking rather annoyed. Interruptions were never welcome in class, and especially not while the Director was there. Each discipline had a single Director, who served as head of the instructors and was selected the same year as the Sovereign. The highest-ranked nonparticipant in the Pathway would be selected for the job, as it was the most prestigious of all non-Court positions. Phillip Edrikson, the Director of Charisma, split his time between all of the Charisma classes, though he'd visited ours most often recently. It was hardly a surprise, given that many of us would be entering the Pathway to Perfection tonight.

"Sorry!" a bright voice called, the accompanying girl sticking her head in with an apologetic smile. It was a conscious effort not to let my jaw drop at the sight of her familiar black hair and dark olive skin. "I've been sent to fetch Willow Aldridge."

I can't believe it, I thought deliriously.

"Sent?" Director Edrikson cut in, brows furrowed. "By whom?"

"The Sovereign," she answered casually, ignoring how the others shifted and murmured at the words. "He's here, you see, and requires his daughter's assistance."

"And who are you?"

"Vi DeLoughery, sir." She grinned. "Discipline of Aesthetics, if you couldn't tell."

The class let out a titter of laughter at that. Even I had to fight to hide a huffed laugh, the joke distracting me from my annoyance. Her unyielding confidence didn't waver for a moment, even as Director Edrikson looked her over with a suspicious glance. She merely stood up straighter, flipped a lock of glossy hair over her shoulder, and glanced at me meaningfully as if to say, *"Aren't you going to help me out?"*

I sighed, relenting at last. I knew I would be pulled into this, whether I liked it or not. Vi had always found a way to drag me into trouble, from the moment I'd met her eight years ago. Seven years old and already obsessed with proving myself, I was quick to introduce myself to the Court-born girl I was seated next to—a girl whom I expected to possess the same poise and sophistication as myself. It didn't take long for that illusion to fade. Despite their high standing in society, her parents had raised her with little regard for Atvas and its rules. Vi got me into trouble often; and yet, like a moth to flame, I could never quite pull myself away.

"Oh," I said, widening my eyes as if in great distress. "I completely forgot to tell you. My father wishes me to help with the..." my voice faded off, and I made a show of glancing at my classmates. "Well, you know."

He couldn't possibly know, seeing as there was nothing *to* know, but that hardly mattered. Pride was what drove men like Director Edrikson. He would never dare admit he didn't know about a highly classified government matter.

"Yes... yes, that's right," he said at last, looking for all the world like a man well-informed. "Go ahead, Miss Aldridge, but please do inform me next time."

"Of course," I promised, gathering my belongings with shaky hands.

I brushed by Vi with hardly a glance, ignoring her wide grin and raised brows as she followed me out. Neither of us spoke until we were down the hall and around a corner, knowing from experience just how far voices carried on the stone.

"You know, you're getting better at that," she commented with a hint of pride. "It's actually kind of scary."

I whirled on her, arms crossed over my chest. "Are you *insane?* That was my last class before the Pathway."

"Don't start with that. I'm sick of that word already." She rolled her eyes. "Besides, it's not like you were paying attention anyhow."

"That's not the point," I sighed, massaging my temples with one hand. "What if we'd been caught? I can't afford a rebellious reputation right now."

"I don't think you have to worry about that." She huffed out a laugh, as if the thought itself was hilarious.

"It's not funny," I reminded her. "This is our future you're talking about."

"Your future. Not mine."

Not hers, because she wouldn't be competing in the Pathway to Perfection. Instead she would join our other peers who wouldn't be participating, either by choice or due to failure to find a Sponsor. Those not competing would continue in their studies, aiming to achieve a higher P-score than the others so that they might be assigned the best jobs. The best jobs besides a position in the Court, that is. I couldn't imagine accepting such a mediocre future, especially if I had the sort of natural talent she did—but then again, it was Vi. She simply didn't care for prestige.

"Come on," she urged, grasping my hand to pull me behind her. "We've got investigating to do."

I huffed indignantly. "I still don't understand why we couldn't do this in an hour."

Vi merely turned around, looking me right in the eyes, and said: "Because your father is *actually* here, and he's angry. Now do you want to find out why or not?"

With that, I stopped complaining and followed her.

We heard the hushed voices before we saw them, my father's ringing out over the others. Pausing at the corner, I risked only a glance at the group. My father was there as promised, speaking to a frazzled-looking Councilman Mullerson. Beside them stood Ruben Bonavich, Auden's father.

"-we already raised the P-score requirement," Councilman Mullerson was saying in a nervous tone. "We can't discriminate based on... personal factors."

"Personal factors?" Yes, that was my father's booming voice, and it was as angry as promised. It was enough to pique my curiosity, to push my feet an inch closer. My father was not an angry man. Cold, somewhat intimidating—but rarely angry. For him to sound so enraged, something big must have occurred. "This is a matter of state security, Mullerson."

"I understand that, but..."

"Do you?" Ruben interrupted, voice low and slippery. "It sounds to me like you're questioning the orders of your Sovereign."

There was a moment of silence as the accusation rang through the hallway.

"All I'm saying," Mullerson continued, and I had to give him credit for the steel in his voice, "is that you put me in charge of the Pathway to Perfection. I am merely trying to act in its best interests."

I inched forward, so eager to hear my father's reply that I failed to pay attention to what was in front of me. I hardly noticed the sting in my thigh as I bumped into the pillar, hardly noticed anything but the panic that arose in me as my boot made a sharp *thunk* on the stone.

Vi and I froze, eyes meeting frantically. The voices stopped, replaced by the daunting sound of approaching footsteps. "Who's there?"

"What do we do?" I mouthed. Vi's eyes darted between us and the hallway beyond before she moved suddenly, linking an arm in mine and yanking me towards the center of the walkway.

"Oh!" she exclaimed loudly, dragging me around the corner and directly into their group. "There you are, Mr. A."

He frowned, his face a web of stress and fading fury. "What are you two doing here?"

"Yes," Ruben murmured behind him, eyes narrowed. "What *are* you doing here?"

Vi looked at me, clearly out of ideas. I gaped for a moment, grasping desperately for any excuse to be out of class and down this particular hallway.

"We, uh... we were sent here," I started slowly, copying Vi's earlier excuse. "By Director Edrikson. He wanted us to...uh...."

"...to ask Councilman Mullerson about the Pathway paperwork," Vi finished for me, a smooth smile pasted on her face. Honestly, sometimes I thought she was better suited to Charisma than I was. "There was some debate about the deadline with the changed rules, you see. Will those unable to find a new Sponsor have additional time to complete it?"

I hardly dared to breathe as they took in our rambling excuse, their suspicious expressions dimming to a faint annoyance.

"The deadline stands," Councilman Mullerson said, waving a hand. "No exceptions."

"Great," Vi said, pulling me to leave. "We'll tell him right away."

We made it all of three steps before a smooth voice stopped us, soft but deadly. "Wait."

Ruben Bonavich always could be counted on to ruin a good thing.

"Strange that Director Edrikson would send both of you," Ruben drawled. "Considering that Miss DeLoughery is a discipline of Aesthetics."

"Alright, fine." Vi made a show of sighing, the picture of a person caught red handed. "I was skipping class, okay? Willow just ran into me on her way to find you, that's all. I was bored and begged her to tag along."

"Willow?" my father asked, brows high and eyes searching my face intently. "Is this true?"

I opened my mouth to disagree, to take the blame that was rightly owed to me. After all, I had chosen to go along with it, had willingly followed Vi out of the classroom and to this hallway. But...well, it *had* been her idea. Besides, she was solidly in the top of Aesthetics and wasn't going through the Pathway—a small infraction would barely touch her position.

"Yes," I breathed, hating myself more with each word. "Yes, that's what happened."

My father peered down at us both, seeming very tall and imposing. Of course, he'd always been tall and imposing to me, both in stature and power. "Very well, then. Violetta, your Director will handle your discipline."

Vi flinched at the full name she despised, but nodded her obedience. "Yes, sir. Sounds riveting."

Punishment, like many aspects of our lives, was decided almost entirely within our own discipline. The punishment for a particular infraction was not the same across disciplines, just as values were not the same. Lying, for example, was utterly intolerable in an obedience-driven discipline like Legality. But in Charisma? You may even be rewarded, if it was done well enough.

"Run along, then," my father said, not unkindly. "We must return to our business."

I wanted to point out that it would be my business soon, and that it would be nice to be involved in the affairs of Atvas since I hoped to run it one day. Perhaps I would have said as much, had Vi not pulled me away. We didn't dare break character until we'd rounded two corners, coming to an empty alcove. Vi collapsed instantly on the stone bench, but I felt no such relief.

"There's no chance they believed us," I said instantly, pacing back and forth as my mind whirred. It was not so bad for Councilman Mullerson to know; despite being a Council member and in charge of the Pathway, he didn't have any real sway. And though my heart was heavy at my father's inevitable disappointment, I could at least count on his desire to preserve our legacy. But Ruben...

"Willow, it'll be fine," Vi sighed, watching me pace with a familiar pity. It wasn't the first time she'd seen me in such a frenzy, and I doubted it would be the last. Honestly, it was what I valued so much about our friendship. I couldn't show this sort of weakness in front of my parents, and I didn't dare show it to Auden. Not with our deep-seated rivalry. But with Vi there was no shame, no need to hide what I truly felt. "I doubt any of them cared."

"I'm sure Ruben Bonavich very much cared." I murmured, teeth sinking brutally into my bottom lip. I realized it only when I tasted iron, a familiar signal to calm down.

"I'm sure Ruben did the same as a child. They probably all did."

I shook my head furiously, making the dangling pearl earrings rattle. "Not my father. He's perfect."

"I didn't say he wasn't," she answered carefully. But of course she would—to say anything different would be treason. "But he's human, Willow. So are you."

I huffed a disbelieving laugh, resisting the urge to rub my eyes in exhaustion. It would only mess up the makeup. "You don't understand."

The words settled uncomfortably in the space between us, for we both knew them to be true. Vi was raised on family and laughter, fed fables of freedom and individuality. She could never understand what it was like to be me, and I would never know what it was like to be her. We were born to the same Court, bred in the same life—and yet, we lived in different worlds.

"I can't believe you called my father 'Mr. A,'" I broke the silence finally, shaking my head lightly.

She glanced up from the bench on which she sat, brows furrowed in genuine confusion. Vi had always been casual with my father, with any authority figure really. "Well, what else would I call him?"

"Oh, I don't know. Maybe the *Sovereign*?" I replied, laughing lightly as I plopped down beside her. Vi just frowned, making a face that suggested she had no interest in that.

"I wish you the dearest of greetings, Your Sovereigness," she spoke in a lofty, overdone accent. "If you should deign speak with a wretched soul like me, I have only the grandest of news for you."

"Ah," I replied, "but you've forgotten to kiss my boots before speaking!"

It was these moments I treasured with Vi, I realized as the sound of our laughter echoed through the corridor—these moments of youthful freedom.

"There you are, I..." Auden's voice cut off as he rounded the corner entirely, brows raising as he took in the scene before him. "Am I interrupting something?"

I clapped a hand over my mouth, stifling the giggles that lingered there, but Vi's face had gone blank. She stared Auden down, as if hoping to burn him to the ground with one look.

"No," I gasped, still short of breath. "Vi just called my dad 'Mr. A,' and then I asked if she knew if he was the Sovereign, and then..." I stopped speaking, frowning as my words fell on deaf ears. Vi and Auden were still staring at each other resolutely, as if answering some unspoken challenge. Auden and Vi had never quite gotten along, despite my best efforts.

"Oh, never mind," I said at last, grabbing Auden's arm to steer him away. "Let's just go." I waved goodbye to Vi, but I wasn't sure she even saw, as she was glaring sullenly at the ground. I rolled my eyes as Auden and I bustled down the hall. We always walked home together, partly because his manor was so close to the Palace and partly because neither of us liked to be left alone to our thoughts. Especially not now, with the Pathway looming like a monster in the dark.

"What's got you all worked up?" he asked, as if it were my fault that I was perpetually caught in the middle of my two closest friends.

"Would it kill you to be friendly?" I groaned, whirling around to glare at him.

Auden frowned at my words, brow furrowed in what seemed like confusion as he replied, "I wasn't *un*friendly."

I just shook my head, looking away. It was ridiculous, really. Of course Vi and Auden wouldn't get along—they're practically opposites, like fire and ice. But still ... was it really so hard to pretend, if only for the few times they actually saw each other?

"What did your father want, anyways?" Auden asked, drawing my thoughts away from the subject.

I snorted. "My father never asked for me. Vi was just being Vi, that's all."

He stopped walking, frowning. "Again? I thought you said she would stop involving you in her schemes."

"I know," I sighed, feeling the sudden urge to defend the very thing I was attacking Vi over earlier. "But this time was different. Wait until you hear what we found out."

I told him what we'd overheard as we resumed walking, from Councilman Mullerson's odd insistence to my father's rare fury. I didn't mention the part where they'd caught us, or the interaction after, if only because I wasn't interested in the "I told you so" I knew I'd receive.

"Do you have any idea what they were talking about?" I asked. "My father said it was a matter of state security, but then why haven't we heard about it?"

Auden contemplated this, face twisting the way it always did when he was thinking hard. I knew every expression of his, knew him like the back of my hand. It was the inevitable result of life-long friendship—and life-long rivalry. Neither of us ever stopped watching the other, not really. "Now that you mention it... my father was riled up last night. Something about a break in at the Palace. A *Service* discipline, apparently."

My blood froze in my skin. "The Palace?"

"I know," he replied, sensing the concern in my eyes. "I was worried about you, but my father said it's been dealt with. Apparently, the Service kid had intended to go through the Pathway—that's why they changed the rules. Their P-score was lowered two points, of course."

I winced despite myself. Two full points was a major setback, more than enough to doom someone for good. To have a lowered P-score was a serious matter, you see—for those who didn't go through the Pathway weren't guaranteed a place in Atvas any more than I was.

Anyone who scored in the bottom half of their discipline by age eighteen would be determined Flawed and cast out of Atvas, alongside all but the top ten participants of the Pathway. They were sent to the Beyond, the wasteland that was once North America, to live out the rest of their days in a society less sophisticated than our own. When I had first learned of the process, I was confused; in the naïve mind of a child, the separation didn't make sense.

When I asked my father why, he had merely shaken his head. *"We simply cannot support those who aren't going to contribute to our society,"* he'd stated. He had plucked a flower from the dirt, the faintest tint of purple visible on the petals, and displayed it to me. *"Just like a weed: allow them on our land, and they will destroy all that we have accomplished."* And with that, he crushed the flower between his fingers and let it fall to the ground.

Of course, that was back when my father cared to pay me any attention at all.

"Serves them right, if you ask me," Auden continued, yanking me back to the present. "I mean, that's your home that they're threatening. You ought to be careful on the grounds. Perhaps you should bring guards when you go to the gardens."

I raised a brow. "You're really upset about this, aren't you?"

His jaw was tight as he replied. "No one should feel unsafe in their own home."

"I'll be fine," I reassured him. "I have the best of Legality protecting me, remember?"

His dubious look made it clear just how much he trusted that, but he said nothing more about it.

"Besides," I added, glancing around cautiously, "I'd be better off worrying about Emmaline. She would stab me in my sleep in an *instant*."

He laughed at that, a light sound that seemed to brighten the mood. "She's harmless."

"Harmless?" I scoffed. "She's our competitor now."

"Oh, please. We both know she'll be nowhere near the Sovereignty. Besides, you can hardly blame her for being jealous."

"You think it's *my* fault?" I tried to keep the edge out of my voice, but it was hard. Anything that implied sympathy for that wannabe was practically a betrayal in my mind.

"I didn't mean it like that," he sighed, raising his hands in mock surrender. "It's just... Of course Emmaline envies you. You have everything she could possibly want."

"Still, she isn't rude to you," I mumbled, belligerent despite the truth in his words. "And she ought to envy you just as much."

Auden laughed, shaking his head as if I'd said the funniest thing. "Please," he scoffed softly, eyes filled with a strange emotion that was somewhere between anger and sadness. "No one envies me."

I opened my mouth to tell him that I did—that I could only dream of being as composed as he always seemed to be, of having words flow from my tongue like water—but he changed the subject before I had the chance. I frowned as he spoke, but the moment was clearly over. There was little use in bringing it back up.

My brow grew oily as we walked, sweat dotting my skin despite the cool breeze. I'd once heard that people used to drive everywhere—another bad habit that had been broken since the decline of the Olden World. Why they had ever wasted precious resources to travel when we were born with perfectly good legs, I couldn't fathom. Although I'd once read that people used to travel thousands of miles at a time, so perhaps that was the reason; I wouldn't know. I'd never left the haven of Atvas, nor had anyone else here. My family owned a car, but it was to be used only for special occasions, and I could count the number of times I'd been in it on one hand.

"I wonder who will find a Sponsor in time," Auden mused suddenly, his mind clearly still on the Pathway. I felt suddenly ashamed of my own thoughts; there wasn't time to be daydreaming about the past, not when I should be focusing on my future. "With the rule change, I mean."

"I wonder who *won't*," I answered, thinking of Emmaline. "Hopefully, it'll knock some competitors out right away."

Auden hummed in agreement. "Luckily, it won't be an issue for us."

Just as my father would be Sponsoring me, Auden's father was to Sponsor him. There was always a fair amount of attention paid to us, but when we were announced tonight, there would be far more. Everyone knew we were the top contenders for Sovereign, and every move would be scrutinized tonight.

Auden bumped his shoulder against mine gently, dimples showing as he smiled. "No need to look so concerned. We were born for this."

"I know," I replied, voice coming out far more certain than I felt.

The sureness of my voice did nothing to soothe the rapid beating of my heart, and I rushed through the Palace upon arriving. There was much to prepare for this evening, but it would have to wait. I stopped at last in front of a large oak door, pushing it open with a desperate sort of gusto. My shoulders relaxed almost instantly as the smell tickled my nose—that musty sort of smell that only books could produce. The Palace library towered in front of me, stacks of books winding around the space. A genuine smile graced my face as I inhaled deeply, savoring the scent of books and ink.

The library was by far my favorite room of the house, if only because of the memories associated with it. A shy, scrawny child with a freckled face and a curious spirit, I was far from the perfect child my parents so desired. Intellect came the easiest to me of all the disciplines, and the time I spent studying in this room had been a welcome break from the pressure of mastering the others. Most children focused only on one discipline, that which they hoped to choose at age eight—yet I was not most children, as my mother reminded me constantly. I had trained for the Pathway long before choosing my discipline, as did many of the children I was to compete against.

I sat for hours in the peaceful quiet, lost in the depths of a history book. I sometimes wished to have books from the Olden days, tattered and withered and filled with stories of different worlds. But those were long gone—lost in the war, like so much else. All the history books in our library had been written back when Atvas was founded, by those who remembered the days before. I could lose myself in them for hours, intriguing as they were. The Olden World may have been foolish and inefficient, but it was *fascinating*. All those cities, all those places that once existed… It was overwhelming to even think about. It was there that I envisioned myself as I read that afternoon, losing myself in the pages and ink. It wasn't until hours later that I came back to myself, a noise near the doorway jolting me from my reverie.

"Sorry, milady," the woman muttered as she entered, a maid whom I vaguely recognized. *Risa*, I reminded myself. "Your mother has requested that I remind you of the time, just in case you forgot."

I frowned, my surroundings seeming to reappear to me all at once. A ray of deep golden sunlight streamed through the window, falling upon the dimly lit space. Finally, my eyes moved to the clock, and I jumped out of my chair.

"It's five o'clock?" I asked, voice high. Risa just nodded, watching silently as I frantically gathered the books into my arms. I had to be ready for the Sponsor's Ball in only an hour—far too little time to look as composed as I needed to.

"Miss, I can help—"

I was shaking my head before her words were out, and Risa hardly seemed surprised. Many women of the Court had adapted to the Olden tradition of having ladies-in-waiting, but my mother had always insisted that I take care of myself. It would help with my Aesthetics training, she'd claimed.

The Palace was bustling with activity, the festivities nearly ready to begin. I almost groaned as bustled into the dressing room and caught a glimpse of my appearance, amplified in the mirrors. I was a disheveled mess, to say the least.

Appearance was a funny thing; one might think it mattered only for Aesthetics, but really, each discipline had its preferences for appearance. For Charisma, that generally included looking as put-together and professional as possible, but tonight was different. For tonight, I was no longer a discipline of Charisma, but rather a competitor in the Pathway to Perfection. I had to look mature, composed, pretty, simple, and severe all at once. In other words, I had to look perfect... as if that were possible with only an hour's time.

I needn't have worried; my gown did everything for me. I knew my mother had spent weeks designing it, but I hadn't been able to bring myself to look at it until that night—as if by looking at it, I had to accept that it was real. The Pathway to Perfection was starting at last.

The gown was a deep emerald, with a full silk skirt cascading from a bodice of matching lace flowers that stemmed into lace sleeves, which came to rest just off my shoulders. My hair fell where the sleeves might have been, a cascade of loose curls with only the front pulled back into a simple braid. I grinned at the girl in the mirror. She was pretty, sure, but she was also serious—a courtier, but also a competitor. Just as I would become, starting tonight.

3

THE BEGINNING OF AN END

The chandeliers glimmered from the vaulted ceilings, seeming to scatter gold beams into the crowd of people below. And the people... A sea of glittering gems in a rainbow of hues, they seemed to glow as they moved, casting a shine of beauty over the entire room. Of course, tonight the crowd was tainted, less beautiful than usual. Most balls were held strictly for the Court and their guests, all high-standing members of Atvas decked out in luxury. Today, all Sponsors and contenders were required to present themselves to the Court, marking the official start of the Pathway to Perfection. The newcomers were obvious, not because they were unattractive but rather because of the way they held themselves. They gaped at *everything*, fidgeting awkwardly with the comparatively cheap fabrics they wore. Still, I smiled at them as I descended the grand staircase, molding my face into the gracious expression I'd mastered so long ago.

"Stay confident, but be kind," my mother had always said.

"They already know you're superior to them," my father would add. "What they need is to think that *you* don't know it."

So, I nodded my head to those I passed, greeting people with every step, and tried my best not to look too pleased with the compliments I could hear from every direction. Any Charisma knew the danger that flattery could present. Be that as it may, no amount of wisdom or Courtly manners could suppress the pride that grew in my chest at the look on Emmaline's face as I passed. She looked absolutely *livid*, and it was with no small amount of satisfaction that I nodded politely in her direction.

"You're ridiculous, you know that?" Vi muttered from beside me, where she sulked as I made my rounds. She'd been acting odd all evening, as if her entire being was shrouded in some unknown darkness. I supposed I couldn't blame her—she was allowed into the ball as a child of the Court, but she didn't belong here. Not tonight, when the focus was on the Pathway.

"I don't know what you could possibly mean." I muttered innocently, nodding over her shoulder to a Council member. He nodded in return, and I flashed a polite smile.

Vi rolled her eyes, turning away suddenly.

"What's your problem?" I asked, the smile on my face fading.

"What's my..." Her words faded off into a disbelieving laugh. "Come *on*, Willow. Don't you see how absurd this whole charade is?"

"Charade?" I raised my brows, beginning to get annoyed. "You do realize this is about my future, right? About the future of *Atvas*? What happens in the Pathway *matters*."

"Trust me, I know." The words were murmured under her breath, so quietly I almost didn't hear them. "It's just... isn't it exhausting playing these games all the time?"

"I'm not playing any games," I said defensively, pausing to grab an hors d'oeuvre from a passing tray before turning to face her.

"Of course you are!" she snapped, voice hushed but harsh, and I drew back. Vi got fired up at times, always ready for a fight, but this was different in a way I couldn't even identify. "That's all you do—you and

Auden and Emmaline and all of you Charismas. Hell, the whole damn thing is a *game.* A stupid, foolish game!"

"*Vi.*" I glanced around worriedly. "Control yourself, for goodness sake."

Indeed, a few of the partygoers around us were paying rapt attention. I cursed inwardly, dragging Vi away from the crowd and towards the outer wall. All logic said that I should avoid her, avoid the stain this could put on my reputation, but... well, she was my friend. She'd do the same for me.

"What's wrong?" I asked again, placing my hands on her shoulders. "Why are you so upset?"

Her eyes flickered to mine, and the moment our gazes met it was as if I could feel every emotion I found there. Anger, fear, bitterness, dread—it was all there, mingling in the deep honey brown of her irises. She looked me up and down, as if assessing me, and opened her mouth. Closed it. Opened it again.

"You have to win the Pathway," she said softly, her voice more passionate than I'd ever heard it. Even more than that time she'd told off Martin Peters for looking down a girl's dress, which was saying something. "If you lose, if you have to go to the Beyond..." She shook her head, moisture glinting in her eyes. "I don't know what I would do."

Oh. Of course she would be worried about me making the Court. It was only logical, even if part of me was offended at the lack of faith. My whole life had been about being number one—top ten had always been implied.

"What do you think I've been trying to do?" I replied, voice exasperated but not unkind. "If I want to win, I have to play these 'games.'"

"I know," she murmured, looking away. She shook her head suddenly, as if coming out of a trance. "I know that, I just...sometimes I really hate it here."

I opened my mouth to tell her off, to warn her to never to say something so treasonous again, but I was interrupted by the sharp tinkling of metal on glass.

My father stood at the front of the ballroom, regal as ever. Lost in conversation, I hadn't even noticed the other participants gathering. They lined one side of the room, ordered by score, with an empty spot in front of Auden—where I should have been standing. I wove quickly through the crowd, heart racing with each glance thrown my way. *Great job, Willow,* I scolded myself. *Fantastic way to start the competition.*

"Are you okay?" Auden mouthed as I slipped into my spot, his eyes searching me for signs of distress. I nodded back, still too shaken to say more. I turned my attention instead to my father, tuning into his speech at last.

"... excellence in all five disciplines, as well as the ability to manage them all. As you are aware, this year's Pathway to Perfection is especially unique. This year, I will be handing the honor of Sovereign to the competitor who proves their unparalleled worth."

The crowd murmured, and I could feel their eyes skate over us all, likely wondering who was to be their Sovereign.

Me, I reminded myself desperately. *I will be the Sovereign.*

"Yes, it's all very exciting!" My father chuckled. "Councilman Mullerson will announce each participant, as well as the upstanding citizen who has chosen to Sponsor them. As always, a Sponsor may endorse only one participant per year. Councilman Mullerson, if you would." My father nodded to the man beside him before moving to the side, heading the line of Sponsors on the wall across from us. I avoided his gaze as Councilman

Mullerson began to speak, choosing to fix my skirts instead. In all the bustle of the night, they had managed to shift from their intended place.

"Thank you, Sovereign Aldridge," Mullerson began. "It is certainly an honor to witness such an event."

I tasted a metallic liquid in my mouth—blood, most likely. I must have been chewing into my cheek again, a nasty habit of mine.

"Without further ado, I shall begin the reading of the participants."

I tried to breathe deeply, as my mother had taught me, and yet the air seemed to catch in my lungs with each word.

"Our first participant is Willow Aldridge, entering the Pathway to Perfection with a P-score of 4.98. She will be Sponsored by the Sovereign himself, Warren Aldridge."

Murmurs spread through the room, yet I barely processed the sound. My heart pounded in my ears as I made my way to the center of the platform, taking the arm of my father before turning to the glittering crowd.

Relax, I scolded myself. After all, I'd been in the public eye for as long as I could remember. A small crowd like this was hardly something to get upset about. Yet this time felt different; as if, for quite possibly the first time, I was in front of a crowd who looked and saw *me.* They didn't see a little girl, just some figurehead by the Sovereign's side; instead, they saw me as something greater. The future Sovereign, perhaps. I shivered at the thought and forced myself to stand a little taller. The life I'd always wanted seemed to float in front of me, dangling just a step ahead of us as my father and I marched through the crowd.

I caught Vi's eyes as I passed, noting the strange glint that lingered in her gaze. She smiled nonetheless, though her last words still echoed in my mind.

"Games," she'd called them, these subtleties that I knew all too well. But that was just the thing; they weren't games at all, and anyone who might mistake them as such would never be able to use them to their advantage. All those poised interactions, those carefully chosen words—they were instruments, well-honed and attuned to the practices of our society. I knew I would say none of this to her, for there would be no point; one could never explain a symphony to those without ears.

"Well done," my father murmured quietly, face still morphed into a proper smile as we exited into an empty corridor. Vaguely, I heard Auden being announced behind me.

"I merely walked across a room," I muttered, confusion clouding my voice despite my best attempts.

"Still." My father fixed me with a stern gaze. "It has begun. You have much work ahead of you."

"I know." I fidgeted awkwardly with the beading on my dress. I couldn't remember the last time my father and I had spoken like this, just the two of us. It felt strange.

My father looked at me carefully for a moment before shaking his head, as if I had failed some unspoken test. "It is no easy thing, being Sovereign. You will be asked to bear secrets heavier than you can imagine, to hold the entire history of Atvas on your shoulders."

"*If* I become Sovereign," I replied, hoping my face didn't reveal the pounding of my heart. "I still have to win the Pathway first."

"You are an Aldridge," my father said simply, waving a hand. "You will win."

"But what if I don't?" I blurted out, even as my cheeks tinged red with embarrassment. Some future Sovereign I was, begging for reassurance when I should be confident and collected.

My father hesitated before stepping slightly closer, clearly as uncomfortable as I was with this new dynamic. We'd spent years speaking as Sovereign to subject. Neither of us, it seemed, knew how to exist as father and daughter. "What makes you say that?"

I looked at my father then, overcome by an overwhelming need to tell him of my nerves, of the unfaltering sense of dread weighing on my heart. After all, he should understand; he too had been the child of a Sovereign, destined for a future seemingly out of reach.

I looked at my still-shaking hands, opening my mouth to share my thoughts.

"Sovereign Aldridge," a voice sounded, and I snapped my mouth shut as a guard rounded the corner. He nodded quickly to me before turning to my father. "Your presence is required in the hall, sir. Right away."

My father sighed, brushing a tired hand across his face as he nodded. He turned to me, the picture of professionalism once more. "Pay close attention to the other participants. Tonight may not be a trial, but the competition has begun. It's best that you act like it."

With that he was striding down the hall, speaking quickly to the guards as if he'd forgotten our conversation entirely. Perhaps that was what the Sovereignty required, all else rendered unimportant when compared to the glorious role of ruling Atvas. It didn't mean he didn't care for me, or that he didn't have any interest in my life.

It was an old, tired argument, one I'd spent my whole life constructing in my mind. I discovered at a young age that my father didn't belong to me any more than he belonged to every child of Atvas. He cared for me as he cared for all of his subjects, ties of duty and obligation that were never quite enough. It didn't take long to figure out that the one thing that set me apart was my potential. I bore the Aldridge name and would carry on his legacy, and for that I would always matter.

It wasn't quite love, but it was better than nothing.

***

Being the first participant announced, I was first to the room where the participants were to congregate for the reading of the rules and opening discussion. The emptiness set me on edge, and the seconds seemed to tick by slowly. I was relieved when footsteps finally sounded in the hallway, yet no one entered. Instead, low voices rumbled in the corridor outside. Auden and his father, having their own conversation.

"... have to take this seriously," Ruben's voice rumbled, a sharp edge to the words. The Bonavich men had distinct voices, low and heavy, and Ruben's always had a snide edge to it.

"I am," Auden replied, clearly agitated. "I've been preparing for years, you know that."

"*Everyone's* been preparing for years," Ruben hissed, "especially your biggest rivals."

There was a pause, as if Auden wasn't sure how to respond.

"I don't have *rivals,* father," he said eventually, and I could practically feel the exasperation he surely felt. "The only one even close to my score is Willow, and I'm sure—"

"Oh, you're *sure?*" I cringed at the harshness of Ruben's tone, at the callousness with which he cut off his son. "Sure of what? That the Aldridge girl isn't set on beating you—that she's just going to roll over and give you the position that's been in her bloodline for decades?" There was a beat of silence, and I heard Ruben sigh. "I know you're not worried, but you should be. The Aldridge family hasn't held the Sovereignty this long by being fair. That girl, your supposed 'friend,' is going to take everything we've worked for with a smile on her face. I've told you time and time again: you're too close to her."

"We *just* started," Auden protested. "Besides, Willow's not like that." His words were certain, but I could hear the wariness and distrust in his voice. The worst thing was, I couldn't even disprove it. I *did* intend to win.

A tense silence followed his words, and when Ruben spoke, it was softer than before. "If you believe that, you're a fool." His voice was cold as ever, and a tremor ran through my body. "We can't afford foolishness, Auden. You *will* win this competition, or so help me—"

"I understand," Auden interjected, as if he didn't want to know where that comment was headed. As if he already knew. "Don't worry, Father. I can do this." The words might have sounded confident had it not been for the desperation in his tone.

A long silence followed, and I could practically see Ruben's cold gaze in my mind. "You'd better hope so," he replied at last. A wave of uneasiness settled in my chest at the words. More than ever, I hated that I had to beat Auden to win.

The door opened suddenly, and I took a few quick steps back as Auden entered at last. I did my best to look uninterested, like I hadn't been listening at the door. It couldn't have been further from the truth. My mind was racing, thoughts jumbled by what I had overheard. I had experienced Ruben's coldness towards Auden before, far too many times to count, but this one chilled me to the bones. I'd heard just one interaction like that before, many years ago. Like this one, the conversation had been intense, the sort of private affair I certainly shouldn't have heard.

"Willow?" Auden said, frowning. "Are you alright?"

"Oh," I said, flustered. "I was just... going to the ladies' room."

"Now?"

"Yes." I turned to face him, heart dropping at the suspicion on his face. "Why?"

"It's just … they're about to announce the rules," Auden said, raising a brow. "And I know you'd never risk missing that."

I cursed inwardly. I never had been able to lie to Auden; to anyone else, sure, but never to him. A tense silence stretched between us, broken only by the sound of the door as the next participant came in. I blushed, turning back around to stare at the table. Auden just sighed, plopping into the chair next to me with no comment.

Neither of us said a word as the other participants gradually filed in, claiming seats at the round table in the center of the room. I took inventory of each participant as my father instructed me to, carefully identifying those who were to be my biggest competitors. There were many Charismas, as expected, and a fair amount of Intellects and Aesthetics as well. Merely a smattering of Legality disciplines entered, and even fewer Service.

A jolt of pain went through my heart as I caught a flash of auburn hair and brown eyes across the room, magnified by the round glasses she'd worn as long as I could remember. Amaris Hewberry: first ranked in Intellect, and one of the most promising participants in the Pathway. Never mind the fact that we'd once been close friends, had once sat on the floor of my bedroom and braided each other's hair. But that was years ago, back before the reality of life tore us apart. Now, she was little more than a competitor. I ripped my gaze away before her eyes could meet mine, turning back to the front of the room.

"Alright, let's get this started!" a jolly voice rang out, and Councilman Mullerson sauntered into the room. He appeared to be alone, and I wondered vaguely where my father had run off to. "Now that the hard part's over, that is."

The room grew heavy with silence, and I stared at him. I knew the old man loved a good joke, but we were all far too anxious to fake amusement.

A titter of laughter sounded from the corner, where Emmaline and her posse had squeezed in. I nearly groaned aloud; so she had found a Sponsor after all. Not that I was surprised; if there was anything Emmaline was good at, it was annoying me at every turn. Now that she was in the Pathway, that would be so much easier for her. Sure enough, it was her who had laughed at Mullerson's awful excuse for a joke.

"Suck-up," someone coughed, a male voice from somewhere across the room. *That* got some laughs, whispers and giggles spreading through the small space. I managed to keep myself from laughing, far too sophisticated to acknowledge such a comment, yet I couldn't help but agree with the anonymous voice as Emmaline turned a bright shade of red, crossing her arms like a furious child.

"There will be none of that," my father scolded, moving into the room at last. A deeper silence settled over us, the guilty silence of scolded children mingling with fear and awe. After all, many of the others had never been so close to the Sovereign before. "You snicker like children, and yet you hope to earn membership in the esteemed Court. Your childhood ends today. It's time to grow up."

I glanced at Auden, and he nodded in return. It was a heavy sort of nod, an acknowledgement of all we had been through and all that was to come.

"Alright, then," Councilman Mullerson spoke, clearing his throat awkwardly. "With that, I shall begin the official reading of the rules." He unrolled the scroll in his hands, clearing his throat once more as if for good measure. "Ladies and gentlemen, I now declare you participants in the Pathway to Perfection. As of this moment, you are no longer of any particular discipline, but rather a student of them all. You will spend your days studying each of the disciplines of Atvas: Service, Charisma, Aesthetics, Intellect, and Legality. Every ten days, you will encounter an assessment designed to measure your prowess in one of the five disciplines. Your P-score is now officially wiped; you begin this journey on even ground."

I tried to ignore the twinge in my chest at the statement. It wasn't as if I hadn't expected it, but no amount of preparation could have readied me for this feeling. A lifetime of hard work, erased with one sentence.

"You will be ranked within the group of participants," Mullerson went on. "Rankings will be updated after each discipline assessment, as well as after the final assessment, a combination of all disciplines. Whichever ten participants receive the highest ranks will receive membership to the Court. You will then be assigned a job based on your rank, the highest of which being the position of Sovereign."

"However..." he called over the excited murmurs, eyes growing serious as the crowd quieted. "The pursuit of true perfection is not without risks. Those not chosen for the Court will be labeled as Flawed, and shall be cast out of Atvas."

A shiver ran down my arms; there must have been twenty-five people in the room, yet most of them were to be cast out. The others must have felt that eerie feeling as well, for a thick layer of tension stretched through the space.

"Be ready for the first assessment in ten days' time." My father's voice was grave as he bowed his head to us. "May you live in the beauty of perfection." He left the room in a sweep of confidence and grace, leaving us staring after him like leaves left without a tree.

"Bet you wish you sucked up, too," Emmaline said to the group, whiny voice oddly serious. "At least I'll be remembered if they kick me to the curb."

And with that, the Pathway to Perfection had begun.

4

OLD FRIENDS AND NEW FOES

It felt strange to wake up the next day. Everything was exactly the same, yet somehow entirely different. I would not attend Charisma lessons that day, but instead would begin training for the first assessment. My mind raced as I got ready, throwing on the clothing I'd meticulously selected the night prior. I knew the details of the assessment wouldn't be disclosed until the day of, but hopefully we would at least learn which discipline it would measure.

I told Auden as much as we walked towards the Cathe, the center of Court business. It was an exciting change of location. For many, this was a first glimpse of one of the most secure buildings in Atvas—one that we all hoped to have a place in one day.

"Of course they'll tell us today," Auden stated, his reply so certain that I felt a bit silly for bringing it up. "How else would we be able to start preparing?"

"I know," I snapped, and Auden shot me a surprised glance. "I mean, that's what I figured. I'm not sure why I even brought it up."

He didn't respond for several moments, instead choosing to gaze at my face as though I were a particularly interesting painting. He did that sometimes, pondering me in a way that suggested he was searching for some hidden meaning.

"You're nervous," he assessed.

It was hardly a question, but I shook my head nonetheless. Auden raised his eyebrows, disbelief on his face.

"I am not." My voice sounded high and whiny, and I cringed. Auden didn't respond, but his eyes were far too knowing for my liking. "Seriously. I'm not," I huffed, glancing purposefully away from the incredulity I was sure to see. "I'm ready for this."

We walked in silence for several moments, the only sound the rustling of dead leaves on the cobblestones.

"Anyways—" he began.

"I mean, why would I be nervous?" I asked, my voice overpowering his. "I've been preparing for this for years. I have no reason to believe I'll have any difficulty at all."

"Alright," Auden said, voice calm and placating. "So, you're not nervous, then."

I pursed my lips, satisfied by his words. And yet, his *tone*...

"Besides, it's not as if we'll be scored today. It's just a formality, really," I blurted out, before cursing myself inwardly.

Great, I scolded myself, *be more pathetic, why don't you?*

"Okay, I believe you."

Somehow, Auden's pacifying reply and knowing smile only agitated me further, and I tasted blood as I bit down harder on my lip. We continued on in silence, our usually casual walk suddenly awkward. Slowly, my anger faded, and I realized suddenly that perhaps Auden was nervous as well. Perhaps he hadn't been accusing me, but merely attempting to open up a conversation. Based on the conversation I had overheard last night, he was certainly under enough pressure to warrant some nerves.

"Auden..." I started, the words rushing out of me as the Cathe loomed closer. I needed him to know that I understood, and that I wasn't out to get him. Auden turned to me, face questioning. I pulled him to a stop, taking a deep breath before opening my mouth once more. "About last night, I—"

"Oh, good!" a voice rang out, and I gritted my teeth as Councilman Mullerson approached us. "Why am I not surprised that you two are so punctual?"

"Just ready to learn," I replied politely, forcing a smile as I glanced behind him. The entryway was practically empty, with only a few older members bustling about. "Are we the first ones to arrive?" It was hardly a serious question; Auden and I were almost always first. Really, I was just hoping to prompt an ending to this talk.

"Oh, no, my dear!" Mullerson laughed, shaking his head. "You may be punctual, but this is the Pathway you're talking about. Someone will always be earlier than you."

I frowned at that. I would have thought half an hour early would be enough, but it appeared otherwise.

"Come with me," he said. "I'll show you to the room where we will be conducting lessons."

I sighed inwardly. It seemed Auden and I would not be finishing our discussion anytime soon.

"That's quite alright," Auden butted in, smiling that suave smile of his. "Willow and I have been roaming these halls since our youth. I'm sure we'll find our way."

I had to admire his tactics: simple, respectful, yet with a subtle reminder of our status here at Atvas. How I had ever managed to outscore him in Charisma was a mystery, that was for sure.

"Sorry," Councilman Mullerson responded with a nervous chuckle. "Rules are rules; no contestants allowed in the Cathe unsupervised."

I raised my eyebrows, glancing at Auden. His jaw was clenched. Generally, Auden was quite skilled at getting his way. As was I, I supposed.

"Come along now."

Auden and I followed Mullerson, trailing a few steps behind as he led us down the halls. The Cathe was just as lavishly decorated as the Palace despite being quite different, the quiet stone to the Palace's glittering jewels.

"Tomorrow, we leave much earlier," Auden muttered, voice low and serious. "I don't care that it's the Pathway. We're first, always."

I glanced at him, taking in the sweat dotting his brow and the tension in his jaw. "I think *you're* nervous."

He didn't reply, which was confirmation in itself.

"Here we are!" Mullerson exclaimed, ushering us inside. "Go ahead and get settled."

I suppressed the urge to laugh as he practically ran down the hall, clearly eager to leave the discomfort of our presence. I couldn't help but pity the guy; I wouldn't want to deal with us, either. I turned my attention to the room, a long chamber with a vaulted ceiling and large windows lining the walls. A soft light flooded the room, casting golden beams upon the few contestants that mulled around speaking softly to each other. Rows of tables filled the room, looking quite a bit like an average classroom. The scene was disarmingly serene, considering the stakes. If I didn't know better, I would have thought we were merely meeting for a casual brunch.

I spotted Amaris at a table near the middle of the room, already jotting notes on a notepad. My immediate instinct was to dart away, to ignore her and hope she ignored me, but... well, we were only children when everything went down. We'd been friends before I met Vi, before we were assigned our disciplines. Funny enough, it boiled down to the same two disciplines for us both: Charisma or Intellect. I went one way, she went the other. That was the beginning of the end, though neither of us knew it at the time. For five years we stayed friends, whispering the secrets of our respective disciplines in the safety of my library. But with age came responsibilities, and increased training, and new friendships. It never mattered to me that we were in different disciplines, not really; yet for Amaris, it was too much. She told me as much the last time we spoke, an argument that had arisen over something foolish but ended our friendship for good. The fight was dramatic in typical teenage fashion, and for a long time I thought it to be the end of the world.

But that was a long time ago. Things were different now—we were no longer separated by disciplines, no longer forced to choose between one ideology and another. If there was ever a time to reconnect, it was now.

Auden trailed behind me as I wove through the numerous rows of tables, exchanging pleasantries with those we passed. Mullerson wasn't lying; there were quite a few other participants there already. Amaris glanced up as we reached her table, a light surprise gracing her features.

"Willow?" Her smile was kind, if a bit weary. "It's good to see you."

"You too," I breathed, fidgeting idly with the straps on my bag. "Do you mind company?" I gestured to the empty seat beside her, currently occupied by a large bag that I could only assume was full of books.

"Not at all," she said, moving to reorganize her belongings.

"What are you doing?" Auden whispered to me as we waited, voice soft but agitated. "We should be sitting at the front."

I merely hushed him, moving towards the seats Amaris cleared. It was strange, this competitive edge to Auden. After all, only yesterday he had mocked me for caring at all. Perhaps his father's words had indeed impacted him, far more than he let on. I wanted to remind him that it wouldn't be awful to make some allies. As our instructor always remind-ed us, connections were an invaluable part of navigating life in Atvas.

"Thank you," I said to Amaris, a sincere smile growing on my face. She smiled back, wide and friendly, and in that moment my heart felt very warm. It was so long ago, our fight—and yet, I'd never quite healed from it. This felt like a step in the right direction, at least.

A hush fell over the room as Mullerson entered, accompanied by three men and two women: the Directors of the Disciplines. I recognized them all, but none as well as Phillip Edrikson, Director of Charisma. He nodded politely in our direction as he filed in—most likely to Auden, as he often stayed after class for more discussion.

"Good morning," Mullerson began, "and welcome to the first day of training for this year's Pathway to Perfection. As you all know, your first assessment will be in nine days' time, beginning at six a.m. sharp. You will not learn the specifics until the day of, nor are you permitted to attempt to learn of them before this time. You are, however, permitted to know the discipline that will be tested."

The room seemed to take in a collective breath, waiting eagerly for the announcement. As usual, Mullerson seemed to relish the suspense, taking the time to clear his throat before continuing. "The first assess-ment will be a test of logic, of understanding, and of mind." He smiled as muttering broke out. "That's right: the first assessment will test the discipline of Intellect."

Amaris was practically glowing beside me, jotting down notes so fast that I wondered if her hand would break right there. My chest twinged as I glanced at her paper, taking in the handwriting I knew so well. The feeling only slightly softened the sharp envy growing in my chest—to start the Pathway in her discipline was an advantage. Luckily for me, Intellect was my natural aptitude.

"Now," Mullerson continued, quieting the murmurs with a raised hand, "please allow me to introduce Mrs. Penelope Ariponas, the esteemed Director of Intellect."

One of the women stepped forward, tall with plain brown hair and a rather unremarkable face. The other Directors filed out behind her, and I realized suddenly that their presence must have been a mere distraction, a way to draw out the drama and suspense of the moment. I would have to keep an eye out for distractions like that. I had a feeling I was to encounter them often.

"Hello," the woman spoke, voice soft but full of an infinite sort of wisdom. "My name is Mrs. Ariponas, but that does not matter. Names do not matter in the discipline of Intellect, for they do not contribute to the matrix of knowledge being built within you. What matters is your mind, and what you do with it."

I waited, pen hovering above parchment, for anything concrete to write down, but it didn't come. No events or dates to memorize, as I had been doing for years of training. Instead, Mrs. Ariponas rambled on in that vague way of hers, describing concepts that were equal parts fascinating and perplexing. I eventually gave up on my notes, choosing instead to sit back and listen to her words. Despite my avid concentration and best attempts to understand, each concept seemed to dance further out of reach than the last. I ended the day with only an empty notepad and a frustrated mood, a feeling made infinitely worse by the full pages of Amaris's pad. I glared jealously at the neat lines of letters, at the ease with which she seemed to understand. I packed up quickly, wanting nothing more than to forget the word *logic* all together.

"It gets easier," Amaris said, voice tinged with pity as she watched me shove my notepad into my bag.

"It's not entirely awful," I replied, as if I were hardly bothered at all. "I rather enjoyed the bit about the Continual Imperative."

"*Categorical* Imperative," Amaris corrected softly, and I huffed out a breath of annoyance. She just laughed, shaking her head softly. "It'll be better in practice—you'll see." She patted my arm sympathetically before disappearing into the crowd, her laugh still echoing in my head like a ghost from the past.

I turned to find Auden, only to find him speaking to the Director. *Great,* I thought sarcastically, *now he'll be better at this, too.*

I couldn't stand to wait in that room, instead choosing to retreat to the small balcony, leaning against the railing to gaze into the gardens below. My emotions seemed to take a dive, free-falling off the very balcony on which I stood. I wasn't sure what about today had affected me so. Perhaps it was the fear of failure, of not being prepared for the biggest test of my life, or maybe it was merely irritation at the ease with which others seemed to understand Intellect, the subject I had always prided myself on. Whatever it was, it alarmed me. At that moment, I cared little for making connections or maintaining friendships. I desired nothing less than perfection, the ability to prove myself to all who doubted me. It frightened me, leaving my hands shaking on the railing.

"You and your plants," a voice sounded behind me. I didn't bother to turn as Auden approached, shutting the door before coming to lean on the railing beside me. It was quiet for a moment before he sighed and said, "I know you heard me last night."

I glanced at him then, at the many emotions fighting across his face.

"... With my father."

"I did," I replied simply, turning to look back at the garden.

"He thinks you're a threat."

"And you?" I replied, looking down at my shaking hands. "Do you think I'm a threat?"

His glance followed mine, brow furrowing. I hid my hands, shoving them deep into the folds of my dress.

"I'd be foolish not to." His voice was dark, and my stomach twisted despite the truth of his words. "But I don't want to fight," he continued, voice breaking slightly. "Not with you."

I turned away from the words, away from the emotion. Perhaps it made me a coward, but I couldn't bear to look at his pleading face any longer.

"We always knew this was coming. It's inevitable."

An awkward silence pressed down upon us. I could sense it in my peripheral vision as he stared at me, face almost pleading, but I didn't turn my head.

"So then, we fight," Auden stated, as if coming to a conclusion.

The words left a dent in my heart, unavoidable as they were. I couldn't help but remember the days of our childhood, playing tag in the yard. We were both so competitive then, back when there were no consequences. I didn't feel quite as motivated now, when winning meant losing something just as precious. I couldn't help but wonder if Auden felt the same.

"And may the best man win," I said softly, the same phrase I'd said back in the days of tag. We'd always laughed at the phrase back then, when life was little more than laughter and sunshine—and yet, somehow it didn't seem quite so funny anymore.

***

Amaris, it appeared, was correct: the vague theories of Intellect made much more sense in practice, and by the final day of training, I was almost *enjoying* myself. We spent much of the days relating the concepts to modern and historical events, so my years of training were helpful after all. I almost felt bad for anyone without prior knowledge, for there was far too much material to realistically learn. Then again, hardly anyone would dare to enter the Pathway without at least *some* interdisciplinary study—a fact made clear as we raced to answer the questions raised, fighting to get our hand in the air before anyone else.

"...this resource crisis was made clear to the first Sovereign, who was..."

A pause, during which dozens of hands shot in the air, then: "Yes, Mr. Liestcher?"

"Sovereign Coldwell."

"Indeed," Mrs. Ariponas nodded in approval. I almost scoffed aloud—even a child would know that answer. Sovereign Coldwell was akin to a deity in Atvas, celebrated and revered in equal measure. "He created the discipline system as a response to the resource crisis. Can anyone tell me why he did this?"

"It creates the perfect society," Auden answered, because his hand was in the air before the question was even finished. "Driven by a fear of change and the connections formed in Atvas, each individual is motivated to reach perfection in their discipline. The Court ties the disciplines together, creating a governing class that ensues cohesion."

"Spoken like a true Charisma." Mrs. Ariponas remained smiling, but there was a glint of displeasure in her eyes. "Yet now we seek to look at the problem from the mindset of an Intellect. Anyone else?"

There were significantly less hands raised this time, uncertainty rifling through the room.

"Ms. Aldridge?" Mrs. Ariponas prompted, though my hand wasn't up. In fact, it was the first time in the entire lesson that I didn't know the answer. For some reason, Mrs. Ariponas seemed determined to expose that.

Think, I urged myself, fingers fidgeting nervously under the table. *Say something, anything.*

"It derandomizes the odds," I answered slowly, heart beating viciously fast. All my life I'd been taught the importance of certainty, warned against guesswork; yet here I was, confessing to a theory I'd only thought about in the dark of night. "Before, survival depended on a variety of random factors. The discipline system eliminates the element of chance altogether, ensuring that those who contribute more to Atvas have a stronger chance of success in society. Those who don't contribute are cast out, which is perhaps unpleasant but better than death. It's a simple risk-benefit analysis, really."

Mrs. Ariponas nodded, a small smile on her lips. "Indeed it is."

I glowed with the praise, trying my best not to look too proud of myself. Emmaline's glare burned into me from a row over, where she was sitting with her usual posse of friends. Others seemed annoyed, too. From the back of the room, a boy with wavy blonde hair glared at me so furiously my cheeks started to burn. I'd seen him before, one of the few disciplines of Service in the Pathway. What he was doing here, I couldn't imagine—he spent most of his time slouched in the back corner, scoffing and rolling his eyes.

I turned back to the front, shaking the image out of my head. The last thing I needed was to be preoccupied by some Service boy who apparently hated my guts. Not that it was anything new—many in Atvas hated me, either because of my father or my status. It was something I'd learned to deal with. Still, the boy's glare haunted me through the rest of the lesson and all the way home. Only when I entered the dining room for dinner did I find a reprieve in the form of my mother, whose intimidating presence seemed to overtake any and all other thoughts in my brain.

"Ah, Willow," my mother acknowledged as I entered, glancing up from the chair in which she sat, poised as ever. I couldn't help but be envious of her, with her smooth russet hair and extraordinarily well-preserved face. She looked young despite her thirty-six years, eternally elegant in a glorious evening gown. I felt almost silly in my day dress, having come straight from training.

"Glad to see you were able to join us," she continued, and I suppressed the urge to scoff. Never in my life had I missed dinner—nor had it ever been an option. A few of our Service staff surrounded me as I took my seat, filling my water glass and setting a cloth upon my lap. I glanced at the head of the table, where my father's empty place sat, sighing internally. We never ate dinner without him, no matter how long it took.

"Any word from Father?" I asked, trying my best to keep the impatience out of my voice.

Clearly, I was unsuccessful, for my mother shot me a reprimanding look. "Your father is a busy man, and he will join us when he's ready. Running Atvas is a very difficult job, you know."

The Charisma instructors would tell me to rebuke the statement, to remind her that I was to one day rule, and she would not. Yet I couldn't bring myself to do it—not with her. No matter how irritated I grew, she was still my mother.

"I haven't heard from him," my mother said finally, sighing at the clock as it ticked again and again. "But we must wait."

Nearly an hour later, the door swung open at last.

"Good evening!" my father called, smiling an infuriatingly casual smile as he settled into his own seat. It seemed to take hours for the Service to pour his wine, and my stomach growled.

"Well, shall we eat?" he asked at last, fixing us with a stare that seemed to suggest he had been waiting for us all along.

"I believe that would be nice." My mother's words were sharper than usual as she fixed my father with a hard stare. He hardly seemed to notice, far too busy beckoning the Service for more wine.

My mother sighed, turning instead to me. "So, Willow. I expect you're prepared for the assessment tomorrow?"

I swallowed down a bite of lettuce, uncomfortable with the shift in focus. Generally, dinner was focused on Father and his rantings about work. That too would change with the Pathway, it seemed.

"I believe so," I answered, hoping she would leave it at that.

Yet luck was not on my side, for my father had turned his attention to me as well. "Now, you know we can't tell you anything about the assessment," my father chided, as if I were a mere child. "But you better keep your wits about you—and think outside the box. Intellect has as much to do with creativity as anything else."

I furrowed my brow. This was the most my father had spoken to me since the night of the Sponsor's Ball. Real advice, too.

"Now," he continued, turning to face my mother. "How is the planning for the upcoming luncheon coming along?"

"Oh, smoothly as always," she answered. "There's the issue of invites, of course, and I've heard..."

I zoned out, pondering my father's advice as I ate. Creativity, sure—but of what type? Wouldn't that be better suited to Aesthetics? I was never permitted to know about the assessments of the previous years—after all, only the Court was invited to those—but Auden had once told me his father said it was mostly historical facts and figures for Intellect, with not much creativity involved. I didn't dare to ask for more details, instead choosing to stay silent throughout the duration of the meal.

I thought of Auden as I crawled into bed, who was likely worrying just as much from a few manors away. I wondered if his father had given him the same advice, or maybe more. I wouldn't put it past Ruben to give away the entire thing—not when I knew he had shared forbidden information in the past. He had always been more involved in Auden's training than my father had been in mine, a fact I had always envied. At least, until that day when I'd witnessed one of their little training sessions firsthand.

The brisk air brought goose bumps to my exposed arms, but I couldn't bring myself to care. I was too annoyed to stay at the Palace, even if it was warm and toasty. I had just finished an especially bothersome lesson in Aesthetics, in which some lady had tried to coax me into penciling charcoal around my eye. Yuck! She would barely even get within an inch of my eye before I flinched away, but I hardly thought that was my fault. As far as I was concerned, the powder and mascara I had been wearing since age six were plenty—a fact with which my mother disagreed. She was always grumpy lately, though I wasn't sure why. It was as if now that I was in my tenth year, she couldn't stand to tell me stories or brush my hair anymore. She was so disappointed in my behavior in the Aesthetics lesson that I ran away, which I knew I would regret later.

I found myself in front of Auden's house at last, a big building that was somehow far scarier than the Palace. Even though Auden and I had been friends for, like, forever, I hadn't been at his house as much as he'd been at mine. I didn't like it at all; it was entirely boring, and somehow always freezing cold. I'd never told that to Auden, but he said he liked my house better anyway. He showed up at our house unannounced all the time, so I figured it was okay that I do the same.

"Auden!" I called, knocking on the door. "Come out, I need help!" I didn't really, but I knew Auden's father wouldn't let him come out unless he believed it was necessary. His father was always mad about something or another, though she never quite understood why.

"Why, hello, Ms. Aldridge." The Service maid who answered the door beamed down at me kindly, red hair tight in a bun. "I bet you're looking for the young Mr. Bonavich, aren't you?"

I frowned, pushing past the woman to peek into the hall behind. "Clearly." Hadn't I just yelled his name through the door? "Where is he?"

"In the courtyard," she replied, "but you may not want to—"

I ignored the words, already set off towards the courtyard. It was where Auden and I played whenever we were here, when Auden's mother, Mrs. Lucille, would shoo us out with strict instructions to stay close.

I skidded to a stop at the sound of voices, one deep and one a bit higher. I was grateful for the doorless arch as I slipped through it, careful to stay out of sight as I ducked behind a pillar. Mother said it was impolite to eavesdrop, but she wasn't here. In front of me stood Auden and his father, clearly in the middle of a training session. I knew Ruben trained Auden personally much of the time, because Auden mentioned it all the time. He never would say what they did, though, and I was curious. I couldn't imagine actually training with my father. It was already awkward enough speaking to him at dinner each night!

"... again," Ruben was saying. I couldn't quite see him from where I stood, but I could see Auden clearly. He held his wooden practice sword in front of him, the sight of which made me grit my teeth. We had received those wretched things three years ago, in our last year of pre-discipline training. I had yet to be able to even pick up the sword, ever since the one

awful day. Mother said the sword wouldn't hurt anyone, that it was just wooden, but I was still afraid (not that I would tell her that). Auden seemed afraid, too, though certainly not of the sword. He held it in front of him in a practiced stance, ignoring the way his hands shook. I wasn't sure if it was from the cold air or from the exhaustion clear on his face. Puffs of steamy air floated with each rushed breath, and his blue eyes were weary. I wondered how long they'd been doing their lesson; Auden hadn't even looked this tired that time we raced from the Palace to the school.

My pondering was interrupted by a sharp grunt of pain, Auden landing on the cold stone floor as the wooden sword slammed into his gut. I gasped aloud, nearly giving my hiding spot away in my surprise. Had I missed the count-off? When my Legality tutor and I had practiced dodging, he always counted to three, and he always stopped before he actually hit me. I waited, breath held, for Ruben to apologize and help him up.

Ruben did no such thing, stepping back as Auden pushed himself up. Auden didn't seem surprised, eyes filled with fear and a hint of frustration.

"Did we not already practice blocking?" Ruben asked, clearly unconcerned with the way Auden was wheezing. I realized suddenly that maybe this wasn't the first time Auden had fallen to the ground that day—a thought that made me very angry.

"We did, sir," Auden replied curtly. I frowned. That didn't really sound like Auden, who was usually all smiles and jokes and comfort. "I just... I wasn't ready."

Ruben muttered something under his breath, something I couldn't make out, but which sounded quite a bit like a word Mother had told me not to say. He began to pace back and forth, appearing every few seconds on either side of the pillar. I saw Auden's eyes follow his movements, ever so carefully.

"*You think the judges of the Pathway to Perfection are going to care if you're ready?*" *Ruben snapped, and as he turned towards Auden, I caught a raised brow. "I've told you a hundred times: you have to be ready for anything, at any time. If you would listen, maybe you wouldn't need all this extra practice." He stopped pacing just within my line of sight, lifting his sword hand once more. "Again."*

"*But Father,*" *Auden replied, voice slow and careful, "Director Edrikson said we're supposed to focus only on Charisma for now. Perhaps I should—*"

I jumped as Ruben's sword swung once more, but Auden was ready for it. He caught the swing with his own, a loud clatter reverberating as they met. A moment of tension ensued as the swords remained engaged, each pushing into the other. Ruben won out, the heavy wood pushing until Auden's wrist snapped back, and the sword fell from his hand. Auden retrieved it quickly, rubbing his wrist.

"*Edrikson is a fool,*" *Ruben said darkly. "Charisma may be your discipline, but it'll be Legality that wins you the Pathway to Perfection, mark my words.*"

"*What do you mean?*" *Auden asked warily. I didn't miss the way his hand clenched around his sword, just in case.*

"*Warren says the Aldridge girl won't touch a sword,*" *Ruben replied, and my cheeks flushed. Why did my father tell everyone about that? "My Legality contacts say she's so afraid that she never will. She's been using a wooden staff, of all things." He chuckled, as if this were highly amusing. "All you need is a good sword fight, and the Sovereignty is as good as ours.*"

I watched Auden's eyes grow wide, watched him bite his lip in what seemed to be uncertainty. "I don't know, she's really good at everything else."

I smiled to myself. I had hoped he'd noticed how much I'd learned from my new tutors!

Ruben scoffed, crossing his arms. "It doesn't matter. She has a weakness—and you know what we say about that." A long pause followed, and I could practically feel the cold stare he gave Auden.

"'There is no place for weakness in perfection,'" Auden recited emotionlessly. "I know that, Father."

"Do you?" Ruben asked, voice mocking. "Because you certainly don't act like it. I swear, you would think you want to lose with the way you cling to that girl. It's embarrassing, Auden." A long, tense pause followed, and I barely dared to breathe. "Well, do you?" Ruben pressed. "Do you want her to beat you?"

A clinking noise sounded somewhere behind me, and I gulped down a mouthful of saliva in my fright. I felt it go down the wrong pipe, a cough fighting to the surface. Face screwed up against the feeling, I slipped carefully back through the arch and into the hallway beyond, practically sprinting to the end before allowing the cough to escape. No one entered the area as I coughed, for which I was extraordinarily grateful. It took a minute or so before my throat felt soothed enough for me to return to my snooping, and I knew instantly I had missed something major. I cursed my throat's timing as I slipped back into my hiding spot.

"... what we talked about," Ruben was lecturing, Auden watching hopelessly with his sword dangling by his side. "There's no place for weakness in this world."

"I understand," Auden replied once more, voice sounding utterly defeated despite his best attempts. "I'll do better."

"You'd better hope so," Ruben replied swiftly. "You know the consequences if you can't cut it."

A wave of fright washed over Auden's pale face, making it appear almost ghostlike in the bitter cold air. I caught a sharp glimpse of panic in his blue eyes, almost desperation—and then, it was gone. A wall seemed to slam over *his emotions as he gritted his teeth, shaky arm extending his sword as if it could guard him from the world. "Let's go again."*

I had never told Auden about that day, never shared what I had seen. I just gave him a huge hug the next day, careful not to squeeze too hard. I went out of my way to compliment his skills, and when he showed up to my house with a cut lip or a sore ankle, I did my best to help. It wasn't enough, though; it never would be. No amount of compliments or warm moments could change the fact that it would be us, at the end. I had always known that, in an inevitable sort of way. I just never imagined how much it would hurt, knowing that the time was near. Tomorrow, the battle would begin—and only one of us could become Sovereign.

5

A RACE TO THE FINISH

The morning of our first assessment dawned clear and sunny—a relief, considering we might very well be outdoors. A weird sort of energy buzzed through my room as I dressed, stepping into the tunic and trousers provided. We had all been given matching outfits to wear, simply colored clothing meant to eliminate appearance from the assessment altogether. Still, I made sure to style myself to a Courtly level, pulling my hair into a sturdy but elegant braid and applying a generous amount of makeup. This was the Pathway, after all—and try as they might, not even the Council could remove the influence of appearance altogether.

I tried my best to remain calm, but my eyes couldn't help but catch on to the portraits in the hall as I passed. Pictured in each frame was a Sovereign, standing tall and mighty and unafraid. I wondered if they had felt the same way before their own Pathway, afraid and excited and unsure all at once. The row of portraits never failed to make anxiety twist in my chest, reminding me of just how much lay in the balance. I was all too aware of how few women were pictured, and of the fact that they all balanced a massive sword on their shoulder.

I had never felt comfortable around a sword. Not since that fateful day ten years ago, when I'd been forced to attend the execution of a rebel, a young girl who had been found guilty of murdering a Court member. It wasn't the first execution I'd attended; though they weren't exactly common, there had been enough in my lifetime for me to grow desensitized. It was, however, the first and only time I saw my father kill someone. Usually Legality was responsible for the actual execution, but this execution, my mother had explained to me gently, was special. Something about movements and the importance of symbols that I was far too young to understand. All I knew was that when the woman screamed, it was because of my father's sword. And when her screams stopped, the sound still mingling eerily with the cheers of the crowd, that was because of my father's sword, too. She was only fifteen.

Needless to say, the image stuck with me. Not the blood, or the girl, or even my father's unbearably calm face; no, it was the sword that haunted me, glinting silver coated in crimson. I wasn't even sure I was afraid of the object itself anymore, but it didn't matter. What began as a childish fear steadily grew into a deep-rooted fear, a mental block so ingrained in my brain that I doubted I could ever overcome it. *I can't even hold a sword,* I thought hopelessly. *How could I possibly win?*

It was a melancholy way to start the day, worry racing through my brain as I began the walk to the Cathe alone. Auden hadn't been waiting outside of his manor, likely there already. It hurt a bit, but then, I'd expected it after our conversation at the fountain. If nothing else, Auden was an all-in sort of person. Besides, what could he and I possibly say to each other today? "Good luck, but I hope I beat you"?

I decided to take the outer route, which added ten minutes to the walk but was far more scenic. Auden always refused, claiming that it made no sense to take more time for the same distance. I was grateful for the views today, the brief glimpses of nature a soothing balm on my nerves. I felt oddly calm as the Cathe loomed, a sort of numbness washing over me. I wished I could claim it was from a sense of confidence, of being prepared and aware. In reality I was empty, as if my nerves were a few steps behind me.

The entire Court was invited to watch the assessments, with my father's hand-picked Council as judges—and yet, the hall was eerily empty as I entered. I furrowed my brows, moving carefully to the large ballroom in which the assessment was to be held. Immediately upon entering, two things appeared very clearly to me. First, although many fellow participants occupied the room, I spotted no Court members here. There was only my father and his Council, seated at a long table near the front. Secondly, a tense silence engulfed the room. There were no contestants mulling around now, everyone remaining seated in a labeled chair around rows of long tables, fiddling with their hands or staring straight forward.

I gulped, sliding into my labeled chair next to Auden in the front. He didn't give me as much as a glance, coolly concentrated despite the shaking of his hands. I swallowed back the nerves beginning to build in my stomach, choosing instead to study the Council in front of us.

My father sat in the middle, smiling jovially as he spoke with Councilman Mullerson. Auden's father, Ruben, glared from his other side, studying the room with an intense gaze. Our eyes met, a strange chill running down my spine at his cold stare. I wasn't sure how Auden ever felt happy with that sort of stare watching him all the time. Then again, Auden rarely did seem happy in the presence of his father, transformed into a terse yet respectful creature. Even now, he avoided looking at the Council, eyes focused determinedly on the table before us.

I looked away quickly, scanning the other members instead. My mother was not present, despite her second-place finish in the Pathway. Second place may have guaranteed her a place in the Court, but only my father could choose his Council. Each Sovereign got to choose their

Council shortly after being coronated, with free pick of anyone in the Court. They would rule on the Council until the next Sovereign was named, unless of course my father decided to replace them prior to that. I wasn't quite sure why he had chosen to exclude my mother; I'd never asked, and I wasn't sure I ever would. Instead, my father had chosen two other men, leaving the Council severely lacking in feminine touch.

Councilman Mullerson stood at last, clearly excited. And yet, there was no embellishment, no big speech as he spoke. Instead, he simply pulled out a scroll and began to read.

"Your first assessment," he announced, booming voice more serious than usual, "begins at the conclusion of these instructions. You shall be split into two teams, with which you will be expected to work collaboratively. These medallions," he said, holding up a collection of platinum medallions, "are the object of the game. Half of you will be in charge of hiding, and the others seeking. The Hiders will have an hour to write a series of three clues leading to a medallion, which you will then hide around the grounds of the Cathe. After this hour, the Seekers will have an hour to find their medallion, using the three clues they will find along the way. This is a double-blind challenge, meaning that Hiders will not know who will be seeking their medallion and Seekers will not know who hid theirs. Points will be awarded or removed according to time and success. The first Seeker to find a medallion and ring the bell stationed at the starting point will receive the most points, while their associated Hider will lose the most. Similarly, any Seeker who doesn't find a medallion will lose full points, while their Hider receives full points. The two groups will be separated during the assessment, and there is to be no conversation between Hiders and Seekers during the assessment."

My breathing grew rapid, mind whirring as I tried to take in all of this information—so much, and all at once!

"You will notice an envelope underneath your chair," Mullerson continued. "Please open it, and read your assignment quietly."

I reached under my chair, fingers meeting the fine envelope. I opened it cautiously, careful not to tear its contents. Inside lay a single slip of parchment, adorned with simple writing:

Willow Aldridge

Team 2 – Seekers

I read it quickly, silently rejoicing. The Hiders certainly seemed to have the harder job, and one in which I was not interested in partaking.

I leaned over to Auden, whose face was falling at his parchment. *Auden Bonavich*, it read. *Team 1 – Hiders.*

He smiled softly, offering me a small shrug before turning forward.

"You may now gather with your teams. Hiders, you will write your riddles in this room, while the Seekers will gather in the room next door. Seekers may not leave your room until the hour is up, but Hiders may leave the room to hide your medallions and clues. However, all riddles must be checked my myself to ensure fair play before you are permitted to leave. Medallions may be hidden anywhere on the property of the Cathe, including outdoors. The Court and Council will then gather in the entranceway, where the Seekers are to meet us to begin the assessment." He beamed at us, pushing the scroll back into his pocket.

I took that as a cue, moving regretfully towards the room next door. I may have been excited about my role, but I hated to be separated from Auden like this. My mood improved slightly as I passed Emmaline, who remained seated with the rest of the Hiders.

"Did anyone else not understand the rules?" a girl asked from the corner of the room, nervous green eyes peeking out from large glasses.

Almost on instinct, I ran a mental scan of her discipline in my head. *Definitely not Charisma,* I thought to myself. No self-respecting Charisma would say something so uncertain in the presence of competition.

"I didn't," another girl admitted, twirling her hair around her finger.

"Me neither," a third voice chimed in, deep and gruff.

"Alright, then," Jerome piped up, a fellow Charisma whom I'd always found a bit dull. "Did *anyone* understand the rules to this thing?"

All eyes turned to me. I didn't understand either, not really—but I couldn't just *say* that. I took a deep breath, carefully casting my doubts aside before speaking. "It's simple," I stated, crossing my arms. "The Hiders hide their medallions and write clues to help us find them. We, as the Seekers, simply have to solve the clues and find a medallion. The first of us to find one gets the most points. Any of us who don't find one loses points. Everyone else is in between, our points depending on how fast we find one." My hands were shaking as I spoke, not from speaking publicly, but rather from the importance of what I was sharing. If I had misinterpreted the rules and ended up steering everyone in the wrong direction, what would happen? Would I lose points—or worse?

Luckily, my practiced voice did its job. The other participants didn't seem to question the summation, breaking into small conversations as if there were no uncertainty at all.

There wasn't much else to do in the hour as we waited, but I was sure to keep busy nonetheless. Nerves were one thing, but to be nervous and bored was infinitely worse; years of pressure had taught me that much. We weren't permitted any books or study materials in the room, but we quizzed each other from memory, keeping our brains as sharp as possible among such nerves and tension. It was funny, how easy it was to forget we were competing against each other; in that hour, sticking together was all we could do.

It felt like days had passed by the time the door opened, Director Ariponas beckoning us out. The entryway was full now, teeming with members of the Court. Murmurs broke out as we emerged, clinks of gold sounding as money changed hands—betting on us, no doubt. It was hardly uncommon for the Court to bet on the contestants. I'd never thought much about it before, but it made me queasy now that I was included in those bets.

I decided instead to focus on the envelopes lying on pedestals in a circle around us. I spotted my name on one of them, moving to stand in front of it. The hiding team was nowhere to be seen, likely locked away in some room after setting out the clues. Moments passed as the others found their envelopes, with Mullerson spouting some elaborate speech about wit and wisdom.

And then, all too suddenly, it was time.

"Seekers, you may open your envelopes in three ... two..."

The nerves hit me all at once, like a ton of bricks. My palms grew sweaty, and I gulped down an unsteady breath as my legs trembled.

"... one!"

I spurred myself into action as papers ruffled, ripping open my own heavy envelope. It took several moments to read the parchment as it shook in my hands, my brain struggling to process anything beyond a blinding sense of panic.

Treasured, but flawed; the imperfect leader of the greatest charade of them all.

I frowned at the words, embarrassingly perplexed. Contestants moved around me, hurrying off to wherever their first clue had apparently led them. Eyes seemed to follow me as I stood, judging my stillness, my silence. I gulped, moving quickly past the crowd and into the hallway beyond. I may have been utterly confused, but no one else needed to know that.

Great job, Willow, I scoffed at myself, *hiding when you should be seeking. What a great start.*

It wasn't the concept of the riddle that confused me, but rather the boldness. No one would so callously call out a leader for being flawed—not if they had a shred of common sense. Perhaps it was merely a jab at my father, at our legacy ... but then again, it wasn't as if the writer of the riddle knew I would be the one to solve it.

I groaned, resting my head on the cool surface of the wall. The paneling smelled old, as if burdened by years of use—one of the leftover bits from before renovation, then. The Cathe had once been a great theater; in fact, the theater still remained within the building itself. It was a historical artifact of sorts, although it certainly wasn't treated as such. We didn't bother to honor the remnants of our ancestors, flawed as they had been. In fact, we didn't have many historical artifacts at all—only the theater, and...

"The crown!" I whispered to myself, laughing aloud. All of a sudden, it seemed so *obvious.* The old crown—the symbol of the Olden kings and queens, fraudulent at best, respected without merit. *Treasured, but flawed.*

I ran along the halls, suddenly grateful for the years Auden and I had spent exploring as children. Why, we must have passed the crown display dozens of times! It had been left in the theater itself, as a lesson more than anything else—a reminder of exactly how much imperfection can cost. Be that as it may, I'd always admired it as a child, with its golden sheen and gems that shone as bright as a rare green leaf. The crown the Sovereign wore was much less elaborate.

It took only minutes to find it again, shining bright in the Olden-style theater. I skidded to a stop in front of it, eagerly snatching up the letter that lay atop it.

A constant reminder of the end.

I frowned at the words. Whoever my Hider was, their riddles were quite depressing. Yet here, surrounded by reminders of the Oldens—surely, that was "the end," the end of the Olden World. And the biggest reminder now...

It took a few minutes to reach the library, even rushing as I was. Luckily I knew exactly where it was, having spent many hours here myself. The Palace library was grand, but no where had quite as many books about the Oldens as this library. Surely this was what the riddle was referring to... right?

I grew less sure as I searched, ripping book after book off the shelf and glancing under each and every table. There was nothing to be found, no envelope or scrap of paper. Eventually, I got desperate enough to start opening books, just in case it was hidden inside. It was in the third book that I saw it—not a clue, but rather the headline of an old newspaper clip pasted into the book.

Fading nature reported nation-wide: Accident or Attack?

Of course—the end of the Olden world was the death of the Earth itself. These books may report it, but what if the riddle meant it more literally? What if it meant...

I grinned as I ran, the wind brushing through my hair as I exited the Cathe. The small gardens were entirely deserted, and I wasted no time in dropping to my knees in front of a peculiarly lumpy portion of the ground. I knew it was the soil that had initially been affected by the bioweapons; in fact, I had studied that particular fact only last night. Besides, my father *had* said to think outside the box.

My carefully polished fingernails grew tarnished as I dug into the ground, scraping at the lump of dirt with my bare hands. Deeper and deeper I dug, with no luck. I was just about to give up altogether when I felt it, wrinkled against my fingertips. I drew out the rolled parchment, cringing slightly at the dirt that poured out of the center and onto my tunic. Suddenly, I was glad I was not in my own clothing today. The paper fared far worse, so browned by the dirt that its message was hardly legible.

Two above the landing, one towards the tree. One more up, inverse from the street.

I glanced towards the tree, hoping to find some sort of clue there. Nothing. And two of what? Steps, perhaps? But from where? The landing could only mean the balcony overlooking where I stood, although I couldn't exactly get above that. Except ... there were windows there. Two windows lined up, in fact, right above the balcony. My eyes widened: *Two above the landing.* I moved my eyes one over to the window next to it, closer to the tree. *One more up,* I counted, *inverse from the street.*

A room—the clue was leading me to a specific room! I counted aloud as I sped through the fifth floor, not bothering to acknowledge those I passed.

I glanced at a clock as I passed, almost stopping dead in the middle of the hall. Twenty minutes—there were only twenty minutes left in the hour. Twenty minutes to find the medallion, make my way back to the main hall, and ring that bell. I spurred myself back into action, forcing my feet to move faster against the hard floor. I'd had yet to hear a bell ring from the main hall, so I still had a chance at coming in first place.

I skidded to a stop at last, not bothering to close the door as I blew into the indicated room. It was a small room clearly out of use, with only a bare desk and mostly vacant bookcase. Still, I searched thoroughly, rifling through each book and looking underneath the desk. I even went so far as tapping the floorboards, just in case one was loose... Nothing.

The medallion was not here.

I gritted my teeth, glancing at the clock on the wall. Fifteen minutes. Perhaps I had counted wrong, or maybe it was talking about steps after all. I took out the dirty note once again, rereading it once, then twice, then a third time for good measure. No... I had certainly counted right, and it could not possibly be anything other than windows. I nearly screamed in frustration, each tick of the clock echoing in my head. For the first time in my entire life, a shred of doubt about my future entered my mind.

Maybe Vi was right, I thought desperately. *Maybe I'll be sent to the Beyond after all. Maybe I was never good enough for the Court, much less being the Sovereign.*

My searching grew more frantic, my arms aching as I struggled to lift the bookshelf. After all, it might very well be hidden underneath. I fell to my knees for a better angle, easing the corner up, up, up, so very carefully...

"It's not there," a voice sounded from behind me.

A curse jumped from my mouth as the bookshelf fell back into place with a loud bang, narrowly missing my fingers. I glanced up from where I kneeled, taking in the vaguely familiar male form blocking the doorway. He leaned against the frame casually, gray eyes full of amusement as I glared.

Oh, I recognized him, alright. We hadn't met, but it was the same appallingly lazy posture I had seen lurking in the back of all our training sessions. The same wavy blond hair, falling in front of glimmering gray eyes and an obnoxiously attractive face. The one contestant in the Pathway who genuinely didn't seem to care.

He certainly didn't seem worried about the ticking of the clock, or the possibility of not finding a medallion. In fact, he held no papers, no envelope with his name on it. It was then that I realized I had seen him this very morning, sitting in the room with the Hiders. That meant he was not on my team, and he was also definitely *not* supposed to be anywhere near me right now.

"Are you insane?" I hissed, my voice a whisper as I shot to my feet. "Get out of here!"

He just stared at me, brow sketched in a way that suggested he was, in fact, insane. "And leave you to move all this furniture yourself? What an awful Service that would make me."

I huffed out a breath of annoyance, glancing once again at the clock. *Twelve minutes.*

"You won't be anything if we're caught in here," I reminded him, peering nervously over his shoulder. "And neither will I." No one had explained the consequences of cheating, but I was fairly sure being kicked out of the Pathway and cast out of Atvas would be included.

Yet the boy didn't look the least bit upset by the idea, instead breaking into a smirk. "How is it that you manage to make my attempts to help you sound so very scandalous?"

I could have screamed, could have cursed at him yet again. Instead, I turned back to the bookshelf, wedging my fingers under it once more. If he wanted to throw away his shot at the Court, that was just fine with me—but he certainly was not about to take me down with him. Not after all I'd done, the lifetime of preparation for this very moment.

I heard a sigh behind me, the first genuine sound from that rough voice I had yet to hear. "It's not there."

I gritted my teeth, lowering the bookshelf to the floor, softly this time. "Care to explain why exactly you're here?"

"I told you," he responded, as if it were obvious, "I'm trying to help you."

I bit my lip. It was insane, but the clock was ticking steadily, and he didn't seem to be going anywhere. "Fine. Then *help me.*"

"It's downstairs. Room 443." His voice was low—a sign that he might be genuine. Yet ... downstairs?

"It can't be," I retorted. "The riddle said it was this room. I'm sure of it."

He frowned, brow furrowing. "Well, it's not. I saw it myself; they put it in room 443. Your Hider must have cheated."

I was shaking my head before he even finished speaking, coming back to my senses suddenly. "This is insane," I whispered, "utterly insane." I had no clue who this boy was, much less why he would be helping me.

Unless, of course, *he* was the one cheating. Tricking me into going down to check, wasting the rest of my time... It made sense. Perhaps that was his game. Fake ambivalence, then cheat us all out of our spots.

I took a slow, careful step back.

His eyes followed me, brows raising at my step. "Right, I'm just a Service. What do I know?" he muttered, a tangy sort of sound dripping from his voice—anger, I realized with a start. Anger at me. "Unbelievable."

I flinched at the sharp words. "I didn't mean..."

"Of course you did." His anger seemed to deflate some as he sighed, turning toward the doorway. "Good luck ruling Atvas without your precious medallion."

I stared after him, bewildered by his reaction. But I didn't have time to dwell on it—not with that incessant ticking reminding me of how little remained. *Ten minutes.* I glanced around the room, halfheartedly sweeping through the desk drawer once more. The clock seemed to move faster with every passing second, the ticking matching the racing of my pulse.

Just then, a faint ringing sounded from far below—a bell. Someone had gotten a medallion. I glanced at the clock. *Seven minutes.*

Back down the halls I raced, back to those stairs and down one level. I felt nauseous as I approached room 443, my hand hovering above the knob despite myself. I didn't have the time to hesitate, and I wasn't quite sure why I was. Perhaps it was the admittance of my wrongdoing, the feeling as if I had cheated myself. Or maybe I simply feared what I would find inside. If the boy was right, and he had been helping me after all... Well, it didn't fare well for my morality. I entered anyway, adrenaline pushing me through the door—and there it was, lying half concealed beneath a desk. I managed only a brief glance at the clock as I lunged for it, but it was enough to see that the hand was almost at the hour. In fact, it seemed *very* close to the hour.

Faces peered towards me as I barreled down the grand staircase, practically shoving aside the Court spectators lining the railings. I saw only in tunnel vision, focused on that bell that stood in the middle of the pedestals. I missed a step, nearly tripping, but an arm shot out of the crowd and stabilized me as I gasped down air. Closer and closer the bell grew, until I could see the detailing on it, the words on the top—and then suddenly it was in my hand, cold and solid against my clammy palm. The accompanying ring was a glorious sound, resounding clearly over the cheering crowd. The sound was still echoing when a deep voice called time—and just like that, the first assessment was over.

6

Something Old, Something New

Amaris smiled at me from next to the bell, a medallion shining in her hand and a smile on her face. She looked calm and relaxed, as if she'd found the medallion ages ago. *Without* sweating like a pig, at that. I pushed down the jealousy in my chest, reminding myself that I was trying to reconnect with her. Besides, it wasn't *her* fault that someone had cheated.

No, I had a feeling Emmaline was to thank for that. She was exactly the sort of person who would write false information, a safe form of cheating that could be easily hidden as a mistake. I felt her icy blue eyes staring at me from across the hall, where the hiding team was clustered, face full of a smug sort of glee.

Later. I'd worry about that later, after I had fully caught my breath. I noted Auden in the clump also, whose eyes went straight to the medallion in my hand. The boy from earlier was there, too, somehow looking as if he'd been there all along. I avoided his eyes, shame flooding my veins. I'd worry about that later, too.

Mullerson was speaking, explaining that the results of today's assessment were to be posted tomorrow morning outside the Cathe. I didn't bother to listen, instead gulping down the glass of water a nearby Service handed me. I was still sticky with sweat. Apparently, no one else's riddles had led them across the whole Cathe. Maybe the judges would consider that when they calibrated their scores. Maybe they would consider the cheating, too, once I told my father about it.

"Are you alright?" Amaris asked softly, eyes wide as she took in my disheveled state.

I sighed inwardly. "I'm fine," I replied, forcing a smile to my face. "My Hider enjoyed running, it would seem. And dirt." I held up my dirt-covered note. Let them think it had been merely the running and digging that slowed me down.

"That's awful," Amaris agreed, holding up her three clean notes. "Mine was boring, really—just three rooms, and all near each other."

"Perhaps boring is for the best," I sighed. "I sort of wish my Hider was less creative."

I glimpsed Auden coming up beside her, his face was pale and drawn. I waited for Amaris to excuse herself before asking, "What's wrong?"

"Nothing," he said, shaking his head. "I'm just... nervous about the scores. Us Hiders won't know our scores until tomorrow."

Indeed, that was one of the benefits of the Seeker role—I already knew I would receive some points, if not as many as Amaris. For Auden and the rest of the Hiders, there was nothing to do but wait.

"You can head back, if you want," I offered, knowing just how jittery Auden could get when nervous. "I'm going to wait for my parents, so I'll be a while."

"Alright." He smiled a tight smile that couldn't quite conceal the tension on his face. "And congrats, by the way. You deserve it."

My heart broke a bit as he vanished into the crowd. My every instinct was to comfort him, reassure him it would all be alright, but...well, we had agreed to fight for the Sovereignty. I didn't have any words to help him, and I doubted he would want them even if I did.

"Oh, look," a voice sounded, that distinctly whiny voice that never failed to irritate me: Emmaline. I gritted my teeth, willing myself to remain calm as I whirled around. She was surrounded with her little posse as usual, as if she were the Sovereign already. "You got a medallion after all."

"Clearly." I kept my voice even, equal parts polite and brutal.

She gave a little half pout that made me want to bash her face in, eyes locking onto the medallion still clutched in my palm. "We were so *worried*. We all assumed you would find yours quickly—you know, since you've been to the Cathe so many times."

I couldn't help but admit it was clever, the way she brought my status into it. Annoying but clever, turning my strengths into weaknesses before I could use them against her.

"Did something happen?" she added, picking at her impeccable nails as if bored by the conversation.

Oh, she was good, alright. She was sniffing me out, trying to find out just how I had located the medallion without a proper clue—and how likely I was to tell on her.

"Not at all," I replied simply, smiling widely. "I just saw no reason to rush." Yes, I would tell on her—but not until I had proof. "But thank you for your concern. I'll be sure to remember that when I'm the Sovereign."

I left as soon as the words left my mouth, not waiting to see the resentment that surely shone on their faces. Ordinarily, I may have gloated, at least for a little bit, but ... I was shaken. Emmaline wanted to win; that much I'd always known. I just never thought she would have the guts to do anything about it, much less to throw it in my face like that. The last time she'd done anything quite so bold we'd been nine years old, and she'd blabbed to the whole class that I was afraid of swords. Since then it had been polite smiles and poisonous words, always hidden behind a mask of niceties. Well, at least until today. She'd surprised me—and that made her very, very dangerous. She needed to be stopped. And to do that, I needed proof.

I watched the Service boy from earlier carefully, tracking him as he headed down a side hallway. I followed a careful distance behind, curiosity taking over any sense I had.

He stopped suddenly, whipping around to face me in the empty hallway. His face was cautious, morphing into surprise as he took me in. We stared at each other for a moment, an awkward sort of tension stretching between us.

"I see you used your brain," he said at last, eyes tracking the medallion still clutched in my hands. "Finally."

I had planned to apologize, to have a good conversation like civilized members of society. I was a Charisma. I knew how to control my emotions, how to use my words to my advantage. And yet, around this boy...

"I wouldn't have needed to, if you had just *told* me why you were there," I retorted, crossing my arms.

"I did," he pointed out, eyes sparkling with something like amusement as he took in my posture. I uncrossed my arms quickly, settling them by my side instead. No need to act *and* look like a child. "I told you I was there to help. It's not my fault you didn't believe me."

"Well, it's not my fault you seemed so suspicious."

"And how, exactly, was I suspicious?" He leaned against the wall, arms crossed over his chest—yet somehow, the posture didn't make *him* look like a child at all. His blonde hair was tousled, as if he had spent hours running a hand through it, and his jawline was a sharp angle. And those *eyes,* that infuriating smirk...

His smirk grew, and I realized with a start that I hadn't responded. I blushed furiously. *Time to change the subject, then.*

"Who did it?" I demanded. "The riddles. Who did you see move them?"

He tilted his head, examining me carefully. "What's the point?"

"Excuse me?"

"What would be the good in knowing who it was?" he asked. His voice was surprisingly pensive, a layer of depth there that I hadn't quite expected.

"The *good,*" I replied, exasperated, "is that I can tell my father and stop them from doing it again."

"Ah," he said, quirking a brow, "off to tell your beloved father. Just as I thought."

"And what's that supposed to mean?" I asked carefully, glancing around us. He may have been spewing pure insanity, but he *did* just help me. Besides, I would rather him not get in trouble before telling me who the cheater was.

"What do you *think* that's supposed to mean?" His voice remained infuriatingly steady, a slight hint of sarcasm the only clue of ingenuity.

"Stop answering my questions with a question."

"Then stop asking questions," he replied, an utterly irritating half smile on his face.

"Fine." I gritted my teeth, turning to leave. I would just have to figure out some other way to prove Emmaline guilty.

"So, when are you going to help *me*?"

"*What?*"

He pushed off the wall, crossing the hall to stand across from me. "You would have failed this assessment," he pointed out. "The way I see it, you owe me. Big-time."

"I didn't ask for your help," I pointed out, voice hard in a way that my mother would say was unbefitting of a civilized woman.

"Fair enough." He shrugged. "I'll just take this, then." And then his hand was on mine, a million firecrackers exploding as his skin brushed my skin. I didn't dare to breathe until he pulled back, my medallion clutched in his hand.

"Give that back! It's mine!"

"Well, I don't think the Council will let you keep it when I tell them you cheated," he said, a smug expression painting his face.

"Let's not forget who started this so-called cheating," I pointed out. "If I go down, you're coming with me."

"Ah-ha," he said, shaking his head. "Except one of us has a lot more to lose."

I narrowed my eyes, glaring at him. He was right, of course. For him, an accusation like that would only further his current downward progression. For me, it would change everything.

I sighed, throwing my hands in the air. "Fine. What do you even want?"

His whole demeanor seemed to soften, and he bit his lip—a habit awfully familiar to me. I did it when I was nervous. If he was the same, this was a serious request.

"You're the most perfect contestant here," he started slowly, watching me carefully. I would have beamed at the praise, yet somehow it didn't seem like a compliment coming from him. "I'm the least. I think it's obvious what I could want."

"So, what? You want me to put in a good word for you with the Council?" I'd been asked that same thing many times, and always refused. I could do it, though. For this, I would have to.

"What?" Genuine surprise shone through his voice, and on his face, too. "No, that's not it at all."

"Oh." I blushed furiously. I really did need to stop making so many assumptions, but I couldn't help it. He was just ... unusual.

"I just need you to teach me some stuff, that's all." He was nervous, I realized with a start—the nerves of someone not used to asking for help. I would know. "Just to get me ready for the assessments."

"Why?" He seemed to care very little for the rules, regulations, and practices of Atvas. Why, then, was he so desperate to improve in the Pathway? Why was he in the Pathway at all, considering he didn't seem to try at all?

"We all have our reasons." His voice was quiet, and I knew not to push any more. Not now, at least. "Will you do it?"

I considered refusing, considered turning him in for cheating and denying any accusations. And yet, as I looked into his eyes ... I recognized them. Not as his, but as my own—for my own desperation shone there, my own drive to do better. Whatever his reasons were, however different from my own, the fear was the same.

"Fine," I sighed finally, the last of my resistance crumbling. "We'll work each Saturday for three hours, beginning at nine o'clock in the morning. We can start tomorrow." His face filled with relief, but I held up a hand before he could speak. "On one condition: you help me with Legality."

That smirk grew on his face again, and I braced myself for whatever comment was sure to come.

"Of course," he said, and I sighed in relief just as his mouth opened once more. "Every princess needs to protect herself."

"I am *not* a princess," I huffed. Princesses were just as bad as the Olden kings and queens—worse, even. There was no bigger insult, and yet ... he hadn't said it like one.

He huffed out a disbelieving laugh. "Yeah, okay. Where should we meet? Here?"

"No. There's no way you'll be able to get in; besides events, no one is allowed in but the Court." I bit my lip, mind racing as I thought through the options. The school building would be closed on Saturdays, and meeting at the Palace would mean explaining this to my parents. The thought alone made me shiver.

"My house, then," he shrugged, as if it were obvious.

"But..." I started instinctively, heart beating impossibly fast. It was the best solution, really—it just also happened to be terrifying. I'd never been to anyone's home outside of the Court, and was more than a bit afraid to.

"Unless you don't want to?" he asked, suspiciously accommodating all of the sudden. "I mean, we could do it at the market, I suppose, but it'll be quite busy. Lots of people around, you see."

Oh, I knew a challenge when I heard one.

"You know," I answered, smiling my sweetest smile. "I think your house would be a lovely option."

"Oh, you do?" There was a glimmer of amusement in his eyes, even as his face remained in that smug smirk. I found the expression oddly distracting as he gave me directions to his house, and I could only hope my mind would retain the words I hardly heard. "...and then you turn right at the bend, and it's right there. Got it?"

"Of course." I shook my head slightly, forcing myself back to the present. "Nine o'clock tomorrow, then. I'll help you prepare for the trials, and in turn you'll assist me with Legality and keep quiet about the agreement."

He looked displeased at the added stipulation, but didn't comment on it as he tossed me the medallion. "We have a deal."

I caught the medallion carefully. Despite my considerable wealth, it was now the most valuable thing I owned. He was already retreating when I glanced back up, off to some unknown location.

"Wait!" I called. "What's your name?"

"Leo," he called, not bothering to stop.

"I'm Willow," I answered awkwardly, speaking to his back. "Willow Aldridge."

Leo looked over his shoulder, those sparkling eyes meeting mine once more. "I know," he said, eyes moving once again to that medallion. "You're welcome, by the way." And then he was gone, leaving me more confused than ever.

"You're welcome for what?" a voice sounded behind me, words sharper than a blade.

I knew that voice. Auden.

"What are you doing here?" I tried to keep the nerves out of my voice, feeling suddenly defensive—which was foolish, considering I hadn't actually done anything wrong. "I thought you were going home."

"I was," he said carefully. "I just wanted to talk to you about something. Besides, you seemed ... upset. I wanted to check on you." His eyes shifted, glancing to where Leo had stood before flitting back to me. "Clearly, someone already did."

A sinking feeling began somewhere deep in my stomach, growing heavier with the confusion and betrayal those blue eyes held.

"It was nothing," I said breezily, crossing my arms as if that could hide the guilty racing of my heart. "I just had to sort something out, that's all."

"Sort out what?" he pressed, and for a moment I wanted to tell him everything, wanted to beg him to figure it all out for me. But...I had no clue how to explain Leo, or the cheating, or any of it. Besides, he was the last person I should be talking to about anything related to the Pathway.

Auden just watched me carefully, eyes more sad than accusatory. "You can talk to me, Willow. You know that."

I remained silent longer than I should have before replying. "There's nothing to tell."

"What is it?" His face was almost pleading, raw with emotion. "Why won't you let me in?"

"We're rivals," I reminded him softly. "We shouldn't be talking, not about this."

"Don't you do that." His voice was sharp with hurt. "We've managed to remain both friends and rivals our entire lives—this is no different."

"Of course it is," I pressed, though my heart twisted with each word. "We agreed to fight, Auden. May the best man win, right?"

"I didn't realize that meant we couldn't even *talk*."

"It doesn't!" My heart raced at the mere thought of cutting contact completely, of losing one of my closest friends. "I just... I don't think we should rely on each other for comfort, not about the Pathway. It'll only hurt us both."

Auden just looked down, shaking his head. His face had grown dark, as If shrouded in shadows of pain. "Who, then?"

"Who, what?"

"If not you," he muttered, voice brimming with undiluted emotion, "then *who* am I supposed to talk to?" The words seemed to weigh down the whole room, the way awful truths so often do. Auden, while incredibly good at making connections, didn't have many close friends. He could perhaps talk to his mother, if she was ever sober enough, but his father...

"Auden..." I started. He must have heard the pity I tried to hide, because his eyes moved downwards and he shook his head again.

"Forget it," he murmured quickly, embarrassed. "You're right, I'm sorry. I don't know what came over me."

"No!" I exclaimed quickly, before he could turn away like he so obviously wanted to. "This whole competition is messing with my mind already," I admitted, sighing. "But you were right. I don't want to lose you."

"Never." The answer was immediate, the dimpled smile returning to his face. "I'll always be there, you know that. Whether you want us to talk or not."

The words made me feel warm inside, as if bathed in a ray of sunlight. Warm and safe, as I always was in Auden's presence. "I do want us to talk. Though I have to warn you—it's a bizarre story."

"What do you mean?"

And so I told him, every detail I could remember. Auden seemed even more surprised by the tale than I had been, eyes growing progressively wider.

"So, then I confronted Leo to find out who it was, and that's why he was talking to me," I finished at last.

Auden's brows were furrowed as he leaned in closer, voice low enough to be a whisper. "Did he tell you, then? That it was Emmaline?"

"No," I sighed, irritation flaring up as I remembered the interaction. "He refused."

"Why?" Auden asked, glancing over to where Leo had stood, as if his gaze might conjure him back and so he could demand that he tell us the truth.

"I have no idea." I shrugged. "But it was Emmaline, trust me. She practically told me herself."

"So, are you going to tell your father?" he pressed, and I smiled. It was far better to see him like this, eyes alight and sharp, curiosity peeking through the pounds of worry he always seemed to carry.

"I don't know," I admitted. "What do you think?"

He tilted his head, pensive. "Ordinarily, I would say you should, but without proof..."

"Maybe the Council could give it to me, though," I remarked, the idea forming in my mind as I spoke. "They must have known who wrote which riddles; they could tell me for sure."

"True." And yet, Auden's voice was cautious.

"What is it?"

"I'm not sure they'll believe you," he admitted, shoulders dropping as if he were relieved to say the words. "I know it's your father, and I mean him no offense, but accusations of cheating have been made in the past."

My brow furrowed. I had never heard of that. How had he?

"My father told me," he continued, as if in response to my unspoken question.

"And...?"

"And, it never turned out well for the accusers." Auden grimaced, as if remembering some unknown tale. "They'll think you're the one cheating."

My jaw dropped. "That's ridiculous!" And it was, really. If I was a cheater, then Emmaline was an angel. Auden, however, didn't seem to agree. With his eyes downcast and jaw clenched, I knew he was holding something in. "What?"

"It's just... I know you didn't ask for it," he started, voice cautious, "but you *were* in the room together. And you *did* follow his advice, so..."

I almost laughed; first Leo, and now him. The one time I'd ever broken such a rule, and everyone felt obligated to point it out.

"I know," I sighed, ignoring the shock on Auden's face. "Leo said as much; it's how he got me to agree to tutor him."

Auden's face was puzzled, realization dawning as he put the pieces together. And then, it was angry. "He *blackmailed* you?" he spat, glaring down the hall. For a moment, I thought he might run down it, might hunt down Leo and demand that he apologize. "He has a lot of nerve, ordering you around like that. Does he even know who you are?"

I smiled a bit as I remembered our conversation, and the way Leo had responded to my name. No awe, no fake politeness. It was refreshing, really.

"We'll find a way out of it," Auden seethed. "You don't have to worry."

"No!" I interjected quickly, biting my lip. "He seemed like he honestly wanted to improve. I can't just ... let him fail. What kind of person would that make me?"

"A smart one." Auden shook his head. "That heart of yours is going to be the death of you some day, mark my words."

I bristled at the words, which sounded more like Ruben than Auden. "Oh, please. I'm just helping him out a bit. I hardly think I'm going to get hurt—unless you think a book is going to attack me, that is."

"I'm serious." He peered at me from under furrowed brows, and I frowned. Serious, indeed. "You don't understand. Those people are not like you and me. They are perilous, and chaotic, and *angry*—angry at

Atvas, and those who run it. More than anything, they're angry at your father. I doubt they're above hurting you to get to him."

I knew he spoke the truth. I had seen the discontentment on the faces of those in the lower ranks, and yet ... Leo hadn't seemed all that angry at me. Sarcastic, smug, even frustrated, but not truly *angry*.

"Just be careful," Auden concluded, casting me a wary glance. "They can be dangerous."

"I know," I agreed quietly, and my thoughts flashed to the fire in Leo's eyes, to the ever-present smirk on his face. *To the sparks still rushing through my veins.* "They can be dangerous."

It wasn't until hours later, as I lay in bed, that I realized: I never did ask what Auden had wanted to talk about in the first place.

7

UGLY TRUTHS AND BEAUTIFUL THINGS

I woke up to realize that I was, quite possibly, the most foolish person alive. It was the only explanation, the only *possible* reason for my agreeing to this idiotic tutoring.

Well, the only reason besides the blackmail, I reminded myself bitterly, throwing the covers off my legs with a groan. The Aldridge family tree was rife with leaders, visionaries who bowed to no one but perfection itself. Yet here I was, ordered around by a mere boy of seventeen. And a *Service,* at that. It was laughable, really—a sentiment Vi certainly seemed to agree with, giggling as I shared the story at the Court brunch the next morning. We'd managed to find a table to ourselves, about as private as one could get at a Court event.

Honestly, I wasn't sure why my mother thought planning a Court brunch the morning after our first trial was a good idea. Every inch of my body was sore, and my brain felt like it had been repeatedly hit with lightning. Yet there I was, dressed in a ruffled white day dress and hair tied back into a loose braid. To make matters worse, there weren't even chairs at the tables. I was fairly sure it was a tactic to encourage mingling, but I'd never bothered to learn more than that. It was necessary information for the Head of Relational Affairs, the pitiful position my mother currently held, but wasn't something a future Sovereign needed to know.

"It's not *that* funny," I groaned to Vi, hiding a smile as I bit into a scone. I was grateful that the brunch was inside at least, the Palace walls shielding us from the brisk winter breeze.

"Sorry, I know," Vi got out, hiccupping through her laughter. "It's just... it's funny to see you like this."

I frowned. "Like what?"

Vi just shook her head, the giggles slowly subsiding. "So ... flustered."

"I am not *flustered*."

"I just wish I had been there to see it," she declared, reaching across the table for the jam. "What's his name, anyway?"

"Leo," I said, and Vi froze, arm still outstretched towards the jam.

"Leo *Hayes*?"

"I'm not sure," I admitted. Leo hadn't told me his surname, and I hadn't asked. It hadn't seemed important in the moment, and I somehow doubted it would make much of a difference either way. After all, Service disciplines rarely had surnames of any influence. "Why?"

"No reason." The words were quick, Vi's usual bravado notably absent. "It's just... isn't he a Service?"

I frowned. Since when did *Vi* care about status? She was practically the champion of discipline equality, always telling me off for looking down on other disciplines.

"I mean, yeah," I said, suddenly defensive. "But it's just tutoring. No harm in that, right?"

She hummed in agreement, still frowning.

"Come on," I nudged her side gently. "You should be glad. Think of it as an opportunity to broaden my horizons, or whatever you're always on about."

"Maybe you shouldn't do it," she pressed, ignoring my words. "It could get in the way of the Pathway."

"Really?" I raised my brows. For the past ten years, Vi had mocked me for caring about the Pathway so much. "Do you know how ironic it is for *you* to tell me that?"

"I'm serious," she said, grasping my hand. Her eyes glinted with that same dangerous intensity as they had at the Sponsor's Ball, that foreign look that held nothing of my light hearted best friend.

"I know." I pulled back my hand, surprised and a little hurt. "I've been preparing for this for years, Vi. I know you're concerned, but you have to trust me. I'm not going to throw my future away for some Service guy just because he helped me in a trial."

She just shook her head, distraught. "You don't know Leo."

"And you do?" I shot back, eyes narrowing. She had claimed not to, but her words said otherwise.

She didn't answer, merely shaking her head once more. "Just... be careful."

"You sound like Auden," I murmured, waiting for the inevitable snort of disgust. Yet Vi didn't seem to hear me, looking off somewhere in the distance. I had a feeling that it was somewhere far, far beyond the confines of these walls, that she was floating somewhere inside her own mind. And though she answered my next question, continuing on with the motions of the day, I wasn't sure she ever really returned.

***

Never in my life had I been so offended by a mere doorway, but there was a first time for everything. I glared at the door, red with peeling paint.

Just knock, I urged myself. *It's really not that hard.*

Only, I suddenly forgot how to knock in the first place. Should I pound on the door, announce my presence clearly? What if his parents came to the door, and demanded to know why I was there? Why *was* I even there?

I forced a deep breath in, releasing in slowly before stepping up to the door. I raised my hand, which shook slightly, and knocked two times. For several moments there was nothing, only a bustle of muffled noise behind the door. I was debating adding a third for good measure when the door creaked open, revealing a disheveled and confused-looking Leo.

"Willow?" He frowned, assessing me with a wary gaze. "You're early."

I huffed. "It's called being punctual."

We both glanced at the clock beside the entryway, the hand halfway to the nine. Admittedly, half an hour may have been a *tad* bit excessive.

"If you say so." His voice was light, his smile devilish. "Too excited to wait?"

"Hardly," I answered, even as my cheeks heated up. "Perhaps I just wanted to get it over with."

Leo just raised a brow, leaning against the doorframe with a casual charm. "Perhaps."

I opened my mouth to spit a retort, but stopped suddenly as my eyes moved past his firm and towards the space beyond. The home was small and untidy, cluttered with a cozy sort of charm, but that wasn't what caught my eye. Behind Leo, eyes peering nervously from under a mop of wispy blonde hair, was a small child. The girl couldn't have been more than six years old, but she remained surprising calm as she watched us with wide blue eyes.

Leo followed my line of vision, and a small smile broke over his lips. It was different from the teasing smirk he'd donned so far, softer and more genuine. "Oh, yeah. This is Eden."

"Hi," I breathed, suddenly feeling very awkward. I hadn't interacted with many children, as an only child myself. Vi had a sister, but she was too close in age for her to ever seem like a child. "I'm Willow."

Eden just stared at me a moment longer, wide eyed, before darting away.

Leo laughed softly, not deterred by the strange behavior. "She's a bit shy."

I shook my head in amazement. "Your sister?"

"One of them." He led me through the doorway and into the home, a journey which only took a few steps. We paused in what must be their sitting room, a threadbare sofa beside a bookshelf that looked like an amateur had made it themselves. "Two sisters, two brothers. Oakley's the oldest; he's thirteen. Then there's the twins, Anya and Axel, who are nine. Eden's the youngest. She'll be eight this year."

"And your parents?"

Leo waved a dismissive hand. "Both gone, a long time ago. It's just us five."

I took this in with no small amount of surprise. To have more than two children was rare—the more children, the greater the risk that one is cast out. Among the court, even two children was rare, as parents usually preferred to focus all of their energy on one child. Five children, and without parents... I almost couldn't believe it. I peered around casually, searching for the other children to no avail. Only Eden was still visible, perched on a chair in the kitchen that adjoined the sitting room.

"The others are in the other room," Leo said, as if reading my mind. He looked mildly amused by my surprise, the corners of his mouth inching up. "You're an only child, I take it."

An incredulous laugh bubbled from my mouth before I could stop it. "Of course I am. Not much use for a second one, is there? They'd only be in the way."

It was a casual statement, a fact that I considered obvious, but Leo frowned. "That's awful."

I fidgeted uncomfortably. "I'm afraid I don't know what you mean."

"No one's worth should be measured by their use," Leo said, brow scrunched and an annoyingly pitying glance in his eyes. "Least of all a child."

"Why not?" I crossed my arms, feeling odd defensive over my parents. "We are little more than what we can contribute to society. Pretending that our worth isn't connected to that will help no one."

The words were taken straight from my father's mouth, the mantra of Atvas that had been fed to me as long as I could remember, but that didn't mean I believed them any less. Besides, what difference did it make if someone realized the importance of utility at a younger age or older one? I'd known that my worth was tied to the future Sovereignty since I was five years old, and I turned out just fine.

Leo laughed, a harsh sound that held no humor. "You really believe that, don't you?"

"I do."

"That's..." He shook his head, eyeing me with a strange look. "I don't even have the words to explain how messed up that is."

Unease crawled on my skin at the criticism, anger beginning to pound in my veins. "Well, good, because I seem to remember you asking for *my* help. Not the other way around."

"Right," he scoffed, "because the great and mighty Willow Aldridge couldn't *possibly* need anyone's help."

"Certainly not yours," I spat, the words escaping my mouth before I even realized it. I closed my mouth quickly, already regretting the words. Yet he didn't look hurt, or offended, or even angry. If anything, he looked disappointed.

"Of course not." His voice was quieter as he shook his head slightly, looking me straight in the eye. "Has it ever occurred to you that maybe, just maybe, that the Court aren't the only people in Atvas with a brain? That they aren't inheritably superior to everyone else?"

For a moment, I wasn't sure what to say. Partially because he sounded just like Vi always did when she was scolding me, and partially because I didn't agree with him. Technically, the Court was superior to the rest of Atvas—it was why they were on the Court. But I couldn't exactly say that, not without starting a fight I didn't have the energy to finish. So instead I merely said, "That's not fair."

"*That's* not fair?" The previous volume of his voice returned as he spoke, face growing red with anger. He took a step towards me, throwing his hands up in exasperation. "Do you even realize how ironic that is?"

"No, I don't," I shot back, matching his step with one of my own, "because I don't spend my time thinking about how *awful* and *terrible* everything is."

"Well, it doesn't take that long to figure out, though I guess you'd never be able to tell from inside your *darling* Court bubble. Probably too busy bathing in your riches and celebrating your own superiority, right?"

"You know, a little respect wouldn't kill you." Never in my life had I heard anyone speak so crudely about the Court, about Atvas in general. This was very dangerous territory, and if this were any other situation I would have been running by now. As it was, some mysterious force kept me rooted to the spot.

"Respect?!" he retorted, incredulous. "What have you done to warrant my respect?"

I puffed out my chest, uncrossing my arms and drawing myself up to my full height. "I am the only offspring of the Sovereign himself. If nothing else, respect me for that."

"I do respect you, Willow," Leo said slowly, "I respect you for everything *but* that."

The room went dead silent as we stared each other down, two stubborn spirits from two separate worlds caught in a battle of wills. We were close now, so close that I could see nearly every detail of his furious face. Despite the anger still pounding in my heart, I couldn't help but notice the smattering of freckles across his nose.

Just as the tension was mounting to an unbearable level, a noise sent both of our gazes flying across the room. A door had cracked open across the kitchen, one of the two doorways in sight. A head of messy dirty blonde hair poked out, a boy who looked quite a bit like Leo emerging from the room beyond.

"Uh, hey." He grinned sheepishly at me before looking to Leo. "I know you told us to stay in the bedroom and all, but I couldn't help but notice things were sounding a *little* tense out here."

"Oakley," Leo scolded him, though he sounded more amused than anything.

"Right, sorry." Oakley—*the thirteen-year-old brother*, I reminded myself—didn't look especially apologetic as he glanced between us once more, a brow quirked. "I'll just go back to pretending we can't hear you, then."

"Please do," Leo answered, slightly exasperated.

The door clicked back shut, leaving behind a thick silence. The tension was gone, disappeared with Oakley's appearance, and the anger drained quickly from my veins. If anything, I felt rather foolish. I rarely lost my head like that in an argument, and I hardly even knew Leo.

"You told them to stay in the room?" My words were quiet, a timid peace offering that he took gratefully.

"Yeah," he admitted, looking almost embarrassed. "I, uh, didn't want to overwhelm you." He glanced at me, lips twitching slightly as he said: "I think I might have messed that up a bit."

I couldn't help it. I burst out into laughter, heart fluttering from all the excitement. "Just a bit."

His laughter joined my own, the sounds mingling like the tinkling of bells in the small room. It was a beautiful sound, so different from the shouts of distaste of the previous conversation. In a way it was almost more painful to hear, if only because I couldn't remember the last time I laughed quite this freely. With Vi, maybe, but... Well, even that had been complicated lately.

"I'm sorry," Leo said at last, once our laughter had finished its symphony. "I didn't mean to insult you the moment you stepped foot in my home, really."

"It's alright," I replied, and it really was. Despite the rage I'd felt during our argument, I truly wasn't bothered by his words anymore. If anything, I was almost intrigued. "For what it's worth, I'm..." I swallowed down the word. So rarely did I apologize to anyone, the practice frowned on by the discipline of Charisma. "I never intended to offend you either. I suppose it's just difficult to anticipate what will upset you."

"Well, that makes sense." Leo offered a half shrug and small grin. "We don't really know each other, Willow Aldridge."

No, we didn't—and yet, I felt as though I'd known him for years. How strange it was, to stand beside a stranger yet recognize him deep in my heart.

"Okay..." I attempted awkwardly. "Then what's your favorite color?"

Leo frowned. "What?"

"Your favorite color. What is it?"

"You want to know my favorite color?" His brows raised, face breaking out into an expression of amusement.

"*Yes*," I said. "Is that so odd to ask?"

Leo stared at me blankly for a moment, before beginning to laugh heartily. It was a deep, genuine sound. Warm as a fire yet free as the wind.

"I'm sorry," he gasped, straightening up at last. I just stared, arms crossed over my chest and trying my best not to succumb to the urge to laugh along with him. "It's just... you're not what I expected."

"Oh, yeah?" I raised my brows. "How's that?"

"Well," he grinned. "I definitely didn't expect you to ask my favorite *color*."

"Fine!" I exclaimed, giving up my composure at last. I threw up my arms in exasperation, even as my mouth found its way to a smile. "Forgive me for trying to be nice."

He just chuckled, shaking his head.

"Well?" I pressed. "What is it?"

Leo glanced up, and it was as if he was seeing me for the first time. His lips molded into a smile, softer than the previous smirk and quieter than the warm laugh. "Brown. Soft brown, like the color of coffee when it's mixed with milk. My, uh... my mom used to drink it like that every morning. Sometimes, if I was calm enough, she'd let me have a sip."

I'd never much liked the color brown, but I suddenly found myself thinking that it was quite beautiful after all.

"Now your turn." Leo tilted his head, looking me up and down. "What color is fitting enough for the esteemed Willow Aldridge?"

"I..." My voice faded off, mind racing to find an answer. The truth was, I'd never given much thought to the question. I'd always said gold as a child, if only because it was the color of the Sovereign's crown, but I couldn't bring myself to say it. Not after Leo's surprisingly genuine answer. "I'm not sure."

I was almost afraid to meet his gaze, to see the pity surely in his eyes. After all, I was almost an adult. How could I not even know my own favorite color? Yet there was no pity as I looked into his gray eyes. Rather, he seemed intrigued.

"Well, then," he smiled. "Looks like we'll have to figure that out."

I snorted, a very un-ladylike sound. "And here I thought I was supposed to be tutoring you."

"About that—am I actually going to learn anything today?"

"Why do you think I brought these?" I gestured to my overly heavy bag, filled with books and weighing heavily on my shoulder. I glanced around once more, cataloguing the layout. One big room, separated into the sitting room, kitchen, and dining room (which was really just the corner of the kitchen). Behind the kitchen table was a small alcove with two doors, one of which I knew to be the bedroom. "Er... I don't suppose you have a library, do you?"

Leo raised a brow, gesturing to the bookshelf beside us. "Sure we do."

"Right," I murmured, cheeks heating up. "An office of some sort, then?"

"Not quite." Leo just chuckled, nodding his head to the kitchen. "The kitchen table will have to do."

I followed him to it, depositing my bag and removing the books. I'd brought one for each discipline, unsure where he'd want to start, as well as a notepad so he could take notes. "We can skip Intellect, seeing as that trial has passed. You of course know Service, and Legality we'll cover later. So, Charisma or Aesthetics?"

Leo watched me, amused, as I began lining up the supplies. "You tell me. You're the one in charge here, Miss Aldridge."

My mind seemed to short circuit for a moment, causing me to freeze for a moment. I couldn't fathom why. There was nothing wrong with what he said, no reason for my pulse to be racing as fast as it was. Only, when I glanced at him he was looking right at me, that maddening smirk on his face.

"Aesthetics, then," I replied once I'd recovered. "But be warned: it's not just flowers and sunshine. It's much harder than you'd think, I can promise you that."

"Great," he murmured, sarcastic, before opening the notepad. I busied myself with rifling through the book I'd brought for instruction, searching for a good place to start.

"You know," I said, keeping my eyes tracked on the pages, "your siblings can be out here, too. I don't mind."

"Are you sure?" His voice sounded surprised, and I was sure if I looked up I would find a similar expression on his face. "They can be pretty distracting. They mean well, of course, and they'd love to meet you. But they're fine, you don't have to... I know that's pretty personal. I don't want you to feel like you have to get to know them, or me, because–"

"Leo." I cut him off, glancing up at last. He was rambling, cheeks tinged red in a way that made my heart swell. For someone who presented himself as smug and sarcastic, he sure wasn't what I expected either. "I don't mind, really."

"Okay, good," he sighed, pausing a moment before continuing. "I know my methods of getting you here were...unorthodox. I do need your help, but I don't want you to feel like you're obligated to do anything else. This wasn't some scheme or trap."

I wished I could express how much I appreciated the sentiment, how much it meant to me to have someone give me even the smallest semblance of choice. "I don't feel trapped, Leo. I want to be here, and I want to know your siblings."

I want to know you. I wasn't bold enough to say the words aloud, was barely even brave enough to think them. It was the truth, though—for some reason, I truly did want to get to know the mystery that was Leo Hayes. In the twenty four hours since we'd met, he'd single handedly saved my score, blackmailed me, insulted me, witnessed me acting insanely childish, and made me blush *several* times. Maybe I should have felt trapped as he suggested, locked into a deal that I had no way of avoiding, but I didn't. If anything, I felt like I was a bird in a cage, only someone had unlocked the door. I did not fly, did not even open the door, but still I was undeniably and completely *free.*

All the good feelings I had felt were gone by dinner that evening, a tense affair during which my mother eyed me like a hawk. My father did the opposite, refusing to look me in the eye as he ate. I frowned to myself. Family dinners were never exactly warm, but they were rarely this cold.

"Well?" my mother snapped eventually, placing her utensils on the table and fixing me with an expectant glare. "What happened?"

I swallowed quickly, forcing the bite I had just taken down my throat. "What do you mean?" I asked carefully. She couldn't know about Leo, right? And besides, it wasn't as if I were doing anything wrong.

"Second place doesn't become Sovereign," she scolded.

I let out a breath of relief, even as my heart dropped to my stomach. The scores from yesterday's assessment must have been released, and it seemed I had come in second. A part of me was ashamed that I had forgotten to stop by the Cathe and check the board. Was I really so easily distracted?

My mother didn't seem to share my feelings, that familiar disappointed expression upon her face. "You said it all went fine."

"It *did* go fine," I argued, cringing slightly at the blatant lie. Far too tired after the assessment, I hadn't even considered explaining the situation to my parents. And now, well ... how could I possibly explain it without getting myself in trouble—or Leo, for that matter? "It was just ... difficult."

"This is the Pathway," my father reminded me, the somber words his first of the night. "It's supposed to be difficult."

I said nothing in return, biting my lip at the truth in the words. He just shook his head, returning to his meal as if reprimanding me were a mere chore to complete.

"At least the Bonavich boy isn't much of a threat," my father continued, voice now lighter in a way that irritated me. "*He* didn't even make the top five."

In all the excitement, I hadn't thought one bit about Auden and his score. He'd been so nervous about it, and it seemed he was right to be. To not make the top five... I had a feeling that his dinner was even less pleasant than my own.

"He'll do better next time." I snapped, strangely defensive of Auden. Foolish, considering he was my competition.

"Then you'll have to try harder," my mother said, moving that gaze off of me at last. She looked as disappointed as ever, but I could have sworn there was something else, too—something that looked a bit like fear. "Winning the Pathway is more important than you even realize. We can't afford any distractions."

"Right," I whispered to myself, Leo's smirk swimming into my mind. "No distractions."

8

WHEN WORLDS COLLIDE

I f helping Leo was a distraction, I wasn't sure I ever wanted to be focused again. Our lessons stretched longer and longer, until we were meeting twice a week for nearly a whole day. My parents hardly questioned my whereabouts, so long as they believed that I was studying for the next assessment. As for Auden, he hardly left his manor—and his father's side, from what I heard. Time passed quickly, preoccupied as I was, and before I knew it the Service trial had come and gone. It was fairly challenging, an all-day event in which we were each tasked with running a tea party for five members of Atvas. It felt extraordinarily unnatural to me, catering to their every need, and it required a unique sort of awareness of others that I found quite challenging. Still, I managed to pull first place, with Auden only a fraction below me.

I had expected Leo to struggle with the assessment too, stubborn as he was, but he exceeded all expectations and got the eighth-highest score. I knew he was a discipline of Service, but he certainly didn't seem to fit their ideals at all. Besides, if he was so good at Service, why would he enter the Pathway after all? Why not excel in Service and stay in Atvas that way? Everything about him was confusing—a feeling that only grew the more I attempted to learn.

"Can I ask you something?" I asked him one Saturday shortly after the Service assessment, my curiosity overtaking me.

"What's up?" His tone was short, gruff in a way that I once would have thought rude but now knew was just exhaustion. It was clear in his face, in the bags under his eyes and the deep lines of worry etched into his forehead.

"What was your score before the Pathway began?"

"Low," was all he said, posture nonchalant but eyes burning with a haunted intensity.

"How low?"

"Does it matter?"

"You did well in the Service assessment," I pointed out carefully.

Leo widened his eyes in mock surprise, holding his arms out as if reaching to the heavens. "Behold! The great Willow Aldridge has bestowed a *compliment* upon me!"

I rolled my eyes, resisting the urge to laugh. It was just like him to laugh this off, the same way he did with anything remotely significant. I balled up a piece of paper and threw it in his direction.

"Ouch!" he exclaimed, but his voice was full of laughter as he tossed the paper back at me. "You know, that's not very proper of you, Miss Aldridge." Once, the words might have sent me into an internal crisis, but I'd spent enough time around Leo to know my propriety didn't exist around him.

"Stop it!" I swatted his arm lightly. "It's not funny. There isn't that much time left, you know. Only four assessments—Aesthetics, Charisma, Legality, and the final."

Leo groaned, pushing his hand across his eyes. "Hasn't anyone ever told you to loosen up?"

I might have found that insulting, except for the amused glimmer dancing in his eyes. "Yes. Some jerk tells me twice a week."

A laugh exploded from Leo's mouth, vibrant and bright with a tone of surprise. It was the same sort of laugh he'd given that first day, as though he couldn't believe I was speaking so spontaneously.

"Well, that must be a very smart jerk." He shook his head, still laughing quietly.

I sighed, shaking off the last bit of laughter as the reality of his situation hit me once more. In only a short amount of time, Leo might be banished to the Beyond—forever. I'd always known it was likely, but now that we'd spent so much time together it seemed much more important. He was ... Well, I wasn't sure exactly what he was to me, but I certainly didn't want to see him cast out.

"I'm only serious because this stuff is important," I said quietly. "Your future hangs in the balance."

Leo just snorted in reply, a sound of disbelief and dismissal. "Don't you think I know that?"

"Well, you don't exactly act like it." I threw my hands up in frustration. "I'm getting a little sick of putting all the effort in here."

"Yeah, well I'm getting a little sick of you pretending that you know everything. I asked you to help me prepare for the trials, not lecture me on the damned stakes."

The language was something that had taken time, too. No one in the Court used such harsh words, or at least not publicly. Vi was the only one I'd even heard curse before, and that was occasional.

Leo crossed his arms, raising a demanding brow. "Have you ever even *known* someone who was cast out?"

I opened my mouth to defend myself, to inform him that of course I knew people who were cast out, only to realize that I couldn't. I wasn't sure I'd ever even spoken to someone who was cast out, except...

"Yes," I answered quietly, the memory sucking all the ire from my body. "There was a woman, at the ceremony ten years ago. She was being cast out, but she spoke to me."

"What did she say?" His reply was notably absent of any anger as well, as if he too found the subject too serious to taint with petty fights.

"Not much," I admitted. "She just ... she screamed, and it was an awful sound. As if her soul was being ripped from her body." I suppressed a shiver at the memory, the screams still echoing in my brain. "She told me to remember her."

"But you didn't know her?"

"No, I'd never met her before. She just thrashed towards me, so close to my face..." I swallowed, unsure of how to describe it. "'Remember me,' she said."

In the silence that followed, I could have sworn I heard the echo of her screams.

"You did." Leo's voice sounded like an alarm in my head, and I was so startled I almost jumped out of my seat. "You remembered her, even after all these years. Why?"

I cleared my throat, forcing my heart to beat at a normal pace. Hearing things that weren't there, jumping at every little sound... the Pathway really was making me lose my mind. I forced myself to get it together as I contemplated his question. "How could I not? She was... Well, I didn't know her, but she was another human and she was in pain. And the way she looked at me, it was like I was both the cause and solution for her pain. That's not something you forget."

Leo hummed in curiosity, face melded into an expression of contemplation. I would never have admitted it, but he looked even more attractive like this—thoughtful, inquisitive. Maybe it was just the intensity of the conversation, the vulnerability of discussing this after so long, but his gray eyes looked oddly appealing in the fading light. It was an insane thought, especially since I'd been angry enough to claw them out only moments ago. Up, down, round and round—my feelings went everywhere around him.

"The point is," I continued, shaking off the uncomfortable intimacy that clung to me with each glance at his face. "Perhaps we both understand the stakes, but I'm the only one who acts like it. If I'm lecturing you, it's because you very well *could* be cast out. You asked me to help you avoid that fate, and that is what I'm going to do."

Leo watched my speech with an amused grin, all remnants of intrigue and contemplation gone. It wasn't the first time I saw that shift in him, as if the door between the mask and the soul was slammed shut, but it was the first time that it mattered to me. For the first time I wished for the key to that door, wished I could peek inside for even a moment longer. For the first time I looked at Leo Hayes and saw him for who he truly was, an entertaining shell that distracted from a layered core. It worked, too; despite my initial determination, we ended that lesson without ever discussing his initial score.

***

After that mess of a lesson, I watched him more closely. I was practically obsessed, determined to unlock the mystery of Leo Hayes. He was a true enigma—achingly kind yet unbelievably rude, surprisingly vulnerable but with walls of unbreakable stone. And though he knew little of the knowledge I had acquired throughout my life, I got the distinct feeling that he understood more about the world than I ever would. The problem was that his knowledge was shrouded in resentment and hatred, blocking him from learning even the most basic of concepts. He was, to say the least, a difficult student.

"This is ridiculous," he'd scoff while learning about the etiquette requirements of Charisma.

"It's a tablecloth!" he'd cry out, nearly exploding from the exhaustion of Aesthetics color schemes. "It doesn't *matter*."

When faced with any other difficulties, he hurdled past them with hardly a second thought. But this anger, this incessant irritation with all things Atvas... it was a roadblock that he just could not get past, mostly because he didn't *want* to.

The issue came to a head at the Aesthetics trial. It was, for lack of a better word, a talent show. There was a stage set up in the ballroom, and judges, and a large audience to cheer us on as we performed for them. We'd prepared for this, the past several lessons spent trialing talents for Leo to hone. He didn't seem to have much experience in any art form at all, so we'd settled on a comedy act that was actually quite amusing.

The performances were given in order of current placement, which meant that I was first. Years of singing lessons left me fully prepared, and I actually enjoyed the performance. I was singing a ballad, the sort of thing that might serve as a slow dance at a ball, and I couldn't help but find Leo in the crowd. There was a gleam in his eyes as he watched me, and I knew with one glance that the doors to his soul were wide open. It made my heart beat faster, made my notes come out stronger, made the emotion of the lyrics more palpable. As the last note rang over the crowd, lingering like a withheld breath, I felt electrified. Not by the applause of the crowd, or even the knowledge that I had delivered a winning performance, but by Leo's gaze. It had remained locked on me the entire song, not shifting for even a moment.

"Good job," Auden whispered as I exited the sage, his eyes wide with amazement. "I mean it, Lo. That was...breathtaking."

I hardly heard myself thank him, hardly noticed as Auden began his own performance. Piano, of course—he was practically a prodigy at the instrument, always had been. Usually I would be drawn into the music, but my attention was elsewhere. So when Leo stood up, edging his way out of the room, I knew immediately. I was on my feet before I had the conscious thought to stand up, my feet propelling me out of the ballroom and into the corridor. Only, Leo was nowhere to be found—not by the refreshments, or the toilets, or even the exit. I was making my way back to the ballroom to check if he had returned when I heard it, a soft snuffling sound past the door to my right.

"Leo?" I pulled open the door, brows furrowed as I took in the scene in front of me. Leo was in a broom closet, of all places, sitting on the floor with a pale face and red-rimmed eyes. He looked up at me, cursed, and pushed himself to his feet.

"I'm sorry," he muttered, wringing his hands anxiously. "I shouldn't... I can't..."

I glanced around nervously before stepping into the closet, shutting the door behind me. I didn't have a clue what was going on, but I was certain that Leo wouldn't want anyone passing by to be privy to this moment.

"My performance was that bad, huh?" I asked, because I desperately wanted to see a smile back on his face. This devastated mess... It wasn't Leo, and it was frankly quite unsettling.

He did laugh at that, a short and exhausted sounding sound, but didn't tease me as I expected. Instead he just looked at me, eyes unbearably sad as he said, "It was incredible. *You* were incredible."

If my heart wasn't beating fast enough already, *that* certainly did it. We were smashed up against each other in a dim closet, close enough that we were practically sharing breaths. "Well, you don't have to sound so sad about it."

I waited him out in silence, curious but apprehensive. This was a sensitive situation, I could tell—the sort I was usually very bad at handling. The last thing I wanted was to push for answers only to upset him further.

"Willow, I can't do it," he admitted eventually, looking down as he said it. Disappointment weighed down his tone, as well as a distinct note of fear. "I can't perform."

I frowned. "You can't... why? Because of the crowd?"

"No. It's not them."

"Who, then? The Council?" I pressed.

The clench of his jaw was answer enough.

"Leo," I sighed, placing a tentative hand on his shoulder. It felt like the right thing to do, but I regretted it immediately as my heart beat impossibly faster. "They're just people."

"I don't care," he gritted out, the fire returning his eyes as he glared at me. The effect was lessened by the moisture still lingering in his eyes. "I won't perform for them. No now, and not ever."

"You've got to be kidding me." My words came out harsher than I intended, but I couldn't bring myself to soften them. "This isn't exactly the time to take an ethical stand, Leo."

"Oh, yeah?" His voice hardened, eyes flashing in anger as he stood straighter. "When, then? There will *never* be a good time."

"You've got to let go of this!" I ran my hands through my hair in frustration, hardly even caring that it disrupted my careful styling. "For all that you complain about Atvas, the only one that's keeping you from what you want is *you*. Can't you see that?"

"It would seem that way to you, wouldn't it?" Gone is the meek, crying Leo; instead, he has grown into a blazing fire that filled the small space with unrelenting heat. Honestly, it was an improvement.

"No!" I replied, hardly hesitating to match his own fire with my own. "No, it wouldn't, because I've been performing since the day I was *born*. My whole life, everything that I am, is a performance. So I'm *sorry* that you have to perform for Atvas this once, I really am, but I think it's time that you get over yourself!"

The statement was met by an icy silence that rested over the fiery anger, sizzling uncomfortably for a moment before fading into a lukewarm quiet.

"I shouldn't have to," Leo said quietly. "We're human beings, Willow. We shouldn't have to earn the right to exist in our own home."

"It doesn't matter." I didn't even let myself think about his words, didn't contemplate them for a moment, because it truly didn't matter. "This is the world we live in. We can either accept that, or..."

"I don't think I can do it," Leo muttered, his head dropping into his hands. "I'm sorry. I know you've put a lot of effort into helping me, but it's just not going to work. I'm going to be cast out. I can't play their game, so they're going to take me off the board."

"No," I stated simply.

Leo frowned. "What do you mean, no?"

"I already told you," I shrugged, "I agreed to help you through the Pathway, and I meant it. Nervous meltdowns included."

He drew back, affronted. "I'm not having a *nervous meltdown—*"

"Here's what's going to happen," I continued, ignoring his protests. "You're going to wipe off your face, walk out of this closet, and get on that stage. You're going to perform the comedy set we practiced, and it'll be great. Then, once this trial is done, we'll tackle everything else. Alright?"

And that was exactly what happened. Leo performed well despite his annoyance, which was clear to me but to anyone else may have seemed part of the act. The crowd gave him a standing ovation, and he even earned the tenth-highest score, pushing his placement up to fourteenth. It all went as it should, and yet I hated it. Something within me couldn't help but recoil at the resigned acceptance on his face, the wide smile that was so obviously fake, the flat tone to his laugh. He lost a bit of his spark that day; even worse, I took it from him.

I showed up to our next lesson prepared to have it out, ready to debate for as long as he needed to understand the necessity of playing the game. In the end, I needn't have worried—Leo showed up with his mask firmly back in place, laughing and joking. The only difference was that his resistance was gone, a weary exhaustion in its place. Even as time passed, as he grew softer and more open in my presence, never again did he bring up that day in the broom closet.

9

—·—

SOMEONE LIKE HIM

What I'd told Leo was true: there was no point in complaining about Atvas when there was nothing to be done about the matter. Still, that didn't mean my brain stopped thinking about it.

In my usual circles, any such discussion would be shut down immediately. It had been that way ever since Chancellor Coldwell began the discipline system, years and years ago. Only Vi had ever dared challenge it, and I'd always chalked that up to her general opposition to authority. Yet recently, after all I'd heard Leo say... it was like poison, infiltrating my mind despite my better judgment. I made the mistake of mentioning this to Vi one day, the words escaping my mouth before I even realized it.

"...of course," I was saying, nearly finished with talking about the Aesthetics assessment, "it would be nice if we all got to stay in Atvas, but as it is there's a good chance that Leo could be cast out, and—"

"What?" Vi interrupted sharply, pushing herself up onto her elbows. We were sprawled on her lavish bed, in the middle of updating each other on every aspect of our lives.

"Well, yeah," I frowned. "It's always been a possibility, even with me tutoring him."

She waved a dismissive hand. "No, not that. What did you say about Atvas?"

"Oh. I mean, I just wish that no one had to be cast out." I fidgeted uncomfortably, twisting the fringe on one of her pillows. "We're all human, right? Why can't we just... exist here without having to prove we deserve it?"

Vi's eyes narrowed. "Leo told you that."

I flopped over onto my back, staring up at the ceiling with a sigh. Vi's manor was almost as large as my own, but while mine was silent and impassive, the DeLoughery home was constantly full of life. I never failed to enjoy my time here, even if her little sister *was* constantly interrupting us with some complaint or another.

"So what if he did?" I said finally, because I never liked to lie to Vi. best friends didn't lie to each other, and she'd be able to tell anyways. "Isn't that basically what you've been trying to tell me for, like, years?"

"Not exactly, but close enough," she admitted, a sour look still on her face. "But that was different. This is dangerous, Willow. You have to stay..."

"...focused, I know." I nearly groaned aloud. "Believe it or not, I can keep up with the Pathway while having independent thoughts."

"I wouldn't exactly call them independent," Vi grumbled, scowling.

"Okay, *what* is your problem with him?" I demanded, pushing myself upright and crossing my arms. She opened her mouth, and I quickly added, "the truth. Please."

She paused, mouth closing slowly, and sat up slowly. For a moment I was worried she would never answer, would perhaps get up and leave the room altogether, but I never got the chance to find out.

I caught a movement in the corner of my eye, and a head peeked in the open door. The fact that she kept her door open all the time was a marvel in itself; I could never imagine being so open, feeling secure enough to do so. Then again, Vi's house *was* very relaxing. It was a manor not much smaller than Auden's, but where his was all silence and ice, Vi's was light and warmth.

"What do you want?" Vi called to her sister, who stepped into the room without invitation. Alia was fifteen now, only three years below us, but she'd always seemed much younger to me. Perhaps it was because she'd always followed Vi and I around as a kid, to Vi's perpetual annoyance. I'd never minded it much; honestly, it was cute. Of course, that was before she entered her teenage years and decided she was too cool for both of us.

"I need my ink," she replied without looking at us, and I could practically *feel* the roll of her eyes as she crossed the room. "Since you never gave it back."

My lips quirked into an amused smile. "Hello, Alia."

"Willow!" she exclaimed, a braid of dark hair whipping around as she turned towards me. "Long time no see."

"I know," I said regretfully. It had been quite a while since I'd been at Vi's, with all the commotion lately. "I've been a little busy."

"Mm-hm," Alia murmured distractedly, shuffling through the drawers of Vi's desk. "You win yet?"

Such a casual question, thrown out in such a casual way. It never failed to shock me, the ease with which the DeLougherys dismissed the seriousness of the Pathway. Both Giselle and Jacob De Loughery were on the Court, having gone through the Pathway themselves—and yet, they didn't expect their children to do so. I couldn't imagine my parents being similarly inclined.

"Uh, no," I replied. "Not quite yet."

"Are you done yet?" Vi snapped.

"Pity," Alia replied, ignoring Vi altogether. "I was really hoping you could issue an official decree against morning lessons."

I snorted a very unladylike laugh. "I'll be sure to remember that."

"Can you please get out of my room?" Vi grumbled, and I frowned. She was always impatient with Alia, one of those sibling things I didn't understand, but she seemed more on edge than usual. Her eyes tracked Alia as she continued to search the desk, an annoyed spark in her gaze that would have made me apologize immediately.

The sisters glared at each other. It was funny how different they were, and yet so similar; like two sides of a single coin. Vi was the deep embers of fire, and Alia the soft rush of water, both wild and free.

Alia just wrinkled her nose, rolled her eyes, and said, "Fine. See if I ever let you borrow my ink again."

The door slammed behind her, leaving us in silence.

"Look, Willow," Vi sighed. Her eyes were pleading as she turned to me, grasping her hands in my own. "I know it doesn't make sense to you, and I know you like Leo—"

"I don't know what you're talking about," I protested, even as my traitorous heart pounded.

Vi just shot me a disbelieving look. "I *know*, Willow. He's charming, I get it. But he's a distraction, one that will ruin you if you're not careful."

"You sound like my mother."

"Just promise me," Vi continued, ignoring my comments. "Promise me nothing will happen between you two. You can keep tutoring him, if you want, but no romance."

The truth was, there was little point in liking Leo. I would be married to Auden, and soon. That would have to be enough. That *would* be enough. I had to convince her.

I have to convince myself.

So I forced myself to crinkle my nose, to say the vile words I once might have meant. "C'mon, Vi. He's a Service, and a low one, at that. I could never like someone like him."

Vi searched my face, and I sensed something like relief in her eyes. "Just promise me."

I hesitated for a moment at the finality of the words. *It doesn't matter if it's true*, I reminded myself, *nothing can happen anyway*. "I promise."

Her shoulders loosened as she breathed a sigh of relief, light entering her eyes once more. "Thank you."

"You're welcome, I guess," I mumbled, eyeing her in suspicion.

"I'm just worried about you," she stated, as if that would make up for the insane behavior. "More than you even know."

"I know," I replied, "but you don't need to be. I know what I'm doing."

***

I had no clue what I was doing. It was a beautiful, sunny *Wednesday* afternoon. I should have been at home, preparing for dinner or resting up from training or preparing for the assessment in two days' time. I certainly shouldn't have been walking alone, trekking down the dirt road to a certain small home. I cursed to myself as I neared the small building.

How do I even know he's here? He could be hanging out with friends, or with someone else altogether...

"Willow!" a voice exclaimed, and I grinned as two small forms barreled towards me: Anya and Axel, two of Leo's siblings. The nine-year-old twins were mischievous at best and downright destructive at worst, constantly getting into one thing or another. The constant bustle of noise and movement in his house had taken some adjustment for me. After all,

I was an only child, and any noise from the staff was smothered by the sheer size of our manor. But now, crying children, curious ears, and the sound of things falling over had grown to be a normal occurrence in my life—and I couldn't say I minded it one bit.

I glanced behind the twins to where Leo stood, his siblings pouring out of the doorway behind him. They all wore packs and clothing meant for the outdoors, clearly on their way to somewhere.

"Sorry," I called to Leo, "I didn't mean to interrupt."

His brows were furrowed in confusion, as if he were wondering if he had the day correct after all. "It's alright, we were just–"

He cut off suddenly, glancing down to where Eden tugged on his jacket. The other kids had all adjusted to my presence by now, but little Eden had remained quiet and timid around me since I met her eyes that very first day. Despite her reluctance, I adored her. She was sweet, innocent, and incredibly calm for her seven years.

"What is it, Edie?" he questioned softly, bending down to her level. My heart swooned a bit, the way it always did when he interacted with his siblings. Despite his general gruffness, he was amazingly gentle with them.

"Can she come?" Eden whispered in that way kids do, so loud it could hardly be called a whisper at all. Leo glanced at me, the question written across his face. I opened my mouth to say no; after all, I didn't even know where they were going. And yet ... all the children looked at me so hopefully, I couldn't bear to turn them down.

"If it's no bother," I answered finally, and Leo's face lit up.

He wants the children to be happy, I told myself. *Surely that's all.*

Anya and Axel whooped in celebration, racing to the front of the clump as we started moving. Eden smiled softly before trotting to catch up with the twins—which was futile, considering how short her legs were.

"If it's no bother," another voice mocked in a posh accent, and I turned to where Oakley stood, laughing at his own joke. At thirteen years of age, Oakley was the second eldest of the siblings. He was the opposite of Leo in most ways, far more sensible at times, although he did seem to take after his brother's sarcasm.

"I do thank thee for bestowing your presence upon us," he continued with mock sincerity. "'Tis an honor—hey, ouch!" he exclaimed as Leo cuffed him on the back of the head.

"Stop mocking our guest and make sure the others stay out of trouble, will you?" Leo said, rolling his eyes despite the laughter he was clearly trying to contain. Oakley huffed, rolling his eyes before darting after the other children.

"Thank you for this," Leo said to me—alone at last.

"It's no problem." I smiled in return. "Although I am curious where we're going." We were nearing the forest, a thick band of deadened nature surrounding Atvas into which I had seldom ventured.

"The glade," Leo replied, pointing to a general part of the forest that meant nothing to me.

"Pardon?"

Leo laughed lightly, eyes sparkling. "It's just a clearing. We've been going there since I was little. It ... means a lot to me."

I glanced at his face, at the tinge of red in his cheeks, and smiled.

As we walked to the glade, my doubt in my decision grew. We were approaching the fence, which made me nervous. Of course, it wasn't as though we couldn't go outside the fence. After all, if someone wanted to leave voluntarily, it would only help with the resource crisis. But Mother always said that the fence was there for a reason. I shuddered at the memory of the words as the fence came into sight.

"Leo?" I tugged on his sleeve nervously as we approached. "The glade is inside the fence, right?"

"Yeah, it's just along the edge here."

My confusion was overshadowed by wonder when I saw we'd arrived at the glade. It was like nothing I'd ever seen before. It was surrounded by trees, although they weren't like any trees I'd ever encountered. They had branches of gray, marred with the occasional scorch of black and covered in pale brown leaves. I reached up to touch one, and my jaw dropped as it crumbled to powder at my touch. This same powder floated off all the trees, shimmering gently in the air before settling on the ground. It gave the whole area the illusion of flickering, and floating powder rained down like glimmering rain. Both terrifying and beautiful, it drew me in with a morbid curiosity.

"Worth the trip?"

I jumped at the voice, startled by the warm breath on my neck. I turned to find Leo behind me, a soft smile on his face.

"It's breathtaking," I said truthfully, staring at the powder as it glistened against the gray of the sky. "How is this place possible?"

He was quiet for a moment, seemingly lost in thought. "Honestly, I don't know. My mother once told me this area was hit especially hard by the bombs, and that the plants adapted to impossible conditions. I never did find out how she knew that."

"What happened to her?" I asked softly, and he flinched lightly at the question.

"She could have saved herself or the baby, and, well ... you've met Eden, so you know what she chose."

Death from childbirth wasn't exactly rare. Without the medical expertise practiced before the war, there was little to prevent it, but that didn't make it any less tragic. Our Intellect medics did their best, but that often wasn't enough.

"She must have been very brave."

"She was." His eyes were cast upwards, and I pretended not to notice the glistening in the corners. Instead I watched Eden as she played, trailing after her siblings around her siblings, and wondered if my mother would have done the same for me. I knew I should let it be, but I couldn't resist the question that slipped from my mouth.

"And your father?"

He clenched his jaw and looked away, and for a moment, I thought he wasn't going to answer.

"Drank himself to death. I guess five children weren't worth putting the bottle down." Bitterness exuded from his tone, and I couldn't blame him. Alcohol was anything but cheap, and if his father drank that much, it was no wonder the Hayes family was left with nothing. "I was fourteen."

A heavy silence settled over us, and I rested my hand gently on top of his without thinking. I was surprised at how nice it felt, connecting with him like this. It was as if despite our differences, despite our scores, in that moment, we were one.

"Leo?" I asked softly, my voice carrying on the gentle wind.

"Yeah?"

"Why did you really enter the Pathway?" I'd asked the question dozens of times now, but never in such a direct manner. In turn, I'd never received a direct answer. But here, in this place of wonder with children's laughter in the air... he turned to me, and something was different. It wasn't the way his hair gleamed gold in the sunlight, or the faint freckles spattered across his nose, or even the sharp cut of his jawline as he clenched his teeth. No, it was his eyes, smoldering gray and illuminated with passion and a hint of something else—something almost like fear.

"Because I had to," Leo breathed, as if the admission was a secret. "I made a mistake, and my score... I told you it was low."

I hardly dared to breathe, hardly dared to do anything other than nod softly.

"1.3. My score was 1.3"

1.3? That was extraordinarily low. He was smarter than that—*better* than that.

"So, you see," Leo continued, huffing out a humorless laugh, "I really did have no choice."

Indeed, a score of 1.3 wasn't nearly high enough to put him in the top half of the Service discipline. He surely would have been cast out, if not for the Pathway.

"You want to know the truth?" he asked, turning to face me with a strange look on his face. I nodded, half afraid of what would come out of his mouth. "I would be okay with it. If it weren't for them, I wouldn't even mind."

I didn't have to ask who 'them' was. His family mattered to Leo more than anything else. You'd have to be blind not to see it.

"I was actually planning to go out that way, but, uh." Leo paused, a sad smile on his face. "Oakley asked me not to. He practically begged me to enter the Pathway, to at least try." There was a moment of quiet before he continued, voice quieter. "He's going to be crushed when it's not enough."

The words carved deep into my heart, so deep that my eyes grew moist. I blinked the tears away quickly, swallowing hard. After all of this, after all we both had given to get to this point, Leo still didn't believe he would make it. The worst part was, he might be right. Leo did nothing but give to others, and here he was with nothing left for himself. Nothing left to put toward the Pathway. The realization settled uncomfortably on my chest, and I felt suffocated for a brief moment.

"Leo?" I asked again, voice considerably lighter. "Do you want to go to a ball with me?"

A moment of shocked silence, then: "What?!"

I resisted the urge to laugh as I turned to him. "The Court has a ball tomorrow, and I thought... Well, we've been working on Charisma, and it might be helpful. And, um, I want you to come." I cut off my rambling, blushing slightly. It had been on my mind for a bit now, something I'd been contemplating but never quite decided. Honestly, I still hadn't really decided, the words escaping before I could stop them.

"I can't go to a ball," Leo said, though his voice was more shocked than anything. "I don't belong there, and everyone knows it."

"But you're in the Pathway," I argued. "When this is all over, you'll be on the Court. You belong there as much as any of us."

"Even if that was true, what about you? I'm no expert at the dynamics of the rich and powerful, but I'm fairly sure it would be bad for your status to bring me."

I paused at his words, conflicted. It was true that bringing Leo to a gala would be scandalous, and although it should have no effect on my actual rank, there was a chance it would. After all, word got around fast—and status was a big part of Charisma. Yet for the first time in a long time, I didn't care about my status, or even my rank. I cared about Leo, and fairness, and giving a chance to someone who deserved it.

"Hasn't anyone ever told you to loosen up?" I smirked, pulling the branch above his head and running away, leaving him covered in powder. He gasped, pretending to be offended.

"Don't you dare," I warned, holding my hands up in surrender as he gathered a handful. He just grinned, chasing after me. Soon enough, we were rolling in the dirt, laughing hysterically and smearing powder on each other like paint on a canvas.

"Okay, okay, I surrender!" I conceded, giggling madly, and he plopped down beside me, panting lightly from the exertion. I turned my head and watched him as he lay gazing at the sky through the canopy of branches above. He was messy, complicated, and utterly improper—yet in that moment, I could think of only one word: *breathtaking.*

The thought surprised even me. When had he gone from irritating to enticing, from making my blood boil with anger to making my heart soar? At that moment, I didn't care that it would never work. I wanted nothing more than to move my hand to touch his, to feel his skin, on mine, to ...

"Leo?" I breathed, speaking before I could do something foolish. "It's going to be alright, you know that? I know it's all very uncertain, but you're not going to let Oakley down. You'll get a Court spot. *We'll* get you a Court spot."

"Why?" Leo didn't look at me, instead asking the air. "Why do you care so much?"

"Because you deserve it," I answered truthfully. "You deserve all of it."

He was silent, but his hand suddenly inched to touch my own. I opened my palm, allowing his fingers to wrap around my own and reveling in the warmth flooding my veins. The powder floated in the gray sky above, swirling throughout the trees as though propelled by the words left unsaid.

10

MEMORY, MOTHERS, AND MAYHEM

The morning of the ball dawned sunny and beautiful—not that it mattered much to me. My morning was spent in a whirlwind of activity, pampering and prepping myself to perfection. By six o'clock, I felt like a different person altogether—shiny, bright, new. An ornate platinum clip pulled my auburn hair into an elegant updo, not a single silky strand out of place. My mother had chosen the dress, of course, but I had to give her credit. Long and flowy with flowers stitched into the cream bodice, it was truly a dress truly befitting a future Sovereign.

"I hope you remember that you have a job to do tonight." The image of my mother appeared behind my reflection, and I met her gaze in the mirror. Her emerald-green eyes, so similar to my own, sparkled with expectations and something that seemed almost like worry.

"Of course," I said without turning around, hoping to end the conversation. I shuffled through my jewelry, automatically setting a large gold necklace aside. Heavy and extravagant, it was an awful thing that I avoided at all costs.

"Are you sure about that?"

I halted at the question, dropping the necklace on my vanity and turning around. Her face was calm, but her eyes were intense, and I knew she had more than the usual reminders in store for this lecture.

"Why wouldn't I?" I asked carefully, narrowing my eyes. Her suspicion was something I wasn't the least bit prepared for. After all, my mother knew how invested I was in my ranking. In fact, it was pretty much the only thing we agreed on.

"I noticed that you added someone to the guest list." Her voice was casual as she moved towards the jewelry I'd dropped, beginning to sift through it. "Someone... new."

"I'm tutoring him," I stated calmly, forcing my voice to stay even. I had hoped she wouldn't notice the addition to the list, but it appeared she was more vigilant than I thought. "Leo needed some experience, so I thought—"

"Willow, we've talked about this. You *have* to start putting your head before your heart."

I bit the inside of my cheek as she cut me off, gently grabbing my hand and turning me to look into her eyes once again.

"I understand that you think it isn't a big deal," she continued, voice somewhere between gentle and scolding. "I can hardly blame you; I was the same as a child."

I tilted my head at this statement, intrigued. Mother rarely talked about her past, but each tidbit she revealed puzzled me more than the last.

"It's not your job to help everyone; it's your job to maintain your position and become Sovereign. That will be help enough." She rested the gold necklace around my neck, heavy and extravagant and awful. Her gaze met mine in the mirror, utterly unyielding. "The boy may come tonight, but please, promise me it's the last you'll see of him. We can't have everything we've worked so hard for collapse." She fastened the necklace on the tightest setting, tilting her head slightly as she took in my image in the mirror. "The necklace works well, don't you think?"

I brought an unsteady hand to my throat, feeling the cool metal beneath my fingers. "Yes," I whispered. "It's magnificent."

The statement echoed off the walls, and then my mother was walking away. I let out a breath, turning wearily back to the mirror. I stared at the image, conflicted. I certainly looked the part of the Sovereign, but I had never felt less in control. I loosened the necklace slightly, yet still it suffocated me, weighing me down. I wanted nothing more than to take it all off and hide—hide from the pressure, from the expectations, from the pain. I knew I should be grateful. After all, I was the ideal, the goal, the dream. I had *everything*.

"My name is Willow Aldridge, and I am perfect." I repeated to myself, seeking comfort in the words my mother had taught me to say. I'd said the words dozens of times growing up, dreaming of the day I would believe it.

As I stared at my pale reflection, I couldn't help but wonder when perfection had stopped being the dream and started to become the nightmare.

***

A tense feeling haunted me in the hours that followed, and by the time I was set to meet Leo I was already wishing the night were finished. I was sure that even his companionship would fail to raise my mood—a doubt I began to question as he appeared in my vision. His eyes scanned the crowd, clearly uncomfortable in spite of his elegance. Despite the clear age of his suit, it fit him well, accentuating his strong form. His eternally messy hair was slicked back tastefully, although his hair clearly resisted the style, creating an appearance of tousled elegance. Gray eyes met green as he found me, and I descended the grand staircase slowly. He grinned as I neared, reaching a tanned hand towards mine. I responded in kind, and he kissed my hand, bowing.

"Good evening, my lady." His actions were proper, but I knew from the twinkle in his eye that he was joking. I giggled softly, sinking into a clumsy curtsy. Courtesies such as bows and curtsies hadn't been used in ages—too reminiscent of the flawed royals of the Oldens—but my childhood tutor had insisted on teaching me anyway.

"Good evening, fine sir," I joked back, grabbing his arm as he offered it to me. It was just as electric of a touch as the day we first met, and yet there was something else, too—a familiar warmth that caused my heart to pound. Something had changed yesterday in the glade, something I couldn't even begin to understand. I pushed it out of my head as we turned, heading towards the ballroom. "Where did you learn all of that, anyways?" The question was genuine. Surely he had never had a tutor, and they were not well-known mannerisms.

"Why, I can't tell you that," he said lightly, eyes twinkling. "That would ruin the mystery."

I laughed gently, but my mind raced. There was something about his tone that told me there was a secret beneath his laughter, and I was determined to discover it.

I was torn from my thoughts by a voice, and I realized we were being spoken to.

"Willow, you look just lovely, of course."

I turned to see Ruben and Lucille Bonavich standing just outside the ballroom. Auden was situated properly between his parents, sophisticated as ever in a white suit and a sleek black tie. He nodded formally as his dark eyes met mine, mouth tightening as he took in Leo beside me.

"Thank you. You do as well." I smiled politely at Lucille, the pleasantries slipping from my tongue easily.

"I see you've brought a... friend." The words came from Ruben, his eyes roaming critically from my hand on Leo's arm to his aged suit. I removed my hand quickly, avoiding Auden's eyes. We both knew what was expected: we would be the first and second-highest scores, therefore designating us to be Paired and married. Bringing Leo here, holding his arm... Undoubtedly they saw it as a threat to our marriage, to the system.

Leo shifted uncomfortably, clasping his hands stiffly behind his back. "Leo Hayes," he said, reaching out a hand awkwardly. His voice was tight, clearly full of nerves. "Nice to meet you."

Ruben smiled tightly, a hint of cruelty behind the nicety as he grasped Leo's hand tightly. "And you, Leonardo." His voice was short, and he turned to leave, clearly disinterested in the discussion.

"It's Leo, actually," Leo retorted suddenly, a subtle blaze behind his words. "Just Leo."

Ruben turned swiftly, eyes hard as they met Leo's. Tension stretched the moment, and I fidgeted uncomfortably.

"Leo," Ruben said slowly, as if tasting the word in his mouth only to find it deeply unpleasant. His face melted into an unpleasant smile—one that reminded me quite a bit of a serpent. Despite his previous attempts to leave, it seemed he had found Leo's answer amusing enough to stay. "You're a participant in the Pathway, then?"

Leo glanced at me quickly, clearly uncomfortable.

"He is," I shot back with a glare, anger flaring up in my veins. Auden just watched the interaction with an increasingly furrowed brow, concern evident in his eyes.

"Ruben, Lucille," a voice stated from beside me, cool and casual. I almost groaned at the sight of my mother. The last thing Leo needed was to meet yet another person who hated him on principle.

"Amelia," Ruben replied smoothly. Lucille didn't bother to reply, merely grasping a flute of champagne from a passing Service. I wasn't offered one myself, as I was too young to drink it. Alcohol wasn't permitted until you entered society as an adult. Yet another thing to look forward to after the Pathway ended, I supposed.

"Is there an issue?" My mother said, eyes darting between Ruben and me. Sometimes I felt as though my mother was a hawk, watchful eyes catching every detail.

Ruben just glanced at me, as if challenging me to cause a scene. Part of me wanted to, but I could see the tension in Auden's jaw and the tightening of Leo's muscles. The last thing I wanted was for either of them to get in the middle of this.

"No," I replied softly, repressing the urge to glare at him.

Ruben smiled, satisfaction in his eyes. "Willow was just introducing me to her friend," he said smoothly. "Theo, was it?"

I could practically feel Leo's fury beside me. Honestly, it was a miracle that he hadn't exploded already. I shot him a warning glance, silently urging him to keep it that way.

My mother made a light humming noise, pursing her lips. "I believe the boy's name is Leo."

I whirled around to face her, shocked. For her to have remembered his name was impressive in itself—but to see her stand up to Ruben? And on Leo's behalf? It was nothing short of a miracle. My mother was all propriety and smiles, never the type to make a scene.

"It is," I added, emboldened by my mother's statement. "Just like he already told you. Twice."

"Did he? I guess I forgot," Ruben said casually, brow quirked. "Funny how that happens." He glanced past me and at my mother as he spoke, voice calm, but eyes dark. "Sometimes we need a little reminder."

His eyes bored into my mother's head, but she wasn't looking at him. She was staring at Lucille, whose eyes had snapped suddenly to Ruben. It was like a bizarre triangle, a standoff that I didn't understand in the slightest. One glance at Auden told me that he was as confused as I was, brow furrowed as he took in the scene before us.

"You can call me Theo," Leo stated, polite with the slightest hint of sarcasm. "If it's so difficult to remember."

"I don't imagine I'll need to call you anything," Ruben scoffed.

The rest was implied: *because you won't be around for long.*

Ruben turned and strode away, Lucille close at his heels. Auden lingered, turning to me with an apologetic look.

"Come, Auden," his father called sharply, and Auden sent me a sad shrug before trotting after his parents.

I expected an interrogation from my mother, but she merely stared after the Bonaviches, oddly distracted. She shook her head lightly before giving me a warning glance and disappearing into the glimmering crowd.

Leo let out a breath, and I shared quietly in his relief.

"I'm sorry about them. I didn't think…" My words faded as I stared after them, my thoughts clouding over in my mind. It wasn't as if I didn't know their views on people of Leo's status; I just hadn't expected quite so much blatant discourtesy. The Bonaviches, while generally cold and unpleasant people, had been closely tied with my family for as long as I could remember. I'd expected more decency—especially with my mother there.

"I thought your Charisma notes said you're not supposed to be rude," Leo joked, though a hint of tension remained in his voice.

"Yes, well, not everyone is as exceptional of a rule follower as I am," I replied, but my heart wasn't in the usual banter—a fact that Leo clearly noticed.

"Don't worry about it," he said softly. "I expected no less."

I cringed at his words, guilty for bringing him into that situation. Still, I couldn't help but feel warm inside. He'd known it would be awful, and he had come anyway. Was it for the experience, or for something else?

Someone else, perhaps…?

I pushed the traitorous thought from my head. Leo and I were just friends, and it needed to stay that way. I couldn't go losing my head just because he looked good in a suit. Even if he looked really, really good in that suit.

"Do you still want to go in?" I asked, gesturing towards the ballroom. "You don't have to; I think you've probably experienced enough of Charisma."

He glanced towards the entrance, tall and daunting before us. "No, let's go in," he stated. "No need to let one conversation ruin a perfectly good night."

Despite our best efforts, it became clear that the conversation had, in fact, ruined the night. The ballroom was magnificent as always, splendid chandeliers sparkling in the light, the arched ceiling entwined with gold, but no amount of splendor could distract the eyes that followed us across the room. The Bonavich family, apparently, were not the only people who found my company strange. It was entirely stifling, and by an hour in, we had stopped pretending to enjoy ourselves. We were sitting in a corner, observing the ball when Leo spoke, his voice sudden in the silence.

"Not that this isn't fun," he said, sarcasm clear in his tone, "but do you want to get out of here?"

My eyes widened, heart sinking. "Oh, sure. I can walk you out."

Leo laughed, eyes doing that twinkling thing I was growing quite fond of. "Who said anything about walking?"

I barely had time to register his hand around mine before he sprung up from his chair, pulling me behind him gently. Then we were off, moving through the crowd like water through rocks in a stream. I grasped his hand tightly, scared of losing him in the bustle of fabric and bodies. I spotted Vi across the room, twirling effortlessly in a gown of majestic mauve. I waved at her as we pushed past, ignoring her confused glance at Leo's and my intertwined hands. Surely she would interrogate me about it later, but at the moment I was focused on Leo's back as we moved through the ballroom and into the entrance hall.

"Wait!" I called, swallowing down an embarrassingly girly giggle as I tugged him to a stop. "We can't..." I started, even as everything in my body screamed at me to stop. I swallowed hard, urging myself to think practically. *Think with your head, not your heart.* "We can't just leave."

"Why not?" he said, brows raising in challenge. "Last I checked, we have working legs. We can go wherever we want, princess."

My heart soared at the words, and I knew it was a lost cause. My heart would have to win, if only for tonight.

"And where do you want to go?"

He grinned, eyes lighting up, clasping both of his hands around my own. "Anywhere."

"Anywhere?" I laughed. "That's your plan?'

"I don't have a plan," he replied, pushing a strand of hair behind my ear. "You should try it sometime."

I thought about that for a moment. It wasn't as if I didn't know that some people lived life like that, moving whichever way the wind blew, but I certainly did not. I couldn't, if I wanted to become Sovereign.

But at the moment, I didn't care.

"Alright, then," I breathed. "Let's do it."

"Yeah?" he asked, raising a brow. I recognized the word for what it was: a chance to turn back.

"Yeah." I answered, heart beating an erratic rhythm in my ribcage.

Leo's face was filled with wonder and a hint of pride as he nodded once, smirk growing, and turned towards the exit.

We were steps from the doorway when Leo stopped suddenly, and I bumped into him. I peered around him to see the doorway blocked by none other than my mother, arms crossed.

"Leaving so soon?" Her voice was composed, but I could sense the tension behind her words. Her eyes flicked towards our hands, still intertwined, before rising to meet my own. My heart twinged at the disappointment in her expression, but I kept my hand firmly in Leo's. "Risa will escort you out," she said, beckoning for Risa absentmindedly.

My heart sank. It felt extremely unfair somehow, like losing a bar of chocolate without even getting to take a bite.

"Actually, Mother, I was going to walk him home," I stated slowly.

My mother stared at me, face impassive, but eyes hard. "Don't be ridiculous. It's the middle of the ball. Besides, it's raining. It'll ruin everything." She gestured to my face, but I knew she wasn't talking about my appearance.

Our previous conversation floated into my mind, and I bit my lip. A crossroads lay before me, two choices with no option in between. My mother's eyes urged me to choose the right path, the clear path, the *safe* path. I could see it so clearly: let go of Leo's hand, go back to the ball, and forget this ever happened.

Just then, Leo squeezed my hand gently, and as I met his eyes, I knew I could never forget this.

"Perhaps it will," I said, voice quiet but certain, "but I'm not sure I care." I turned without waiting for a reaction, tugging Leo with me.

"Willow Aldridge, you come back here!" my mother hissed, clearly torn between anger and embarrassment. We sped up at the words, breaking into a jog at the sound of heels on marble behind us, and suddenly we were running through the manor, winding through halls of marble and doorways of gold. The sound of my mother's heels had long since disappeared, yet still we ran, laughter rebounding off the walls as we tumbled by, throwing ourselves through door after door until suddenly we were plunged into a damp darkness. I stopped abruptly at the sensation, squinting through the onslaught of rain at our surroundings.

"Where are we?" Leo's voice called, muffled by the downpour.

"The gardens," I shouted back, pulling him under the cover of a nearby tree. The drooping branches covered us, and the droplets rained slowly through the leaves. We paused for a moment, panting lightly from the exertion. My heart was beating fast, adrenaline highlighting my surroundings with a brightness like never before.

I felt a hand on my hair, strong yet gentle. I looked up to see Leo, eyes twinkling as he plucked a flower from my soaked hair. It was a pale purple, rare and vibrant amongst the brown of the garden.

"Willow." His voice was soft, barely audible over the volume of the rain, and I glanced at him in confusion.

"Yes?"

"No, the tree," he said, laughing gently as he gestured to the hanging leaves. "It's a willow tree." He moved closer, pressing the flower into the hair behind my ear.

"How do you even know that?" I asked, laughing softly.

He smiled gently, his hand dropping to linger by my cheek. "Because it's beautiful," he murmured. I shuddered at the intimacy of the moment, noticing for the first time just how close we were. "Because I make it my business to know the names of beautiful things."

A memory echoed in my mind, of when I had first told him my name. *"I know,"* he'd said.

I glanced at his face, and it was as if I were seeing him for the first time. His eyes were gentle but intense, burning into my soul, and raindrops clung to his eyelashes, occasionally rolling down his smooth skin to rest on his lips—lips that moved towards mine, and I leaned forward as if by instinct. The moment was perfection like I'd never experienced, but...

"We can't." The words were a sigh of regret, torturous as they left my mouth. I pulled away from him quickly, before my body could act to the contrary. I cursed inwardly as the air grew tense, heavy with discomfort as Leo's face crumbled. I shouldn't have even let it get this far, shouldn't have tempted my brain so.

"I'm sorry, I thought—"

"No, you were right. It's just..." my voice faded off as I scrambled for the words. How could I explain the promise I made to Vi?

"I know. The Pathway. It's alright."

I winced. After all that had passed between us, he still believed me to be so shallow. *Not that I can blame him.* "No! This has nothing to do with my score. I promise." I grasped his hands in mine despite my better judgment, desperate to make him understand. I wished I could say my resolve didn't waver as our skin touched. "It's just—"

The words were interrupted by a sharp rustle behind us, propelling my body backwards and away from Leo instinctually. Hurt flashed in his eyes, but he said nothing as I turned towards the source of the noise. My heart dropped into my stomach as a figure emerged from the drooping branches.

"Am I interrupting something?" Vi's voice was harsh, bitterness seeping through the betrayed look upon her face. It took several moments for my frazzled mind to process the situation, the hurt and rage in her tone seeming utterly out of place in the beauty of the moment.

"It's not what it looks like," I started slowly. "I promise."

Vi merely scoffed at my guilt-ridden statement. "Yeah, okay," she spat, rolling her eyes and turning to leave. "You *promise.* As if your promises mean anything."

Leo glanced at me sharply, and I cringed. Really, the timing couldn't have been worse.

"Wait, Vi!" I called desperately, fighting to follow her through the damp leaves. Droplets rained onto my face from above, the rain pouring down harder than ever. "Listen..."

"No!" she spat, whipping around to face me. "I'm done listening. I *always* listen." She wiped a frustrated hand across her soaked hair, pushing it out of her eyes. "I have been there for you through *everything.* Every little problem you had, every tantrum, I listened."

"I know!" I exclaimed, my voice breaking slightly around the words. "I know, but—"

"Even now!" she interrupted with a harsh laugh. "Even now, you refuse to hear anything other than your own thoughts."

"I'm listening!" I yelled, cringing at the loudness of my voice. I took a deep breath and tried again, softer. "I'm sorry, okay? I'm listening."

"It doesn't matter," she whispered. "It's too late."

At that moment, I knew this wasn't about Leo. It wasn't even about me lying. No, this was about something bigger—something I didn't even know I was doing wrong. It was completely unfair.

"Vi, I…" My voice trailed off in my confusion; I was suddenly unable to find any words at all. I wasn't even sure why she was so upset. "I don't understand."

"I know," she laughed bitterly. "I think that's the worst thing of all."

I gritted my teeth. Nothing she was saying made any sense, and I was getting pretty sick of being blamed for something she had never told me. "Maybe I would understand if you just *told* me what's going on, instead of blowing up at me for no reason."

"No *reason*?" she exclaimed. Her voice was high and thin, almost delirious. "Oh, Willow, your naivety never fails to impress me."

"That's enough," Leo cut in sharply. "You're being unfair, Vi. Willow hasn't done anything wrong."

"Oh?" Vi raised her brows. "You think she's such a great *friend*? Loyal?"

Leo glanced at me. His brows were tight, and I knew he was still annoyed about what had happened under the tree.

"Yeah," he said anyways, a fact which warmed my heart. "I do."

My returning smile wasn't enough to explain what it meant to me—what *he* had come to mean to me these past weeks. Some days it felt like we had been merged from the beginning, but others I struggled to understand how we were connected at all, as if passion and practicality were eternally warring in my heart.

"That's funny," Vi said, voice uneven. "Considering what she said the other night."

I noted her glassy eyes, glistening dangerously in the dim light, and in that moment she wasn't my best friend. The brewing darkness had taken over at last, fear and anger and bitterness clouding her bright soul.

"Vi, don't," I begged, nausea rising within me as I realized what would come next. "Don't do this."

She hesitated for a brief moment, face unsure, and I had begun to think maybe she would listen after all when her eyes shifted to the flower in my hair, damp and broken and so vividly *violet*.

"Because that night," she continued almost numbly, eyes tracking the flower, "that night she said you could *never* like someone like *you*."

The words were poisonous and final, killing any chance at reconciliation. I didn't stop her as she walked away, shock gluing me to the spot where I stood.

"Leo, it wasn't like that." I turned towards him, frantic. "Please, you have to believe me!"

"Is she telling the truth?" His voice was unusually quiet and pained, the sound wounding me somewhere deep inside.

"Leo..."

"Did you say it—yes or no?" The words seemed to harden his voice, leaving it angry but tainted with a deep pain.

I swallowed hard and nodded, searching his face for any sign of forgiveness. He merely stared at me for a few moments before shaking his head and turning to leave.

"No need to come next weekend," he spat without turning around, voice strangled by something that sounded almost like tears. "I won't waste any more of your precious time on 'someone like me.'"

I wept as his form retreated, sinking to the ground slowly as my knees gave out beneath me. I yanked the flower from my hair, and it fell to the ground, rain pounding it into the dirt until it was hardly recognizable. I half wished it would do the same to me; at least then I wouldn't have to feel this ache within me, an abrupt feeling as though I had lost a piece of my heart.

Two pieces, a nasty inward voice reminded me. Raindrops streamed down my face, mingling with the bitter salt of my tears as I stared at the dark sky and wondered just how long it would take to drown in this ocean of my own creation.

11

— · —

WHEN THE CROWN SLIPS

It was my mother who found me, splayed flat on my back in the dirt. I imagine she planned to lecture me, but decided my current state was punishment enough. I knew I should be grateful, but I couldn't find the energy to feel anything but empty.

"Oh, honey," she said, rubbing my back as she guided my shivering form through the manor halls, the walls that had once echoed with laughter silent once again. "I tried to warn you; it's not worth it."

The melancholy of that night plagued me in the hours that followed, time crawling by slowly. Life seemed suddenly monotonous, and I was haunted by the realization that this was my future. Auden was the only light in the darkness, steadfast as always. He stayed with me all night, despite the assessment to come in the morning.

"Thank you," I whispered at some point, once my tears had stopped long enough for me to say anything at all. Darkness surrounded us, lights off as if either of us were getting any sleep. "I know you should be at home getting a good night's rest for tomorrow."

Auden was silent, and for a moment I thought maybe he was asleep after all.

"It's alright," he murmured, voice less poised than I'd come to expect. "I didn't much want to be home, anyways."

I stayed quiet, waiting for him to say more, but nothing came. I cursed my awkwardness; I really was quite awful at comforting people.

"Want to talk about it?" I said at last, the words seeming to float in the darkness. I didn't expect much of a reply; Auden rarely spoke about his life at home, but I'd always known it wasn't pleasant. It couldn't have been—not with the way Auden worked so hard to keep me at a distance from there, the way he was always over at the Palace, the way he sometimes came back from a long weekend with a perpetual frown and dark bags under his eyes.

"My father is under the impression that I am at fault for Leo's presence at the ball," he admitted softly. "He's not pleased."

"What?" I exclaimed, propping myself up on two pillows. "How does that even make sense?"

Auden didn't reply for a moment, as if he were ashamed of what he was about to say. "You're soon to be my wife. It's my responsibility to ensure you're behaving properly." The words were flat and monotone, as if he were reciting them from memory—no doubt from an unpleasant discussion with his father.

"Auden," I said slowly, goosebumps rising on my skin, "you know that's ridiculous, right?" As much as I trusted Auden, the words concerned me. Sure, I understood the importance of familial structure; after all, it was a staple of life here in Atvas. Still, the extent to which Auden was presenting it... Only the most traditional of families followed such stringent guidelines. Like the Bonaviches.

"Yeah," Auden replied quickly. "Of course. You know that's not what I want for us. It never has been."

"Then, what?" I pressed gently.

"I may not be responsible for your actions," he answered, "but it is my duty to protect you. And tonight, seeing you so hurt..." His voice faded, but his meaning was clear enough.

"Tonight wasn't your fault. If anything, it was mine." And wasn't that just the cold, hard truth. "I know you want to protect me, but sometimes you just can't. That is not your fault, no matter what your father says."

"I know," Auden sighed. "It's just ... sometimes it's hard to tell where he ends and I begin." His voice was oddly hoarse, vulnerable and full of pain. "Other times, I wonder if I'm myself at all."

"I'm sorry," I replied softly, emotion choking my voice.

"It's not your fault," Auden whispered. "It's just ... well, you're in first place right now."

I gulped. I hadn't even thought of that.

"That's not what I meant," I admitted, because I couldn't honestly say I was sorry for that.

"What else would you have to apologize for?" he asked, and I imagined he was probably frowning in confusion, although I couldn't be sure in the darkness.

"For not being there," I answered honestly. "I've been so focused on ... well, everything, and I haven't been there for you like I should have."

Auden didn't answer for several moments.

"It's my fault, too." His voice sounded almost ... guilty. "I haven't exactly made things easier for you, being on your back all the time. I just... I *knew* he would hurt you somehow."

I shifted uncomfortably. Tonight was hardly Leo's fault, but I didn't feel like getting into it right now.

"Still," I said instead, "we're ... well, we're *us*. I should have known things would be hard for you right now. I should have been there for you."

"You were," he said again, though I knew it wasn't true. "You always are."

"For the record," I whispered, so quietly I wondered if he could hear, "I think you're a better man than your father could ever be."

He didn't reply, but I knew he had heard—and that was enough.

***

Auden either hadn't slept at all or hadn't slept enough, because he was up and ready by the time I was awoken by Risa.

"Morning, sunshine." Auden's greeting was brighter than usual, and he glanced at me carefully as I approached. "How are you feeling today?"

"You know, you don't have to treat me like I'm made of glass," I scoffed, rolling my eyes as we started down our morning path. "I'm not *that* fragile."

He quirked an eyebrow, and I hit his arm playfully. "Hey, I'm not!"

"I know you're not," he groaned in mock pain, rubbing his arm softly. "I'm just worried about you, that's all. Yesterday was emotional, and I want you to be able to focus today."

His eyes were soft as he glanced at me, and I blinked rapidly as the gentleness of his tone surrounded me like a hug. I met his serene blue eyes, a wave of appreciation washing over me at his presence.

"I know." My voice was soft, and I smiled gently at him. "And I appreciate it, honestly. But I'm fine."

It was the truth, honestly. Surely it would hurt when I saw Vi or Leo, but I'd concluded it was for the best. Leo, the glade, leaving the ball... It was all a phase, a temporary lapse in judgment, and it was over now. I had to focus on what mattered: the Pathway.

If I say it enough, maybe I'll start to believe it.

I shook my head free of the thoughts as we approached the Cathe, keeping my eyes focused on the doorway at the front. Despite my new-found conviction, I felt shakier than I cared to admit. I hadn't slept more than an hour or two, and my eyes were still red-rimmed from cry-ing—not exactly the best good shape to be in for a Charisma assessment. The halls were loud, bustling with spectators eager to catch a glimpse of us as we hustled down the corridors. I couldn't help but blanch a bit from the attention. I should have been used to it, but I felt oddly vulnerable.

A flash of blonde hair crossed my vision—a tall figure that I knew all too well. I hadn't forgotten that Emmaline had tried to sabotage me in the first trial, that she was watching my every move for an opportunity to strike. I found myself wondering if Vi were here as well, waiting to watch me fail. Maybe they would become friends now, would form a Willow Aldridge hate club.

"... right?" Auden finished, and I realized suddenly that he must have been speaking this whole time. My brow furrowed as my brain raced, trying to remember a single sound I had heard in the past five minutes. It was hopeless; I may as well have had no ears, for all the good they'd done me.

Auden just sighed softly, steering me gently towards a chair. We had somehow migrated from the hall to a large ballroom, one of the more decorative rooms in the Cathe. A large stage sat at the front of the room, with rows and rows of benches spanning the remainder. Up front sat several rows of individual chairs, labeled for each of the Pathway participants. I wondered vaguely what the assessment would be, with a setup as bland as this—a thought I probably should have been pondering minutes ago.

Focus, I reminded myself. *I just need to focus.*

I watched as participants and spectators filled the room, the volume growing steadily. I really should have been interacting, talking it up the way Auden was beside me, but I couldn't find the energy. I found my mother in the crowd, seated with the rest of the Court just behind us and looking strangely happy. Then our eyes met, and the strangest thing happened: she *winked.* An uneasy feeling simmered in my gut. My mother hadn't winked at me in years, if she ever had at all.

What is she up to?

"Welcome!" a voice exclaimed, so bright and excited that my headache intensified instantly. "Today we will witness something magical: the fourth assessment of the Pathway to Perfection!" Councilman Mullerson paused, as though waiting for a cheer to rise up from the crowd. A few people clapped politely, and I heard quite a few stifled snickers. I almost felt bad for the guy as his face fell. Really, it wasn't his fault he was so awkward. "Alright, then," he continued, face beet red. "Let us get started with the rules."

Auden shifted next to me, practically on the edge of his seat. It occurred suddenly to me that perhaps I should be the same.

"Those with Charisma are clever," Mullerson said. "They are able to say the most in the smallest number of words. Even better, they are able to extract the meaning of a conversation from the most subtle cues."

What a great Charisma I am, I thought bitterly. *I couldn't even tell that my best friend was upset.* It suddenly seemed extraordinarily clear to me that I knew nothing at all.

"This assessment will put these attributes to test right here, right now, in a magnificent round of Charades!"

There were mutters around us, but I frowned. Charades? What was that?

"They did this one a few years back," Auden murmured to me, clearly catching onto my confusion. "That's why everyone knows it."

I huffed quietly; of course no one had ever bothered to tell *me* about this seemingly well-known game. As much as I didn't envy Auden's relationship with his father, I couldn't help but wish my own had prepared me more.

"It will proceed as follows," Mullerson called over the murmurs, clearly agitated that everyone seemed to know the game already. "Each participant will come up to the stage individually and receive a card from a Council member. This card will show a term or concept we believe is central to Atvas. Each participant will be permitted three words. They must use these to describe the term on their card, and the other participants will attempt to guess the term. Points will be awarded to the correct guesser, and will also be awarded to the participant doing the describing, based on the speed of the correct guess, as well as speed of their description of the term. An incorrect guess will result in negative points."

My mind raced. This would be tricky. The describer role would be easy enough; three words were more than enough for any concept. But the guessing... That was where the real game would be played. It would be a careful balance, weighing a desire to guess first against the temptation to wait longer and reduce the points of the describer. I would have to pay very, very close attention to the other guessers, would have to judge their proximity to guessing on body language alone. *Subtleties, indeed.*

"We will start with the top of the current standings and work down from there," Mullerson announced, and a jolt ran through me; I wasn't even close to prepared. "Willow Aldridge, please make your way to the stage."

I gulped down my fear as the syllables bounced around the room, rising onto my shaking legs.

"Hey," Auden whispered, gripping my arm gently as I stood. "Just focus; you're ready for this. Don't think about him, alright?"

And just like that, all I could think about was Leo—his face, his caring words, the hurt in his eyes when Vi spoke those awful words. I nodded anyway, forcing one foot in front of the other as I made my way towards the stage. Before I knew it, I was staring at the sea of faces blending together like paint in the rain.

Mullerson strode towards me, a card face down in his palm. "Willow Aldridge," he said, and I gulped again. "Once you take this card, your time will begin." He looked at me then, and I could have sworn there was pity in his gaze. "Good luck," he muttered softly, so quiet that only I could hear.

A shaky hand reached out in front of me, floating over the card as if of its own will. *Focus,* I reminded myself. *Stay focused.*

And then the card was in my palm, and it suddenly all made sense. The pitying glance, my mother's wink—it all made perfect sense.

Service

I almost laughed at the absurdity of it all, at the unfairness. It was no coincidence that I had been given that particular card—not after bringing Leo to the ball. As my mother always said, reputation was everything. Especially in the discipline of Charisma.

I glanced at the crowd helplessly, wishing for a chance to run off stage and hide from this nightmare. I knew what the Council wanted me to say, knew why I had received this card. It was my chance to denounce Leo altogether, to show that I was a vicious Charisma through and through. It was my chance to redeem myself in their eyes. But if I did that... Well, Leo would be a lot more hurt than he already was. He would be humiliated. His whole *family* would. I wondered suddenly if they were here, too, if they would see whatever came next and judge me for it.

Mullerson glanced at me nervously, clearing his throat. I opened my mouth to say the words, three simple words that any former Charisma could guess in an instant: *Servant. Working. Below.* Just then, I met a pair of gray eyes in the crowd—eyes I knew all too well. My mouth grew dry as Leo and I stared at each other. His eyes flickered to the card in my hand, then to the panic on my face, and he nodded slowly, as if he knew what I had to do. He probably did, smart as he was.

"Go ahead," His eyes seemed to say. *"Do it."*

I knew then that I couldn't do it. I wouldn't. Not when I knew him the way I did, had seen the way he was with his family. *The way he was with me.*

"Family." I choked out, the words scratching their way out of my throat. "Caring." The card fell from my shaking hands, but no one seemed to notice. They were all too busy staring at me, faces scrunched up as they fought to decipher my words. "Beautiful," I gasped, a feeling of utter catharsis flooding me as the word floated into being. Whatever consequences would come, the words were out—and the right words, at that.

The hall was utterly silent for a moment, the participants frowning in concentration. I almost felt bad for them, but the feeling lasted only a moment. If they couldn't recognize Service from that description, maybe they needed a wake-up call anyhow. Never mind the fact that *I* wouldn't have been able to until recently.

"Court?" someone called from the back of the participant group, and I cringed for them.

"I'm sorry," Mullerson announced, glancing at me with a strange look in his eye as he spoke. "That is incorrect."

Murmurs broke out across the room, the participants watching each other warily. No one wanted to guess wrong—not after that.

"Friendship," another voice called out, and I snapped my head toward it. Auden.

Oh, no. I knew he was thinking of our friendship, knew it from the bright look in his eyes as he glanced at me, dimples showing. In that moment, he looked so happy, like a little kid being complimented for the first time, and my heart broke a little on his behalf.

"I'm sorry, that is incorrect."

I glanced away from him, not willing to watch the hurt that surely flashed across his face. I locked eyes instead with Leo, who stared at me with his mouth ajar. It was almost satisfying to see him like that, so surprised—a nice change from the usual smugness. Although if I were honest with myself, anything was better than the coldness of last night.

"Service," Leo muttered, so quietly that I could barely hear. Only his lips gave it away, curving upwards around the word, as if he couldn't help the smile it brought.

"Sorry?" Mullerson called awkwardly. "Speak up, please."

"Service," Leo repeated, voice strong. He let out a laugh, as if he couldn't believe what he was saying. "She's describing the discipline of Service."

A few snickers sounded from the crowd, those who had heard Leo's proclamation eager for the denial they thought imminent. I could recognize Emmaline's obnoxious giggle from here, her sneer clear in the crowd. Auden just stared at me warily, disappointment painting his face.

"That is correct!" Mullerson's voice was disbelieving, as if he weren't quite sure what he was saying. "Service is the correct answer."

A tense silence filled the room, a hundred eyes on me. My mother's seemed to shine particularly bright, green tinged with displeasure. I fidgeted awkwardly, unsure what to do next; was I to sit down, or wait for dismissal? Mullerson seemed unsure as well, glancing at his papers as if new instructions would appear out of thin air. I wondered what those instructions would be titled: *What to do when your top participant does something irrevocably stupid,* perhaps.

Suddenly, a noise rang out from near the back: the sound of hands coming together. After several moments, I realized someone was actually *clapping.* Oakley stood there, clapping his hands. It appeared Leo's family was here after all. The twins joined in next, hollering in typical rowdiness, followed by little Eden. I wasn't sure she even knew why she was clapping, but she bounced up and down anyway, blonde hair leaping jubilantly. Leo joined in after a moment, gray eyes latched onto mine as he stood carefully. A few other people began to applaud as well—whether out of respect or confusion, I wasn't sure. My eyes welled up with tears nonetheless, and I wished I could bottle this moment and keep it forever. Sure, there would be hell to pay for that little demonstration. My reputation might never recover. But in that moment, I could only see what was in front of me: undeniable, unstoppable support.

Family, indeed.

I kept the image with me as I returned to my seat, Auden's stare like a weight as I lowered myself into my chair. He certainly hadn't been applauding me.

"I'm sorry," I murmured, "I just couldn't do it."

He said nothing, and I gulped down the guilt in my throat as he made his way to the stage. I cursed inwardly. After all he had done to prepare me for today, I had sent him in upset and distracted. Still, he seemed steady enough as he reached for his own card and flipped it over. He barked out a very un-Auden-like laugh, lacking all his usual mirth.

"Confusing," he listed almost instantly. "Inconsistent." He met eyes with mine, blue on green. "Unrequited."

"Scores," someone called.

"Emotion," shouted another, almost instantly.

"Both incorrect," Mullerson announced, although he sounded distracted. Most likely, he was too busy enjoying the drama in front of him as Auden stared me down. I shook my head slowly, but the words left my mouth of their own accord.

"Love," I said finally, because I knew it was the answer. I knew it from the bottom of my soul, because this was *just* like Auden. Of course he had to make this a lecture, had to remind me that love wasn't worth it. I knew he was trying to help, trying to keep me on track, but *really*? During an assessment in front of the entire ballroom was the absolute best time to do this? I glared at him as he returned to his seat, and he looked away.

A thick tension stretched between us, only worsening as the assessment went on. We were at each other's throats practically the entire time, shouting our guesses in tandem. By the time Leo was up on stage, we were about equal in guessing points.

Leo took his time strolling up to the stage, a new-found confidence propelling his steps. He picked up his card leisurely, smirking as he read.

"Palace, running, awkward," he said quickly, and I grinned. I knew what he was getting at, even if the rest of the participants scrambled to make sense of the odd words.

"Ball!" I called, grinning as I did so. Leo grinned back as Councilman Mullerson laughed.

"Very good, Ms. Aldridge," Mullerson exclaimed. "That's our fastest answer yet."

Exhilaration filled me. It would do little to enhance my own score as the guesser, but that kind of boost would do wonders for Leo. That excitement stayed with me throughout the rest of the assessment, driving me to answer faster and faster. Auden grew increasingly frustrated, and by the end of the assessment, he seemed almost defeated.

It seemed like hours later that the last participant made their way back to their row, Mullerson dismissing us at last. I nearly groaned in relief. Despite the boost of adrenaline from Leo's inside joke, I was exhausted.

Auden sat frozen beside me, hardly seeming to realize the commotion around him.

"Look…" I began, any anger I'd had at him long gone in the face of his distress.

"It's fine." His words were short, and his tone clearly suggested it wasn't fine at all.

"Auden…" I started again, but a tap on my shoulder cut me off.

"Oh," Amaris said, glancing between us awkwardly. "I hope I didn't interrupt anything. I just figured I'd let you know, the rankings have been updated."

I frowned. That couldn't be right. The assessment had *just* finished.

"Already?" I asked, but Auden was already moving. I sighed heavily as the door slammed shut behind him, exhausted in the wake of his anger. I hated that we had to fight like this, hated that we had to fight at all.

"He's changed," Amaris observed, voice neutral as she glanced at me.

I huffed out a laugh, the sound more tired than amused. "Haven't we all?"

Amaris hummed in agreement, pausing for a brief moment before saying, "You certainly have."

I half wanted to remind her that it had been six years since we last spoke, and that anyone would change in that time, but I bit my tongue. Perhaps that action alone was enough to prove her point. "Look," I said instead, gnawing at my cheek nervously, "I'm… sorry, for how things went with us. For our fight." The apology felt foreign in my throat, the word grating uncomfortably against my instincts.

Her brows raised in surprise. "Oh."

"I mean, I know it was a long time ago," I rambled, my anxiety mounting by the second, "but I just wanted you to know that. If I did anything to hurt you, or push you away, I'm sorry."

"No, it's fine," Amaris cut in, seeming quite confused. "That's all... I mean, we were just kids, Willow. I barely even remember it."

Oh. I'd spent years avoiding her in crowded halls, missing our friendship in the dark of night, thinking of her every time I saw the spots where we used to frequent. In all that time, I'd never considered that our friendship simply didn't matter as much to her.

"Right." My cheeks were red, eyes downcast. "Of course. I just meant, since we were so close."

She shrugged. "In the way children are, sure."

"Sure." I tried to laugh, but it came out sounding all wrong. "I, uh, I guess I'd better see the scores, then. Thank you for letting me know."

I wondered if she could sense the urgency in my steps, if she could see the flaming of my cheeks. *Stupid, stupid, stupid.* I'd been so stupid to bring that up, just when we were starting to grow close again.

The conversation fled my mind as I entered the main hall, where the score board was posted. I found Auden almost immediately, finding him staring open-mouthed at the board. There was no longer a singular column of names. No, *two* names sat atop the stack, side by side, with the exact same number beside them.

"Oh," I said dumbly, "we're even."

Indeed, Auden and I were both in first place. Unexpected, considering the way I had renounced everything the Council stood for. Auden should have been in first, should have taken my place solidly. He would have, had he not used his turn to make a point.

Auden went pale beside me, and I winced. "I'm sorry."

He shook his head. "It's my own fault," he muttered, blue eyes more worried than I had ever seen them. "I shouldn't have lost my head like that. I wasted my description. It was foolish."

"It wasn't foolish," I replied softly. "You were just trying to help me. I know you think my love for him is doomed and not worth it; I know you just wanted to warn me. That isn't foolish at all."

"Yeah," Auden scoffed, "it is."

I frowned. There was a hint of something else in his voice, a hidden emotion I couldn't quite distinguish.

"You were trying to protect me." My voice broke slightly.

"You're right," he muttered. He looked over me once more, as if coming to a revelation. "All this time, I've been trying to shield you from the world, but I shouldn't have. Sometimes hurt is inevitable."

I nearly sighed in relief; it was exactly what I had been trying to tell him all along.

"It is," I agreed, "but you know I love you for trying."

I hoped the words would comfort him, perhaps force some blood back into his increasingly pale face, but they just seemed to make him more sad. "Yeah," he said. "I know that."

I smiled softly, grabbing his hand and squeezing it. A moment passed between us of understanding and the sort of tenderness only decades of friendship can bring.

"Go," Auden said, smiling sadly as he nodded over my shoulder. "Get your prince charming."

I turned, and there he was: Leo, disappearing from the room before my eyes. I squeezed Auden's hand one final time before turning towards

Leo, pushing through the crowd to keep my eyes on his back. I looked back over my shoulder once, only to see Auden leaving the room as well, Ruben's hand heavy on his shoulder. His head turned, and I could have sworn a shadow passed over his gaze as our eyes met once more—and then, he was gone. I gulped once before turning back towards Leo, eyes trailing his mop of blond hair as he wove his way out of the Cathe.

"Leo!" I called softly, searching for his messy hair as I exited the Cathe and rounded the corner. The crowd had thinned here, leaving only a few stragglers making their way out of the building. I veered off the road, weaving through brick ruins. Finally, I spotted him, shoulders hunched and hands deep in his pockets as he walked. He started as I touched his elbow, spinning around to face me.

"Willow?" His face was surprised. "What are you doing here?"

"What do you think?" I panted, breathless. "I'm here to see you."

"I don't think that's a good idea." He frowned and turned his back, as if to walk away, but I grabbed his arm once more.

"Wait!" I commanded, sounding every bit the Charisma I was raised to be. "You can't just *do* that."

"Do what?" Leo's voice was bewildered, as if he genuinely had no clue what I meant.

I huffed, indignant. "That!" I exclaimed, gesturing wildly in the direction of the Cathe. "You can't just ... connect with me like that, and then act like nothing is going to change."

"Watch me," he said shortly, pulling his arm out of my grip.

I stomped at the ground, feeling quite a bit like one of his kid siblings as I crossed my arms. "Why?" The word resounded loudly through the alleyway, bouncing off the brick and seeming to penetrate his skin. Leo froze, muscles tense as he turned around. "I thought we were good," I continued, voice desperate. "I thought ... I thought you liked me again."

"Of course I like you," Leo sighed. "That's the problem."

I blinked. The confusion must have shown on my face, because he sighed again, rubbing a hand across his face. "Don't you see? Today was a reminder. I can't be the reason you don't become Sovereign. You *need* to be Sovereign."

"It's not your fault I tied," I insisted. "It's my own fault, no one else's."

He shook his head, shoving his hands deeper into his pockets. "Come on, Willow. You killed that trial, and Auden messed up a ton. You know the only reason they docked your score is—"

"Because *I* didn't do what they wanted. My fault." He clearly didn't believe me, so I grabbed his face in my hands, meeting his eyes. "Really, I'm flattered you want to take the blame, but this one's on me."

He stared into my eyes for several moments before pushing away, looking down once again. "Still, I don't think we should keep doing ... this."

I raised my eyebrows. "Who's the one making things sound scandalous now?"

"Damnit, Willow, I'm serious!" His voice was pained as he pushed past me abruptly, moving to lean on the opposite wall.

I frowned at his anger, at his refusal, at the space he put between us. "So am I! I don't get the problem." Anger flared up in my own stomach, a bubbling heat that started in my gut and spread towards my heart. "It's *my* rank; why do you even care?"

"Why do I care? Willow, if you don't know why I care, then what are we even doing here?" He ran his hand through his hair as he spoke, frustration seeping into his voice.

"I don't know; why don't you tell me?"

"I'll tell you what we're *not* doing—what I'm not doing." He met my eyes, and the guilt was back, the brief reprise of anger now faded. "I'm not letting you destroy everything you've worked for."

"It's not your choice!" I was yelling now, and I knew it, but I couldn't resist—not when the anger had bubbled into my throat, into my voice. "I'm so sick of everyone trying to control me! First my mother, and Auden, even Vi, and now you too?"

"I'm not trying to control you," he interrupted, infuriatingly calm, "but we can't just ignore the problems this is going to cause."

I nearly screamed in frustration at the words. "I don't even know what you're talking about."

"Willow, I'm *ruining* your life!" The words were loud, piercing the air with a pain so raw that it sent chills down my spine. He breathed in deeply, turning towards the wall for a few moments before turning back to face me. "I'm ruining your life—and you don't even care." He met my gaze, eyes peering into my soul as he spoke. "That is a *big* problem."

I stared at him, speechless. My brain whirred rapidly in an attempt to process the words, process the pure *emotion* of the moment.

"You're not ruining my life." My voice was a whisper in the alleyway, but it seemed to echo in the space between us. "Leo ... I think you're saving it."

The moment the words were out, I knew it was the truth. Before Leo, I had been an empty shell, a mask of perfection to hide the vacant soul beneath. Before, I may as well have been a corpse, but now I felt life flowing through me in a way it never had before.

Leo glanced at me, shock filling his face. Silence hung heavy in the air, and for a few moments, we just looked at each other—past the hair, the clothes, and even the faces. In that moment, we looked into each other's souls.

"I guess someone has to save the princess," he said finally, that trademark smirk gracing his face once again.

I laughed, pulling him towards me. "Leo Hayes, how many times do I have to tell you that I am *not* a princess?"

"Maybe just one more time," he breathed.

He didn't move this time as I leaned in, and suddenly we were kissing at last. It wasn't as I had imagined it; it was better. The usual electricity raced through my veins, but I almost didn't feel it. It was as if there was no air in the alley, as if he *was* my air and I was his, and in that moment we were one, surviving only through each other.

I'd never felt more alive.

12

Turning Tables

The time with Leo left me light and happy, as if walking on air. I forced myself to calm down as I neared the Palace, sealing my joy in a special box before burying it in my mind.

"No one can know; it must be a secret." His words floated through my head like tendrils of smoke, suffocating me. He was right, of course: I *did* want to be Sovereign, and that wouldn't happen if my reputation was in question. If the choices were keeping us a secret or leaving him forever, well, the choice was obvious. Nevertheless, it unnerved me, and goosebumps dotted my skin at the mere thought of the deception. I would have to lie to my parents, to my mother. I'd done my fair share of lying over the years—to my classmates, to the Council, to myself—but not to her. *Never* to her.

I took a deep breath as I opened the door to the main corridor, stepping in as quietly as possible.

"Willow."

I startled at the unexpected voice, whipping around as the noise echoed in the usually empty corridor. My mother was perfectly poised in the chaise lounge beside me, body calm, but face sunken with the depths of her disappointment.

"I'm surprised to see you in such great spirits." Her chin lifted as she spoke, her eyes burning into mine. "All things considered."

I fought the urge to roll my eyes at the words. Even as her worst nightmare loomed close, she danced around the subject, her ever-present propriety defeating even the worst of her panic. Honestly, part of me was a little jealous; I needed some of that poise if I hoped to pull this off.

"I'll recover, mother. I have Legality and the final still to go. We both know two assessments are more than enough time for me."

Her eyes narrowed as I spoke, and I resisted the urge to fidget. "Do we?" she pressed. "I'm not sure how a person could know such a thing. Given the evidence."

"I can get my score up." The words sounded as forced as they were, making their way through my gritted teeth as my patience ran thin.

"Not if you keep seeing that boy," she spat, face hard. "The Council gave you an out! Do you even know how few people would be given that?"

"It wasn't fair, I—"

"Oh, Willow, nobody cares about *fair*! There are much more important things than fairness!" She moved closer, laying her hand on my shoulder. Her voice was soft, moving through the air like silk, yet I knew any argument would be useless. "You cannot see him again."

"I know," I replied, molding my face into a mask of disappointment. "I won't." My mother's stare burned into the side of my head as I glanced away, doubt clear in her eyes. I swallowed deeply, already regretting the words I forced up my throat. "I'm not stupid, mother. I wouldn't throw away all our hard work for a Service."

She eyed me, clearly not convinced—not that that was surprising, given the events of today.

"He doesn't want me, anyways," I admitted in false defeat. "He's still mad." I couldn't help but think about the alleyway, about the evidence that he most certainly was *not* mad at me.

"Well, it doesn't matter anyhow." My mother's voice yanked me from the depths of my mind, sharp and abrupt against my lucid thoughts. "He'll still ruin you if you let him distract you."

Her words were an echo of Leo's own words, bouncing through the marble hall just as his had filled the alleyway. The thought of earlier, of *Leo,* gave me enough energy to push out the words I knew would convince her, once and for all.

"Of course, mother." I smiled brightly, channeling the girl she wanted me to be—*the girl I once was*—as I grabbed her hand in mine. "After all, Leo is no match for a future Sovereign. It's over. I promise."

My stomach churned uncomfortably in the hours that followed, simmering with uneasiness. My mother had always been able to see through me like glass, and with every moment that passed, I feared my façade would shatter. Yet she remained out of sight as I dressed for dinner, not a sound echoing across the vast manor.

Dinner, Risa informed me as she dusted my room, would be at the Bonavich's tonight. I shuddered at the thought. Usually I enjoyed Auden's presence, but dinner with our parents was the worst thing for our friendship right now, especially considering the events of today. Even more frustrating, dinner at another household warranted more formal dress than usual—something I was hardly in the mood to do. I huffed, settling on a silky cream dress with a short but flowy skirt. The loose sleeves trailed down my arms, bunched at the wrist with fabric that splayed slackly over by hands. As I slipped into a pair of strappy heels, I glanced in the mirror across from me. I looked good, of course, but I didn't look like the top-ranked participant, didn't look perfect. *Fitting,*

I thought candidly, *because I'm not—at least, not alone.* It hadn't hit me yet—the loss, the pain, the way the one thing I'd ever really wanted was slipping slowly from my grasp. With Leo by my side, I wondered if it ever would. With Leo, I was *more,* better than any number or position. I was myself, open and free as a bird that soared through the sky after a storm.

A soft smile graced my face at the thought, providing me with the courage to push through this dinner. It was bound to be awkward—not just between Auden and I, but also with our families. The Bonaviches had always wished for our status, and it seemed as if they might just get it. The thought didn't bother me as much as it should have, but then again, this was *Auden.* If there was anyone I trusted to run the government, it was him, with his soft nature and calming presence. Even if he was probably still angry with me. I took a deep breath at the thought, releasing the tension in a gust of air. *Maybe this won't be too bad after all.*

***

By the time the second course slid in front of me, I had realized just how wrong I was. Friction hardened the conversation, evident in the sharp edges of each word. Even the silence was hostile—so much so that I was grateful for each scrape of metal against the fine china.

My mother cleared her throat gently, and I glanced up.

"Lucille, your home looks as lovely as ever," she asserted, clearly attempting to ease the tension. "It's only been a short time since I visited, and yet it looks even more elegant."

Lucille offered a polite smile, but it was Ruben who responded. "Why, thank you, Amelia." His voice was cold as he spoke, face sneering. "We've seen many improvements over the past month." His gaze slid slowly to Auden, and then to me.

Auden's eyes met mine, and I knew he hated this as much as I did. I had hoped he would be looking better today, more like himself, but he seemed more shaken than ever. Dark circles decorated his eyes, as sure a sign as his pale complexion that he wasn't sleeping well at all. Even his mannerisms were different, his usual comforting smile tinged with a hint of weariness.

"Ah, yes, I'm sure you must be very proud of Auden," my father spoke at last, voice jovial, but face alert. "To catch up with my daughter is no simple task!" I knew the words were said out of pride, but not for me. No, my father was defending his own ridiculous pride. What I would have given for him to say those words and actually *mean* them.

"Of course, what's done one month is easily undone the next," my father continued, a warning tone tainting his words.

Ruben seethed at the statement, stabbing his steak with startling ferocity. "Ah, yes," he responded, voice dark, "how fragile a rank can be." His penetrating stare rested on me, and I glanced down at my food, inspecting the salacious meat as if it were the most interesting thing I'd ever seen. "One mistake, one distraction, and you lose everything."

A blush fought its way across my face as everyone fixed their eyes on me—everyone besides Auden, that is. Auden stared instead at his father, some sort of unspoken conversation seeming to pass between them. Whatever it was, Auden seemed to lose, his eyes flitting away from his father and to me at last.

"But you would know that, wouldn't you, Amelia?" Ruben continued, and a harsh silence cut through the air.

Auden shook his head slightly, looking almost disappointed as he turned to his plate. I tried not to feel too relieved as all eyes moved to my mother, but unlike me, she did not blush. She met his eyes unflinchingly and smiled.

"It's a funny thing," she replied, voice quiet but deadly, "how I could lose everything; and yet, I'm the one to call the Palace home."

A deep silence followed her words, heavier than the rest. It continued throughout the remaining courses, broken only by a scrape of metal or squeak of a chair. No more words were spoken, no more truths told. After all, there were none quite as startling as the one my mother uttered. I knew my mother lost the Pathway by a mere margin, but I'd never dared ask for more details. Had she really lost due to a distraction? What sort of distraction? I ate the rest of my meal as quickly as possible, forgoing manners and pleasantries in an attempt to escape the discomfort. I needn't have worried; the rest of the table was doing the same.

"Well," Lucille piped up, speaking for the first time as we all pushed out of our seats. "It was lovely to dine with you this evening."

I nearly scoffed; "lovely" was the last thing I would call this meal. I glanced at my mother, the look on her face suggesting she felt similarly.

"Indeed, it was," she managed, that ever-present poise acting in my stead. I nodded my farewell, unwilling to add any fuel to the conversation. Auden did the same, and I caught his eyes. I had the sudden urge to comfort him, to draw him into a hug, as I might have before this whole thing began. He just glanced away, stepping back as their maid led us to the door.

Our fathers said nothing in the way of farewells, settling for terse nods, and then we were gone. My mother and father were quiet on the walk home, surprisingly; I had expected a lecture, instructions, *something*. I was thrilled to be spared, but the quiet made me uneasy. It wasn't unusual for my family to be quiet, but after such a horrendous dinner, I expected at least *some* admonishment.

My cursed curiosity got the best of me as usual, and I lingered outside my parents' room long after I usually went to bed. I pressed my ear against a particular spot on the mahogany door, which I had long ago discovered was easier to hear through. For a moment, I felt extremely silly, like an immature child, too juvenile for an adult discussion. I was about to pull away when I heard a voice at last: my father's, hushed and irritated.

"... can't afford childish mistakes right now. It's too important."

"Don't you think I know that? As your *friend* reminded me, I know the cost better than anyone. No thanks to you, by the way." It was a feminine voice, tight and high: my mother.

"This isn't about *you*, Amelia. You know what hangs in the balance. They're already—"

"It wouldn't hang in the balance if you would grow up and just do the right thing for once."

I furrowed my eyebrows, confused. I knew my parents wanted me to become Sovereign, but I had no clue what "hung in the balance" besides our status and wealth.

"Don't start with that. You know I can't," my father began, voice exhausted in a way that suggested they'd had this conversation before.

"No, I know you *won't*."

"The point is, we cannot allow Willow to throw away this position. You need to make sure she gets rid of that boy."

I stiffened at my father's words. *Does he know...?*

"She already has, Warren. She told me so today. She promised."

"And you believe her? She's a *child*; she lies."

"Not to me." Guilt bubbled in my stomach at my mother's words, and I swallowed it down anxiously. "Trust me, she's done with him. Besides, you've seen her lately. She's clearly smitten with Au—"

I pulled away from the door suddenly, almost crashing into the wall behind me. I stumbled back to my room, aching to understand the conversation I had just overheard. It might as well have been in code, for all I understood. But one thing was abundantly clear: for the first time in my life, I had successfully lied to my mother.

***

I expected scrutiny in the week that followed. After all, if I knew one thing about my mother, it was that she was persistent.

"Graceful as a dove, but stubborn as an ox." Even the shadow of Vi's words made me laugh, and I shook my head softly at the memory fighting its way into my consciousness—one from a time before the name *Leo* was even mentioned. I shook it away, forcing myself to ignore the sting in my chest. It faded a bit each day, but I doubted it would ever vanish completely. Vi's friendship was the brightest ray of sun in the dreary moments of life, illuminating the parts of myself I liked best—a role that Leo now attempted to fill.

"You're going to have to learn some time," he pointed out one sunny afternoon, crossing his arms against my glare. "Besides, you made me promise, remember?"

I huffed. I had made him agree to help me with Legality, back when this whole thing began, but that didn't mean I wanted to do it *now*. I scowled at the wooden practice sword on the grass, the sun lighting it up in an irritatingly unintimidating way.

"Well," I stated matter-of-factly, "I changed my mind. I don't need your help after all."

Leo just sighed, rolling his eyes in a way that suggested he'd figured I'd say something like that. "Willow, you know the Legality assessment is next. You really think you can get through that without picking up a sword?"

He was right, of course: Legality was all about strength, the ability to protect yourself and your community.

"Now who needs to loosen up?" I mumbled, but Leo didn't rise to the bait. He remained where he stood, brows raised.

"Just pick it up," he insisted. "You'll have to use one in training anyways."

I blew out a breath of air, staring down at the wretched object. I never had gotten over my mental block with swords—not really. But Leo was right: I was out of time. Training would start tomorrow, and I would have to participate if I had any hope of doing well in the assessment. And as my mother loved to keep reminding me, I had to do well. She was all too happy to learn that I would be practicing today with Auden. Somehow, lying to her was growing easier and easier.

"Oh, you've got to be joking!" Oakley called, bounding out of their hut towards where we stood. Anya and Axel trotted beside him. "You *still* haven't picked it up?"

I shot him a glare, half wishing Leo would cuff him on the head again, but Leo just shrugged.

"It's wooden," Oakley pointed out helpfully.

"I don't care." I crossed my arms, stepping back from where the sword lay. "It's not about the sword itself; it's a mental thing. I just can't do it."

"I know how to use a sword," Axel announced proudly. It wasn't exactly helpful.

"How did you get through pre-disciplinary training?" Oakley wondered aloud. I expected the question; after all, showing a basic proficiency in each discipline was expected in order to be assigned a discipline in the first place.

"I used a staff through it all," I replied, wrinkling my nose at the memory. It was a source of embarrassment for me, being the only child in class to use a staff past age six.

"Oh," Axel said, eyes wide. "You used a staff the whole time?" Indeed, staffs were usually only used for ages four and five. For anyone to use it past then was unusual—and embarrassing.

"My friend Sarah hates swords, but they said she had to use them anyways," Anya piped up.

Something in my chest twinged at the question in her eyes. Times like this, I realized how naïve these children really were. They knew too much, had experienced prejudices against Service their entire life—and yet, the subtle interactions of power in Atvas were lost on them. I knew that was due to Leo, protecting them from the harsh realities of the world. It warmed my heart; at that age, I had already understood politics all too well.

"Uh..." I glanced at Leo, unsure of how to broach the subject. How could I explain to them the constant shifting of rules that had accompanied my childhood? How could they possibly hear that and not blame me for their hardships?

"That's 'cause Sarah's annoying," Axel replied, nose wrinkling. I was grateful for the intervention.

"She is not!" Anya glared.

"Is, too! Girls are gross." Axel's voice was serious, as if the grossness of girls was his largest concern in life.

"I'm a girl," Anya huffed in reply.

"Yeah—and you're gross."

Leo just rolled his eyes before turning towards me. "I can train you with a staff, if you really want. Not sure how helpful it'll be in the trial, but it's better than nothing."

I frowned. "You have a staff still?"

"Oh, yeah," Oakley piped up proudly. "We have all sorts of weapons."

My brows flew up, surprise making my eyes widen. Each child was given a standard practice sword as part of year seven pre-disciplinary training, but all other practice weapons were only issued to disciplines of Legality. Even the weak staffs of childhood were returned after the sixth year of pre-disciplinary training. Sure, plenty of people snuck in a few others—but rarely Service, and rarely so many.

"Shut up," Leo snapped at Oakley, far stricter than he usually got with the boy.

"What does he mean, 'all sorts of weapons'?" I pressed. "How did you get a hold of weapons?"

"I'll just go inside," Oakley murmured, looking guilty as he trudged towards the door. He dragged Anya and Axel behind him, still arguing. I watched them go before spinning back to Leo.

"Please don't ask," he murmured, and I froze. I had been planning to interrogate him, to press him until I got answers, but ... he looked so *tired*. Exhausted, really. I realized suddenly it was how he always looked when the kids weren't around, when he wasn't busy putting up a strong front.

"Fine," I sighed. "As long as we forget about this whole Legality thing and go inside."

"Can't do that," Leo replied, and I could see in his eyes he wouldn't be changing his mind. "Not even your parents can get you past this trial, Willow. You need to figure out a way to fight—and fast."

I groaned. I wasn't so sure I enjoyed this serious version of Leo. "Fine. The staff, then." I had little doubt that there would be a full arsenal of Legality weapons at our disposal for this trial, staff included. It was hardly the most popular weapon, but I knew some Legality disciplines specialized in it anyhow.

Leo's grin returned, and I felt a bit lighter. "Stay here."

I frowned as he disappeared into the house, no doubt off to wherever his illegal weapons were stored. The thought made my heart race. Here I was, the daughter of the Sovereign, willingly ignoring an obvious display of illegal activity. I felt as though it should bother me more than it did. Then again, my parents themselves had been bending rules since the day I was born, if not before.

"Here," Leo called, tossing me a staff as he approached. I caught it with a stumble. It was far larger than the one I had trained with as a child, and heavier, too.

"Alright," I replied. "I'm holding it. Now what?"

"What do you remember from training?" he asked, gesturing for me to demonstrate.

I breathed in deeply, swinging into a move I remembered vaguely. It was much harder than I recalled.

"Woah, woah!" Leo exclaimed, and I realized I had nearly missed bashing in his head. I lowered the staff slowly, color tinging my cheeks. "Watch the angle."

I tried again, a weak and pathetic swing that wouldn't have bothered a tree branch.

And so it went, for hours and hours. Leo was patient and kind, correcting me with a smile. At one point, he had me put down the staff altogether, working on my posture and body control. It was advanced knowledge, especially for a discipline of Service.

"Am I allowed to ask how you know all this?" I huffed, sweat dripping down my face despite the coolness of the day. My arms ached from holding them up, weak muscles trembling in protest.

"No," he replied simply. "Let's try with the staff again."

I tried not to look too upset as I bent to pick up the staff, but I couldn't hide the sting of his refusal. All this time we'd spent together, the bond between us ... and he still didn't trust me.

"Willow." His voice was soft, and I tried not to look hurt as he met my eyes. "It's not you, okay? You just... You don't want to know."

"And if I *do* want to know?"

"You don't," he said, hard and unrelenting. It grated on my nerves, that tone—as if I were a child, as naïve as Anya and Axel.

"It's not your decision what I do or do not want to know." My voice was petty, hardened by years of Charisma. I hated the sound, hated that it was being applied to Leo once more.

"Maybe not," Leo replied, "but it's my choice what I tell you."

A beat of silence pierced the air, pulsing furiously with tension. It dissolved, albeit slowly, leaving us standing there in the quiet.

"I'm not made of glass. I can handle it," I sighed finally. It was the same thing I'd told Auden so many days ago, the morning after that awful fight in the rain.

"I have no doubt that you could," he replied, voice calm, "but you shouldn't have to. Not yet."

Not yet ... as if I would have to someday. A chill went through me at the thought.

"Fine," I relented, though I didn't like it. "Let's go again."

It wasn't until hours later that we stopped practicing, finishing just as the sun began to sink into the horizon. I couldn't help but be relieved for the reprieve. Enlightening as it was, our lesson left me sweaty and coated in a fine layer of dirt. I didn't think I'd ever been this filthy before, and I certainly had never been so exhausted. For a weapon so simple, the staff sure knew how to wreak havoc on my muscles ... although that could have been the core exercises Leo had put me through, insisting that I needed more strength to throw with proper form. Why exactly Leo knew proper form, I never discovered.

"I'm never touching a weapon again," I groaned, throwing myself into a chair at the kitchen table. "Actually, forget weapons—I'm never going to so much as *walk* again."

Leo watched me with no small amount of amusement, a small smile on his lips. At least he had the courtesy to not laugh outright. "Too much work for a princess?"

"If I say yes, does that mean I never have to do it again?" I groaned, resting my head between my arms. The rough wood of the table felt cool against my flushed skin, and I couldn't help but wish I could stay there forever. I might have, had I not heard Leo's muttered curse. I raised my head, frowning, to find that Leo had crossed the house, peering into the bedroom.

"What's wrong?"

"It's Oakley. He took off." He sighed, brushing a frustrated hand through his hair.

"He left? To go where?"

"Exactly where he's not supposed to. *Damn it.*" He took a few steadying breaths before turning to face me, eyes apologetic. "You should probably go home. Get some rest before training tomorrow."

It was true, and not just because of the exhaustion in my bones. It was nearly time for dinner, and missing that would bring questions I couldn't answer. Yet I couldn't bring myself to agree, not with the panicked look in his eyes. "I'll go with you."

"Willow, you're exhausted."

"So are you," I pointed out. He was *always* exhausted, even if he'd never admit it. I pushed myself to standing, grasping one of his hands in my own. "Let me help."

He let out a long breath, staring deep into my eyes as if searching them for some unknown answer. "Alright," he said finally. "But you can't tell anyone what you see tonight."

"I won't," I answered without thinking. Only once the words were out of my mouth did I realize that it was a mistake, that I could be agreeing to anything.

For some reason, that didn't scare me as much as it should have.

"Here, put this on," he added, plucking a hat off the coat rack and tugging it over my hair. "Tuck the rest in, too. We don't want you to be recognizable."

"Okay?" I replied uncertainly, complying even as my eyes narrowed.

"Just... trust me." His smile was grim as he clutched my hand, leading me out the door.

I followed a pace behind as we moved through street after street, the buildings growing sparser and more decrepit as we reached the outskirts of Atvas. Here the buildings had never been renovated, left untouched since the war that ruined them in the first place. I was about to ask what Oakley could possibly be doing all the way out here when I heard a murmur of voices echoing across the silent landscape, the distinct sound of a crowd of people. The sound increased with each step we took, growing into a roar of chaos just as we rounded the corner and saw them.

I'd heard about the parties, of course—everyone had. Groups of people would meet up at the ruins and engage in all sorts of prohibited activities, allowing their inner demons to escape in the dark of night. I'd never dared to so much as ask about them, never dared to risk seeming too interested. Not when the last party that was busted had resulted in

Lisa Redding, a well-respected daughter of the Court, losing one and half points off of her P-score. Last I'd heard, she was barely clinging on to the top half of Aesthetics and was at high risk of being cast out this year.

"Woah," I breathed, heart racing as I took in the space. "So *this* is what you meant when you told me those stories about bonfires."

A huge bonfire had been lit in the center, its flickering flame the only light in sight besides the stars above. It kept the space in half-darkness, contributing that much more to the atmosphere of secrecy. The party-goers didn't seem to mind. They laughed and joked and yelled, some with words so slurred I could hardly understand.

"What, not what you pictured?" Leo joked, but his face was guarded, as if worried I would bolt. Honestly, the fear was well founded. Part of me cringed away from the scene, the obedient part of myself that I'd spent all these years crafting. Yet the other half of me, the part that basked in the glow of freedom, of running in the rain and kissing in alleyways...it thrived here in the chaos and noise.

I turned to face him, forcing a reassuring smile onto my face. "Let's go find that brother of yours."

In the end, it didn't take long. Oakley was exactly where you might expect a thirteen year old boy to end up—at the edge of the party, attempting to flirt with girls way older than him and significantly out of his league.

"Hey!" he exclaimed as Leo grasped his arm, dragging him away. "What are you...oh." His grin faded as he registered who, exactly, was holding his arm.

"What did I tell you?" Leo demanded, letting go of him with a soft shove.

"To live a miserable, boring life," Oakley grumbled under his breath. "And to have no fun at all."

Leo didn't rise to the bait, merely crossing his arms. "We talked about this. No parties."

"Like you're one to talk!"

"*Oakley.*"

The boy sighed, defensive stance dropping at last. "I'm sorry, 'kay? I just wanted to have a bit of fun."

"I know," Leo said, voice a bit gentler, "but these things are getting busted more and more these days, and you have a good score. Don't throw that away."

Oakley looked away, clearly still annoyed, but he nodded sullenly anyhow. There was a moment of stiff quiet, the noise of the party floating over us, before Oakley spoke again. "So... does that mean I have to leave?"

Leo laughed, shaking his head in disbelief. "Are you serious right now?"

Oakley just shrugged, completely shameless. Leo rolled his eyes. "One hour. But that's *it*. And no more parties after this."

Oakley didn't reply, just shooting his brother a quick grin that suggested he would not be obeying that rule before darting away. Leo watched him go with a sigh, shaking his head.

"He's just a kid," I offered cautiously. "He could do worse things than sneak out to a party."

"I know," Leo muttered, letting out a short laugh. "I mean, I did worse myself."

It took everything in me not to ask what exactly he was referring to.

"I just..." he shook his head again, clearly still frustrated. "I wish he were a little older. A little more mature."

"He'll learn in time."

"He may not have the luxury of time." He looked at me then, and I almost flinched back at the sadness in his eyes. No, not quite sadness—emptiness.

"What makes you say that?" I asked slowly, heart pounding.

"He'll need to take care of them," he continued, looking away as if he hadn't even heard me. "I hate it, because he's still so young, but..."

"Leo."

"...it's not even a choice, really, and..."

"*Leo.*" I moved into his line of vision, grasping his face in two hands. "Would you *please* shut up?"

His jaw snapped closed, eyes growing wide in surprise.

"Oakley isn't going to take care of them," I asserted, not allowing even a shadow of doubt onto my face, "because you're going to be here to do it."

He didn't respond, but the way his gaze shifted to the floor was answer enough. He didn't believe it for one second, and that was the problem.

"But if for some reason you're not..." I hated saying it, hated even *thinking* it. "If you're cast out, then your siblings will be just fine. I'll take care of them, okay?"

His eyes flicked back up. "You promise?"

"I promise."

"Thank you," Leo said quietly. "For that, and for tonight."

I glanced at the sky, an expanse of inky darkness above us. Already I was dreading the interrogation sure to come when I returned home.

"I can walk you back," he said, as if reading my mind. "We'll come up with an excuse."

It was certainly a smart thing to do. I was exhausted, still grungy from our lesson, and had to be up early for training. And, of course, I shouldn't be there in the first place. Every second I spent there was another person who could see me and begin a deadly rumor. But... well, maybe I'd been seen already. The hat could only cover so much. Most likely, my mother would ground me the second I returned home. What if I never had another chance to experience something like this?

I hummed in agreement, meeting his eyes with a small grin. "In an hour?"

Shock spread across his face like a puddle in the rain, building into a wide-eyed stare. "Are you sure? But your score..."

I rolled my eyes, grasping his hand to pull him towards the center. "Really, Leo, you must learn to be less uptight."

He grinned, wild amusement glinting in his fire-lit eyes, and followed me into the fray.

13

The New World

It only took a few minutes to realize that I was entirely out of my depths. It was nothing like a ball, polite small talk replaced by sarcastic jokes and playful laughter. Not to mention the people—there were so many of them, and yet I knew so few. I'd never realized just how many peers remained under my realm of knowledge, always present yet crouching just out of sight.

"Leo, my man!" A loud voice called from behind us, loud and wild. A grinning face appeared a moment later, a boy with carmel skin accompanied by wild brown hair who seemed vaguely familiar. "I was wondering when you'd show up."

Leo just crossed his arms, glaring at the newcomer. "You're lucky I'm too tired to punch you right now. What were you thinking, bringing Oakley here?"

The newcomers' face twitched slightly, but the cocky grin remained firmly in place. "Who said I brought him?"

"Who else would?" Leo pressed. "He's only thirteen, Abner."

"So? We were younger," Abner shrugged, though he had the decency to look guilty. "Let the kid live a little."

Leo just shook his head, looking away.

"He'll be fine," Abner said, voice gentler as he clapped a hand on Leo's shoulder. He looked past him as he did so, eyes widening as he took me in. "What is *she* doing here?"

"This is Willow." He introduced me, albeit a bit nervously.

"I know who she is."

"She's a friend," Leo murmured. I did my best to ignore the twinge in my chest as he lowered his eyes, kicking at the ground uncomfortably.

Abner shook his head in disbelief. "Dude, you're an idiot for bringing her here. She'll get us caught by dawn."

"*She* can hear you," I cut in at last, awfully sick of being ignored, "and believe me when I say I have *no* interest in telling anyone about this."

"Right," Abner replied, voice full of disdain. "Because then you'd have to admit to speaking to the likes of us. What could *possibly* be more shameful?"

"Abner." It was a warning, Leo's voice low and unamused. The two boy's eyes met, a wordless exchange between two people who knew each other very well. However Leo knew Abner, they had clearly been friends for a long time.

Abner looked away first, rolling his eyes. "Whatever. Bex can watch her."

I raised my brows. *Watch me?* I opened my mouth in retort, but it was too late. Abner had already turned, calling for this mysterious 'Bex.'

"I'm sorry," Leo said under his breath, soft enough that only I can hear. "My friends, they can be a lot."

If Abner was any indication, that was an understatement. Yet Leo had come to the ball with me, had let Ruben Bonavich mock him with hardly a word in retort. The least I could do was at least try to be supportive. "It's fine."

I began to second guess that statement as a young woman came towards us, tall yet slim with dark hair that fell just below her chin. Everyone at the party was dressed casually, but none quite as much as her. She wore plain black trousers and a black tank top that showcased her exceptionally pale shoulders, as if she was trying her best not to look put together. If that was the intention, it didn't work—everything about her exuded a bright sort of confidence, from her smooth walk to casual grin. She looked close to our age, but the pin she wore that caught my eye, placed on the pocket of her trousers as if to hide it. I would know that pin anywhere—the pin of the Court, marking someone as a successful participant of the Pathway.

"Sorry I'm late," she called with a grin.

"But you've still got the goods?" Abner pressed, brows raised eagerly.

The woman just rolled her eyes, pulling a small flask from her pocket and tossing it to him. "Go crazy."

Abner whooped in appreciation, taking a hearty swig of its contents. I had the distinct feeling that it wasn't water. He grasped Leo's arm and began to pull him away, going on about the people they needed to see and talk to. I stepped after them, panicked at the thought of being left alone, but Leo just mouthed a pained "sorry" before turning to follow his friend.

"They tend to do that," the woman said from behind me, and I almost jumped. I hadn't heard her move closer. "Practically attached at the hip, those two."

I whirled to face her, hoping I looked less frazzled than I felt. It was a difficult feat, considering how viciously my heart beat in my chest.

"The name's Bex," she continued, sticking out a hand.

"I'm Willow," I said, taking the hand gratefully. "Willow Aldridge."

"Oh, I know. All of Atvas has been talking about you lately."

I winced at the reminder. Sometimes it was easy to forget just how many people were watching me, waiting for me to slip up. "Don't remind me."

She laughed, a friendly sound. "I know how that feels. I was a bit of a conversation piece during my own Pathway."

"Really?"

"Unfortunately," she sighed. "But that was three years back now. Who cares anymore?"

None of it made any sense. She was on the Court, and it was a perfectly fine evening. She should be anywhere but here, surrounded by rule-breaking teenagers.

"What?" Bex asked, brows raised. "Go on, ask it. I don't bite."

"It's just..." I bit my lip, trying my best not to sound offensive. "What are you doing here?"

Luckily, she didn't seem offended by the inquiry. If anything she'd expected it, face unchanging as she considered the question. She looked me over, brown eyes seeming to look right into my soul. "I could ask you the same thing."

Fair enough. It wasn't a question, but I knew she was fishing for an answer all the same. I just didn't have one to give.

"I'm here," she said finally, filling the silence so I didn't have to, "because despite what everyone thinks, the Court life is difficult. It is harsh and unforgiving, and more often than not it feels like a cage." Her gaze remained on me, steady and surprisingly serious. "I suspect you're here for a similar reason."

I nodded along with her words, hating myself as I did so. It felt like a betrayal, speaking of the Court like this when I would soon rule it. It was hard to imagine that, though; here, I felt like a different person entirely. Someone not bothered by a little fun and mischief, someone who could criticize Atvas and get away with it. Of course, that didn't mean it was the truth—genuine as she seemed, I didn't know Bex well enough to trust her alliances. Not right now, with the Pathway underway.

"I came to help Leo find his brother," is all I dared say "That's all."

She hummed in reply, a sound that indicated she didn't believe me but didn't want to push it. "Nice of you."

"I tutor him," I blurted out, if only to distract from any other ideas she may be forming. No one could know about our relationship, not if we wanted to stay safe from rumors. "That's why I was with him."

"I know," Bex replied simply. "I'm his Sponsor, so he keeps me updated on his trainings."

My eyes widened. It made sense—honestly, I'd been wondering how he'd found a Sponsor—but it was a surprise nonetheless. To sponsor someone was to vouch for them, to put your reputation on the line. And given Leo's lack of preparation...it was a risk. "You trust him enough to sponsor him?"

"I'd trust Leo with my life," she answered sharply, the first sign of anger I'd seen the whole conversation. It was gone as fast as it came, dissipating into the fiery haze around us. "He's family, if not in blood then in every way that counts."

I frowned. How close *were* Leo and his friends, and why had he never told me about any of them? I might've asked for more details if it wasn't for the flash of dark hair across the ruins, a glimpse of a familiar face. Vi—that was *Vi* walking towards us, her eyes alight with happiness and mouth open in a grin.

Well, at least until she saw me. Then she stopped where she stood, ten feet away. Her face morphed first into shock, followed by anger and finally a blank grimace.

"Hi," I breathed, moving towards her slowly. "It's really good to see you."

"What are you doing here?" was all she said in reply, arms crossed tightly over her chest.

I opened my mouth, only to close it as I realized I had no acceptable answer to give. Nothing that wouldn't give away Leo and I, nothing that wouldn't ignite her anger all over again. "I..."

Leo chose that moment to find me again, bursting out of a nearby crowd of people. He saw me first, breaking into a guilty smile. "Sorry about that."

"Of course," Vi scoffed, eyes like pure fire as she glanced between us. "I should have known."

Leo finally pieced together the situation, taking in the bizarre scene. "Oh. Hey, Vi."

She ignored him, merely shaking her head before whirling around.

"Wait, Vi!" I cried out, but it was no use. She was already striding away, the conversation officially cut off. I watched her go, heart wrenching as if a piece of it had been sewed back on only to be ripped off once more.

Leo looked over my shoulder to Bex, the two exchanging a meaningful glance. Bex just shook her head, seeming annoyed.

"I'll talk to her," was all she said before disappearing into the crowd, weaving between bodies like water in a stream.

I turned to Leo, huffing a confused sigh. I didn't even know Bex knew Vi. "Is *everyone* at this party friends?"

He merely laughed, wrapping an arm around my shoulder to guide me away. "Guess we'd better get going. I'll explain on the way to the Palace."

So he did, telling me all about his friend group on the walk home. I'd met most of them tonight, he said, except for a woman named Cera who was a bit older than Bex and apparently would never be caught dead at a party. He'd known Abner most his life, just as I'd expected. The two of them had later met Bex and Cera, who had also been friends for a long time. Vi had joined their group only a few years ago, as a friend of Bex's. It was something else I didn't know about Vi, yet another sign that I didn't know her as well as I thought I did.

"It's sort of been us five since then," Leo finished. "They're a lot sometimes, but they're like family."

It was the same thing that Bex had said. Interesting.

"What are you thinking?" he asked, voice low as we neared the Palace gates. We stopped just outside them, hidden behind a large tree.

"I'm thinking that there's a whole half of Atvas that I haven't seen and know nothing about," I answered truthfully. "I'm thinking that that's a shame."

Leo shrugged. "Sometimes, it's better to not know."

"No." I grasped his hands, looking deep into his eyes. I needed him to understand how serious I was about this. "I want to see that world, Leo. I *need* to see it."

He looked at me then, a serious glance that told me he was contemplating something. At last he nodded, taking both of my hands into his. He slowly lifted one of them to his lips, brushing a soft kiss over my skin. "Okay, then. I'll show you my world."

***

Leo's world, apparently, included being heinously sore—a fact that was all too clear as I crawled out of bed the following morning. I hadn't noticed it much the night before, too filled with adrenaline from the party and nerves about sneaking in unnoticed to care. But now, between the training and the party, my body was aching from head to toe. I nearly groaned aloud with each movement, which was hardly a good sign for the day of Legality training ahead.

"What's wrong with you?" Auden asked, brow furrowed as we walked to the Cathe. I had wondered whether he would show up to walk with me at all after our awkward dinner, but sure enough, he was waiting. Just like always. He seemed a bit happier, too. Dark circles still marked his eyes, but there was a certain sureness to him that had been absent at that wretched dinner.

"Nothing," I said, nearly groaning again as I flexed a sore muscle. "I'm just … sore." His brow furrowed. "I was running yesterday," I amended quickly. "To prepare." I couldn't bring myself to tell him about what I had done all the past day. Not only was he my direct competition, but it would lead to questions I couldn't answer. Especially considering that, at least as far as he knew, Leo and I weren't in contact at all.

As we approached the Cathe, it grew increasingly clear that these trainings would be quite different. People milled around on the grass outside, but the true treasure lay behind the Cathe, where the majority of participants had gathered. There were no chairs set up. Instead, there were large stuffed sacks that I assumed were to be used as dummies, as well as targets painted onto large bales of faded hay. Racks of wooden practice swords were scattered throughout, but my attention was drawn to the far side of the space, where a row of specialized weapons sat. I spotted a single staff at once, near the bottom, and grinned.

"Oh no," Auden said beside me, and my face fell. "Willow, I'm sorry."

"What is it?" I glanced around worriedly. What had happened to put such a pitying look on Auden's face?

"I know you were hoping it would be something else," he continued, nodding towards the swords. "I mean, I know you still … struggle with that."

"Oh—" I started, blushing slightly, but a voice interrupted me.

"Participants!" a booming voice called, issuing from a middle-aged man with bulging muscles near the center of the group. I recognized him instantly as Kane Borkin, Director of Legality. "Gather around."

Auden and I moved towards him as instructed, hands shadowing our eyes from the brutal morning sun. It was an oddly warm day for spring, the sun bearing down on my carefully braided hair.

"You are here to learn about Legality," he instructed, staring us all down in a rather intimidating way. "You are not here to gossip, or play, or complain about your sore muscles."

I could practically feel Auden grinning beside me, and I elbowed him lightly in the side before turning my attention back to Borkin.

"You all know what's at stake, so use your time wisely. Grab any weapon you would like; I don't care. I will circle around to instruct you, but in the meantime, spar with your companions, or use one of our provided tools." He turned then, heading suddenly towards some unknown location without any sort of dismissal.

"Well, that was abrupt," I noted, watching the man as he strode away.

"Typical Borkin," Auden replied, nodding for me to follow as he made his way to claim a sack dummy. "Quite rude—even for a Legality," he elaborated, and I glanced worriedly at the staff before following him deeper into the crowd. "Fantastic at his job, though," he finished, drawing a wooden sword from the rack and holding it out to me, hilt first.

"Actually," I stated awkwardly, "I think I'm going to try a different weapon instead."

Auden frowned, confusion overtaking his face. "But ... those are for disciplines of Legality," he argued.

"None of us have a discipline anymore," I reminded him. "And Director Borkin did say any weapon."

That didn't seem to be good enough for Auden, who frowned even deeper as he gazed at the row of weapons on the faraway rack. "You don't know how to use them," he pressed, something like concern filling his eyes.

"I don't know how to use this, either," I retorted, eyes sliding to the sword he still held in his hand.

"Yes, but *I* do." His voice was impatient, as if speaking to a child. "I can teach you."

And there it was: that sweet but insufferable need to defend me from all harm.

"Auden," I said softly, "I can protect myself, remember?"

He gazed at me for several moments, scanning my face before letting out a breath. "Alright," he relented. "Stay in sight, will you? And be safe."

I huffed out a laugh. "Auden, they're wooden."

He raised a brow, looking towards the wooden sword I had yet to touch.

"Point taken," I admitted. "But fine, I promise to be super safe. Ten feet from you."

He smiled, clearly relieved, and I shook my head softly before leaving him to his sword. Something was still off with him, that was for sure. He was clingier than usual, still a bit shaken up for some unknown reason.

I arrived at the weapons rack at last, finding the staff in no time. I went over what Leo had taught me the day before, though I eventually grew bored. And so, I tried other weapons—daggers and slingshots and even a small axe. By the end of the day, my mood was bad and my muscles were even sorer. My temperament was helped only by occasional glances over at Leo, who watched from afar with pride in his eyes.

When Director Borkin blew the whistle at last, announcing that training was finished for the day, I practically sagged in relief. I jogged over to Auden, who somehow had managed to evade the sweat that coated my body.

"How did it go?" There was a certain brightness to his tone, and I could tell the exertion had done him some good as well. Color flooded his cheeks for the first time in weeks, and his grin was teasing as he took me in. "What, did it rain over there or something?"

"That's just unfair!" I wheezed, hitting his arm lightly as I neared. "I was throwing things. Much harder than swinging wood."

He laughed, watching amusedly as I gasped for breath. "Seems like that jog affected you more than you care to admit." His voice was light, joking, but I knew a real question lay behind it. He handed me a clean rag from a nearby table, eyebrows raised and awaiting my response.

"Maybe it did." I snatched the rag from his outstretched hand, wiping my forehead immediately. He was right, of course: Leo and I had spent all day working, but he couldn't know that. *No one can know.* "Besides, what does it matter? At least *I* went on a jog."

His eyebrow quirked upwards at the taunt, and I turned my back to him.

"So, that's what Leo and you did all day? Jogged?"

I whipped around at the question, eyes wide as I scanned our surroundings carefully. No one was near to us, or at least, not near enough to be a liability.

How could he know? I racked my brain, searching for the moment I had given myself away, but came up blank. I was so sure he couldn't possibly know; I was so careful, so persistent. A blush worked into my face as I contemplated my response. *Should I confirm it, or deny it? What if it's just a guess, and I give myself away? Does he know about the party?*

"Oh, don't do your panic face." Auden's voice jerked me from my thoughts, and I searched his face. He seemed calm, if a little hurt. "Willow, I don't care that you're still seeing Leo. In fact, I'm not even surprised. I just don't understand why you thought you couldn't trust *me*." He met my gaze, eyes pleading. "I'm your best friend; you can tell me anything."

I contemplated that for a moment. I'd never thought of Auden as my best friend, although I supposed he was. In my mind, that had always been Vi. Auden was just, well... He was just *Auden*.

"I'm sorry." My voice was quiet, and shame swam through my heart as I gazed at the deep blue of his eyes. "I just knew you didn't like him, and after what you said about love at the assessment... I just figured you wouldn't understand."

"You're right, I don't like him. But I like you, and you obviously care for him." he stated, giving me a small smile. "Honestly, Willow, it's not my choice—it's yours. I respect that, even if that choice *is* a scruffy Service boy"

I rolled my eyes at the subtle diss. Clearly, there would be no reconciliation for those two, but if Auden accepted the relationship, that was enough for me. Besides, he didn't seem to know about the party—that, at least, was still a secret.

"Well, since we're being honest," I smiled at him sheepishly, "I may have told my mother I was with you yesterday. Until late. So if anyone asks..."

"Really? I'm your cover up now?"

"You know how she is!" I defended myself, throwing up my hands in frustration. He did, after all, know my mother quite well. We'd spent most of our youth at the Palace, and my mother was not an uninvolved woman. "Please?" I asked, eyes wide and begging.

"No need for that look." He gestured to the path back to our homes, and we moved towards it together. "You know I've always got your back."

"Auden?"

He turned towards me, a grin still upon his face. "Yeah?"

"How did you know? About Leo and me."

"Please, Willow. I've known you my whole life." He shook his head, laughing lightly. "You really think I don't know when you're hiding something?"

I smiled, his words resonating in a deeper part of me, a part that yearned to be seen—the part that everyone else failed to acknowledge. "Thank you."

He didn't ask me what for. He just pulled me into a hug, warm and gentle and comfortable. I took in the feeling, bottling it up in the back of my mind for a rainy day. It was a reminder that no matter how complex the future might be, some things were constant—*Auden* was constant—and because of that, everything would be alright.

***

"You look ridiculous."

I glanced up at the voice, finding Oakley glaring into the cluttered bathroom space. The thirteen-year-old gazed past me, stare resting irritably on the makeup smeared across Eden's small face. I had to agree with him; with bright splotches of blush donning her cheeks and a mess of color upon her eyelids, she certainly looked ridiculous. Not that I would ever say it aloud—not when she was just opening up. I had finally managed to get a soft giggle to escape her bashfulness, only moments before Oakley appeared. She had looked terrified when Leo first mentioned the idea to her, staring wide-eyed at the vanity bag I held. Even I had questioned it when Leo asked during training, a part of me dreading the loss of sleep I would surely suffer the next day. Yet I *had* asked him to let me into his world, and this was a big part of it—caring for his siblings. Given that they had no mother figure to rely on, someone had to teach her the basics of makeup.

"Hey, she's just learning," I shot back, shooting him a warning glare. "Be nice."

"That *was* being nice," he grumbled under his breath, shaking his head before retreating from the room. I sighed as he left, watching as he plopped onto the couch. He was a responsible boy, and kindhearted, too, but the sass of an early teenager shone through more often than not.

"I look ugly." Eden's voice was tight, and her emerald eyes watered as she examined her reflection. Despite my careful instruction, wisps of blond hair escaped the loose braid, framing the mess that was her face.

I cringed inwardly, but kept my face calm as I knelt beside her. "No, you don't," I said softly, brushing a teardrop from her soft skin, "and I don't want to ever hear you say that again, okay? All this stuff—makeup, hair—it's just for them, for the Council. You're gorgeous with or without it; never forget that."

She sniffled, face full of doubt. "B-but ... I want them to like me." She turned back to her reflection, yanking the hair tie from her braid. "I wanna be like *you*." The tears fell faster, and something like nausea churned in my gut. I'd always wanted to be a role model, to be looked up to. Was this really what I wanted—to make little girls stare at their reflection and cry? I stared at myself in the mirror, at the practiced makeup coating my face. When was the last time I had gone without it?

"Don't be like me," I whispered, and I meant it. "And don't worry about the evaluation. They'll love you."

"R-really?"

I forced a smile as she met my eyes, sniffling lightly. "How could they not?"

She smiled then, a watery smile that ignited joy within my heart. Suddenly, she launched herself at me, grabbing me around the middle tightly. I wrapped my arms around her lightly, blinking rapidly to diffuse the wetness gathering in my eyes. Leo watched from where he sat, perched upon the ledge of the bathtub. He was smiling, but doubt danced his eyes, and he nodded towards the bedroom. I nodded, squeezing Eden one final time before releasing her hold. "Now, why don't you clean this all up, yeah?"

She nodded, and I edged into the hallway carefully before following Leo to the bedroom.

"Is it true?" he questioned immediately, voice hushed as he shut the door behind us. "Does it truly not matter?"

I flung myself down on the nearest bed, rubbing my temples against the oncoming headache. "No," I said quietly, avoiding his eyes. "Unless she figures out the hair and makeup before her assessment, it's unlikely she'll get any result besides Service."

A child was permitted anywhere from one to three choices, depending on their natural skills and parental history. They could choose either of their parents' disciplines, or they could choose the discipline in which they display the strongest talent, as identified by the Council. As for me, with parents in Charisma and Aesthetics and a natural strength in Intellect, I had been given the choice of those three options. Well, more accurately, my parents were given the choice; I was eight years old at the time.

Choosing disciplines was a risky business, indeed—a balancing game. The object was to place the child in a discipline in which they would do well, but still have sufficient opportunity. Aim too low, and the child would be limited in opportunity for the entirety of their lives. Aim too ambitiously, and the child might not score high enough to qualify for emergence into society. Often, the natural inclination of the child was ignored entirely.

With both parents being Service, Eden's only chance at another discipline would come from the Council's determination of her natural placement. If she couldn't manage to pull off the put-together appearance of Charisma or the flowery attitude of Aesthetics, that gave her little chance at anything besides Service. She simply was not built for Legality, and, well... She was clever in the same way as Leo, but not smart in the way Intellect would require. I didn't say this to Leo, though; there was no need. It had worked out just about the same for him.

Frustration rolled off of him in waves, and I knew without looking that he was upset. Recently, I always seemed to sense what he was feeling, as if our very souls were connected in some way. "Service could be alright," I tried, although my words were halfhearted. "She could soar to the top easily, settle into a nice life—like Oakley." Despite his sass and humor, Oakley truly was an amazing Service, and his score reflected it.

"No, she can't," Leo bit out, voice pained. "Not her. She's different; you know that."

And I did know. Eden's soul was bright, innocent in a way that so few Atvasian children were. She was a dreamer, wrapped up in a system that would trap her in a nightmare. Being forced into the life of a Service, a field so completely wrong for her ... it would stifle her, crush that beautiful spirit into a poison. I saw that future in Leo, another dreamer tied to the ground.

"You shouldn't have done that," Leo continued, voice tense but soft. "She needs to hear the truth. You *know* that. It's why I asked you to help; you know better than anyone how the game is played."

"I *know*." It came out in a harsh snap, and I took a deep breath to calm myself. The ceiling swam before my eyes, and I realized with sudden embarrassment that my eyes were tearing up once again. "But she needed to hear what I told her, too. I know *that* better than anyone." I didn't mention how much I had needed to hear that when I first doubted myself—or that I had only been five at the time.

I heard the creaking of the bed as Leo lowered himself beside me, but I didn't move my gaze from the ceiling. I felt a hand on my cheek, and a warmth filled me. I turned towards him at last, surprised to see sadness splayed across his features. It was a weird sort of sadness, not as deep as when he spoke of his mother; no, this was a rumbling, crawling sort of sadness, the type that you can feel in your bones. A shiver ran down my spine as he grasped my hand.

"I hate that you grew up like that," he said finally, "and I hate that I never saw it. I always assumed you and the other Court children were doted on, frolicking in paradise while the rest of us rolled in the mud. But the things they told you, the things you were forced to believe..." His voice faded off, and he shook his head. "It's abhorrent."

I shifted uncomfortably. "Oh, I don't know. It wasn't so bad. Most of the time I just ran around and played with Auden."

"Right." His frown deepened. "You and Auden have been friends a long time, then?"

"Practically since birth." A smile grew on my face as I recalled the days of our youth, the memories bathed eternally in a golden glow. "He was always there, supporting me in every way. He was... he was my rock. He still is, in a lot of ways."

Leo's resulting snort suggested he highly doubted that fact.

"Oh, stop it," I chided, rolling my eyes. "He is. He's even okay with us still seeing each other; he told me today."

"You *told* him?"

"No! He just guessed." I shrugged. "Like I said, we know each other well. But he won't tell anyone, he promised."

"And you believe him?" The bed shifted as he jolted upright, eyes narrowed. "You do know he's your biggest competition, right?"

I didn't deign to respond to that, merely shooting him a deadpan look that conveyed my feelings quite well. Leo, stubborn as he was, glared right back. We stayed like that for several moments, frozen in a battle of wills. It reminded me distinctly of our first session, when everything began. The memory was enough to soften my rough edges, enough to make me look away first.

"I don't trust him," Leo asserted, as if that wasn't obvious.

"Have you even *met* him?"

"I don't need to. He's a pompous jerk, walking around like he owns the place."

"The same way I used to?" I quirked a brow.

"It's different," he insisted. "It's the way he looks at people like me, like we're dirt on the bottom of his shoe. He never would have agreed to tutor me, not in a million years."

Now that I couldn't argue with.

"You know," I replied finally, letting out a deep breath, "when we were nine years old, Auden came to me one day with the widest grin on his face. He wouldn't shut up about something his maid brought him to, some sort of clinic where they helped sick children who couldn't afford proper care. It was all he talked about for weeks, and each time he was more excited than the last. On the last day, he told me determinedly that he was going to fix everything. I didn't know what he meant; to this day, I still don't. All I can remember is his face, bright and smiling and so damn proud." I paused for a moment, the image still swimming in my memories. "I think it's the happiest I've ever seen him."

Leo was quiet for a moment, and then: "And?"

"And, nothing." I shrugged. "He never talked about the clinic again, and anytime I brought it up he insisted that it was a dumb idea in the first place. I never figured out why; perhaps the pressure of the Pathway got to him. Perhaps he figured such behavior would never lead to the Sovereignty."

"The Sovereignty?" His brows scrunched together. "You were nine."

I almost laughed aloud at the surprise in his tone. For a pessimist, Leo could be strangely optimistic. Pressure waits for no one. It is the monster under the bed when you're nine and it is the face in the mirror when you're eighteen. It comes in the dark of night and it *takes* and *takes* and *takes* until fear is all you know. Perhaps, in a better world things could be different; but not here. Leo, of all people, should know that.

"All my life," he continued, voice low, "I've been angry. At my father, at myself, at the whole damn system. Hell, for a long time, I was even angry at you. I was angry at you before I even met you, just because you existed." His voice was distant, speaking as if in a trance. "I've been so *livid,* so blinded by rage, that I forgot what I was even mad about."

I furrowed my brow, turning to face him completely. "What do you mean?"

"Don't you see?" His voice was tired, and he stared wearily at the ceiling above. "We're all so *screwed up* by this system. I thought it was just people like me—people who searched ceaselessly for their next meal, people who were doomed from the start. But I was wrong. It's me, and you, and all of my friends, and all of *your* friends, and everyone in this damned place."

My stomach clenched instinctually at the criticism, and I opened my mouth. "Leo... we've talked about this. There's no point in ruminating about hating Atvas, not when there's nothing we can do about it."

"Nothing we can do?" he shot back, gray eyes seeming to stare into my soul. "Is that what you really believe?"

I averted my gaze, resting it instead upon the light that filtered through the window, coming to rest upon the shabby but clean floor. I wondered vaguely how Leo managed to keep it so clean with so many children running around.

"I mean, come *on* Willow," he pressed, voice growing passionate. "Don't you ever even *think* about it? The things you would change?"

"Why should I?" I asked, although what I really wanted to ask was, *"Why me?"* Why was everyone so insistent that I, of all people, think deeper?

"Because you have the power to make a change," Leo replied quietly, watching me carefully. "And you have a heart strong enough to persuade you to."

That same heart leapt in my chest at the words, even as my brain raced at the meaning behind them.

"You're going to be the Sovereign, Willow. Things don't have to be like this, not once you're in charge."

Honestly, I'd never thought about it that way. Sovereign meant following the years of tradition before me, meant enforcing the rules of Atvas and maintaining status quo. The Court of Atvas was highly resistant to change, and tradition kept us grounded. At least, that's what my father always said. I'd never thought about the power I would actually have, the ability to make changes.

"Then they won't be," I answered simply, as if the words didn't make my chest tighten in anxiety. I knew I'd been distracted lately, paying far too little attention to training. I made a mental note to try harder, to remember that there was more than my parent's expectations on the line.

"I sure hope so," Leo stated darkly, "for all our sakes."

14

— • —

UPSIDE DOWN

I t was late when I returned home for the day, well past dinner, and yet no one awaited me in the entryway. I frowned as I examined the empty halls, perplexed. It was unusual for my parents to be away on a Saturday night without prior arrangements, and even more unusual for them to allow me to miss dinner without questioning. Especially when I'd already missed dinner only days before.

"Mother? Father?" I called cautiously, straining my ears for movement, but silence answered. I shrugged, heading towards my room. Just then, I heard a sound at last: a soft sigh, followed by light footsteps. I frowned; surely I was hearing things, exhausted by the day. *I should just go to my room, sleep it off.* Even as I decided it, my feet already moved towards the noise, driven by that annoying curiosity of mine. I passed the doors quickly—kitchen, dining room, my father's office—but as I rounded another corner, I bumped into someone. They swore as we tumbled to the ground, and an obscure hand reached out to me. I followed the sight, my eyes roaming up the familiar tan arm.

"*Vi?*"

Vi looked different than the last time I had seen her; face sharper, eyes darker. I gaped up at her, and she smiled tightly.

"Well, are you going to take it or not?"

I tilted my head, utterly perplexed, and she gestured to her open hand. I took it cautiously, and she pulled me up with surprising strength.

"What are you doing here? And where are my parents?" The words came out flustered and uncertain. It had been so long since we'd spoken and, well, she was in my house.

"Are they not here?" she asked, a perplexed expression gracing her features as I shook my head. "I just assumed they were in bed already," she said.

"Why are you here?" I asked again, eyes narrowing at her diversions.

"I-I wanted to apologize." She blushed, seemingly flustered. "I haven't been fair to you."

"No, it's my fault," I insisted, relief flooding my chest. "I promised you, and I should've stopped it sooner. I'm sorry."

She was shaking my head before I was even finished. "No matter—what's done is done." I opened my mouth to respond, but she spoke before I had a chance. "I want to be friends again."

My chest lightened at the words, a month's worth of pain melting in just moments. "I want that, too," I whispered, a smile working its way onto my face. "It's all I've wanted for weeks."

She grinned as well, and as the smile lit up her face, she looked just as I remembered.

"Now," she said, pulling me towards my room, "tell me everything."

I opened my mouth, and the words began to flow once again. We talked for hours, learning every detail we'd missed in the past weeks. I glazed over the parts with Leo—no need to rub salt in the wound—but told her of Oakley's sass, my struggles with training, and even my fight with my mother. The conversation streamed from topic to topic effortlessly, natural in a way Leo's and mine could never be. Even Auden couldn't draw the words out of me like Vi; no one could. I was just telling her of my time with Eden and the changes I hoped to one day make when she cut me off, a strange look in her eyes.

"You've changed," she said quietly, but it didn't sound like an insult. No, it was *pride* that I saw glistening in her eyes, tangled up with something sadder—something like regret.

"Thanks?" I replied, unsure. "So have you." I meant it. Gone was the Vi of our youth, the crazy rebel who sought chaos with every passing moment. She still had the mysterious sort of glint in her eye, but it was different now—more focused, as if the energy inside her had finally found direction. As if she was at peace.

"Promise me something," she said finally, dark eyes seeming to stare directly into my soul. "Promise me you'll become Sovereign."

I frowned. She'd made her desire for me to win no secret these past months, but I'd always chalked it up to concern for me being cast out.

"Why?" I breathed out, scanning her face carefully.

She seemed on the border of panic now, grasping my hand tightly in hers. "I always knew you would make a good Sovereign, given the time," she began, present yet somehow distant at the same time. "You're ready; I see that now. You *have* to become Sovereign." The words were insistent, her hold on my hand increasingly painful. Her eyes snapped back to mine, as if she were trying to drill the message into my soul. "Promise me, please. It has to be you."

"Alright, I promise," I relented. "Just ... let go of my hand."

Vi started, dropping my hand as if it were a hot iron. I shook it out, the blood flooding back into it painfully.

"Sorry," she murmured, eyes wide as if coming out of a trance. "I guess I got a little passionate there."

"Yeah," I groaned, glancing at my hand. "A bit."

She laughed, a melodic sound that put warmth in the air. "Speaking of passionate..." She grinned mischievously, eyes glimmering. "Do you remember that food fight in Year Eleven?"

I snorted. "You mean the one *you* started?" I replied, and she laughed.

"Hey, it wasn't my fault that..." I watched as she launched into a retelling of the event, noting the wariness on her face. Despite the lightness of the story and the giggles she regularly emitted, there was no doubt that something was weighing on her—something big, if the bags under her eyes were any indication. I didn't think about it too hard; there would be plenty of time for that later, now that we were friends again. For the moment, I was content just to laugh with her again. For a moment, we were eight and ten and thirteen, mere children giggling in the dark of night.

I could have talked all night, but Vi insisted we sleep eventually, claiming she didn't want to be responsible for screwing up my training tomorrow. I didn't argue too much, though; my eyelids had grown heavy hours ago, and I *did* have training in the morning. I drifted off to sleep happily, comforted by Vi's steady presence beside me.

***

I awoke violently, jerked into reality by the sound of heavy feet outside my room. I wiped the sleep from my eyes just as the door was thrown open, wincing as a beam of light was cast into the room. Two silhouettes stood in the frame: my mother and father.

"What is it?" I yawned, voice still sleepy as they rushed into the room.

"Who was here?" my father demanded, tight and loud.

I sat up straighter as the sleep left my body, the urgency on their faces finally registering in my dazed brain. I glanced over at where Vi lay—but where her body once was, there was only a faint dent in the covers. *When did she leave?*

"No one," I said, watching confusedly as my mother strode out to examine the balcony. "I mean, just Vi, but she—"

"Violetta DeLoughery?" my father barked, surprise on his face.

My eyes slid to my mother, whose face was crestfallen.

"Yes," I responded, grabbing my robe before following my father from my room. "But she was just here to see me. We'd had a fight—"

My father was out the front door before I could complete the sentence, and I turned to my mother, mystified. She stared at me for a moment, sadder than I could recall seeing her, and put a hand on my shoulder.

"Your father and I were sent a note regarding urgent business at the Cathe. When we arrived, it became clear there was no business. It was a diversion, meant to distract us so that a thief could gain access to our home."

The pieces clicked in my head as she spoke, and I began to shake. "No." I sputtered, shaking my head. "No, it can't—"

I stopped abruptly. I never *had* found out what Vi was really doing here, and I did find her right outside my father's study.

"I'm sorry," my mother stated softly, "but Violetta DeLoughery is not who you thought her to be."

I didn't sleep for the remainder of the night; no one in the Palace did. Council officials rushed in and out in preparation for Vi's arrest. In natural form, I eavesdropped shamelessly, peeking my head around corners and pressing my ear to doors. I heard nothing of value, though—at least, not until I came upon my father and Ruben in an empty hallway, speaking in hushed tones.

"What should we do when we find her?" Ruben asked, voice grave.

"Take her home," my father sighed, exhaustion clear on his face. "We'll have to dock her score, of course. Two points should do it."

There was a long pause, and I could tell from the shifting of Ruben's body that he disagreed.

"Need I remind you that this isn't the first attempt to break into the Palace? They're getting closer, Warren."

I had no clue who "they" were, but a memory flashed through my mind, from the day of the Sponsor's Ball. Auden had told me something about a break-in at the Palace, a failed attempt that the guards had managed to catch. Was this related?

"Two points is what we took off the last perpetrator's score," my father retorted, but Ruben shook his head.

"That will keep her in the top half of Aesthetics," Ruben pointed out, voice tight. "We need to send a message they can't ignore."

"She's been friends with Willow for years," my father said, face distressed. "She's not what you think."

My heart twisted. I hadn't thought my father noticed my friendships at all, much less how long they lasted.

"Don't be weak," Ruben hissed, and my brows raised in surprise at the harsh tone. He was an aggressive man, but he knew how to play the game, and usually it was all cold smiles and veiled insults for my father. In fact, some may even say they were friends. "Friendships mean nothing when it comes to this; you know that. This is bigger than all that."

My father looked as though he were going to throw up, and I couldn't help but pity him for the pressure on his shoulders. *The pressure that will be on my shoulders, soon enough.*

"What would you recommend?" My father murmured at last, and I nearly groaned aloud at the satisfaction Ruben seemed to exude.

"She must be cast out."

I froze at the words, terror coursing through my veins. Sure, I knew she would get in trouble; in fact, she *should* get in trouble. But this was Vi. She was always getting in trouble, and she always ended up just fine. Besides, she was one of the top-ranked disciplines of Aesthetics, and the daughter of two Court members as well. Surely they couldn't just throw her into the Beyond. My father wouldn't do that. I watched him carefully, noting the dismay on his face with a sense of certainty.

See, I thought hopefully, *he's stronger than that. He'll never allow it.*

"Yes," my father said at last, and a tiny corner of my heart seemed to harden. "I don't like it, but you're right. It will be done." And then they were gone, moving carelessly down the hall as if they hadn't just ripped the ground out from under me.

The orders were given within the hour. For the attempted theft from the Palace, Vi would be held in the prison until the next Sovereign was crowned, and then she would be cast into the Beyond, along with the unlucky half of our year. The thought of her locked up in a room made my skin crawl. I was unbelievably mad and inexplicably confused, but I still couldn't stand the idea of her bright spirit trapped in such a grim, dreary place as the prison. I had never seen it, of course—there were no pictures, not when camera technology had been lost in the war—but my mother had told me of it, and it was no place for a light like Vi. By some small mercy, my father allowed me to stay away from the frenzy of paperwork and plans, permitting me to mope in my room. It wasn't much better, the space I normally loved tormenting me in a cage of memories. I stared at the wall all night, and by dawn, I was aching to escape.

By the time the sun crested the horizon, I was out of the manor and well on my way to Leo's. Honestly, I wasn't even sure why—it was only six o'clock in the morning, far too early to warrant a visit. Yet my feet moved there anyways, driven by a mysterious pull in my chest. *Leo. Leo. Leo.* The chant ran in a loop through my panic-addled brain, the tension in my chest easing slightly with each step I took towards him. Leo was safety, was peace and laughter and love. Leo was the only person I could stand to see, to even think about speaking to.

I knocked on the door frantically, barreling in as it was pulled open.

"Willow! What—"

"We should go on a picnic again," I said breathlessly. "We should go to the glade, and bring food, and—"

"What?"

"I mean, it'd be nice, right?" I continued, breaths coming in shallow puffs of air. "It's just, who even knows how much time we have left together. We should make the most of it, just in case... in case..."

"Shh, it's okay." Leo pulled me into a hug, cradling my shaking form carefully. He still looked unbearably confused, but didn't comment on the random visit. "Why don't we talk inside?"

He pulled me into the small bathroom, the most private room in the house.

"Please," I continued, though I wasn't sure why it was so important all of a sudden. All I knew was that I needed to get away from it all—away from Vi and my parents and Ruben. That I needed an escape, and Leo always gave me that.

"Alright," Leo began, backing towards the opposite wall as if retreating from a crazed animal. "Let's just talk for a second."

"What?" I asked breathlessly, frustrated. I didn't want to *talk,* or think, or anything that required remembering Vi.

Leo stared at me as if I were insane, clearly confused. Not that I could really blame him. "What's... What are you doing?"

"I was *trying* to plan a nice day," I huffed. I took in his appearance. He looked tired, hair ruffled still from the sleep he had most likely just awoken from. I sighed. "Look, I just don't want to think about it right now, okay?"

"Think about what?"

I bit my lip, sighing. Talking it was, then. I moved to sit on the rim of the bathtub, pushing my hair away from my red eyes.

"It's Vi. She's been arrested. She's going to be cast out."

I expected him to be upset, shocked, worried—but I did not expect the pure panic that appeared on his face. "Vi got caught?" he breathed, eyes wide and face pale. "How?"

I frowned at the question. "Well, I saw her, and then my parents asked who had been in the house, so I said–"

"You told them you saw her?" His voice was stricken as he spoke, almost accusing, and I nodded cautiously. He began to pace the small bathroom rapidly, wringing his hands. "This is bad," he muttered, "this is *very* bad."

He stopped suddenly, a sharp shadow overtaking him as he did. "Willow..." He spoke slowly, as if afraid to hear the answer. "Why are they casting her out for this? Shouldn't it be simpler—two points off?"

"I don't really know," I admitted, frowning at the question. "I guess somebody else already tried to break in a few weeks ago. They said something about sending a message."

Leo grew very, very quiet, but I could sense that his mind was anything but. He seemed almost frozen in time, face stuck in an expression of absolute horror.

"This is my fault," he whispered eventually. "It's all my fault."

And it all came together then, pieces finding their match at last: Leo's lowered score, so last minute that the Pathway was the only way to redeem himself; the blame he so clearly felt now. *Two points.*

"It was you," I whispered, the words seeming to sizzle in the tense air. "You were the one who broke into the Palace weeks ago."

I felt almost numb, the confusion and distress of the past twelve hours taking their toll. I knew I should be furious at the revelation, should feel utterly betrayed, but ... I couldn't. Not with the way Leo looked right now, so torn up and guilty and utterly remorseful. Besides, I was still reeling from Vi's betrayal; I doubted I could handle another. So, I took Leo's shaking hand in mine, hardly believing the two words that made their way from my mouth. "It's alright."

He glanced up at me with wary eyes, a child expecting to be chastised. "It's not, and I'm so sorry."

I knew, deep in my bones, that he was. No actor, not even the best of the Aesthetics, could fake the sense of authentic guilt that radiated from him at that moment.

"Maybe she'll like it," I tried, a far-fetched attempt at reassurance that clearly missed the mark. I watched as his face grew more pained with my words, once again cursing my inability to comfort. "She's never been a fan of our society, after all. Maybe she'll enjoy the freedom of the Beyond."

"No, she won't." His voice was dark, and he paused his pacing suddenly. "Willow, listen to me carefully," he stated. "I need you to trust me, okay?"

I furrowed my brows. It was an odd thing to say, considering the revelation I'd just had, but I nodded nonetheless. After all, it was Leo; how could I not?

"I'm going to tell you something—something you won't want to believe. But you have to."

A cold feeling came over me, and I had a sudden sense that something bad was approaching. Chills worked their way down my arms, and I took a deep breath as he held my cheek carefully.

"The Beyond isn't the Americas," Leo said slowly, "and you can't get there on a boat."

I shook my head, confused. "I don't understand. You mean they're sent to a different continent?"

Leo looked me in the eyes with a searing gaze, and something seemed to scorch my gut.

"Willow, those who are cast out aren't sent anywhere," Leo said softly, gaze pitying. "The Flawed are killed. And this year, Vi will die with them."

I laughed.

"You're joking," I realized, the weight lifting off my chest with the realization. "Wow, you really had me going, too." I appreciated that about Leo—his ability to take my mind off of anything with his humor. I wasn't sure what it was—perhaps the lack of sleep, or the stress of the assessments, or maybe the emotions of the day, but this joke was getting me more than ever. I was practically delirious, laughter pouring out in wheezing gasps.

Leo didn't give up the gig as easily, made clear by the somber expression painting his face. "Willow, I'm serious," he said, and the laughter dried up.

"No," I choked out, breath speeding up at Leo's continually solemn expression. I gasped for air that didn't seem to exist, lungs burning and burning and burning and—

I heard a door open behind me, causing my hyperventilation to double as Oakley peeked into the bathroom.

"What's wrong with her?" he grunted at Leo, clearly unhappy about being woken up so early in the morning.

Leo just shook his head, watching me grimly. An uneasy feeling began to seep into my bones, brain racing loops around an empty track; there were too many thoughts and no thoughts, all at once.

"I think she's in shock," Leo murmured, and my hands began to shake as I began to shake my head.

No, no, no. Not in shock. There was nothing to be shocked about. *No, no, no.*

"Willow?" Leo asked, approaching me cautiously. "Did you hear what I said? This is real, princess. I need you to realize that."

The nickname jolted something, a lever pulled within me.

"Oh," Oakley stated, voice startlingly serious. "You told her."

And then, it hit me. This was no game, no practical joke, no attempt to make me feel better.

No, no, no...

"You're delusional." The realization hit me suddenly, my breath slowing even as my heart sunk. "You're insane." I backed towards the doorway slowly. Was it only yesterday that I'd sat in this room with Eden, enveloped in her warm embrace?

"I should have told you earlier, I know. I just thought you would panic," Leo started.

"An absurd thought, really," Oakley added under his breath, cringing as Leo shot him a sharp glance. "Right—not the time, sorry."

"Get away from me, both of you!" I snapped as Leo advanced towards me, and he flinched back as if I had hit him. "You're lying!"

He must be lying, because if he's not...

"You know I'm not lying," he said, voice serious and hard, "You *know* it, Willow. You just don't want to admit it."

"I'm leaving," I stated, voice as low and dangerous as I could manage.

He just looked at me sadly, shaking his head slightly. "You'll change your mind," he responded softly. "Meet me after the assessment—ten o' clock, at the edge of the forest."

I shook my head vigorously, backing fully out the door and onto the path beyond, the voices from within seeming to haunt me as they floated out the open doorway.

"I think she took it well," Oakley said.

A faint cuffing sound followed, then a muffled, *"Ow!"*

I forced the faint smile from my face. I couldn't think like that about them—not anymore. They were delusional, the whole lot of them, probably brainwashed by whoever had told Leo that insane rumor in the first place. A part of me pitied them for it.

I sprinted all the way back home, not slowing until I reached the front gates of the Palace. I caught my reflection in a window as I passed and gave a humorless laugh. I looked rabid, deranged—sweaty, pale, and shaking, with tufts of hair sticking out of my once perfect braid. I pushed through the front door rapidly, running straight into my mother. She scanned me distastefully, taking in the smell radiating off my body with a scrunched nose.

"Where have you been?" she demanded, crossing her arms. "Why have you been missing dinners? And why aren't you at training?"

"I've been with Leo," I said candidly, because I couldn't find the energy to lie.

A sick part of me reveled in the betrayal that flashed across my mother's face, and I pushed past her towards my room.

"Are you joking?" she snapped, finally losing that irritating composure. "You can't see him!"

"Watch me!" My voice was a yell now, echoing sharply in the entryway. It was a ridiculous argument, especially considering the last thing I wanted to do was see Leo anyhow, but I couldn't stop myself.

"You don't understand," Mother pressed. "He... Willow, he tried to break into the Palace several weeks ago."

"I know," I spat out bitterly, "but I'm so glad you decided to tell me."

And there it was, the true source of my anger—because she had known the entire time. She'd known, and yet she never said a word to me about it, instead spouting lame excuses for me to stay away. Even now, she wielded the truth like a weapon, sharing it only to coerce me into acting as she wished.

My mother just gaped, staring at me for several moments as though I were a stranger.

"I couldn't tell you," she said finally, glancing away. "It would get you too involved."

All of a sudden, it was all too much—Vi, Leo, my mother, and her persistent ability to never answer a direct question. I needed to be alone. Immediately.

"Fine," I snapped, turning on my heel and stomping towards my room. "And by the way, I'm not going to training."

I didn't add that I couldn't bear it, couldn't stand the pitying glances the others would afford for the best friend who'd gotten played—not to mention that Leo would be there. No, what I needed was a nice long nap to get me back on my feet.

"You promised!" my mother called, her voice surprisingly unsteady. "You *promised* me you were done with that boy."

I froze in place, not daring to turn and see the hurt I knew I would find on her face.

"If you wanted me to keep my promises," I said, voice low, "you shouldn't have raised me as a Charisma."

And then I was gone, the cold words settling like a weight on my shoulders.

15

— · —

FACE THE MUSIC

The following few days passed in a blur, a haze of sleep interrupted only by the thoughts racing relentlessly through my mind. Risa brought me meals regularly, but it didn't matter. I had no appetite, shoveling the undoubtedly delectable food into my mouth for sustenance alone. I didn't go to training, a fact that surely would haunt me in the assessment scores, but I couldn't bring myself to care. I didn't want to see Leo. Besides, everyone assumed I was recovering from my best friend's heart-wrenching betrayal. I couldn't help but wish that were all I was recovering from; in all honesty, Vi's actions haunted me the least. It was the uncertainty that plagued me, the overpowering sense that I knew nothing at all.

I was torn between two worlds, two stories with only one truth. Once I had time to process it, I had to admit Leo made some fair points. I knew next to nothing about the Beyond, and we never did hear anything more from someone who had been cast out. But on the other hand ... this was *murder* he was suggesting. How could that go unnoticed? And more importantly, how could so many people I trusted possibly be alright with it? As much as my parents irked me, I knew in my soul that there was good in them, had seen it with my own eyes. To think that the same mother who had tucked me in as a child, who told me stories of lands far away, could be complicit in the murder of dozens of people a year... It simply wasn't possible. My head ached from the constant battle, the struggle of a puzzle I never wanted to solve. It felt as though as I were trapped in another assessment, except this one never ended, and there was no true winner.

It made the thought of my Legality assessment even more tiring, yet I managed to drag myself out of bed anyhow. It was hard to care about being Sovereign right now, but it would be harder to deal with the consequences of missing the trial. And so, I dressed in the standard blacks, forced another meal down my throat, and hauled myself out to meet Auden.

"What's wrong?" he demanded instantly, scanning me with a worried glance. I wasn't surprised; to anyone else I would look normal, if a bit tired, but not to Auden. He knew me well enough to sense the deep weariness within me, even if it wasn't visible.

"You don't need to worry about me seeing Leo anymore. We're done," I replied easily. I had tossed and turned for quite a bit, contemplating what exactly to tell Auden. As much as I needed to talk to someone about this, I knew it wasn't the time. I didn't want Auden going into the assessment shaken, and besides, I didn't want to get Leo in trouble—especially since I wasn't entirely sure what to believe. Besides, it was sort of true; we hadn't exactly left things on a positive note.

"I'm sorry," Auden responded, although he didn't look especially sorry.

"I don't want to talk about it."

The remainder of the walk was silent, just as I'd hoped. With very little energy and a long day ahead, I needed to save it for what mattered. The cool morning air grounded me, reminding me just how important this assessment was.

With Auden and I coming into the trial tied, I had to make sure I scored close to his score or above it. If either of us scored low enough… Well, then the last round would be quite pointless, for there wouldn't be enough points to make up for a low score today. I couldn't help but think about just how important this assessment was for Leo as well. He was currently ranked tenth, but the eighth- through twelfth-ranked scores were all within a point of each other. That meant Leo could leave the assessment today securely in eighth place going into the final assessment next week, or he could leave without a chance for Court at all.

I'd fully expected the assessment to be outside, but upon arriving, it became clear that was not the case. We were ushered into another ballroom, this one without a stage. There were no swords in sight, to my relief. In fact, there were no weapons at all. Instead, the room was set up in long rows of tables with chairs. A wooden divider separated each chair, creating a private desk space for each participant. Behind these rows was the normal arrangement of chairs for the audience, most of which were already full. Beside me, Auden's brow furrowed as he took it all in.

"Are we sure this is the right room?" he muttered, eyeing the desks with confusion. I was inclined to agree. I had never been to a Legality assessment before, but even I knew they usually involved more than desks and chairs.

"Pretty sure." I nodded towards two desks in the front, labeled with our names. I vaguely noted the order; our scores may have been even, but my desk was still first. "I guess I don't need to swing a sword after all."

"Guess not." Auden scrunched up his nose at the wooden dividers as we took our seats, leaning back to see me. "What, are we taking a test?"

I shrugged. For all my worry about missing training the past few days, it seemed that would hardly matter at all.

It quickly became clear that Auden and I weren't the only ones surprised by the unusual layout. In fact, almost everybody who entered seemed perplexed. The energy in the room grew increasingly jittery, the uncertainty tainting the usual excitement of assessments.

"Welcome all!" Mullerson began, and I groaned inwardly. I couldn't wait for this competition to be over, if only so I could stop hearing these ridiculous speeches. "I hope you're all prepared for an intense spectacle, because today we will watch these young participants battle it out in … the assessment of Legality!"

I glanced at the rows of desks, raising a brow as I met Auden's gaze. *Intense spectacle?* He seemed to be thinking the same thing, a twinkle of amusement glinting in his eyes.

"The discipline of Legality is complex," Mullerson continued, and I forced my attention back to the front. "It is the craft of swordsmanship, of defense and attack. But more important is knowing when to use this—and how. That is, the ability to make decisions and follow orders. Our Legality assessment is going to be a little different this year, for a Sovereign must understand the latter aspect of Legality as much as the former. A basket is currently being brought around the room. Please select two slips of paper, but do not open them."

There were several moments of quiet rustling as we did so, the papers seeming to weigh a thousand pounds as I lifted it out of the basket and into my palm. My mind raced. What exactly could we be doing with two slips of paper? And more importantly, what was written on them? The temptation to open them was overwhelming.

"Good!" Mullerson exclaimed, far too happy for a person holding our fates in his hands. "Now that you have your slips, we can begin. You will each be given a paper and pencil—a test, of sorts." Auden peered around the divider, shooting me a *"See?!"* look. "Once you receive your paper, you may read your slips and begin. You will have five minutes to complete this."

I nearly jumped as a sheet of paper was set in front of me, no further instruction given. I frowned. This was it—a test? It seemed so easy, and yet I had to admit it threw me off guard. I focused on the paper quickly, determined to maintain some semblance of focus. There was a list of questions, "what if" scenarios with a blank space beneath them. I opened the slips next, my shaky hands making it take far longer than it should have. I finally managed the first one, frowning at the writing upon it.

Auden Bonavich

I bit my lip, repressing the urge to glance at Auden. I turned to the second slip instead, opening it with increasingly unsteady hands.

Leo Hayes

I almost laughed. *Really?* Of all the papers in the basket, *this* is what I had gotten? It was a cruel trick of fate—one I certainly did not appreciate. I inhaled deeply, exhaling shakily. *Focus, Willow.* I wasn't sure when the words had become such a necessity, a mantra that I found myself repeating more often than not—probably around the same time that my ability to focus began to melt like wax under a flame. I forced my attention back to the paper in front of me, letting out another slow breath. *Start at the beginning,* I reminded myself. *Instructions first.*

SIMON SAYS

SIMON SAYS read these instructions carefully. SIMON SAYS do not follow any instructions that do not begin with the words "SIMON SAYS." SIMON SAYS complete all others. Skip number five, even though it says SIMON SAYS. SIMON SAYS use the names received from the basket to complete all items.

I nearly sighed in relief; it made sense at last. It was a test, that much was sure, but not on swordplay as I had thought. No, this was a simple test in following directions. I filled out the "SIMON SAYS" scenarios quickly, each answer coming to me easily. Some were rather obvious, questions like, "You come across a dagger and a sword. Who do you give the dagger to (Leo, because apparently he had all sorts of weapons), and who do you give the sword to?" (Auden, because swordplay is what he's best trained in) I was suddenly glad to have picked names of those I knew so well. It was an exercise in observation—hence the trainings. As Director Borkin had said many times this week, knowing your opponent was half the battle. With other names, my time would have been awful; but as it was, I finished with a minute to spare. Except for number five, of course. Left with nothing to do but wait, I decided to read over number five anyhow, curiosity overtaking me.

5. SIMON SAYS choose one to lose 2 points on this assessment.

I frowned. What an awful scenario! It didn't even have to do with Legality. Perhaps it was just boredom from the extra time, but I couldn't help wondering why they would include this at all. I glanced at the clock: forty-five seconds remaining. *It did say not to do number five, right?* I chewed my lip, suddenly unsure. I re-read the instructions once, twice, three times—and then I caught it, the trap that I had foolishly fallen for. Before the line about number five, there was no "SIMON SAYS." My heart pounded, and I checked the clock once more: twenty seconds to answer this question.

Twenty seconds to betray a friend.

It was an impossible decision. On the one hand, Leo and I weren't speaking. He had tried to break into my home, *and* lied about it for months. Not to mention the murder accusations. Auden was the one to pick me up each time Leo broke my heart, the one who supported me unconditionally. The one whom I'd let down too many times already.

But on the other hand... Well, Leo was one place away from being cast out of society. And Auden was my direct competition.

My palms were sweaty as I picked up my pencil, poised over the line with nothing to write. It occurred to me then that I had a third option as well: leave it blank. Save them both, but doom myself. The ticking of the clock echoed in my mind like a time bomb, ready to implode at a moment's notice. I decided just as the time ran out, flipping my paper over in tandem with Mullerson's shout of "Time!"

The room seemed to let out a collective sigh at the words, the relieved sound of those who assumed the worst was over. It was clear who had read the instructions and who had not, both from the facing of the paper in front of each participant and the look upon their face. It took only moments for the papers to disappear, whisked off to wherever they would go next. Somewhere secret, I hoped.

"Wonderful!" Mullerson exclaimed. "Now that the fun part is over, it's time to evaluate our choices." *The fun part?* I thought bitterly, rubbing my temples to rid myself of the ache. "The discipline of Legality requires adherence to all orders and the ability to make difficult decisions—a task which *some* of you completed." His emphasis was not missed by the participants fidgeting nervously around me. I was suddenly very glad I had decided to re-read the instructions after all. "However," he continued, "making decisions is only the beginning, for disciplines of Legality have an even more difficult assessment: accepting responsibility."

My heart sunk in my chest, suddenly heavy. *He can't mean...*

"Oh, yes," Mullerson said, voice unusually serious. "Now, you will read your answers aloud."

My whole life, I'd always been first—first to walk, first to talk, first-ranked in the top discipline of Atvas. Rarely had there been a time when I resented that fact—until now. Now, I wished to be anything but first.

"Miss Aldridge, if you would," Councilman Mullerson repeated, hand still extended towards me. I glared at the wretched paper lying innocently in his hand, painfully present despite my wishes for it to be far, far away. I could feel the eyes of the audience as I raised myself out of my seat, each step towards the front of the room heavier than the last. I reached towards the paper slowly, as if my arm were moving through a heavy tide. The paper felt weighted down as I held it, loaded as it was with treachery.

"Good," Mullerson said, eyes seeming to urge me on as if he knew how uncomfortable I felt. He probably did; *everyone* probably did, with the way I was acting. "Now, if you could read me number five."

I gulped, saliva like glue in my throat. "Simon says choose one to lose two points on this assessment." The words grated against the sandpaper of my throat, coming out in one scratchy rush.

"And which names did you receive?" Mullerson asked, a seemingly innocent question that tore at my heart.

"Auden Bonavich," I said carefully, "and Leo Hayes."

"And did you answer this question, as the instructions directed?"

For a moment, I considered saying no, taking the fall myself. But it wouldn't have mattered anyway; Mullerson had already seen the paper, even if no one else had.

"Yes." The word was a whisper, drifting cautiously into being. I met Auden's eyes, which were achingly hopeful with a hint of apprehension. I wished that hint were larger, wished he were more prepared for the blow to come.

"And who did you choose?" Mullerson prompted, voice suggesting that I was taking far too long.

"Auden," I attempted, but it came out as an awkward squeak. I cleared my throat, cheeks burning. "Auden Bonavich," I repeated, voice far stronger than I felt. "I chose Auden Bonavich."

A wave of déjà vu rushed over me as the crowd began to murmur, the situation far too similar to the last assessment. Same pitying look from Mullerson, same surprise on Leo's face, same uncertain reaction from the crowd. *Same betrayed look on Auden's face.*

"Go now," Mullerson murmured, voice sounding strangely muffled to me, as though he spoke through a thick wooden door. I couldn't help but feel as though I were back in the Palace, a child eavesdropping on some discussion or other. "Go in peace, with the knowledge that your decision has been revealed."

Yeah, I thought indignantly. *Peace is definitely what this little game brought me.*

I let the bitterness propel my feet, carrying me to my chair. I was suddenly quite glad for the dividers between us, separating Auden's despair from my own guilt. I barely heard his own responses, listening only enough to know my name wasn't involved. It wasn't until later, when Auden was seated beside me once more, that I jolted to attention.

"Willow Aldridge," Amaris was reading from the front of the room, "and Emmaline Vanouten."

I sagged in relief, suddenly quite thankful that I had reconnected with Amaris. Besides, she'd always hated Emmaline as much as I had. It was something we had in common, even as children.

"... who did you choose?" Mullerson was asking as I zoned back in, only partially listening.

"Willow Aldridge." I froze. "I chose Willow Aldridge."

It was pain of a different sort—the sort I had seen on Auden's face only moments ago. *Betrayal.* A laugh sounded from the row behind me, and

I turned to glare at the perpetrator. It was Emmaline, of course—smug, irritating Emmaline. I met Amaris's eyes as she headed back to her own seat, but she didn't seem to realize the blow she had dealt. She just shrugged, a casual gesture that didn't seem to fit the tightness in my chest. "Sorry," she said, that same small smile upon her face. "It's nothing personal."

It never was with her. It wasn't personal when we were ten and she'd ignored me in the courtyard, out of shame or annoyance or something I'd never understand. It wasn't personal when we were twelve years old and she'd ended our friendship, leaving with a dry face as I sobbed into my pillow. And it wasn't personal now, six years later yet no wiser than we'd been then. Amaris, just like always, did the logical thing; I, just like always, failed to see it coming. It was like we were doomed to repeat this cycle, her apathy and my persistence eternally at war.

"Get yourself together," Auden whispered, and I cringed at the harshness sharpening his tone. Not that I could blame him; I'd betrayed him publicly twice now, and *he* wasn't losing his mind. Besides, he was right: I was a mess, and everyone could tell. Perhaps it was the realization of Amaris's true motives, or the guilt about betraying Auden, or the lack of sleep. Perhaps it was the sinking feeling in my gut that whispered a secret I didn't want to know. Whatever the reason, my normal tactics were failing entirely, that unspeakable emotion drowning me slowly. It was all I could do to keep the tears from spilling. I didn't hear a single other answer, didn't hear if Leo had answered at all. I didn't even hear Mullerson's high-pitched voice, no doubt congratulating us on a job well done.

Good job, I thought bitterly. *You successfully betrayed your peers.*

The thought struck a chord within me, deep in my bones. I couldn't explain how, but I knew then: that had been the real test. Not whether we *could* follow instructions, but whether we *would*—especially when it involved the harming others. The realization settled like acid in my stomach, bubbling uncomfortably against my insides. For the first time, I truly understood what Vi had been telling me all these years. It was a game—all of it. A terrible game that we had grown far too comfortable playing, any care for others buried under an overwhelming desire to succeed.

Auden didn't speak to me after the assessment. In fact, he barely even looked at me. I couldn't help but be grateful. In my current state, I wasn't sure I could handle his disappointment and anger as well. I wondered miserably if we were still friends at all, or if I had neglected him one too many times. It was a disheartening thought, cemented as I walked home alone. The silence seemed to taunt me, reminding me that I had managed to lose every friend I'd ever had. Amaris—gone, if she was ever there at all. Auden—gone, if his farewell was any indication. Vi—gone, soon to be shipped off to who knows where.

Leo knows where, a voice in my head whispered. *He knows, and you do, too.*

"Well done." My mother's voice sounded from the space in front of me, and I glanced up at the Palace entry hall that surrounded us. Lost in my thoughts, I had hardly noticed the walk home. "I wasn't sure you could do it," she continued, and I noticed then that she was actually *smiling.*

"You're ... glad? Even though I betrayed Auden?" The words were shaky, unsure as they left my mouth. I had expected my mother to be angry, disappointed that I had chosen Leo once again. The sudden flip threw me off center, and I felt nauseous once more.

"You didn't *betray* anyone," she replied, tucking a strand of hair behind my ear before continuing. "You just made the smart move for yourself. He would've done the same, trust me."

I almost forgot that choosing to dock Auden's points *was* the smarter move for me. A weight seemed to alleviate in my chest, lifting suddenly as I realized Auden *would* do the same. It was hardly my fault I had chosen those names, after all. Besides, my decision had allowed Leo to do well on the assessment, pushing him up to ninth place. Despite everything, I couldn't help but be relieved at the news.

"Wait," I said, the word bursting out of my mouth without a thought. "What did you mean, you weren't sure I could do it?"

"Don't be so offended," Mother warned, sighing delicately. "I just... wasn't sure you could handle that sort of competitive edge. You have too much heart, you know that. You always have." Her eyes seemed to reveal a deeper meaning, and I suddenly wondered if my mother was talking about the assessment at all.

"I can handle more than you know."

"Yes," she murmured. "You did prove that today." She stared at me contemplatively, eyes scanning me carefully.

Tell me, I urged her silently. *Tell me whatever you're thinking about.*

"Not yet," she murmured to herself. I almost screamed in frustration as she turned to walk away.

"Stop!" The word was a command, perhaps the most regal I had ever sounded. I crossed my arms, staring my mother down. "Tell me," I said, aloud this time. "Tell me it's not true. Tell me that we don't murder *dozens* of people a year."

The blood seemed to drain from her face. "I don't know what you're talking about."

The thing was, I knew it was a lie. I knew it the same way I knew the frustration on her face was covering up something far worse: fear. Perhaps it always had been, from the day her stories stopped and the training began. That damned acidic bubbling began to simmer once more, nausea overtaking me, because *I knew*.

"It's true?" The words were a whisper, seeming to stop all motion as they floated into the air. "We're really ... murderers?" I was shaking by then, trembling with the knowledge.

"No." My mother's voice was a sharp knife, pointed with pain as she reached for me. "Not you. You've done *nothing* wrong."

I slapped away her hand, denying the attempt at comfort. "Don't touch me!"

Her mouth gaped, opening and closing as if she couldn't find the words to say. "How did you find out?" she asked finally, and I almost felt like laughing at the question. I had just found out that my parents had been murdering innocent people for my entire life, and *that's* what she chose to ask?

"How could I not?" It was the question that was burning in my mind, pushing against a wall of pain and shock. "Did you think I wouldn't find out when I was the *Sovereign?* Were you planning to hide this forever?"

"Of course not!" Her eyes shone with unshed tears, her face crumpling under the onslaught of my words. I'd never seen her so upset, so utterly distraught. "You would have to find out, one day—but you weren't *ready.*"

"How could anyone ever be ready for that?!" I asked incredulously, although I really wanted to ask how *she* had ever been ready for that. Despite all evidence to the contrary, I felt deep down that my mother was not an evil person.

"You don't understand," she tried, "I never wanted this. *Any* of this."

I opened my mouth to speak, to scream that it wasn't enough, but she held up a hand. For some reason, I found myself obeying.

"Just ... let me explain," she pleaded. "Let me explain, and then you can talk. I promise."

I pursed my lips, nodding tightly.

"We didn't start this," she began. "It was already in place. It has been ever since the very first Sovereign. There was never a real solution to our population crisis, never a real Beyond."

"But that was decades ago!" I exclaimed, unable to stop the words from escaping my mouth.

"Yes," my mother answered solemnly. Her face was grey as stone at the admittance, at the utter amount of people who must have died since then. I knew the feeling—my own body had begun to tremor, from exhaustion or shock or some mix of the two.

"Like you, I knew nothing of this. Not until after my own Pathway. If I had known..." Her voice trailed off, and she shook her head tightly. "It doesn't matter. The point is, I had little power by the time I learned of it. I was horrified, as you are now. And your father... He's not a bad man, Willow." I raised a brow, and she sighed. "He's not. He hates it too, but he's afraid. There is no real solution, and our society cannot sustain a full population. Men like your father aren't built for fear."

"You could have done something," I insisted. "Anything."

"I did do something!" my mother snapped, the first sign of anger she'd shown this whole conversation. "I *have* been doing something, since the day you were born. I knew I had no power over your father's decisions, knew it would be unwise to attempt to exert any. Coup d'états are not taken kindly, and I couldn't risk an execution; after all, I would do little good dead. I looked for other solutions, looked places I never thought I would, but there was nothing of use. And yet, I knew there was always a way to find power; you just have to know where to look. So, I raised you. I raised you to be perfect, ensured that you had every tool to succeed, to become Sovereign." She smiled at me, eyes holding rare tears. "Don't you see, Willow? You have to become Sovereign, have to stop the murders—it's the only way."

"No." The word rushed out on a wave of red-hot rage. Suddenly, I didn't care about the tears in my mother's eyes, or the clear pain in her voice. Suddenly, I was *angry*. "You're a coward," I spat, drawing only satisfaction from the hurt that flashed across my mother's face. "You blame father for being afraid, but you're just as much to blame."

"Don't you dare!" she exclaimed, voice unsteady. "Don't you dare blame me for something you don't understand!"

"You're right," I retorted. "I *don't* understand. How many people?" I demanded, seeing red. "How many died because you were too afraid for your own safety?"

Mother was crying now, ugly tears that didn't suit the poised archetype she had always presented. "Not just for my own safety," she cried, almost pleading. "For your safety, too."

"Don't," I hissed. "Don't pretend that you care for my safety. Don't you see? All you've done is pass your burden on to me!" I was yelling by this point, tears streaming down my face, because it just wasn't *fair*. All those years, a lifetime of anxiety and pressure placed on me, and for what? My mother's fear of upsetting the societal order? "You raised me, alright; you raised me like a lamb for slaughter."

"It will all be alright," Mother tried, attempting comfort once more. "One more assessment, and then you can stop it."

"No," I argued, "I can't. Not until after my coronation—not until after my best friend is cast out!"

My mother shook her head, face taking on an irritated expression, as if the fact was insignificant. To her, it probably was. After all, what was one more year of murder after so many?

"She betrayed you!" Mother retorted, an edge of anger in her tone. "I know it's hard to comprehend, but sometimes friends can't be trusted."

My head shook side to side slowly, bitterness oozing from my tone as I replied, "She's not the one who can't be trusted."

Vi, who had always been there, who was a ray of light in my life. *Vi, whom I turned in.* I choked on my tears, gagging at the realization. If Vi died, it would be my fault.

I killed my best friend.

The thought echoed in my head as I backed away and ran, sprinting out of that wretched place where my world fell apart.

16

—·—

In the Dark of Night

Surely, I was drowning. Surely, that was the reason for the air that ran from my lungs, leaping, bounding, springing as if it knew of the poison that lived in my soul—this poisonous guilt that spread through me, paralyzing my every muscle and leaving me gasping for air. Surely, drowning was the reason my world collapsed into waves around me, drifting memories sinking further and further away from my consciousness as the moments passed.

Of course, my life could never be so simple. There was no water surrounding me, not even a spray of rain on which I could blame my misery. It was not rushing water that pushed me to the brink of unconsciousness but rather my own gasping breaths, ripping the air from my lungs with a burning sharpness.

Dozens of people are murdered each year. By my parents. My parents are murderers. Vi is going to die next. I'm a murderer.

I murdered Vi.

I barely saw the front gates in front of me as I stumbled past, staggering through them and onto the vast crumbled road. I only got a few yards before collapsing against a nearby tree, mind still running even as my body twitched in exhaustion.

It's true. Mother confirmed it, and it's true. Leo was telling the truth.

I gasped at the realization, heart beating impossibly faster. He'd been telling the truth, which meant that he knew. He knew and he never told me, not even when he was mere places away from death himself. Even now, he told me to save Vi—not himself. Never himself, not for selfless Leo.

Leo could die.

The thought erased any composure I might have had, my breaths growing shorter and faster than before as a sob tore out of my throat. It was all I could think as I fought for air, the awful words running a loop through my panicked mind.

Vi will never play a prank on someone again. She'll never bail me out of a boring meeting, will never meet my children and I will never meet hers. They'll never exist in the first place. And Leo... Leo will never see Eden be assigned a discipline. He'll never watch Oakley grow out of his teenage phase. He'll never kiss me again, will never smile at me or hold my hand or kiss my head or—

The mental cacophony continued as the sun bore down upon my tired body, a rare warmth in the bitterness of early spring that taunted me. I felt raw, exposed, as if my soul was bared for all passing by to see.

"Willow?" A large form kneeled in front of me, grasping my shoulders. "Are you alright?"

I glanced up to see Auden, brows furrowed in concern. Blue eyes studied me carefully, taking in my disheveled appearance and tear-streaked face. His kindness only made me sob more.

"Auden," I breathed, the word a warning and a prayer at the same time. He couldn't be here, couldn't find out what I knew. It would ruin him, ruin him like it ruined me. Yet I wanted to tell him. More than anything, I wanted to tell him. Maybe it was wrong, a selfish desire. But...

maybe he *should* know. Hadn't I just been thinking how awful it was that my mother hadn't told me, that Leo had kept it from me for so long?

"What's going on?"

"I can't tell you," I breathed, carefully avoiding his eyes. I knew my resolution would break if I looked into them, if I saw the calmness surely lingering there.

He frowned, grasping my face gently in his hands. "You can tell me anything, you know that." I didn't answer for several moments, eyes still tracked on the ground. "Willow, please. I'm worried."

I glanced up ever so slowly and took a deep breath.

"Those who are cast out—they're murdered. By the council. By our *parents*," I blurted out, the words escaping my mouth before I could rethink it. "There is no Beyond, and there never was. There is only the awful truth, passed down through the decades."

Shadows danced across his shocked expression, highlighting the wideness of his eyes. For a moment he said nothing, simply staring at me. "Are you sure?"

I nodded slowly, and his jaw dropped. "My mother told me herself. I didn't—"

"I believe you." His words cut through the air, propelled by a sharp certainty.

"You're not surprised?" I knew I sounded accusatory, but I couldn't gather the effort to soften my words. "I mean, this is our *parents*. You really believe they'd do this?"

Auden just laughed harshly, extending a hand to pull me up. "Have you met my father?"

A leaf floated down from the tree beside me, fluttering slightly in the breeze. I watched it fall as if in a trance, Auden's words seeping sluggishly through the fog that enclosed my brain.

"I have," I said slowly, "and I know he's awful. But Auden, this is *murder* I'm talking about."

"Yeah," he murmured, shrugging as he released my hand. "I know."

I watched him carefully, my own pain momentarily dimmed as I observed his. It was easy to forget Auden was suffering, too. He was impossibly resilient, ignoring his pain so resolutely that it was almost impossible to tell it was there at all. But I knew Auden, perhaps better than anyone. He may have shrugged off the revelation, but the stiffness of his shoulders and twitching of his fingers revealed the truth. He was panicking, plain and simple.

"C'mon," he said, shooting me a soft smile as he snaked an arm round my shoulders and led me to the road. "Let's get you cleaned up."

An odd feeling worked its way throughout my veins as we walked—a warm feeling of calmness and safety. I realized with sudden clarity that it was the same feeling that had rushed through me only weeks before—the one that I had bottled up for a rainy day. I glanced up at the clear sky above and shoved the feeling back inside its bottle, for I knew without a doubt there were far more rainy days to come.

***

Everything, it appeared, could be improved with a bath—even finding out your entire life has been a lie. Auden helped me to his manor, assuring me it was empty before calling a maid to assist me. Where my mother had insisted the hired help stay out of the way, his did quite the opposite. I barely had to move as the maid cared for me, bathing and dressing me in a simple tunic and trousers. By the time their maid set a steaming plate in front of me, I had stopped shaking and the fog had cleared from my mind, leaving behind a pleasant lull. Auden glanced at me carefully as we ate, reminding me so painfully of the glances he used to send me, after that night in the rain.

"I'm not that fragile," I had said, but it couldn't have been further from the truth. I'd had no idea how thin the veneer was, hadn't understood that my life was based on a lie. Of course I was fragile—I had been walking a tightrope, only I didn't know it.

"How did you find out, anyways?" Auden's voice broke me from my thoughts, and I glanced up.

"Leo, but it was my mother confirmed it."

"Leo?" His voice was surprised—shocked, even. "How did *he* know?"

"I don't know," I admitted as I stuffed food into my mouth. "All he said was..." My words trailed off as my mind whirred, suddenly awake.

"Meet me when you change your mind—ten o'clock at the edge of the forest."

I glanced at the clock above the mantle: 9:45 p.m. The chair let out a squeak as I jumped up, hurrying towards the doorway.

"Where are you going?" Auden called, hurrying only moments behind me. I didn't answer as I shoved my feet into my boots, mind frantic. I barreled out into the darkness, stumbling clumsily over the stairs as I hurried in the direction of the forest. Auden followed silently behind, jogging lightly. The warmth of the day had seeped away into an icy-cold darkness, and I rubbed my arms to keep warm. Auden trotted the last few steps towards me, extending an arm when he approached.

"Here," he breathed, handing me a jacket—his jacket.

I paused momentarily, but the cold won out, and I took it. "Thanks." I pulled the jacket tight around me as we set off towards the forest. It was long on me, and baggy—not exactly stylish, but I didn't care.

"So, where are we going?" Auden asked, breaths still shallow and rapid.

"I'm not sure," I admitted, pushing my legs faster with each step. "Leo just said to meet him, once I knew it was true."

"Meet him *where*?"

"The edge of the forest." We were approaching the outskirts of town, where the buildings grew old and corroded.

"Right," Auden murmured, glancing around uneasily. "Because that's not suspicious at all."

I ignored him as we neared the edge of the forest, spotting Leo almost immediately. He leaned against a tree, arms crossed and face worried. His face lit up as I approached, before growing suddenly dark.

I ignored the look, launching myself towards him with a relieved sigh. My thoughts from earlier hadn't quite escaped my head, and I couldn't help but fear that our hugs were limited. How many more times would I feel his warmth, experience his shocked arms wrapping around my form?

"You were supposed to come alone," he whispered, voice both surprised and worried as he glanced at Auden behind me.

I shook my head, waving his concern off. "Don't worry, he knows everything already. You can trust him."

"I'm not so sure about that." Leo's voice was low enough that only I could hear him, though the daggers he glared in Auden's direction were hardly welcoming. "Listen, Willow, you need to know—"

"Care to share with the rest of the class?" Auden interrupted, voice loud and mocking. I could hear the annoyance behind the words, mingling with a well-hidden edge of hurt. Auden hated being left out, so his response was hardly a surprise, but I found myself annoyed anyhow. I was trying to get Leo to trust him, and this wasn't exactly helping. "It's rude to whisper about people in front of them, Hayes."

"It's also rude to show up uninvited, Bonavich," Leo pointed out, matching his tone, "and yet, here you are."

The two boys glared at each other, their eyes meeting with no small amount of animosity. The air seemed to stand still with tension, and I glanced between them nervously as I detached from Leo. I noted the rigid stance of Auden's body and curled shape of Leo's fists before clearing my throat. "Look, we all know the truth. Let's just go together."

Leo shook his head adamantly, giving me an apologetic look. "I can't bring him, Willow. They'll be upset enough about you."

"They?" Auden frowned. "Who's 'they?'"

I ignored both, merely crossing my arms and turning to Leo. "If he doesn't come, I don't either."

Leo considered this for several moments, face looking like he'd swallowed something very sour. "Fine. Let's go."

I let out a breath and set off beside him, Auden trailing behind us.

"Are you okay?" Leo's voice was quiet, and he looked at me tenderly. All animosity was gone now that Auden was out of the conversation, his features more relieved than anything. Guilt curled in my stomach—he probably thought I'd never speak to him again.

No, I'm not. The words died on my tongue at his glance, warm and gentle. I knew he would blame himself for my unhappiness, knew how guilty he would feel.

"Yeah, I'm alright." The words seemed timid in the cold air, utterly unconvincing, but he just grabbed my hand, squeezing it.

"No," he replied, "you're not."

A weight seemed to lift off my chest at the words. "I'm sorry for earlier." The words were small and quiet, my gaze on my shoes as we walked. "I may have overreacted a bit."

"I'd be worried if you didn't," he reassured me, eyes shining with a glimmer of humor. It seemed strange, to see such a light emotion on such a grim day. "It wouldn't be in character."

I rolled my eyes, hitting his arm softly. Even in the darkest of times, he brought a smile to my face.

"Where are we going?" Auden's voice demanded from behind us, and I cleared my throat guiltily. A part of me had forgotten he was there at all.

"You'll *see*," Leo snapped in return, voice sharp once more. Auden didn't reply, choosing instead to glare at the back of his head. Minutes passed in an awkward sort of silence, the air seeming heavy and stiff.

"You're gonna freeze, man." Leo's voice was rough as he glanced at Auden, but not entirely unkind. "You should've brought a jacket."

I glanced back at Auden, who stared him down with hard eyes, and cleared my throat. "Auden gave me his jacket." I fingered the heavy fabric nervously. "I was cold."

"Oh." Leo's voice was short and uncomfortable as he met my eyes, and I cringed as the tension increased tenfold. "You can have mine, if you'd like."

"It's okay," I said, "I'm not cold now."

Silence returned, and we walked quietly for a few minutes longer before another voice emerged—or voices, more like. I grew nervous as we approached a pocket in the wood: the glade. I wasn't sure what we would find here, but I couldn't help but dislike it on principle alone. It was a place of peaceful memories, but tonight it seemed like anything but. Voices danced across the clearing, and the closer we moved, the more there seemed to be. Young, old, male, female—all sorts of tones rang out across the forest, so loud that I glanced around to see if they'd gathered any unwanted attention. It was foolish, though; this far in the forest, no one could hear or see us.

I drew closer to Leo as we walked, more and more of the scene becoming visible with each step we took. The glade was filled with people—at least forty, from what I could see. They lounged around, talking and laughing loudly. Some even went as far as to perch in the lower branches of the trees. I fought to keep the shock off my face at the *wildness*. It was chaos, plain and simple.

"Leo," Auden said slowly, "who are all these people?"

"This," he motioned towards the disorder ahead of us, "is the Defiant."

As a child, my mother would whisper stories to me while my father slept. She did it for years, adding story upon story until my brain was so full of fantasy that I forgot to worry about reality. The stories had stopped over time, and my imagination along with them, but I didn't forget. I remembered many of the stories long after, running them through my head constantly. Fantasy stories were my favorite, of course—stories of a world that ran on technology, where you could have anything you wanted with the tap of a finger.

But she told me stories of our world, too. She told me about the founding of the discipline system, and about the people who refused to follow it. They were too attached to their freedom to realize that Atvas would perish within years without change. There was a group, she had said, called the Defiant – and they were the worst of them all. I always got scared then, tearing up until she reassured me not to worry. After all, the Defiant were long gone.

As I stared at the chaos in front of me, I realized just how wrong she was.

"They're real?" Auden breathed from behind me, staring at the glade with an expression of shock that was surely reflected on my own face. Leo didn't seem to notice our surprise, moving easily into the clearing. I followed, drawing closer to Auden as we entered the space.

"You're joking," a voice scoffed, rough and harsh. I glanced around, searching for the source, but found no one who appeared to have spoken. Just then, a rustle sounded from above, and a body dropped directly in front of me. I shrieked, jumping back at the sudden movement. Laughter sounded around me, and my face grew red as I drew Auden's jacket tighter around myself. It took me a few moments of disorientation to realize it was Abner, Leo's chaotic friend who I'd met at the party.

"Really?" Leo raised his brows. "Was that necessary?"

Abner ignored him, crossing his arms. "What the hell are they doing here?"

"We're..." I began, only to be cut off by his scoff.

"I wasn't asking you." However annoyed he'd been to see me at the party, that was nothing compared to the rage in his eyes now. I could see nothing of the laid back jokester I'd met before, no sparkle of joy or glint of amusement. That night I'd assumed he was nothing more than a rambunctious Service looking for fun, yet in front of me now stood a true rebel.

"Let them explain," another voice sounded, light and familiar. I couldn't help the gasp that escaped my mouth as Bex approached from behind Abner, placing a hand on his shoulder. Sensible, wise Bex was a *rebel*? She smiled at us, though her eyes were wary. "You'll have to excuse Abner. He tends to be a bit dramatic."

"A bit?" Leo murmured under his breath, a hint of amusement in his tone. That got a few laughs from the crowd and a vulgar gesture from Abner.

"We'll see who's laughing when they turn us in," he complained darkly.

"We're not here to get you in trouble." My hands shook slightly as I spoke, all too aware of the glares cutting into me from every direction.

"Then why are you here?" Bex's voice was quiet but sharp as a blade, her eyes panning between Auden and I. I knew that my next words were critical, that they could determine how the rest of this meeting went. There were so many stiff stances and wild eyes, as if we were heinous creatures in need of slaying.

I opened my mouth to respond, only to realize that I didn't have an answer to give. Honestly, I had as little information as they did. I was only here because Leo had told me to come, because I was drowning in the terror of what I'd learned and this was the only life raft in sight.

"She asked a question, *princess*," Abner snarled.

I bristled at the nickname, glancing at Leo. That name, that joke... it was *our* thing. To think that he'd shared it with Abner set my cheeks ablaze, embarrassment pouring through me as a few laughs echoed from the surrounding group.

"Why don't you ask your friend?" a voice rang out from behind me, strong and steady. The eyes of the crowd shifted to Auden, and I breathed a little easier. "Leo's the one who brought us here."

"I'm sorry," Abner said, voice mocking. "Who are you?"

"My name is Auden Bonavich," he answered, voice like steel. "A fact that you'd do well to remember." A strong anger radiated from him, from the glare gracing his docile features. Abner glared right back, and the crowd watched the silent battle with intrigue. Abner was certainly intimidating, but Auden's protective nature was stronger. Abner glanced away at last, spitting in the dirt by his feet.

"They know." Leo's voice seemed sharper here, a voice fitting to the hard persona he'd slipped into as soon as we crossed through the trees. He shared a glance with Abner, a wordless conversation occurring between them just as it had the night of that party. I almost felt like laughing—how foolish I'd been then, assuming they were merely normal friends. It was no wonder they were all so close. They shared a bond of secrets and treason. "They know about the murders, and they're here to help."

Outrage erupted at his words, the murmurs growing into shouts. "Yeah, right!" someone yelled from my right, just as another voice sounded from my left: "To betray us, more like!" I glanced towards Auden, finding the same uncertainty I felt reflected in his eyes. It was clear Leo wouldn't be defending us as the voices grew louder, propelling my heart into my throat. I was all but ready to flee when one voice rang above the crowd, cool and calm against the madness.

"Settle down." It wasn't hard to locate the woman, not when she stood out so starkly from the crowd. She was dressed similarly enough to the others, and yet she looked the opposite of disorderly. Strands of dark hair escaped a loose braid, framing her sharp features and tan face. Perhaps it was her stance, or the clear tone of her voice, or the way she met my eyes, cool and unflinching; whatever the source, authority radiated off her in waves. The crowd must have felt it, too, for they obeyed. I marveled as the bestial group grew quiet, even taking a seat as she strode towards where I stood.

She was older than me, no doubt, but younger than many of the Defiant. Still, they listened. As she neared, it became clear to me that few remained standing. In fact, besides me and Auden, only two others remained standing: Abner and Bex.

The intimidating woman reached us at last. She nodded to us, the first polite gesture I'd seen since arriving at the glade. "Willow Aldridge," she said, "and Auden Bonavich. What a surprise." Her words were swift, leaving no time to reply before she continued. "I see you've met some of our leaders already."

Surely, Leo wasn't a leader. Indeed, he'd sat down as the woman approached. I turned to Auden, who was once again staring towards Abner.

Oh. I nearly groaned aloud. *Of course he's a leader—the one person here who absolutely hates my guts.* Abner smirked at me, cocky and rude as ever.

"My cousin, Abner, heads our weaponry and combat," Cera continued. "You're in the same year, I believe."

Cousin? No wonder he had so much power in the Defiant, if he was related to this intimidating woman in front of me. No wonder he was so harsh, too.

"And Bex," Cera motioned past him to Bex, the only other person left standing. "Head of training and our main source of intelligence."

"But you're on the Court!" I exclaimed before I could help it. It was one thing for her to be in the Defiant, but as a *leader*? My eyes flew to the new woman's shirt, checking for a pin that wasn't there. She wasn't in the Court, then; it was only Bex.

The woman's eyes tracked me as I glanced at her empty shirt, then back up to her face, where she met me with a glare. I resisted the urge to cringe away from the judgment searing from her eyes.

"Status matters very little here," the cold-eyed woman said quietly. "If you really are here to help, I suggest that it matter little to you as well."

I flushed a deep red. "I-I didn't mean to..."

My pathetic sputters were cut off by a childish groan, the type I'd heard Leo's siblings give a million times. I turned toward the noise to see Bex rolling her eyes.

"Gee, Cera, think you could meet just *one* person without terrifying them?" Bex's voice was light, joking, but her gaze was intense. Warning, almost, as if cautioning Cera to back off. Cera seemed to sense it too, because she sighed and turned away from me at last. I realized suddenly that this must be the other friend Leo had mentioned, the one who'd never be caught dead at a party. I could see why. Cera didn't exactly seem to be the party sort.

"We have more important things to discuss, anyhow." Cera's cool voice grew somber as she spoke, addressing the entire crowd. "Vi was captured. Our sources reveal she is to be cast out."

Noise spread across the clearing, but my thoughts were louder. *Why would they care about Vi?*

"We're not sure how she was caught, just that she wasn't found until after the mission," Cera continued—and suddenly it all made sense.

My mind reeled, and I realized with a jolt that Vi was not a thief at all. No, she was a rebel. A *Defiant.* Anger pumped through my veins at the betrayal. How long had she hidden this from me? And not just her—Leo had lied too, had spun some story about meeting through a friend group. We'd need to have a conversation about that particular conflict, but I knew now was hardly the time.

"Did she get the proof?" a voice rang out from across the glade, and I tensed in shock once more. It was Director Kane Borkin, Director of Legality. He gave me a little nod from where he sat, the same sign of approval he had given me many times throughout training.

"What proof?" I asked softly, the question directed towards Bex. She seemed to be the kindest of the leaders, or at least the most likely to answer without a glare. She opened her mouth to respond, but Abner spoke before she got a chance.

"Of the *murders.*" His eyes seared into me, as if it were my fault those cast out were killed. I had wondered how Leo knew of the murders, but it was clear now; it appeared all of the Defiant knew. Perhaps that knowledge was what brought them together, just as it had brought me here.

"Vi was looking for proof of the murders," Bex clarified, voice gentle, "to expose them."

"It's the same thing I was doing," Leo admitted softly, avoiding my eyes. "When I broke into the Palace."

Another conflict unresolved.

"Then what?" Auden asked, speaking for the first time since his stare-off with Abner. He met Cera's glare with a steady gaze, calm and collected in a way I could only wish to be. "What happens next?"

"Then," Cera said, voice steady, "we revolt against it all—the Pathway, the Sovereign, the whole damn system."

I cringed at the words, at the pure hatred in her voice. I may not have agreed with the murders, but the *whole system*? It wasn't perfect, but it was the only thing that kept us alive.

"And what of the resource crisis? What of the chaos that will ensue?" Auden shot back immediately, utterly unphased by her exclamation. "The system may be brutal, but you can't deny its necessity. It'd be better to wait until the Coronation Ceremony, when we can make change the legal way."

Cera's eyes narrowed to slits, the clearing erupting into whispers once again. "Trust me, boy," she hissed, "we've tried the legal ways. It's no use."

"Well, you've never had *us* before," I pointed out. "We know the Court better than anyone. We can figure it out." I cringed as the words left my mouth. I sounded just like my mother.

"Don't flatter yourself," Cera hissed. "We've had Court members before, and we'll have more in the future."

"This is different," I replied, forcing myself to meet her cool eyes. "One of us will be the Sovereign."

"It doesn't matter." Abner crossed his arms as he spoke, shaking his head. "We can't put our entire cause in *your* hands."

"What's that supposed to mean?" My voice was strong for once as anger seeped into my veins.

"It *means*," Abner spat, "that I don't trust you for one instant. The second you get over this charity phase of yours, you'll have us all cast out in moments."

"How *dare* you?" My voice was harsh now, losing the polite edge I'd tried so hard to maintain.

"Oh," Abner shot back bitterly, "so it wasn't you who snitched on Vi?"

Ice ran through my blood, and my eyes widened as the whispers of the crowd erupted into cries of outrage. I whipped my head towards Leo—the only person who knew what I'd done, the only one who could've told them.

He glared at Abner, a look of warning that told me all I needed to know. I ignored his guilty eyes as I looked back towards the crowd. A third unresolved conflict, then. *A big one.*

"I didn't know," I said in a meek attempt to explain. "I thought she was just there for me, to visit..." My voice trailed off as the words were devoured by the noise, and I glanced at Auden worriedly.

"Quiet!" Cera barked at last, and the crowd grew begrudgingly calm. "Are you going to help us, or not?"

My heart beat furiously in my chest, my breaths shortening as the group looked at me. I knew then that there would be no more delaying, no more questions—I had to decide, and fast. These people were brutal, heathens that aimed to destroy everything I'd ever known, but what choice did I have? I was powerless on my own, and my mother certainly wasn't going to help. I was out of options.

"Yes." There was an odd finality to the word, and I had the sudden feeling that I'd committed to something far greater than I knew.

"Then prove it." Cera smiled at me then, a cold, calculated smile. "You're going to help us break into the Cathe."

17

WHATEVER WE MUST

The plan was simple enough, really: the raid was set to occur the following evening, during the Council Ball. The whole Court would be there, ready to celebrate the outgoing Council and Sovereign before a new one was ushered in. Which meant, as Cera pointed out, that everyone would be distracted. Even better, they'd all be at the Palace, far from the Cathe.

"No," Auden interrupted her explanation. "That's wrong."

"Excuse me?" Cera's brows shot up. Clearly, she wasn't used to being interrupted. Or being told she was wrong.

"The ball isn't at the Palace," Auden continued, unphased. "At least, not this year."

Bex shook her head, frowning. "The invitation was clear. 'Palace ballroom, seven o'clock.'"

"Right," Auden agreed, "but that was before Vi broke in. They're locking down the Palace, allowing no one in except for necessary personnel. The new invitations are going out in the morning."

"And you're certain?" Leo pressed, arms crossed. "You're sure you didn't...mishear?"

"Positive," Auden replied, voice icy. "It'll be at the Cathe instead."

Leo glanced at me, waiting for a confirmation I couldn't give. I just shrugged—it wasn't like I'd paid much attention to ball planning these past few days, and I wasn't exactly speaking to my mother.

"This changes nothing." Cera crossed her arms, commanding attention once more. "If anything, it makes it easier."

"Easier?" Abner snorted. "You call conducting a raid in the same building as the most powerful people in Atvas *easy?*"

Cera ignored him, looking instead to Bex. The young woman appeared thoughtful, nodding slowly. I remembered suddenly what Cera had said earlier—*our main source of intelligence.* It made sense, seeing as she was on the Court, but it made my skin crawl. Is that what they'd expect of me, if I went along with this? To spy on my peers, on my family?

"It does eliminate the issue of getting in," Bex agreed. "The entrances will be far less guarded, and the guards will be distracted. It'll be tricky, of course, and dangerous. Stealth is a necessity."

With that the planning commenced, a tense process that involved far too many opinions. I couldn't help but breathe a sigh of relief when they picked a small team for the mission, dismissing the rest of the group and leaving only a few of us left to contribute. Cera and Bex dominated the planning, with Abner and Leo butting in occasionally. Auden just watched with an intrigued expression, taking in every word with curious eyes. I wondered if he was as conflicted about being here as I was.

It took hours for a concrete plan to be made, yawns breaking through our words by the time it was done. It was decided that Kane Borkin would inconspicuously use his Legality connections to leave a back entrance unguarded. From there, four members would enter—Cera, Abner, Leo, and a girl named Quinn who was apparently very stealthy. She was a quiet girl, a few years older than me, hanging in the back for most of the planning. I liked her, if only because she was one of the few in the clearing who had yet to glare at me. While the four of them searched the Cathe for evidence, Bex and Kane would function as double agents in the ball. They would monitor the situation, keeping the Court in the ballroom as much as possible and alerting the others if something went awry.

"What about weapons?" Abner asked, suddenly very engaged. Head of weaponry and combat, Cera had called him. It seemed he lived up to the title.

"Weapons?" Quinn asked, voice uncertain. "What for?"

"Don't worry," Bex assured her. "We shouldn't need to use them—it's just a precaution." She reached into her pocket, drawing out a small silver dagger. I took a small step back, just in case; a good idea, seeing how a moment later she'd sent the dagger flying across the clearing and into the trunk of a tree. She shrugged casually, as if chucking knives into trees was a casual activity. "You know what I'll use."

Cera, unamused by her little show, just rolled her eyes. "I'll take a sword." She eyed Quinn, who still looked very uncomfortable. "Perhaps you should, too, if you're uncertain."

Abner nodded, seemingly cataloging this all in his head. "Got it. I'll take a sword as well, and Borkin will have one in his uniform. Which just leaves... Leo."

Leo, who had been watching all of this with a small smile, glanced up. "Oh, right. Uh..." He paused, seemingly thinking about the question. Suddenly, I realized that this must be why he had all those weapons in his shed. "I'll take a crossbow."

I imagined Leo with a crossbow, looking dangerous and mean, and shivered. It was so at odds with the Leo I knew, with the gentle brother who raised his siblings. There were no traces of that kindness in the man who stood before me, eyes glimmering with excitement at the thought of a deadly weapon.

"And us?" I asked, sick of being ignored. "What do Auden and I do?"

Abner scoffed. "You keep your mouths shut, that's what."

"Seriously?" I asked. After everything, after all I was betraying to even be here... "That's it?"

Cera shrugged. "Unless you have information on where we might find evidence, then yes. You will go to the ball, you will dance, and you will say nothing to anyone."

I bit my lip. I'd been to the Cathe dozens of times, but never anywhere important. Even my father's office had always been strictly off limits to me. I hardly even knew where it *was*, much less whether it would hold evidence.

Bex smiled sympathetically, patting my arm. "We'll need your help after, trust me."

"And what *will* happen after?" I pressed, crossing my arms. "You're just going to tell everyone the truth, and that'll be it?"

"That's the plan," Abner said, exhaustion shining through his taunting. "Take it or leave it."

"It'll never work." Auden pushed off the tree he had been leaning against, voice tight. He snorted as Abner met him with a glare, throwing up his hands. "I'm just telling you the truth. You really think all those Court members will just turn on their Sovereign, on their system? They fought for their spots. They have no reason to want change."

"But you're here. I'm here." Bex spoke from where she had retreated, perched upon a tree branch. "We've got no reason, either, yet we're fighting. Why wouldn't they?"

"Auden and I... We're different than most of the elite. I may not know you, but you clearly are as well." I said simply. Auden was right. The others wouldn't fight, wouldn't care. It was the very reason that I'd had such difficulty finding friends as a child, why Vi had always fascinated me so much. "He's right. They will stay loyal to my father."

And maybe they should, I thought once again. I pushed the thought aside. I could worry about morality later. For now, I just had to talk these people out of pure insanity. I wanted the same change as them, but... well, I was sensing that I might not like their methods.

"Then we get rid of *him.*" Cera emerged from the shadows of the crowd, eyes burning.

I gaped at her. Surely, she didn't mean...

"You can't be serious." The words slipped from my mouth, tone breathless with disbelief. Despite the fact that this was my parents, it was also *murder.*

"Actually, it could work," Abner stated slowly, tone solemn. At least he had the decency to look ashamed, unlike Cera. "It would leave them with no one to idolize. They would have to place someone in charge. Surely, they would choose Willow."

I noted the hurt on Auden's face at the assumption. After all, we were still tied.

"Or," I shot back, "you could just wait a few days for us to get the same power *without* murdering anyone."

"It'll be too late for Vi, though," Bex pointed out. "We need to take control before the ceremony. I'm not saying this is the way, but..."

"...but it would work," Cera finished, nodding.

"That is my *father*!" My voice was a hiss of steam in the cold air, and I aimed it towards Cera and her infuriatingly calm demeanor. Suddenly, I understood what Vi had been talking about at the Sponsor's Ball. The world of subtle insults and petty fights... yes, it was a game. *This* was real life, and it was ugly. "He thinks he's doing the right thing."

"So did the people he's murdered."

I ignored Cera's words, instead turning towards Leo. "Tell them how crazy this is."

He glanced at me, biting his lip in the way he always did in stressful situations. It was that movement that triggered my memory of another day in this very glade, a beautiful day of happiness and sunshine.

"You know I love you, right?" Leo's voice was soft as he glanced at me, biting his lip in a way that suggested he'd been meaning to say it for a while. There was a sort of boyish nervousness about it, his anxious smile illuminated by a beam of sun that filtered through the trees.

"You what?" I exclaimed, pushing myself up onto my elbows on our makeshift picnic blanket.

"You heard me." He grinned, still sprawled on his back like a cat with his arms tucked behind his head. "I, Leo Hayes, am in love with you."

"You can't be," I insisted, even as my heart fluttered viciously in my chest.

Leo didn't falter, merely smiling wider. "Well, too bad. I am."

"Leo..."

"Is that so awful?" he asked, brows furrowed slightly. "To be loved by me?"

I huffed out a breath as I glanced at him. There were a million things I wanted to say to him, but... "There's only a few weeks left."

The words were enough to cut off his grin, to remind him of the harsh truth. In only a few weeks we would be separated, if not by distance then by law. "Right." He shook his head, suddenly forlorn. "Man, that's gonna be hard."

"What?"

"Seeing you with him," Leo continued. "Knowing you're right there, but we can never be together again. I don't know how I'll keep sane."

I just stared at him, heart leaping in joy. For the things he said were awful, even if undoubtedly true, but the way he spoke... as if he would indeed be here. It was the first time I'd heard him speak so confidently about his future in Atvas.

"What?" he asked, catching sight of my face. "How is that something to smile about?"

I merely leaned down, pressing a tender kiss to his lips. I took my time drawing back, studying every inch of his face as I did so. The freckles dotting his skin, the small birthmark on the right side of his nose, the light eternally dancing in those beautiful gray eyes.

"I love you, too," I breathed. "It's unbearably foolish and utterly improper and I'll regret it for the rest of my life, but I love you."

Leo laughed in wonder, amazement painting his features. "You've really got to work on your compliments, you know that?"

I shrugged, shooting him a mischievous smile. "Maybe I just need a tutor." I cut his grin off with a kiss, and all my fears seemed to float away in the wind.

The memory seemed to shatter the moment Leo opened his mouth.

"It would be too risky," he said, avoiding my eyes. "There would still be the other Council members to consider. The power would have to pass through all of them before it got to Willow. And that's assuming Amelia wouldn't be an obstacle."

I stared at him for a few moments in utter disbelief. Was he seriously considering this? I waited for him to laugh, to tell me he was joking. Instead, he just kicked uncomfortably at the leaves coating the ground.

"It wouldn't work. At least, not with just him," Leo finished.

No one spoke, watching the tension unfold before them.

"I don't like it," Bex piped up, shaking her head slowly. "One person is one thing, but ... this is different. You're talking mass assassination here."

"No." Cera's voice was inexplicably cold, and I felt suddenly that I did not like her one bit. "What they've been doing for years—*that's* mass assassination. This is justice."

"Revenge will do nothing," a deep voice broke in—Kane Borkin. The man was frowning, burly arms crossed in a disappointed stance. "We must be better than them. Take the high road."

"Screw the high road!" Abner spat, throwing up his hands in frustration. "Where's the high road ever gotten us, huh?"

"I've heard enough of this." Auden sidled up behind me, voice hard and eyes fiery as he placed a protective hand on my shoulder. I was grateful for the touch, a lifeline in the stormy sea. "Willow, let's go."

Cera just watched us, eyes narrowed and a small smirk on her lips. "If you're trying to threaten us, boy, it won't work. We don't need you."

"Have your little raid, if it pleases you. It'll fail anyways," Auden waved a dismissive hand. "But if you so much as *touch* Warren Aldridge, or any other member of the Council, I will end you. You leave our families out of your games." He smiled, but there was no humor to be found in the expression. "How's that for a threat?"

It was all I could do to keep my jaw from dropping as he spoke, far harsher than I had ever seen him. Something stirred deep inside me, and when I blinked it was like I was seeing him in a completely different light. *Here* was someone standing up for me, for common human decency. Why Leo didn't do the same, I couldn't imagine. He even had the audacity to look horrified at Auden's threat, as if asking them not to murder half a dozen people was an atrocity.

"You don't need us," I said, voice quiet but anything but soft, "and we don't need you." I turned to Auden. "Let's just go."

And so we did, weaving back through the trees with a certain ferocity. It faded as we walked, the silence losing its tension as exhaustion set in. Auden stopped us and wrapped his arm around me at one point, drawing me into his arms. They were cold, goosebumps lining the skin—I still had his jacket.

"I'm sorry," he murmured. "I know you wanted this to work."

I didn't know if he was talking about the meeting or something else entirely, but it didn't matter. It all went wrong anyhow. Was it only days ago that my biggest worry had been my rank being even with his? I longed for those days, ached for the normalcy I had taken for granted. Everything seemed incredibly grim now, a black hole with no light in sight. No matter how hard I tried, I couldn't conjure up any emotion but melancholy and panic.

Anger, too, I thought, Leo's face floating to the forefront of my thoughts. I huffed at the thought, pushing him from my mind. Tomorrow, I would have to deal with that—with everything.

"What are we going to do?" I asked into Auden's chest. The words were a plea, a whisper of hopelessness in the dark velvety night. The Defiant were our last hope, the last resort, and now even that was gone. I didn't even know what else there was *to* do.

"The only thing we can do," Auden replied after a moment, voice pained. "We do whatever we must."

18

BLOOMING OF THE RAREST FLOWERS

I woke up the next morning feeling undeniably refreshed. Despite the anxiety pounding in my chest, I had managed a few hours of good sleep. Leo, it appeared, had not been so lucky, a fact made clear by his appearance below my balcony the next morning. I had only just awoken, stepping out for a dose of fresh air, when I spotted him—or rather, spotted the burst of color that accompanied him. Leo was holding a bouquet of blossoms; special flowers, vibrant and violet like the one he'd once tucked in my hair. I couldn't help the drop of my jaw as I beheld him pacing nervously in the garden below. I rushed down the main staircase and out the garden doors.

"What are you doing here?" I breathed, marveling as he grew closer. Rare—flowers that bright were so *rare*. He must have spent hours searching for them, to have so many in one place. I was so amazed, I almost forgot I was angry. Almost.

"I'm sorry," he rasped, voice filled with emotion. "I didn't mean it—any of it. You have to know that."

"Leo..." My voice was a whisper in the crisp wind, carried through the gardens softly. I didn't retreat as he stepped closer, pushing a blossom behind my ear.

"You let the last one fall for her," he whispered, "for Vi." He handed me the bouquet, and I took it with shaky hands. "We'll give her these when we free her."

I glanced at the flowers, at the emotion on Leo's face as he awaited my answer. I knew then that he really was sorry, that he truly hadn't meant it. And yet, the things he had said, how he had made me feel, the *person* he'd become...

"Thank you," I said softly, and I meant it. I grasped his hands, squeezing lightly as I spoke. "But you can't expect flowers to solve everything." He opened his mouth to speak, but my voice rose louder. "I know you're sorry, and I know you didn't mean it."

His brow furrowed as he snapped his mouth shut, glancing at me with confusion. "Then why..." His voice trailed off as he glanced at me, at our hands still intertwined around the flowers.

"I know all that, Leo. But I also know you weren't *you* around those people. At least, not the you I love."

He looked down, ashamed. "I know. It's just..." he bit his lip, as if searching for the words. "Before I met you, I *was* that person. I was angry and hateful, so lost in loathing that I couldn't find my way out. But then you came along, so bright and full of hope, and you showed me that there is more to life. Loving you... it changed me, Willow. But being there last night, with those people, made me forget who I've become. Who *you* helped me become."

I couldn't help the wetness that gathered in my eyes at his words, the swelling in my chest. I wanted nothing more than to forget this space between us, to throw myself into his arms and stay there forever. It was an effort to keep my feet where I stood, to say my next words. "I just... I need some time."

He shook his head lightly, staring at me with disbelief. "We have less than a week."

"It was always going to end." My voice cracked, and I cleared my throat.

"Not like this," Leo murmured. "Never like this."

"Does it really make a difference?" The flower slipped down in my hair, jostled by the wind. "In a week, I'll be married to Auden, and you to another."

He shook his head rapidly, as if he couldn't bear hearing the words aloud. "That's what you want?"

"It doesn't matter what I want."

"Of course it does," Leo replied. "I want to be with you. And I think you want to be with me too. What if..." he swallowed deeply, as if nervous. "What if we can make that happen?"

I let out a shaky breath. "Leo..."

"No, listen," he begged, grasping my hands in his. "I've been thinking about this for a while, and I have a plan. We can run away, far from here. We'll bring my siblings, of course, and we can sneak Vi out too. We'll go to the *real* Beyond, outside the fence."

I recoiled, pulling my hands away. "You're insane. That's... I mean, it's practically suicide! We'd never survive."

"We could," he pressed. "I know how to live off the land, and so do my siblings. I could bring supplies, and you know I'm handy, and you could help, too, and there's practically nothing that Vi can't do when she puts her mind to it, and—"

"Stop!" I exclaimed, on the verge of tears now. Partially because it really was insane, and partially because I wanted it. More than anything, I wanted it.

I could see it so clearly, a beautiful future flashing every time I closed my eyes. Living together, all of us, farming the land and sewing clothes. Raising a *family* together. Images flashed in my mind, little girls and boys with dirty blonde hair and green eyes. We'd be poor, sure, but we'd be *happy*. More than that, we'd both be alive—which is more than I could say for the future looming before us. With Leo in ninth place and the scores so close, the final trial could go either way.

"Just... stop," I breathed, voice cracking.

He fell silent, but his eyes remained bright. "Tell me no, Willow. Tell me that you don't want to be with me, that you actually want to stay, and I'll never mention it again."

I opened my mouth, then closed it. Of course I wanted to say no—the Sovereignty was everything I'd ever wanted. And Auden... I didn't know what Auden was to me these days, but it wasn't nothing. I wanted to spend my life with him, wanted to feel safe and happy in his arms.

But then there was Leo. He always came along just when I'd accepted my future, always did something like *this* and blew me away. He was passionate, and caring, and so unbelievably good that it hurt. It was like looking into the sun, only to find it was looking right back. How could I ever say no to that?

"I can't." The words were quiet, floating into the open air. "I can't say no."

Leo's face morphed quickly, surprise followed by pride and finally a bright, open happiness. "Are you serious?"

Despite myself, I smiled. I couldn't help it—his joy was contagious. "No, I'm Willow."

Leo let out a surprised laugh, picking me up by the waist and spinning me around. I squealed, drunk off of his joy. "Your sense of humor can be the first thing we work on."

I raised a brow. "Really? Before finding shelter?"

"Oh, yes," he answered, mocking a serious tone. "It is of the utmost importance that you learn to make good jokes. Otherwise we may all die of cheesiness."

"Hmm," I replied, smirking slyly. "Then I guess we need to change your definition of 'good jokes'."

The answering laughter echoed in my mind even after his lips met mine, effectively silencing the sound. It was like a sword in the brush, beating away the vines of tension the last few days had wrought. It was a drink of water on parched lips, a fireplace on a cold day. It was exactly what I needed—*he* was exactly what I needed.

He drew away first, scanning my face carefully as if afraid I'd changed my mind. Our faces were close enough I could see each freckle on the bridge of his nose, could feel the warmth of his breath on my face. "You really want to do this?"

"I do," I breathed, lost in his eyes. "And you?"

His lips curved into a small smile, and he shook his head in disbelief. "I do. Of course, I do."

In that moment, looking into each other's eyes, something passed wordlessly between us. Something like excitement, only far more solemn. A promise, more like; an agreement that he was everything to me and I to him. We remained there for several moments, lost in the feeling.

"We'll go tomorrow," he said finally, stepping back slightly. I shook my head, disoriented from the raw emotion still coursing through my bones. "I'll meet you in the glade at first light. Bring everything you can carry."

"Tomorrow?" I frowned. Now that I committed to the idea, I didn't want to spend one second longer here. "Why not today?"

Leo just shook his head. "There's too much to do. We have to gather supplies, I need to tell my siblings, and we need to figure out a plan for rescuing Vi."

It made perfect sense, but... "That's it?" I pressed, suspicious. "No other reason?"

"Like what?" he asked, brow furrowed.

"Come on, Leo," I sighed. "You know what."

The raid. I didn't know if it was still happening, didn't know what they'd decided. Not that it mattered much to me anymore, but I still didn't want anyone to *die.*

"Oh," he said, shaking his head. "No, we're not doing it. I convinced Cera to wait. We think that if you—or Auden now, I suppose—speak up at the ceremony, right after being crowned, you might have the power to stop things. Worth a shot, at least."

"Really?" I narrowed my eyes. "And *Cera* agreed to this?"

"Well," he laughed awkwardly. "I wouldn't say 'agreed' is the right term, but she got outnumbered."

I shook my head in amazement. "Okay, then. Tomorrow it is."

"Tomorrow it is," Leo confirmed, grinning before pressing a quick kiss to my lips. "I can't wait to start our lives together."

If the rest of the conversation wasn't enough to get butterflies in my stomach, *that* certainly was. I couldn't help but smile as I watched him disappear, climbing a tree to get over the tall gate.

"I suppose we should get better gates."

The voice sounded from behind me, and I turned suddenly. My mother stood in her nightclothes, plainer than I usually saw her. I opened my mouth to explain—to lie, if I had to—but stopped short at her expression. It was soft, gentle, almost kind as she took in the bouquet of violet.

"Those are beautiful," she said gently, sniffing them lightly. "Rare, too. That poor boy must have gone all over Atvas for them."

"You're not upset?" I asked, glancing at the place Leo had recently abandoned.

My mother smiled that soft smile once again—an expression I recognized only from my childhood. She nodded her head towards a stone bench, and I followed her cautiously to it. We sat close, far closer than I had been to her in quite a while.

"I've made a lot of mistakes, Willow. With your life, and my own." She grasped my hand in both of hers, regret turning her beautiful features to sadness. "I lost my first love. I never wanted that for you."

My eyebrows raised in surprise, and I searched her face for any sign of a lie. "You ... you loved another? You never told me that."

She shrugged. "It's a very long story, and not a happy one."

The pieces clicked suddenly in my brain: her dislike of Leo, her insistence that it would bring nothing but sadness... "He was cast out, wasn't he?"

"He wasn't supposed to be," my mother stated quietly, "not at first." Her eyes turned distant as she gazed into the distance, eyes focused on the rising sun in the distance. She did that often, examining each sunrise as if it were a particularly moving piece of art. "But rumors are dangerous. And the rumor that pushed me down to second pushed him into eleventh."

"He died," I said slowly, carefully.

"Yes."

"Did you know?"

"Not at the time," she admitted. "If I had... I think things would have gone very differently."

I paused, unsure of what to say. I imagined Leo being cast out, imagined finding out the truth months afterwards. It was an awful image.

"But you didn't avenge him. You didn't stop the murders." The accusation pushed through my tone, and my mother cringed at the sharpness as if it wounded her.

"I started to, once." Her eyes explored my face, as if conflicted. "The Defiant... they're real." I schooled my features at her words, forcing an expression of shock onto my face. "I met them once," she continued. "I had hoped they could help, could reveal the truth once and for all."

I didn't have to fake the shocked expression that crossed my face then. The idea of my refined mother in that clearing was almost laughable. A part of me wished I could have seen it.

"Did they help?" I asked softly, though I knew the answer before I opened my mouth.

"No." The word was definite, echoing in my mind eerily. "They wanted change, sure—but they were too radical, too unpredictable, and I feared for your safety."

"*My* safety? Why mine?"

"You were only a child at the time," she whispered, "and yet, they feared you. Feared your future, what it might mean for them." Her hair shifted in the wind, and I watched the dark strands twisting as she spoke. "They knew who you were, watched you constantly. One even went so far as to speak to you, at her casting-out ceremony."

My mother watched me, waiting for a reaction, but none came. I'd known about that instance since the day it occurred. *"Remember me,"* the woman had said—and I did. Little did I know at the time that it was death she was begging to escape, death that she fought so valiantly against. Little did I know that she was a Defiant.

"You stopped working with them for me?" I whispered, guilt weighing down my heart. All those deaths, maintained for my safety alone... It was too much to bear.

"I stopped working with them for everyone. They want far more than they claim, more than I could afford to give." Now that I could understand—after all, hadn't that been the same reason I left the meeting? "Even as a child, there was goodness in you. I knew that you would stop the deaths, should you have the power."

"So, you made sure I would have the Sovereignty." It wasn't a question, and it didn't require an answer. It was all so clear to me now: the lessons, the lectures, the obsession with my score... A necessity, in my mother's mind. If I thought I had known pressure before, I was dead wrong.

"Do you, uh... think they've changed?" I asked, fighting to keep my voice even. "The Defiant, I mean."

My mother watched me carefully, her eyes narrowing slightly. I nearly groaned aloud—I knew that look. "Willow Aldridge," she demanded, "what aren't you telling me?"

I remained silent, kicking at the dirt beneath me. The last thing I wanted was to get the Defiant in trouble, especially if they weren't doing the raid after all. But... could I trust them? I trusted Leo, of course, but...

"Willow," my mother said again, gentler, "Did you go to the Defiant?"

I let out the breath I was holding. "Yeah."

A moment of silence passed, and I waited for the eruption. This broke pretty much every rule my mother had, not to mention that I'd unknowingly trod directly on her painful past.

"And?" was all she said, and with a glance I realized she wasn't angry at all. No, she looked afraid. I didn't know how to tell her that she should be, with what had been suggested last night. Uncertainty hit me like a wave as I recalled the awful suggestion, Cera's call for revenge and Leo's blank acceptance. Could I really run away with a man who was willing to murder the woman who sat beside me?

"I can't tell you everything," I answered carefully. "But they had plans. Some not so great, some very bad. But I don't think they're happening anymore," I cut in quickly, seeing my mother's panic. "I'm just... I'm still nervous."

My mother took this information in with an understanding nod, though she still looked concerned. "I see." She leaned forwards, looking me directly in the eyes. "I know you don't think I trust you, Willow, but I do. I trust you more than anyone. So I won't push."

I blinked, surprised. "Thank you."

"But," she continued, holding up a stern hand. "I need you to promise me that you have good reason for believing these 'very bad' plans will not occur. You need to be one hundred percent certain, you understand? We can't risk anything less."

My heart beat furiously in my chest, but I nodded. I trusted Leo. I *had* to be able to trust him. "I promise."

She watched me for a moment longer before nodding, a sense of finality to the gesture. "Good." Her next words were quiet, and I had to lean forwards to hear them. "You weren't wrong, before. I have not given you an easy life, in choosing this for you. You will suffer."

"That's not exactly comforting." I snorted—an extraordinarily unladylike behavior.

"No," she agreed, laughing softly. "It certainly is not. But trust me, my love, it will be worth it, when you change the world."

Wetness threatened to spill from my eyes, tears forming at her words.

"Besides," she continued, smiling slightly, "I never was great at comforting anyone."

The tears fell at last, breaking through the surface as a laugh bubbled out of my throat. Another similarity between us—one that I had never known.

"Well," I said, laughing slightly, "a hug always helps."

And then she hugged me, pulling me tight to her form. It felt just as I remembered from my childhood so long ago: warm, and so unbelievably *safe*.

"It'll be okay," she was muttering into my hair. I was shocked to feel a wetness there—she was crying, too. "It'll all be alright."

19

THE LAST NIGHT

I spent the rest of the day preparing to leave Atvas. I called for obscene amounts of nonperishable food from the kitchens, chose a few items of clothing, and gathered them into the largest bag I could carry. Only once I had everything fully set did I allow myself to pursue the hardest task—saying goodbye.

I found Auden at his manor, where I was met at the door by a maid. I had a terrible sense of déjà vu as I stared her down, as if I were a mere child once more.

"I need to see Auden," I insisted for a third time, wringing my hands anxiously. "I'm not leaving until I see him."

"Oh, alright," she sighed finally, waving me behind her. "This way, miss."

I followed her down the halls, rubbing my arms to keep them warm. The manor was always cold, probably because the fireplaces were rarely lit. I once asked why, and the resulting argument was so bad Auden didn't speak to me for days. The maid led me to the parlor, nodding once before disappearing—probably hoping to avoid being seen letting me in. I couldn't blame her. She'd probably get in trouble for this, seeing how many times she attempted to explain that the Bonaviches weren't allowing visitors. If it had been any other occasion I wouldn't have insisted, but this was too important.

Auden sat at the grand piano, so enthralled in playing that he didn't notice me enter. It was a simple but melancholy melody, one I was reluctant to interrupt. His face was forlorn as he played, eyes somewhere far away even as he stared at the keys. I allowed myself a few moments to simply watch him; after all, it was the last day I'd get to do so.

"I like that one," I said as the last note faded off, causing Auden to jump. He whirled around, surprise coating his face. Rarely did I come to his manor, especially without an invitation.

"What are you doing here?" he demanded, voice only slightly above a whisper. "Who let you in? Elise?"

I sighed. "Oh, don't get mad at her. I'm very persistent."

Auden's lips twisted at that, amusement breaking through his annoyance. "Yes, you are." The smile dropped as he examined me, taking in my serious face. "Why are you here?"

"I always forget that you play," I deflected, sliding beside him on the piano bench. I lightly placed a finger on a key, resulting in a deep pitched note. "It makes perfect sense, though. You're good at everything."

"Oh, I am?" he teased, but I could tell his heart wasn't in it.

"Yeah," I whispered, throat suddenly tight. "You are. You'll make a good Sovereign, too."

"Willow?" I raised my head at the word, meeting his eyes at last. They were wide and concerned, not to mention confused. "You're sort of scaring me."

I breathed out slowly. "Auden, I'm leaving."

An odd combination of notes sounded as the hand he had sitting lightly on the keys pressed down, his jaw dropping in time with the clamor. "What?"

"You can't tell anyone," I added quickly, though I knew he didn't need to be told. "It's all very secret. But I couldn't..." My voice faded off as my throat tightened. I swallowed deeply, forced myself to continue. "I had to say goodbye."

Auden just stared, mouth still ajar.

"Auden," I urged gently. "Say something."

His mouth closed, then opened. Closed again. He shook his head, as if that would change the words filtering through his ears. "You're... leaving? Leaving Atvas?"

I nodded, biting my lip.

"That's..." He shook his head. "You'll die. You know you'll die, right?"

"I'm not going to die."

"Yes you are!" He stood up quickly, hand running anxiously through his hair as he began to pace. "I mean, you've got to *eat*, for one, not to mention shelter and clean water."

"Leo knows—"

"*Leo?*" Auden stopped suddenly, eyes filled with fire. "You're leaving with *him?* After last night?"

"He apologized for that," I retorted. "And the Defiant aren't even doing the raid, he told me."

"Right," he spat, "because we always trust the word of people who suggest mass murder."

"I know," I sighed. "Trust me, I know how it sounds. But you have to understand, that wasn't him. He's... he doesn't belong here. That's part of why we have to go."

"Sure," Auden scoffed. "That's why *he* has to go, maybe."

"*Auden.*" I scolded, crossing my arms.

"I'm sorry," he said, though he didn't sound very sorry, "but you *do* belong here, Willow! You belong with me, ruling Atvas!"

I crossed my arms. "I think I know where I belong."

"Out there, starving to death?" Auden threw his hands up. "*That's* where you want to be?"

"If it's with him." The words were quiet, but they said more than a yell every could. Auden stopped pacing, eyes full of pain and anger and an undeniable hint of fear. "Listen, I don't expect you to understand. But he makes me *happy*, Auden. Happier than I knew I could be. And... maybe I did belong here, once, but that was a long time ago. I don't... I don't think I want to rule Atvas, not anymore."

"You don't?" His voice was confused and hurt, but calm. He collapsed back onto the bench once more, seeming years younger than eighteen as he gazed at me.

"No," I admitted, and a thousand pounds lifted off my chest at the word. "But you do, and you'll be great at it. You just... you have to let me go."

There were several beats of silence as he contemplated this, a thousand emotions flashing in the deep blue of his eyes. I could practically see the moment when he gave up, his shoulders sagging. "I don't like it," he insisted, though there was no fight in his tone.

I laughed softly. "I don't expect you to."

"It's not safe," he continued, frowning deeply. "And it sounds utterly miserable."

"I'll manage." I leaned my head on his shoulder, taking a moment to remember the way it felt. For years we'd been doing this, the never ending cycle of admission and confrontation and comfort. No one knew me like Auden did, that was for sure—and no one knew him like I did. There was a special sort of comfort in that, in the intimacy of knowing.

"I can't do it without you," he said at last, his voice far weaker than I'd ever heard it. I glanced up to see tears lingering in the corners of his eyes, a sight I'd rarely seen.

"Of course you can," I answered, forcing back the wetness in my own eyes. I'd already felt far too many emotions that day. "You've always been the better Sovereign, Auden."

It was the truth, though I hated to admit it. I knew the rules of the game better than most, but I didn't know how to play it. Not in the way Auden did.

"Well," he said suddenly, voice returned to its normal strong tone. "It's not over yet. We have tonight."

I frowned, the evening's ball coming back to my memory. I'd nearly forgotten. "Oh. Right."

"Hey," he nudged me gently, "No need to look so glum. Tonight is going to be the best ball you've ever had. You'll need it, to tide you over years of staring at fields with no entertainment."

I rolled my eyes, hitting his arm. "Oh, shut up."

He wasn't wrong, though. A sharp pain cut through my chest as I dressed for the evening, each mundane motion seeming more meaningful than ever. Each removed curler brought a smile to my lips, and even the sharp pain of waxing my legs didn't feel quite so bad. I almost felt like crying as I zipped up the dress of the evening, gazing at the beautiful girl in the mirror. I wasn't sure what life would be like in the 'real Beyond,' but I was fairly certain that it wouldn't include pretty dresses and glamorous balls.

The feeling stuck in my head, clinging to each thought as I approached the ball. Passing through the front doors of the Cathe was like a portal to the past, taunting me with memories of childhood and the Pathway. I felt a sharp pang in my chest as I nodded to Court members and peers, people I had never given much thought to but was certain I would miss. Yet worst of all were the people flanking my sides—my parents. As rocky as my feelings were towards them, they'd been by my side my whole life. How was I supposed to leave them?

"What's the matter, darling?" My mother's voice pulled me from my preemptive sorrow, her frown piercing my soul. "You've hardly said a word." I could see straight through her polite glance, knew what she actually meant: *Get it together, before someone notices something is amiss.*

"Oh, it's nothing," I replied, forcing my face into an acceptable expression of weariness. I could feel the stares of the surrounding Court members with whom we were mingling, reminding me what I *wouldn't* miss about Atvas. "Just thinking about the final task. It's rather soon, isn't it?"

The excuse worked perfectly, the suspicious faces melting into sympathetic expressions. Priscilla Moore, whose son was a Pathway participant the year before, began to lament the difficulty of the final trial. "It is an awful time, between the two. Really, I don't see why there needs to be a gap at all..."

My mind began to wander once more as the conversation took off, though I was careful to nod and smile at the right moments. Would I miss this, these silly balls and small talk conversations? It was hard to imagine now, but...

"Excuse me," a voice interrupted my train of thought. I glanced up to see Auden approaching, armed with a charming smile that softened the interruption. "I don't mean to intrude. I was merely hoping to steal Willow for a dance."

The couriers ate that up, cooing softly as Auden extended his arm. It was no surprise—a future couple, sharing a dance despite the upcoming competition. It was all very heartwarming, I supposed. I took his arm with an equal amount of elegance. Only once we had stepped several feet away, conversation slowly rebuilding in our wake, did I dare to release the deep breath I'd been holding.

"That's what I thought," Auden muttered, the corners of his mouth turning up at my deep sigh. "You looked a little...distressed."

"Was it so obvious?"

"To me, sure. To anyone else, I doubt it." He pulled us to a gentle stop on the dance floor, and we moved mechanically into a proper position and began the dance. It was second nature to us both, so I knew that couldn't be the reason he was frowning. "Thought you'd be happier. Considering..."

His voice faded off as he looked around pointedly, clearly unwilling to say anything more while we could be overheard. I was immensely grateful for the caution.

"I am happy." It was the truth—as much as I would miss Atvas, nothing had changed. I wanted that life with Leo, more than anything. "It's just a bit overwhelming, that's all."

Auden opened his mouth to speak, but I never got to hear what he planned to say. We were interrupted by a tap on my shoulder, Auden's eyes going wide as he glanced over my shoulder. I turned cautiously, already dreading what was to come. It was the end of the song, and I was fairly notable. It wasn't surprising that someone else would cut in for a dance.

I just didn't expect it to be my father.

"Willow." He addressed me with a little bow before turning to face Auden. "I hate to break up the happy couple, but forgive an old man his whims."

Auden merely nodded his head in return, eyes still glowing in surprise as he backed away. "Of course, sir."

My heart beat impossibly fast as the dance began, my body on high alert as I placed a cautious hand on his shoulder. I could count on one hand the number of times I'd been touched by my father, and most of them were a mere hand on my shoulder in public. Honestly, we barely even spoke to each other most of the time. Why he wanted to dance now, of all days, I couldn't imagine.

"You're a good dancer," he remarked suddenly, filling the awkward silence. Somehow, it just made things more uncomfortable.

"I should be," I answered stiffly, uncertain how to interact with the man before me. "I had plenty of lessons."

"Ah, yes," he sighed, "I recall that. I didn't think they were strictly necessary, but your mother insisted you learn."

Suddenly, it was my turn to be surprised. I knew it was my mother who spearheaded my training, but I'd always assumed the etiquette portion was my father's influence. After all, my mother was born in the lower ranks of the Court while my father was the son of the Sovereign himself.

"I know I haven't been as helpful in the Pathway as I might have," Father said with a sigh that made him seem twice his age. It was hard to tell with all the spinning, but it almost seemed like he glanced towards the head table where Ruben sat. "It's forbidden to share information, of course, but you likely expected that I'd disregard that rule. Many in high positions do."

"Why didn't you?" I'd always assumed it was a moral high ground, but after learning about the murders I found that incredibly hard to believe.

My father looked at me then, meeting my eyes with his own intense gaze. I realized with a twinge in my chest that this, too, was a rarity. His eyes were so different from my own, watery blue to my emerald green. "When you're in the public eye as you are now, and will continue to be, very little is truly yours. You've been sheltered from that to an extent, but that time has passed. No matter the results of the final trial, you'll no longer belong to yourself. You'll belong to the people of Atvas, as any good ruler should."

No, I won't, I thought with no small amount of relief. *I'll be free.*

"But this competition, this victory," he continued, face growing pained. "That's yours, and no one else's. You're the one who did that, not your mother and not myself. Perhaps it was a risk, but I couldn't bear to take that away from you. Without that you never have the Sovereignty, at least not in the ways that matter. Without that, you have nothing."

A million emotions warred in my chest as I listened, anger and fear and guilt fighting valiantly to the surface. Yet it was joy that prevailed, an undiluted happiness and immeasurable relief. For within his confusing speech was definite proof that somewhere, deep down inside, my father cared about me. At least enough to spare me this small bit of anguish.

It was enough to force the next words out of my mouth, the question I had pondered a dozen sleepless nights. "Did you ever not want to be Sovereign?"

Were you ever like me?

Around us the music stopped, dancers coming to a halt as the last note hung in the air. My father dropped his hands, stepping back as if burned. Yet his face didn't look angry. Rather he looked contemplative, brows scrunching together as he considered the question. "I don't think anyone's ever asked me that," he answered finally, huffing out a surprised laugh.

Around us, a tinkling of metal on glasses began—a sign that they were about to start the Council toast. My father gave me one last nod, my question left unanswered as he wove towards the head table. It made sense; as guest of honor, it wouldn't do for him to be on the floor during the toast. Still, I couldn't help but wish he would stay, would prioritize me over the Sovereignty even once. Then again, he'd soon step down altogether. Maybe things could be different, after.

Except there would be no after. I was leaving tomorrow, and I'd never see my father again. For some reason, the thought didn't seem so happy anymore.

"Ladies and Gentleman, please gather around." My mother's voice boomed across the room, echoing in the high ceilings. I'd nearly forgotten—my mother's Court position was Head of Relational Affairs, meaning that she ran Court events and would be responsible for giving the evening's toast. She didn't look nervous at all, smiling graciously as the crowd tightened. A hand wrapped around my waist, and I looked behind me to see Auden. I leaned back against him, comforted by his steadiness as my mother began her speech.

She spoke about the trials and difficulties faced by the Council, about their strength and cooperation. I allowed my mind to wander, scanning the Council members as she spoke. Were they strong? Ruben wasn't, at least not in character, and I wasn't sure my father was either. Councilman Mullerson was kind and sort of amusing, but he was a huge pushover. The other two men, Councilmen Jameson and Peters, I'd never gotten to know. Considering they must know about the murders and allowed it to happen, I doubted their strength of character as well.

My mother, though—she was strong. Whatever doubts I had about her methods for the past eighteen years, that much had always been clear to me. Especially now, watching her sing the praises of men who sat in her rightful place, I was in awe. Could I ever command a room in such a way, pleasantly and without an ounce of fear?

Of course, I wouldn't have to. There wouldn't be much of a room to control outside of Atvas.

"Now, if everyone could raise their glasses," my mother was saying, prompting me to quickly grab a glass off the tray of a Service passing by. A quick glance told me that this was real alcohol, likely allowed as a special gift as we were nearly of age. I was ecstatic—at least I'd taste it once before leaving.

"I'd like to offer a final toast to our wonderful Council. Your hard work will not be forgotten, but rather continued by the next generation." Mother raised her own glass, the room mirroring the movement. I followed, glancing at Auden as I did so. A forlorn look passed between us, a somber acknowledgement of everything tomorrow would bring. I would be gone with the wind, under the influence of none but destiny itself. It was Auden who would belong to the people, who would suffer the burden of a crown on his head.

"To the Council!"

"To the Council!" we echoed, a room of voices mingling into one everlasting chant. I brought my glass down perhaps too quickly, eager to try the alcohol forbidden to me since birth.

I'd only just felt the first drop on my tongue when everything fell apart.

20

TIME STANDS STILL

First came the screams, not of joy but rather fear. They sliced sharply into the once joyous atmosphere, cutting deeper and deeper until it was bleeding, spewing thick pools of terror that flooded my senses and suspended my consciousness. For a brief moment I saw nothing and no one besides the woman in front of me, clutching a toddler to her chest. She turned as if in slow motion, face suspended in grotesque horror.

"What is it?" I wanted to ask. *"What's wrong?"*

Then I saw it, and I understood. Everything was wrong, and nothing would never be right again. For even from here, a great distance from the head table, I could see the blood that blossomed from my father's chest, flowing from the crossbow bolt embedded over his heart. In my delirium, I couldn't help but think it looked like a flower.

Tine surged forward like a turbulent wave, crashing and dragging and pulling all at once. My ears ached with the cacophony around us, desperate calls for a medic ringing over the fray. My feet moved of their own accord, pushing me through panicked courtiers as if they were little more than air.

"Willow!" I could hear Auden call behind me, fighting desperately to keep close. "Wait, you shouldn't—"

I broke through the front of the crowd, catching sight of my father at last. He looked so frail, skin pale against the white satin of his shirt. It was the same shirt I'd gripped only minutes ago as we danced, yet now it was covered in blood, *he* was covered in blood, and...

A harsh hand pulled me back, gripping my arm firmly enough that I couldn't pull away. It was just in time, too—only moments after Auden pulled me away from the head table, Councilman Mullerson fell to the ground.

This time, it was me who started screaming. I screamed as the life left his eyes, as the Council member next to him fell as well. I kept screaming as they dropped like flies, the whole Council taken down one after another. Auden held me upright through it all, arms wrapped around me with unrelenting strength. Even as Ruben Bonavich fell, face frozen in eternal anger, Auden's arms did not falter.

"It's the Defiant!" a voice called out from the fray, only resulting in further panic. Through the mass I could see a Legality guard enter, a black-clad figure wriggling in his grip. The figure wore a black mask, covering her identifying features, but I recognized the calculating blue eyes and confident stance instantly.

"I know nothing about this," Cera insisted, voice far less calm than it had been the previous night. She held out a hand, as if to calm he angry crowd. "We mean no harm."

The Defiant decided to raid after all. The realization hit my heart like an acorn on a hollow tree, thudding dully against my heart. Perhaps they lied to Leo, excluded him from the plan since he'd shut it down. It made more sense than the alternative, at least. Because Leo couldn't have... he wouldn't lie. Not to me, and not about this.

"There's one in the rafters!" someone yelled from the crowd, pointing at the arched ceiling above. My heart nearly stopped in my chest as I glimpsed a shadowy figure, crossbow loaded and aimed down. Auden's eyes met my own, a sharp terror resounding in the space between us.

There was a beat of silence, and then chaos erupted. In one swift motion, Cera knocked her elbow into the man behind her, startling him enough to let her go. They were a rush of motion and violence as they fought, him with a sword and her with her fists. In mere moments more guards flooded the room, followed by more black-clad Defiant members. The fight broke out all at once, knives flying and swords swinging. Only the figure in the rafters remained frozen, still as a statue despite being discovered. The crowd morphed from afraid to desperate, trampling over each other as they flooded towards the doors. Any sense of decorum was long gone, societal niceties pushed aside in the face of survival. I couldn't fault them for it, not as I watched a Court woman drop to the floor, bloody, simply for being in the wrong place at the wrong time. The Defiant in front of her, the actual target of the swing, had dodged just in time.

"Auden!" I shouted over the fray, a single panicked word. I pointed desperately to the head table, where the corpses lay abandoned. Even the Intellects practiced in medicine had left, favoring their own survival over the faint possibility of prolonging certain death. Yet two people remained—our mothers. Lucille was curled over Ruben's body, anguished cries wracking her body. Above her stood my mother, tugging her arm desperately. I couldn't hear her words over the noise, but the intention was clear. *Get out, now.*

Auden and I started running at the exact same time, our destinations identical. I didn't let myself look down as we stumbled over chairs, didn't let myself think about the corpses we passed. My only focus was on my mother, a beacon of light and hope shining in the midst of the carnage.

Even as the fight grew closer to the table, swords swinging dangerously close to our path, I focused on her.

"Come *on*, Luci," I could hear her urging Lucille as we drew nearer. "We've got to go."

"No!" Lucille exclaimed, hysterically. "I can't leave him."

"Amelia, you have to go," Auden panted as we trotted to a stop beside them. He crouched down beside his mother, rubbing soothing circles into her back. "Take Willow and get out of here."

"No!" I exclaimed indignantly. "I'm not leaving you."

"I'll be fine, and so will my mother," he said, voice impossibly calm despite the fear lingering in his eyes. "They killed the whole Council, and the archer's still in the rafters. Who do you think is next?"

Suddenly, the Defiant's words came back to me. They'd suggested the Council die, yes, but also… my mother.

"We have to go," I breathed, grasping my mother's hand. "Mother, we have to go *now.*"

My mother, who had tears running down her face, just glanced past me. "Auden, she won't leave him."

He looked up slowly, meeting her gaze with a sad smile. "I know. I've got her."

My mother nodded solemnly, as if finding something unspoken in his gaze. She turned to me, face determined. "Let's get out of here."

I turned, leading the way around the table and towards the crowd. My heart beat faster as we approached, metal clanging ominously. Far too many sword tips were coated in blood for my liking, but there was no way around this. Like so many things, the only way out was through.

It was indescribable, the sensation of weaving through the horde of violence. We moved as fast as we could, dodging weapons and pushing through bodies. I was floating through a sea of agony and terror, anchored only by the feel of my mother's hand on mine. The crowd had thinned some, but not nearly enough to make the exit quick. I gasped aloud as I ran directly into someone, sending us both reeling back onto the floor. The woman, wearing the Defiant black, had lost her hood somewhere along the way. I realized with a start that it was Quinn, the Defiant girl who'd been part of the plan. We stared at each other for a moment, little more than two frightened animals encountering each other in the woods. Her fingers twitched around her sword, but she made no move to use it. I opened my mouth to say something, though I didn't know what, but I was interrupted as the tip of a sword appeared in the middle of her stomach, sliding back out with a sickening squelch. Her eyes met mine one last time before she fell, dead.

I didn't even know her last name.

"Are you alright, Miss Aldridge?" the owner of the sword asked, a Legality guard I'd never met before. He let the sword hang by his side, crimson dripping onto the marble floor. I watched it fall, mouth hanging slightly open. "We need to get you to safety."

Safety. Only then did I realize that my tether had disappeared. I was drifting at sea, drifting slowly into panic as I whirled around, searching, searching, searching...

"Mother?" I called desperately. "Mother!"

"Willow." Relief flooded my body at her voice, though I still couldn't locate it. I went to retrace my steps, only to find my path blocked by a fallen body. Ice cold terror flooded my veins as I glanced down to find my mother, bleeding out on the floor with a bolt embedded in her neck.

The world stopped as I fell to the floor next to her. Nothing else mattered, the battle around us rendered unimportant as I watched the shallow rise and fall of her chest. Her blood was warm and thick as it rushed around my fingers, my hand pressed desperately to the wound.

"Don't...don't take it out," I gasped through my tears, my Intellect training kicking in despite the chaos. "You'll be fine, we just need a medic. They didn't get your heart, you'll be fine."

My mother just smiled, the soft and beautiful sort I'd rarely glimpsed on her face. Like the calm blue beneath the flames, a gently flickering warmth that filled my chest. I would see that smile again, I *had* to, because otherwise...

"Oh, my darling," Mother whispered, hand coming to rest on my cheek. It was shaky, as if the exertion was too much for her body to handle. "My perfect daughter."

A sob escaped my chest, raw and painful. "Perfect? But I don't... I haven't..."

"Always," she rasped, letting out a hacking cough that made my heart wrench. "You've always been perfect to me."

I couldn't speak through the tears that wracked my body, blurring my vision and running filling my mouth with the taste of salt. "I love you," I choked out, wiping my eyes furiously. "Mom, I love you."

When my vision cleared, she was already gone.

Nothing mattered, not the yells of anguish or the blood raining down around me. I cared for nothing but the sight of my mother's lifeless eyes, the feel of her blood on my hands. How had it become cold so fast?

Vaguely, I was aware of someone pulling me up. Auden's face appeared in my blurry vision, yelling something I didn't care to hear. He looked sad, too. I allowed myself to be pulled through the rest of the crowd, only slightly aware as a sword grazed my skin. Auden looked very concerned about that, but I felt nothing. There was too much agony in my heart already, no room left for the mundane discomfort of a scratched arm.

I drifted away, untethered, my unconscious sunken deep beneath vicious waves of agony. These waves didn't come and go but rather remained omnipresent, pushing deep into my lungs until there was no room for air. I didn't care, content to live amongst the suffocating depths of despair. It wasn't until we came to a stop, confronted by the sudden silence of the hallway Auden had pulled me down, that I dared to kick back to the surface.

Later, I would wish I never had. For there I found Leo, dressed in black and holding a crossbow.

"No." It came out as a whisper. I backed away from Leo, away from his familiar eyes and gorgeous face, *away from the truth*. I jumped as my back hit Auden, warm and sturdy behind me. He placed a comforting hand on my shoulder.

"We found this one near the entrance to the rafters," the guard holding Leo's arm huffed.

"I'll take a crossbow," he'd said at the meeting.

"Willow, I'm sorry," Leo cried. I could barely stand to look in his direction, but I could hear the guilt in his voice. "I wanted to tell you, I did. I'm so sorry."

I opened my mouth, then closed it. There were no words, not when my mother's blood still stained my hands. I hoped he saw it, hoped it haunted him for the rest of his life.

"Willow, *please*," he tried again, but I just shook my head.

"Get him out of here," I heard Auden instruct the guard. I made no move to stop him as he was led out of the room, but I couldn't resist a glance at his face. I regretted it immediately, heart splitting in two as his gaze met mine. Two minutes ago, I would have thought I could feel no more pain. But this... It was different from the grief weighing down my heart, different than the lingering fear that made my hands shake. It was sharp, disbelief edged with anger. It was betrayal. My blood was fire, simmering angrily through veins of ice. I almost wished it would boil just a bit stronger, so that it might be powerful enough to break the shards of ice that encased my very soul.

"I'm sorry." Auden's voice was gentle as he approached, hands tender as they gathered me into his arms, wiping away a tear I didn't realize I'd cried.

"No," I whispered again, because it couldn't be true. It was just today I had been held close to my mother's chest, had felt the warmth of her body and heard the study beat of her chest. Less than an hour ago I was dancing with my father, having a real conversation for the first time. They couldn't just be... gone.

Suddenly, the ice melted, rushing out of me in an almighty stream.

Auden held me through it all, fingers brushing through my hair with each jolting sob. I cried for what seemed like hours, enclosed in the warmth of his embrace. Occasionally the tears would slow, ceasing just long enough for an image to flash in my mind—my mother's face, her amazing stories, even my father's indifferent nods. Occasionally Leo's face would appear, too, filling me with a rageful pain that started the tears once more.

"I'm sorry," Auden whispered again and again, guilt clouding his features. "I should have realized it sooner. I'm so sorry."

His face seemed to blur as I sobbed on the floor, the world nothing but salt and melted ice.

21

— · —

DRIFTING AT SEA

The following morning, the sun rose above Atvas. The sun rose, and perhaps somewhere a girl awoke, happy and ready for a new day. Maybe she would eat breakfast with her parents, hugging them goodbye before going out into the world. Surely, she would eat lunch with her best friend, whispering about the boy who made her feel like the world was ten times larger than it was. Most of all she would smile, secure in the life she was living.

Perhaps that would happen, somewhere... But this was not that place, and I was definitely not that girl.

In fact, I wished the sun hadn't risen, wished there was no new day. Everything I thought I loved was gone, and everything I thought I knew was wrong. There were no parents to say goodbye to, no best friend to eat lunch with, no boy to whisper about. There was only myself, an empty Palace, and Auden. Auden, who had always been with me, who had held me until I cried myself to sleep. Auden, who had taken every bad thing and made it a little bit better. It was for him that I forced myself out of bed that morning, despite every inclination telling me not to.

I found him on the balcony, staring aimlessly into the distance. I inched up beside him, leaning against the stone railing. We said nothing for several minutes, reveling in the peaceful silence. It was almost *too* peaceful, a beautiful tranquility that didn't match the agony in my heart.

"I thought the calm is supposed to come *before* the storm." My voice rang quietly through the morning air, and Auden glanced over at me. His eyes seemed tired, and I wondered vaguely if he had slept at all.

"It still could come." The wind rustled through the garden below, the plants swaying ominously as if they'd heard the words he spoke. I glanced at him carefully. There was a haunted quality to his face, and for a moment he appeared years older than he was, almost archaic in the early morning light. "There is much to consider now."

I hummed in agreement, even as the words twisted into my chest like a knife. There wasn't supposed to be a future for me to worry about, at least not in Atvas. I was supposed to be in a field of flowers, building a home with *him.* Part of me still craved that future, craved the tranquility he'd promised me.

Why is it that promises of peace always fall victim to violence? What is it about human nature that makes it so *difficult* to be gentle?

"The final assessment been moved up," Auden said bluntly, effectively silencing my inner turmoil. "It'll take place the day after tomorrow."

My heart dropped to my stomach. "Two days? That's not nearly enough time."

Auden shrugged. "It'll have to be. They're all gone, Willow. The whole Council, wiped out at once. Everyone's trying to step up, all at once, and no one is listening to anyone else. Atvas is in a state of chaos, and it needs a leader."

A lump grew in my throat at his words, formed both by grief and fear. There were regulations in place for the loss of a Sovereign, but loss of the whole *Council*? It was uncharted territory. I knew Auden was right, knew that each passing day was an opportunity for any scorned citizen to grasp power. Yet still...

"Look, Willow," Auden sighed, "You don't have to compete. No one would blame you."

Something inside me recoiled from the thought, a sharp instinct honed by years of training and dreaming. The feeling must have shown on my face, because Auden's eyes grew wide.

"Or do compete," he amended, hands up in surrender. "I just thought... Well, you said you didn't want to be Sovereign."

His point was valid. Only yesterday I'd renounced my desire for the position, far more inclined to live out my days unbothered. I didn't feel that way just because of Leo; or at least, I didn't think so. I'd honestly, truly desired to be rid of the pressure for good. But now...

"It's not about what I want," I replied honestly. "I have to at least try. For my parents."

Auden took this in with a contemplative expression, nodding slowly. A shadow of grief seemed to pass over him, clouding his eyes as he turned to me. "I'm sorry," he said, a cracked edge to his voice. I realized suddenly how unwell he looked, his eyes rimmed with red and darkened by distinct circles of purple. "They were good people."

"They condemned dozens of people a year to death." The statement came out flat, unemotional. The anger it once might have held was gone, buried under layers and layers of grief. Now there was only the truth, untainted by the delicate intricacies of emotions.

Auden's brow furrowed. "I know, but they thought they were doing the right thing. Sometimes it's more about the intent than the actions."

"I suppose so," I said, though I wasn't sure I meant it. It was all so confusing, contrasting opinions clashing in my head angrily. None of it was black or white, right or wrong. "I'm sorry about your father, too. I know your relationship was … complicated, but no one deserves to die like that."

He just shook his head, an odd expression on his face. "It feels… strange. Devastating, of course, but I can't help feeling relieved." His blue eyes met mine, brimming with emotion. "Does that make me an awful person?"

"I don't think so." It was an honest answer. I felt no relief from my own parents' demise, but Ruben wasn't exactly a kind person. "You're just grieving; it's normal."

"No," Auden replied with a sigh, "it's not. But my father, he…"

His voice trailed off, eyes fixed somewhere in the distance. A million different emotions seemed to be warring within him: sadness and anger, relief and guilt.

"He used to train me himself, you know that? In everything, but his favorite was Legality," Auden said suddenly, lips curling into a bitter sort of smile.

"Yeah," I said softly, the memories of that day I'd overheard his "training" still fresh in my mind. "I know."

"He said he wanted to make me strong," Auden continued, as if I hadn't spoken at all. "Said that if I wasn't, I might as well not exist. Did you know that?"

"No," I whispered, "I didn't."

"I always wondered," he murmured, voice catching as it left his throat, "what he would do if I failed. Guess now we'll never know." He turned to me, and his face was vulnerable in a way I had never seen him before. It was as if for the first time, I was seeing Auden with no wall of a smile or mask of certainty. It was sort of unsettling, like seeing a fireplace coated in ice.

"What do you think he would have done if you were cast out?" I wasn't sure what made me ask. Maybe it was because I had been wondering the same thing about my own parents. For all our preparation, it could have happened. Had we failed more than a task or two, we would have been cast out just as easily as the next person.

"I'm not sure," Auden admitted. "But I'd like to think he'd have let me die." He scoffed out a laugh—as if any of this were funny. "Makes me feel less guilty."

My brow furrowed. "Guilty for what?"

Auden stared out into the distance for a moment, watching a browned leaf drop to the ground. "For not missing him. For being glad he's dead."

I tried to imagine that for a moment, but I couldn't. For all my issues with my parents, I missed them the same as if I were missing a limb. Then again, my parents were not Ruben. "I'm sorry."

Auden just shook him head, as if coming out of a trance. "We'll need to plan their funerals. They'll have to be tomorrow, I suppose." He glanced at me with uncertainty. "I'm sorry. I know it's sudden."

I almost wanted to laugh at the statement. Yes, it was sudden. Everything about this situation was sudden. Instead I shook my head, offering him a small smile that felt wrong on my face. "We'll get it done."

***

It wasn't easy, especially considering the state of Atvas. Auden hadn't been exaggerating when he said it was chaos. We were interrupted constantly, some Court member or another knocking at the door to propose a new governance or offer *themselves* up as Sovereign. It became irritating quickly enough that we decided to split the load, Auden disappearing to deal with Atvas while I arranged the funerals.

Of course, that wasn't easy either. Every step of the process was a stark reminder of why we were doing this, of the fact that they were gone and never coming back. In a weird way, it almost didn't feel real. I half expected my mother to knock at the door, to peer over my shoulder and correct my work.

"No, no," she would probably say, brow wrinkling in the disappointed look I'd hated so much but now ached to see. *"Proper etiquette dictates that the Sovereign give the speeches."*

"But, Mother," I'd respond, arguing just for the sake of arguing, *"there is no Sovereign. He's gone."*

Each imagined conversation sent me into a spiral of grief, all planning suspended as I curled up into my father's office chair and sobbed. Did the office smell like him? I searched the deepest crevices of my mind, begging my grief-addled brain to *think*, to recall even one memory of his scent, but it was no use. Memories were mere ghosts of the past, pale and fading and utterly useless when there were so few to begin with. I'd never known my father enough to know if the office smelled of him, and now I never would. For some reason, that seemed like an atrocity. Even worse was the way my mother's scent seemed to linger everywhere, the sweet aroma of her perfume clinging to each room. It smelled fresh, as if she'd only just walked through. I couldn't help but wonder how long that would last, how long before that memory, too, would fade.

I almost wished that Auden and I had switched roles, wished that I could ignore the gaping hole in my chest for even a moment longer. Almost wished it would disappear altogether, would leave me in blissful emptiness. But that was a foolish wish—and I never had been afforded the luxury of foolishness. There was no choice but to push through the pain, to allow the memories to flood me as I planned. For my mother and her best intentions, for my father and his skewed morality, for Mullerson and his jokes, and for all the Council members who had ever been kind to me, I would plan a magnificent ceremony—even if it took what little strength I had left.

By the time Auden found me I had moved to a hallway of the Palace, a sparse area near the kitchens that I'd rarely been in. It was the only place I could find that brought up no memories, effectively rendering it the only space in which I could get something done. I was just looking over the final arrangements, squinting in the fading light, when his footsteps neared.

He didn't comment on the strange location, merely lowering himself to the floor next to me. I leaned back into him as he looked over the plans, feeling quite a bit like a hollowed-out shell. I'd ordered the victims of the accidental deaths, those harmed in the fighting, to be returned to their families. Only the Council and my mother would be buried tomorrow, a mass funeral that all of Atvas was welcome to attend. Everything was drawn up according to etiquette, just as my mother would have liked it.

"The speech will need to address the battle," Auden murmured thoughtfully, looking up from the plans. "Are you okay to do that?"

I frowned, pushing myself upright. "Really? At the funeral?"

"Unfortunately. There's already an uproar about it. The families of the dead want answers, and they want them now."

"What about the Defiant? Where do they stand in all of this?" I asked, voice small. As always, Auden saw right through me.

"We have *him* in custody," he said slowly, carefully. As if the wrong word would make me fall to pieces. "The others have disappeared. I've sent guards looking, but they're very good at hiding. We'll have to pick up the search once things have settled down some, but we'll find them. I promise."

"What do we tell everyone, then?" It was a difficult question, especially considering the Defiant were on the loose. Telling them that there was an anarchist group currently running amok in Atvas would only cause paranoia and panic, but too many people saw it happening to lie.

"The truth," Auden stated, as if it were a simple thing. "We tell them that a deranged boy gathered a following and led them into a coup d'état. Paint it as a desperate attempt of a kid who knew he was about to be cast out. We'll tell them that we're searching for his accomplices, but make it clear that they're not a threat on their own."

I couldn't help but frown at the words. It wasn't exactly the truth; after all, he wasn't even a leader in the Defiant and they certainly were a threat without him. But I couldn't deny its effectiveness. It would work, at least for now.

"What are we going to do with him?" My words were little more than a whisper, an uncertain inquiry. "With all of them?"

There would be no more bloodshed, no more murder. That much I was certain of. The Flawed had to be dealt with somehow, thought, and so did the criminals. How did we change the system without destroying it? Was such a thing possible?

"I've been thinking about that," Auden admitted. I wasn't surprised—this was Auden, after all. Hypervigilant, overthinking, always one step ahead Auden. "Honestly, the solution's been there all along."

"Oh?" I quirked a brow.

"Sovereign Coldwell started the murders because it was easier than dealing with an actual population existing beyond Atvas," Auden sat up straighter, eyes glowing with an assured glint. "But what if we took the harder path? You and Leo were ready to live beyond the fence. Why can't they?"

"I don't know," I said uneasily. "Survival is a gamble out there, even if you're prepared. Voluntarily deciding that is one thing, but throwing them out there? It doesn't feel right."

Auden waved a hand, unconcerned. "Then we send them out over-prepared. Food, building materials, everything they could need to start a civilization of their own. After a few years, they'll be flourishing."

"And if they grow too strong?" I challenged, brow furrowed. "What happens in fifteen years when they decide they want to attack us for wronging them, or when Atvasians decide they'd rather try their hand out there?"

Auden merely shrugged. "Then we deal with that in fifteen years."

The thing was, there really was no other choice. I wasn't willing to risk the collapse of Atvas by demolishing all order, the way the Defiant wanted. But I also wasn't willing to sit back and watch dozens of people be murdered each year. Auden's plan wasn't perfect, but it was an improvement. Maybe in fifteen years, things could be different. But for now...

"Alright," I agreed. "Let's do it."

***

Only an hour later, I was already regretting the decision. Because what I'd failed to consider, the factor that hadn't even crossed my mind since yesterday morning, was Vi. As I stared up at the imposing walls of the prison, I couldn't believe I'd ever forgotten. It wasn't just Leo whose life I was gambling with this plan. It was hers, too, a fact which I intended to change.

The inside of the prison was cold and utterly uninviting. A group of three guards surrounded the entrance, nodding their heads in reverence and pity as I approached. I nodded back, swallowing the lump in my throat.

"I'm here to see Violetta DeLoughery," I announced, eyeing them critically. Prisoners weren't technically allowed visitors, barring cases of special circumstance. If they chose to deny me, I wasn't sure there was anything I could do.

The guards looked at each other, then back at me. The one closest to me, a middle-aged man, spoke first. "The thieving traitor?"

"That's the one." I pushed down the anger rising in my chest. After all, Vi technically was a traitor to Atvas. She'd betrayed me, too, even if it was for a noble cause. "I need to question her."

The guards looked at each other once more, clearly uncertain. The prison was one of the most secure buildings in Atvas, and no one was allowed in without approval from the Sovereign or his Council. I doubted there was any protocol for this; no one was officially in charge of Atvas at the moment, but Auden and I were closer to it than anyone else.

"Very well," the same guard said. "Follow me, Miss Aldridge."

I controlled my breath as we advanced through the door and down the hall, trying not to think about what this building was. I knew Leo was in here somewhere, knew it in my bones. The knowledge haunted me, a phantom pain that weighed down each step.

We stopped in front of a door at last, the guard unlocking the door and gesturing for me to go ahead. I forced myself to breathe as I raised my hand, knocking three times.

She might not even want to see me, I reminded myself. *After all, I'm the reason she's here in the first place.*

The door opened tentatively, and Vi peeked out at me.

"Only you would knock on a prisoner's door," she scoffed, walking back into her small space and sitting cross-legged on the bed. I hovered on the threshold, observing wearily. "Well?" she asked, brow raising, "are you coming in or not?"

Just like that, I flung myself into her arms.

Vi looked good, or at least as good as someone who'd been in prison for weeks could. Bags lined her eyes, but she seemed well fed, and her room was certainly nicer than any prison cell I had imagined. I glanced around the space, taking in the small cot, bookshelf, and dresser with clothes. They were plain clothes, but clean nonetheless.

"Nice room," I said awkwardly, if only to fill the silence.

She smiled gently, as if peering right through me, but responded nonetheless. "Yeah. Someone must be looking out for me."

I noted the title of the books on the shelf—classic books I had grown up reading. I recognized one that had been read to me as a child and smiled.

"My mother," I replied, voice curving around the lump that grew in my throat once again. "I think she did this."

Vi frowned, an incredulous look on her face. "Your mother? She hates me."

"You haven't heard?"

The question lingered in the air, and Vi shook her head. "Willow, I'm in prison. It's not exactly a reliable outlet for gossip."

Everything poured out at once, every awful day since she was captured laid bare. I didn't cry; no, there were no tears left for me. I instead began to shake, softly at first and rapidly by the end. Vi's arm wrapped around me somewhere in the middle, holding me as I forced the painful words from my throat.

"And then I came here," I finished. "I think it's about time we talk, don't you?"

"Willow," Vi said, grasping my hands. "I know you don't want to hear this, but... are you sure Leo's really guilty?"

I huffed a dark laugh. "Trust me, I didn't want to believe it either. But the evidence doesn't lie. He was holding the crossbow, and he basically confessed."

"Yeah," she murmured, though her brows still scrunched together. "It just doesn't *seem* like something he'd do."

I almost asked how she would know, before remembering they had known each other for years, had been in the Defiant together.

"Really?" I said. "You don't believe that he has enough anger in him to do this? Because I do. I think the world hurt him really badly, and he burned the world down in return." I shook my head, staring at the books on the wall. "In a weird way, I almost get it."

Almost, and not at all. Because the anger brewing in me, the things I'd felt since that night...it was downright terrifying, but it would never be strong enough to warrant that sort of bloodshed. Not in a million years.

Vi was quiet, observant as she watched me. It was a strange reflection of our usual roles—she'd always been the passionate one, and me the one watching from the sidelines.

"You have to understand," she said softly, "that I never meant for any of this to happen. When I broke into the Palace, I had no clue that it would set off that sort of catalyst. I didn't even know you would be home. When I discovered you were, I did everything I could to leave you out of it."

I shook my head. "I know that. I don't blame you, but...you should have told me sooner." After all, she'd been in the Defiant for *years*.

"It wasn't like that," she replied, as if reading my thoughts. "I started hanging around the Defiant at fifteen, but I wasn't *in* the Defiant until much later. I didn't learn how to fight until last year, and it wasn't until the night of the Sponsor's Ball that I found out about the murders."

The night of the Sponsor's Ball, when she'd looked so panicked and afraid. When she'd begun insisting that I must win.

"Growing up, I never wanted you to be Sovereign," she admitted. "Not because I didn't think you'd be good at it, but because I didn't want that for you. You were always too burdened as is, and I figured that the Sovereignty would only make it worse. I'd hoped you could be content someday, if not happy. But once I knew the truth, even that wasn't an option. It was all I could do to leave you blissfully ignorant for as long as possible."

It was so eerily similar to what my mother had said, and moisture grew in the corner of my eyes despite their already red rims. I'd never realized just how many people were watching out for me—not just for my future, but for me as a person. For my happiness. For some reason, it didn't feel comforting. All those people wishing for me to be happy, yet I was miserable. How disappointed they'd be.

"I think I could be content as Sovereign. Once things die down, at least. With Auden by my side and you in my corner, it won't be half bad." I knew she could see through the false cheeriness, but she didn't call me out on it. She only looked down, biting her lip.

"You know I love you like a sister," she began, and a slimy feeling began to curl in my stomach as tears gathered at the edge of her eyes. I gulped nervously; I had a feeling that I wouldn't like whatever words came next. "But I have to go."

The air seemed to leave the room, yet I tried to suck in a breath nonetheless. The air was grating on my throat, as if poisoned by the words she said. "Why?" I choked out, emotion filling my voice. After all we'd done to save her from the Beyond, and she wanted to *go*?

"You know me!" she exclaimed, flinging her arms out. "I hate it here, and I'm not afraid to say it. I hate the people, and the rules, and the whole system. Out there... imagine what we could do, what we could create! If what Auden said is true, then we will have plenty to get started. We could create a whole new society, just the way we want it."

I shook my head in refusal. It made sense, sure—but it was still *insane*.

"It's too big of a risk," I insisted. "I won't allow it."

The claim was absurd. I would, and Vi knew it. She just smiled that infuriatingly calm smile, gathering me in her arms for a final hug. "I'm going to miss you," she whispered, "more than you know."

And then I cried again.

22

—·—

WORLD OF DREAMS

Auden didn't ask questions when I stumbled into my room hours later, eyes puffy and red—although that was because he was asleep, sprawled out on the large bed. Utterly drained, I fell into bed next to him and drifted off to sleep almost immediately.

It turned out that having Auden there was more to my benefit than his, a fact that became painfully apparent when I woke up screaming, sweat clinging to my body. The images clung even harder—images of blood and death and my mother's smile. I dreamed that I was back in that ballroom, watching my parents die over and over again. I didn't hesitate to melt into Auden's open arms, shaking lightly.

"Shhh," Auden muttered softly, brushing away the sweaty strands that stuck stubbornly to my forehead. His warmth seeped into my clammy skin, his embrace a shelter from the storm of my mind. "It'll be okay," he muttered, "I promise."

For hours, the only sounds were my rapid breaths and his comforting murmurs, until both faded into the nothingness of sleep.

Until the second time ... and the third. On the fourth, I threw up, barely missing Auden's feet. And yet, he held me through it all, keeping me safe until an uneasy sleep brought me to morning. I was still rattled when I awoke, shrouded in darkness despite the sun that crept over the horizon. Not that it was surprising; I was to bury my parents under that very sun. Getting to my dressing room was a monumental feat, and I groaned to think of the effort it would take to look like my usual self today. As I dragged my aching body into the room, my heart skipped a beat. A figure stood there, rustling through the clothing.

"Risa?" I murmured groggily. "What are you doing here?"

Risa was never in my chambers when I was, as mother had always insisted I get myself ready. A part of me whispered that perhaps she'd wanted me to have that small piece of self-sufficiency. It wasn't as obvious as sword-fighting skills, but I knew better than anyone that independence could be a weapon worth wielding.

"I thought you might want assistance today," she said, a sadness deep in her eyes. A part of my brain screamed at me to refuse, to maintain that last grip I had on myself. Yet a far larger and more logical part reminded me of all I had to face today, and suddenly all strength seemed to melt from my muscles.

"Yes, please," I said, collapsing onto the bed.

For the first time since I was very young, I felt pampered in my own home. It appeared Risa was just as knowledgeable as myself in fashion, and she found me a suitable funeral outfit in moments. We chatted about anything and everything as she curled my hair, watching as I did my makeup in the mirror. She even got a giggle out of me once, a short but bright sound that ended as soon as it began. There was no room for brightness in my heart, no room for anything but heavy grief. Still, she was a welcome reprieve from the gloominess that had hung over me the past week.

"I can't believe you've worked here for years," I said at one point. "How have we spoken so little in all of that time?"

Risa blushed slightly, eyes focused on the curl she was working on. "I was instructed to stay out of your way," she confessed. "The first family I worked for, before yours, felt that I interfered too much. Your father was kind enough to employ me anyways, but I didn't want to risk getting too close."

"Where did you work before?" I asked, suddenly aware that I knew nothing about her at all.

She stopped curling, setting the iron down for a moment. "Auden didn't tell you? I worked for the Bonaviches for eight years."

"No," I replied, surprised, "he didn't mention that." The admittance floated through the air between us, heavier than it ought to be.

"We spent a lot of time together, when he was young," she admitted. "I thought he might have remembered me, but..." I met her eyes in the mirror, taking in the depth I saw there. "Well, never mind that."

"What was he like?" I asked suddenly, though I wasn't sure why. I'd known Auden as a child, after all. Yet to have lived in his home, to have seen *everything*...

"He was kind," Risa said softly, a sad smile upon her face. "Soft, too, in the best way possible. I assume he's lost that, with that father of his."

"He was soft?" I grinned at the thought. Ever since I could remember Auden, he'd been a rock, strong and constant. Sure, he was gentle with me, but not exactly soft.

"Oh, yes," Risa said, and I could tell by the fondness in her eyes that they'd been closer than she claimed. "A real mama's boy—though I can't say that Ruben much enjoyed that."

Now *that* I hadn't expected. Auden had always seemed to resent his mother, though he'd never spoken about it. "Did Lucille know about how Ruben treated Auden?"

Risa pursed her lips, swallowing deeply. "I've been warned not to speak of this," she said quietly, "but between you and me, she didn't care half as much as she should have. She was more interested in her wine, if you know what I mean."

I couldn't help but wonder if I knew anything about Auden at all, because he'd certainly never told me *that*. Though now that she mentioned it, I had never seen Lucille without some form of alcohol. "I didn't know that."

"I always wondered how he had turned out," Risa mused. "He's got a kind soul, but with a home like that..." She shook her head, as if shaking the memories from her brain. "It's a miracle he's himself at all."

"Sometimes it's hard to tell where he ends and I begin," Auden had said that night so long ago. *"Other times, I wonder if I'm myself at all."*

In that moment, I was very glad Ruben was dead. As horrible as it was to be murdered in such a way, a part of me couldn't help but think he deserved it. At least now Auden could be free.

It turned out Risa was quite the stylist, and even in my distracted state, I had to admit I looked good. Grim, sure—but good. I adjusted the velvet fabric of my dress, black as night beside the white lace collar that lay across my collarbones. My hair was beautifully curled, pushed back by a headband of black pearls. I couldn't stop touching it, surely ruining Risa's hard work as I waited for Auden to emerge. My eyes moved to the grand staircase as if by instinct, and memories flashed before my eyes before I could stop them.

"Good evening, my lady."

Anger coursed through my veins, at both Leo and myself—and yet, there was something else there, too. A devastating feeling, as if something found had been lost once again.

He made his choice, I reminded myself, *and now my parents are dead.*

Auden emerged at last, and I couldn't keep my eyes from following him as he moved sleekly down the staircase. Even without a stylist, he managed to look just as primed. Auden always looked good, of course, but something about today seemed different. It appeared he sensed the difference, too, for he gazed at me in a way like he never had before. I fidgeted with my hair once again.

"Risa found me," I explained, blushing slightly.

Auden's eyes moved over me, slowly, coming to rest on my face. "So I see." The words hung in the air around us, dangling above us like an omen.

A small smile grew on my face at the attention. I immediately hated myself for it, for daring to care about a foolish compliment when my parents were about to be buried. The smile dropped at the thought, and I swallowed deeply. "We'd better go, before we're late."

Auden sighed, looking inexplicably sad as he said, "Okay, Willow. Let's go."

We walked in silence, the wind tearing mercilessly through my hair. I was just beginning to feel sorry for Risa, who put so much effort into my hairstyle, when we saw it.

Across the pavement of the road, painted on in crimson, were the words:

The Dead Rise In Us

Goosebumps rose on my arms as I took in the message, suddenly feeling quite unsafe. The paint shone in the light of the sun, and I couldn't help but think it looked distinctly like blood.

Auden sucked in a breath behind me, seeming upset but not especially surprised. "I was hoping they had cleaned it up by now."

I whirled on him, frowning. "You knew about this?"

"I was told yesterday," he admitted grimly, mouth in a straight line. "I didn't want to worry you."

"What does it mean?" The crimson letters seemed to brighten as I looked at them, a scalding image I was certain I'd never forget.

Auden sighed. "Apparently, there are many in Atvas who sympathize with the massacre. It's all whispered rumors and anonymous messages, so it could just be the Defiant. I'm not certain yet."

"The dead rise in us," I whispered, the words rolling uncomfortably in my mouth.

"It's a slogan of sorts," Auden explained. "They've been using it to justify the murders. Because... Well, they believe that they're getting revenge for those who have been cast out. It's how they rationalize extreme actions."

I didn't resist as he took my arm and led me away, too shocked to care. Red hot anger rose in my chest. "It was cold-blooded *murder*. How could they..."

"We must pity those unable to see the truth," Auden stated, voice distant, "For they live in a dream world."

I nodded in confirmation—and yet, as I imagined the anguish one must feel to justify such a thing, I couldn't help but think that no dream world could be quite that unpleasant.

The service was long and anything but serene. Much of Atvas had shown up to pay their respects, Court and disciplines alike. It should have been touching, seeing so many people there to remember my parents and the other Council members, but I hated it. Their eyes were greedy in their wetness, daring to cry over people they didn't even know. It was everything I could do not to scream at them, scream that my parents were *mine,* they should have been *mine,* and yet I never got to have them because they always belonged to everyone else. It wasn't fair before, and it was especially unfair now. It was all I could think as I looked down at my parents' corpses, as I tracked the age lines in in their faces and realized I'd never get to see them form more.

It isn't fair.

Auden ended up giving the speeches, stepping up without question when I asked. It was all I could do to stay upright and quiet, to quell my anger and suppress the agony that threatened to escape with every breath. Tears traced down my face as Auden spoke, spewing our pretty lies.

If we lead them into a dream world, I wondered idly, *do they deserve our pity, or our envy?* As I watched my parents' coffins be lowered into the earth, I couldn't help but think it was the latter, for the real world was harsh, and cruel, and terrible.

***

I was drained by the time we arrived back at the Palace, Auden and I together once again. We had never discussed our current living arrangements, but with our houses swathed in emptiness and our dreams haunted by memories, I couldn't imagine being anywhere but by his side. Still, I was sure he would have to return home soon, if only for his grieving mother.

Risa was long gone—probably at home preparing for the ceremony tomorrow—so I drew my own bath. It was tiresome, but worth it. As my mother used to say, a good long soak will do wonders for stress. When I emerged, clean and clothed, a bowl of soup and warm bread waited for me beside the bed. I practically leapt towards it, stomach grumbling.

"I figured you'd be hungry." Auden's voice rang out from the bed. I was so focused on the food that I hadn't even noticed him lying there. To be fair, it *was* very dim, only a single flickering lamp flooding the space in a warm glow

I looked up, forcing myself to eat a little slower. "You were right," I muttered, leaning into him, "like always."

"Always?" he quipped, eyebrow raising.

I hit his arm lightly before placing the bowl, now empty, on the night stand. "I take that back."

Auden laughed gently, and I settled back into the warmth of his chest. In that moment, clean and full of warm soup, the weight on my heart felt a bit more manageable. It would be a comforting life, to always be taken care of like this. I could imagine it clearly: Auden running that same hand through my hair, calming me down as our children drove us mad. And unlike the dream of a life with Leo I'd once had, this one was real. This, I could actually have.

A dream world within reality itself. I almost smiled at the thought, lips turning down at the last possible moment as I remembered how awful reality really was. For even in the dream future of my mind, my parents were gone and there was nothing I could do to change it. That fact alone made it a nightmare.

"Willow," Auden said slowly. I didn't look at him, but I could hear the frown in his voice. "You know you're allowed to be happy, right?"

I stiffened. "I'm *not* happy. My parents just died."

"And you think they'd want this for you?" he replied, voice low and intense. "You're not betraying them by smiling for a moment, you know."

It was as if he'd reached directly into my soul, stealing the words that lingered there. I hadn't even realized it myself, but that *was* how I felt. My parents were gone. What business did I have being *happy,* of all things?

"I don't know what they'd want." I pulled myself away from him, glaring. "I'll never get to find out."

Instead of backing down, Auden just snorted. "Well, I can tell you that they wouldn't want this."

"Oh?" The word was harsh, filled with a venom I didn't really mean. "Because you knew them so well?"

"Of course I did!" Auden exclaimed, looking inexplicably hurt. "You know I loved them like they were my own parents."

"Well, they weren't," I spat, tears blurring my vision. "I'm sorry if that hurts, but it's the truth. They were *my* parents. Not yours, not Atvas'. They. Were. Mine."

I almost wanted him to yell back, to get in my face, to demand I stop being so selfish. Anything to ignite the anger in my blood, anything to feel something besides this aching despair that clung to my every thought like an ill-fitting bandage. But Auden, being Auden, merely extended his arms in surrender.

"Okay, Lo," he said softly, carefully. "You're right. I'm sorry."

The words were like a needle to my emotions, my anger deflating as quickly as it had come. I settled back against his chest reluctantly, still disgruntled but mostly just exhausted.

"Do you want to talk about it?" he asked after several moments of silence, in which he pretended not to hear my sobs.

"No," I breathed, sniffling. "Can you just... tell me something good? Something about the future?"

"Of course." The words were quiet and intense, and they sent a shiver down my spine. "I actually..." His voice faded off, a blush working its way across his cheeks. "Never mind. It's embarrassing."

"What?" I pressed. Considering he was never flustered, I was intrigued. "Tell me."

"No, I couldn't," he answered bashfully, looking down.

I raised my head to send him a pouting glare. "You have to, because I'm sad. That's the rule."

"Oh, is it?" He raised a brow, smiling slightly.

"It is," I declared, forcing the corners of my mouth to stay straight. Despite what he'd said about being happy, I couldn't bring myself to smile.

"Fine, fine," he relented, sighing so deeply I could feel it along my side. "I'll tell you, but remember it was under coercion. I take no responsibility for any embarrassing admissions."

I nodded, satisfied, and leaned back into his chest.

"When I was younger, my parents fought a lot," he started, voice shifting to a somber tone. His hand started to fiddle with the ends of my hair, almost unconsciously. Whatever he was about to say, he was nervous. "Well, my father fought. My mother just tried to keep the peace, only it was never there to begin with. Eventually she'd give up on that, too, and that's when it'd get really bad."

I hardly dared to breathe, afraid to break his trance. So rarely did Auden ever discuss his childhood, and this was twice in two days. I wondered if he was grieving his father after all, in his own way.

"Anyways, that's hardly the point," Auden laughed humorlessly. "The point is, I spent a lot of time sitting on my floor and waiting for it to end. And... well, I'd think about us. Every time, I'd remind myself that one day I wouldn't live there anymore. I'd live in the Palace with you. I imagined every aspect of that life, but the most important thing is that we wouldn't be like them, not ever, because we have something they didn't."

"Good anger management skills?" I muttered, cursing myself the moment it came out. It was hardly the moment for humor, but Auden didn't seem to mind. He merely huffed out a laugh before shaking his head.

"Respect." His voice was genuine, his hand going still in my hair as our gazes met. "My parents loved each other, in their own way. But they never understood each other, and they never respected each other."

"My parents were the opposite," I admitted. "They never loved each other, but they did respect each other."

Auden smiled. "How lucky are we to have both?"

I froze at his words. It wasn't like when Leo said he loved me, but the intention was just as clear. Only, unlike the last time, I didn't know if I could say it back. I'd never thought about it, not really—until this year, I'd never considered that love might be important. But... didn't I love Auden? The warmth in my chest when he was near had to mean some-thing, and he'd been there for me in ways no one else could. He knew me better than anyone in the world, and I knew him. It was different from the passionate burning I'd felt with Leo, but it certainly wasn't less meaningful. Sometimes, in the depths of my heart, I was grateful Leo and I had never run away, if only because it meant I didn't have to lose Auden. Was that not love?

"The luckiest," I answered finally, and the way my heart lightened at his smile was confirmation enough. I let out a deep breath, utterly relaxed as his hand started moving in my hair once more. "Tell me more about this life of ours."

Auden was silent for a bit before speaking, and for a moment I was afraid I had invaded too much. "Well, make no mistake," he began at last, "things aren't easy. We're extremely busy."

I huffed out something that might have been a laugh. "Of course we are."

"But we always make time for each other," he continued. "We eat dinner every night at five thirty, but it isn't tense and awful like our dinners were growing up. It's filled with laughter, and jokes, and fun." He paused, as if imagining it. I did the same, feeling almost warm inside. "On the bad days, when things are hard, we sit by the fire in the parlor. Sometimes we talk through it, allowing each other to alleviate the pain. Other times we just sit there in silence, watching the flames together."

"Even during the heat of summer?" I quipped, raising my brows. "Seems impractical."

"Even then," he insisted. "Our home will always be warm. Always."

I hummed in agreement. Considering Auden had lived in the objectively cold Bonavich manor for eighteen years, I could accept that. Anything that separated him from those horrible people, anything that eased the pain I'd just heard in his voice... I would do it, no questions asked.

"We have children, of course." His voice had grown distant, as if he were talking to himself. In a way, I supposed he was—reverted back to his childhood mindset, wishing for a better future. "Two boys and one girl."

"Only one girl?" I sat up so we were at the same level, fixing him with a glare. "What if I want two girls?"

"Hey, it's just what I wanted as a child." His voice was placating, a hint of amusement at the edge of his tone. "I wanted a brother, so I figured our son would as well."

"Well, I always wanted all girls," I retorted, crossing my arms.

"Should I be offended?" He quirked a brow, still smiling slightly.

"I was a child, too," I reminded him. "Boys were gross and scary."

"But not me?" he all but whispered, leaning in slightly. "Was I scary?"

"Not you," I answered immediately, voice growing gentle. We were close now, so close I could feel the heat of his breath on my face. "Never you."

And then he was moving towards me, lips coming closer and closer, and every part of my mind screamed at me to stay still, and yet...

"Wait," I breathed into the dimness.

His lips paused, but he remained close, those tantalizing blue eyes startlingly close to my own. "What's wrong?" he asked, voice so soft and *broken* that I almost took it back, almost moved towards him once more.

"Let's wait," I whispered. "Until the ceremony, when we're Paired. It's... it's improper." I tried to ignore his warm breaths upon my face, upon my neck.

"I think we've abolished all sense of propriety already," he pointed out, eyes searching my own for an answer to his unspoken question. "*What is it, really?*"

I'm not over Leo yet.

I couldn't bring myself to say the words, to admit the weakness. My eyes teared up at my body's betrayal. *He killed my parents—and I'm still not over him.*

"Can this be one of those days you were talking about?" I answered, voice breaking slightly as tears pricked the back of my eyes. "The ones where we just watch the flames?"

His eyes lit up with understanding, and he nodded quickly. "Yeah, Lo. We can watch the flames." He hugged me close to his chest, and I breathed a little easier. Auden was my rock, and I couldn't afford to lose that.

When we're Paired, it'll be different, I reminded myself. We'd have the life he spoke of one day. And yet, the thought did nothing to stop the weight that seemed to hover over my chest, threatening to crush me entirely.

"We should sleep," I forced out, turning away awkwardly. "Our final assessment is tomorrow."

"Yeah, alright," Auden replied. "Good night, Lo."

"Good night." The word was a whisper into the darkness, a quiet prayer to have just that: a good night, free from the terrors of my dreams. It was little use. I still awoke frequently, utterly convinced we were in great danger. It was with great relief that I awoke the next morning to a rising sun, an escape from the agonizing darkness.

23

——— • ———

READY OR NOT

Waking was only a partial escape, the weight upon my chest pressing down harder than ever as I swam into consciousness. I sighed as I forced my body to sit up, awake, but more exhausted than ever. I couldn't help but wonder when it would get better, when I would wake up with anything other than weary despair. *When I would wake up and see anything other than my parents' faces.*

"Hey, Auden?"

He stirred beside me, and it occurred to me suddenly that perhaps I should have checked if he was also awake before speaking. "Yeah?" he replied, voice groggy.

"Do you still... see him? Your father?"

Auden groaned, rolling over to face me. "Good morning to you, too."

I blushed at his words. "Sorry."

"No, it's fine." Auden pushed himself up beside me, in all his morning glory. It was strange, seeing him this disheveled. Strange ... but not bad. There was something appealing about the disarray, the way his tousled hair seemed to flop in front of his eyes. Perhaps it reminded me of a simpler time, when we were younger and far more carefree. *Perhaps it reminds me of someone else entirely.*

"It's just not what I expected to hear first thing in the morning, that's all," he continued. "Usually I save the dead father talk for *after* breakfast."

"Do you, though?" I pressed, mind too stuck on the topic to appreciate his joking. "See him?"

"In some ways," Auden admitted softly. His eyes were on me, but I could sense that his mind was somewhere else entirely. "More than I'd care to admit."

"Yeah," I replied, guilt twisting my gut. "Me, too."

It was their faces that floated through my mind as I dressed absent-mindedly, mind anywhere but on the assessment ahead of me. Winning the Pathway, becoming Sovereign... It all seemed so small now, insignificant compared to all that had passed.

It was only Risa's assistance that kept me from looking like an utter slob, all motivation regarding my appearance abandoned. It didn't help that each step of the process reminded me of my mother. I couldn't help but wonder what today would be like if she were here, helping me prepare instead of Risa. No doubt I would have grumbled the entire time, endlessly irritated with her presence. Tears welled in my eyes at the realization, at the knowledge that I would do anything to feel that presence once more. Overbearing as she was, my mother had never failed to calm me with her sureness. That sense of security, the knowledge that everything would be alright—it was long gone. If anything, I had a distinct sense that nothing would be alright at all. I was to enter a life of pretty lies and ugly decisions, floating alone at sea with only Auden to hold onto.

"All done, miss," Risa piped up from behind me. "You look perfect. Like a true Sovereign."

I glanced at myself in the mirror, hair braided back elegantly. Makeup dusted my face, heavy enough to cover my flaws, but light enough to suggest I wasn't wearing any at all. Risa had managed to dress up the boring mandated attire, somehow transforming it into a far more intimidating ensemble. She was right: I did look like the next Sovereign.

If only I could feel like it, too.

I wondered if Auden felt as unprepared as I did. He certainly didn't appear to. He seemed ready as I met him in the front hall, as focused and concentrated as I'd ever seen him. I wondered for the millionth time why I couldn't be more like him, composed no matter what the circumstances.

"Are you ready for this?" he asked, taking my hand as we walked. It felt nice—warm, secure.

"Are you?" I countered, partially to deflect the question and partially out of curiosity.

"Ready as I'll ever be," he replied, dimples appearing as he grinned. I didn't reply, offering a noncommittal grunt instead. I certainly didn't feel as ready as I'd ever be; in fact, I had half a mind to ask to postpone the whole thing.

"And you?" Auden pressed, not taking my grunt as an answer.

"Ready for it to be over." It was the truth; if there was anything I was happy about, it was the fact that this whole competition would be done soon.

"I suppose," Auden responded lightly. "Although I don't imagine things will get easier for a long while."

"What do you mean?" I wished I could say my voice didn't shake at the thought.

"Well," he continued, regarding me carefully, "whichever one of us is Sovereign will be under an immense amount of pressure. Right now, no one knows where to turn, with no definitive Council or Sovereign. They're disorganized, and that's not to mention the brewing rebellion. But when the confusion settles, that's when the chaos will begin, mark my words. I mean, you saw that slogan yesterday." Auden shook his head as he spoke, voice far too casual for the words exiting his mouth. "Honestly, this will feel easy compared to what's to come."

I gulped at his words. As much as I hated to believe it, he made a valid point. This was far from over. My chest constricted at the thought, breathing suddenly quite difficult.

The Dead Rise In Us.

The panic only intensified as we drew closer to the Cathe, heart pounding increasingly fast. A sharp wave of nausea overcame me as we entered, as we passed the room of the battle. The doors were open, and I stopped abruptly.

No, no, no... Not here.

The marble was still stained red with the blood of those whom I had seen here only days ago, those whom I saw fall *down down down*. I gasped for air, gulping in gusts that didn't seem to satisfy the burn in my throat as acid crawled up it, scraping against my insides in an attempt to escape from the horrors of this place.

Not here not here not here...

"Willow?" Auden was calling beside me, shaking my arm lightly. "Willow, what is it?"

My head shook rapidly, *right left right left.* "I-I can't," I choked out, "not here."

A hand landed on my shoulder, guiding me gently to the floor. "Here," Auden soothed me, rubbing my shoulders, *right left right left.* "Why don't you sit down."

I stumbled to sitting, only to be interrupted by a scream.

My own scream.

"No!" I shouted, launching off the floor as if it were on fire. There I was, crouched on the diamond pattern and holding my hands to my mother's neck, watching in slow motion rewind as her breaths slowed *down down down* then stopped, and her blood turned cold as ice—

"Willow!" I snapped back to reality at the feeling of hands on my face, gripping tightly enough that I couldn't fall, couldn't go down like Quinn, sword through her gut. "What in the world is wrong?" Auden's voice floated into my vision, and I shook my head suddenly, tearing the hands from my face.

"My dream," I sputtered, suddenly quite dizzy. "They're here."

It didn't make much sense, even to my oxygen-deprived brain, but Auden seemed to get the point. He swore softly, running a frustrated hand through his hair before turning to a nearby guard. "Close those doors, now."

My chest slowly began to inflate with oxygen once more, and I began to feel quite silly. "It's fine. I'm fine."

"Clearly," Auden muttered, guiding me carefully to a different ballroom, where the competition would be held.

Neither of us had time to say anything more as the room grew increasingly crowded. Hordes of "well-wishers" approached us, some seeming genuinely sorry and others hoping to gain information. I kept hold of Auden's hand as he handled the conversations, his calmness my only lifeline in the sea of people. It seemed like ages before a monotone voice rang out, silencing the crowd.

"Hello," a man said, standing center stage where Councilman Mullerson once had. "This is the final round of the Pathway to Perfection competition, in which all disciplines will be integrated. This assessment will determine the future Sovereign of Atvas."

My heart twinged at the blandness, at the loss of a certain announcer. Councilman Mullerson may have been irritating, but he didn't deserve to go like that. Bile tainted my throat at the memory of his merry face, frozen in an everlasting scream as he fell. Whoever had arranged this new announcer, they'd done a poor job of replacing him.

"Ready," the man onstage said steadily, "set ... go!" He stepped back, and chaos erupted.

I glanced at Auden where he stood, seemingly as confused as I was. He peered at the crowd from under furrowed brows, evaluating as they moved. The spectators were leading the charge, dragging their chairs hurriedly to the corners of the room. Clearly, they had been given some instruction that we had not, for the rest of the participants looked as perplexed as we did.

Auden started forward beside me, and I followed without question. As the chairs were moved, a picture was slowly emerging: arrows, drawn on the floor in faint lines of paint. There were three of different sizes and colors, all pointing towards a different exit from the room. I gaped at them, mind still not entirely caught on to the fact that this was happening.

I knew I should choose an arrow, should at least do *something*, but I was frozen in place. Frozen in place, because *it wasn't right.* This wasn't how it was supposed to happen. There was supposed to be a speech—an annoying speech by an annoyingly cheerful man. There were supposed to be rules, a name for the test, anything at all to guide us in the assessment. I was supposed to feel ready, was supposed to be confident in my abilities and training. I was supposed to have support on the sidelines, a best friend and mother and father cheering me on. My whole life had been spent imagining this moment—*and it wasn't supposed to be like this.*

I was jarred out of my thoughts by a body colliding with mine, sending me tumbling to the ground. I yelled out in surprise, glaring up at whoever had knocked me over, only they had already moved on. In fact, nearly everyone had. Only a few other participants remained in the room, the walls of spectators seeming to close in on us. I had an abrupt feeling that if we didn't choose soon, they just might. I cursed inwardly. I should have watched where the others went, should have followed Auden and Amaris. But now there was no one left to follow, no one to tell me what to do. There was only me, and what little sanity I had left.

I gulped in a breath, studying the floor carefully. Three arrows: one blue and thin, one red and large, and a yellow one in between. *Primary colors,* a voice whispered unhelpfully in my head. As if that would do me any good. I swallowed slowly, dashing in the direction of the small blue arrow without a further thought—because if there was anything I knew about Atvas, it was that the smallest things could make all the difference.

The exit led down a back hallway of the Cathe, one I hadn't been in since childhood. My heart raced as I ran down the hall, the door at the end a beacon that called to me. The walls seemed to shift and change, swimming along with the rest of my vision as I gasped for breath. Every muscle in my body screamed at me to stop, to rest for just one minute, but I ignored them. It seemed like hours had passed as I crashed through the door, although it couldn't have been more than a minute or two.

I practically fell into the space beyond, skidding to a stop as I took in the chaos surrounding me. The small office was filled with other participants, some searching the room, some pouring out the door opposite me. Many were simply standing, tearing open blue envelopes and reading the contents. I spotted a head of brown disappearing out of the opposite door: Auden. He already had his letter, then. I gritted my teeth against the pounding in my head—yet another sign that my body was done with this insane day. A body bumped into me from behind, and I realized with a start that others were still trickling into the room. Dazed, I moved out of the way, beginning a half-hearted search for a blue envelope with little luck.

The atmosphere grew increasingly tense with each failed attempt to find a letter, the others murmuring about the lack of envelopes and *maybe there weren't enough for everyone.* Just then, the girl to my right jerked, rushing in a way that could only mean one thing: she'd found an envelope. I wasn't the only one who noticed, a fact made clear by the stampede in our direction. Yet only from my vantage point did I find myself able to see it: a light blue envelope, tucked discreetly into the corner of the bookshelves beside us. It seemed to glow in the dim light, a final beacon of hope.

We reached for it at the same time, her fingers inching just ahead of mine, and I knew I wouldn't make it, knew I was too slow—and then it happened. As though of its own accord, my other arm reached out from my side, pushing her just hard enough to throw her off balance, and then it was *mine.* I gripped the paper tightly, hardly caring if it got crumpled as I sprinted towards the door. I slammed it closed behind me, shutting out the sharp shout of "That's not fair!"

What just happened? I wondered to myself, braced against the wall of the hall beyond as air rasped out of my chest. *Did I just ... cheat?* Could it even be called cheating, when there were no rules in the first place? I opened the envelope with shaky hands, ignoring the screaming guilt inside me as I ripped out the paper within.

Congratulations!

If you are reading this, you are one of the cleverest members of your partic-ipating class. You have demonstrated Intellect, both in picking the correct path and finding this letter.

Sure, I thought uncomfortably, *because it sure took a lot of Intellect to shove a girl.* I shook the thought from my head before continuing. If I was going to fight for this chance, I should at least use it.

Yet the assessment has only just begun. This is a race to the finish, comprised of elements of all disciplines. There is no time limit, but know this: only the first-place member will win a full amount of points, so do not dally. Follow the blue arrow to continue to your next obstacle.

The words were enough to spur me onward, down the hallway and to the next room. I took in a deep breath and cracked the door open slightly, mentally steeling myself against whatever chaos I would find inside.

24

——— • ———

POINT OF NO RETURN

The room was practically empty, a dining table set up in the center. A woman sat at one end, a man at the other. On the sides sat a young girl, perhaps nine years old, a teenage boy, and a crying toddler. They all appeared to be arguing, the plates of food forgotten as they shouted at each other. I would have questioned my sanity altogether if it weren't for the final member of the room. Only one boy around my age stood at the other side—another participant, with a distressed look upon his face.

"No, don't argue!" he exclaimed. "I don't understand!"

Just then, the man stood up from the table and grabbed the boy's shoulders, steering him to a third door on the side of the room. "You have failed," the man said. "Please return to the finish line and await the end of the race."

The participant disappeared, leaving me alone with the chaotic family scene. The man returned to his seat, snapping his fingers as he sat. The others ceased arguing at once, sitting up straight and falling silent almost immediately. Even the toddler stopped crying, the woman bribing him with something I couldn't see. It was eerie, the way they sat up so straight and silent, but I forced myself to enter anyhow. They didn't look at me as the door snapped shut, but rather began speaking to each other.

"How was your day, darling?" the woman asked, a tight smile on her face.

The man glanced up from the half-eaten ravioli he'd begun to consume, grunting. "It was fine. The usual."

The boy beside him rolled his eyes, muttering something under his breath.

"What was that?" the man asked, voice hard. "Speak up, boy."

The air seemed to grow tense, and I cursed inwardly. I wasn't sure what exactly I was supposed to be doing, but I was fairly sure keeping them from arguing was part of it.

"Nothing," the boy mumbled, and I blew out a breath. The sharp pain that had taken up residence in my chest loosened a bit, though not enough to lengthen my pants of breath. Thoughts and emotions sped through my brain far faster than I could handle, and it was all I could do to keep my attention on the conversation in front of me. I eyed the door across the room. If I ran through it, would they stop me? Perhaps this was meant to be a distraction, and by taking part in it, I would fail.

"That's not true," the little girl pointed out, and I tensed, my attention snapping back to the table. "You did say something, I heard it."

The boy glared at the girl, the man and woman exchanging a long glance.

"Mary, honey," the woman said, "What did your brother say?"

It was then that I noticed the empty chair beside the little girl—more accurately, the empty place setting in front of it. I was moving without another thought, sliding into the seat before the conversation could worsen any further. It was either the right thing to do, or very wrong, for they all looked at me at last. I waited for them to speak, to give me a clue about what to do next, but there was only silence.

"Sorry I'm late," I said at last, voice shaky and unsure. I wished my head would stop hurting for a moment, if only so I could *think*.

"Where were you?" the woman asked, clearly the mother figure. "We were worried."

Perhaps it was the pain in my head, or the emotion of the past week, or maybe this woman was just too good of an actress, but I couldn't keep my eyes from welling up. "Got distracted on the walk home," I choked out, keeping the excuse vague, since I had little clue who I was supposed to be. "How was everyone's day?" I asked, directing the question first to the boy.

He seemed to perk up, as if no one had bothered to ask him that in quite some time. "It wasn't half bad," he replied, before spinning into an amusing tale about his day of classes. The entire family was engaged, even the father laughing once or twice. I looked around at the group, this fake family that wasn't mine, and a piece of my heart broke. For just a moment, I wished it were real. I wished I were simply eating dinner, with siblings and parents who still breathed. With people who cared for me, who would protect and guide me.

"Ba ba!" the toddler babbled from across the table, laughing. This seemed to trigger something, for the table suddenly went silent. They returned to their initial position, backs straight and faces bland. The father stood, gesturing for me to stand as well. I did so shakily, still reeling from the sudden change in atmosphere.

"Congratulations," the man stated, the previous fatherly tone of voice forgotten. "You have shown abilities in both Service and Aesthetics, by sensing the family's needs and acting as a character to fulfill them. Continue on through this door." He led me to the door opposite the one I'd entered through, opening it and guiding me into the following hallway. I wiped the moisture from my eyes as the door clicked shut behind me, steadying myself with a breath. I continued on with as much vigor as I could muster, jogging raggedly down the short hall and wondering for the hundredth time why I hadn't postponed this assessment.

The next room brought familiar faces once more. There were six people in the room besides me: Amaris, Emmaline, two other participants whom I recognized vaguely from my childhood, an older Court member, and … Auden. They were all speaking at once, practically shouting over each other at the Court member. Only Auden refrained from such behavior, speaking quietly and calmly. Yet it was to him the woman listened, nodding slowly along with his whispered words. She turned, unlocking the door behind her. By the time the door clicked shut behind me, Auden's head was disappearing through the doorway parallel to me. The woman shut the door behind her, ignoring the words of the other participants as she fixed her eyes on me.

"Willow Aldridge," she spoke softly, a soft tenderness in her eyes that I couldn't help but despise. *Pity.* "Why should I allow you to pass? *Convince me.*"

It all made sense then: Auden's success, Amaris's lack of it, the desperation of the other participants to be heard. This was made to test our Charisma, to see how we used our strengths and weaknesses in a persuasive environment. I could think of a million ways to win this woman over: my status, her pity, every little weakness of hers that years of Charisma training had taught me to detect. And yet … I couldn't find the energy for all of that, not with the pounding of my head and exhaustion deep in my soul. For once I didn't bother with strategic wording; for once, I told the truth.

"Because my parents are dead," I said plainly, "and so is every adult who helped raise me. My best friend is soon to be cast out, and I haven't had a good night of sleep in over a week." The room fell silent, all eyes latched onto my words. Emmaline met my eyes, but I couldn't find the energy to decode her expression.

"Very well," the woman conceded, voice heavy with sympathy. She reached for her keys and unlocked the door. "You may pass."

The door swung open behind her, wide enough for me to pass through, but not so wide that the others could see through. I walked towards it slowly, floating like a ghost towards the light beyond. A foreboding feeling settled in my chest, as if there were something awful beyond. The feeling only intensified as I stepped into the hallway, the wallpaper old and the lights dim. I knew where this hallway led; I had run down it only last month, at the first assessment when all this began. How excited I'd been then, how certain of everything. That Willow would make a good Sovereign. This Willow... I wasn't so sure.

It wasn't supposed to be like this.

The door to the Olden theater appeared far too fast for my liking, looming in front of me like an omen.

Only Legality was left to be tested in this assessment, the remaining discipline to determine. My stomach protested violently as my hand landed on the doorknob, twisting in a way that suggested I would be better off running in the other direction. I ignored it, thrusting the door open before I could convince myself otherwise.

I was met with a frenzy of noise. It appeared all the spectators had migrated here, leaving the small theater overflowing. The stage was left empty, one lone figure standing smack center: Auden.

"Willow Aldridge." The room fell silent. The announcer from earlier stood just in front of the stage, extending a sword in my direction—a *real* sword, sharp metal glinting in the light. "Come retrieve your weapon, then join Mr. Bonavich on the stage."

My head pounded in time with my heart, twinging sharply with each step towards the weapon. The shine of the metal assaulted my senses, reminding me of screaming and panic and death. I was no less afraid of the weapon than I'd been before the massacre, but I no longer had the luxury of ignoring it. My hands shook as I took the sword, every inch of my body screaming to stay far away. I weighed it carefully as I ascended the steps to the stage. It felt awkward in my hands, heavy and foreboding. A clatter sounded, and I realized suddenly that I had dropped it. My cheeks grew heated as I rushed across the stage to retrieve it from where it had slid by Auden's feet.

"The rules are simple," the announcer stated, voice sounding almost bored. "At the sound of the bell, you will spar. The goal is to keep yourself on stage, and to get your opponent off the stage. Whoever remains on stage will win this assessment, and..." He rustled through some papers in front of him, as if double-checking something. "Yes: because your scores are so close, whoever remains on stage will win the Pathway to Perfection!"

Excited murmurs spread through the crowd—as if everyone didn't know it would end like this. Auden and me, fighting for the Sovereignty. As if it ever had a chance of ending any other way.

Auden caught my eyes, staring straight into my soul as if sending me a message. "I'm sorry," he said aloud. "I don't have a choice."

And there it was, that ugly truth: neither of us had a choice. We never had. It was inevitable that we would end up here, rivals despite it all. I smiled softly, because if there was anyone in the world I didn't mind being my rival, it was Auden.

"I know," I replied softly even as my stomach clenched again. A wave of nausea sending acid up my throat. Auden's brows furrowed, eyes scanning me as he seemed to take in my state.

"Are you alright?" he asked, as if this were a normal day and we were having a normal conversation. I almost laughed at the thought. Here we were, about to start our final battle, and Auden was asking if I was alright. It was just so... Auden.

"No." I laughed, because I couldn't be bothered to care about the spectators. "I'm not."

And then the bell rang, and it began.

"You need to rest after this," Auden said, beginning to circle me. I mirrored the action, forcing my arm to lift the sword to attention. I suddenly wished that I'd paid any attention at all when the instructors taught the rest of the class how to spar. I still stood a chance, though, for as little as I had learned about swordplay, I had learned an awful lot about dodging. Besides, Leo's lessons had taught me how to move my body in a fight. Even if the weapon was different, the steps were the same. I was quicker than Auden, lighter on my feet. All I'd have to do was get him to swing close enough to the edge.

"I'm fine." The words were short and harsh.

Auden's eyes flitted to my wrists, noting the way the sword shook in my weakened grip with a raised brow.

Gritting my teeth, I forced myself to tighten my grip. It didn't help; if anything, the sword seemed to shake more. Then Auden struck, sword swinging towards my left side. I jumped to my right out of reflex; I'd moved much closer to the front of the stage. He took the opportunity to move where I had stood previously, facing me as he swung again, high and close enough that I would need to back up to avoid the swing. I ducked it instead, taking the time of the swing to move behind him.

"Nice," he admitted—and it was. I didn't know how, but I'd managed to force Auden to near the front of the stage, with me behind him.

Apparently, the years of dance I'd been forced to take had done some good after all. At least for a moment, I had the advantage.

"I didn't even realize you could hold a sword now," Auden added, nodding towards the weapon.

"It's new," I replied, my voice sounding muffled, as if spoken through a tunnel. "I wish I couldn't." It was the truth; the days when I couldn't hold a sword were simple. If I could go back, reverse the events of the past week, I would have done it in a heartbeat—even if it meant I couldn't hold a sword, couldn't fight in this assessment. I'd give it all, the Sovereignty and all that came with it, for one more day with those I'd lost.

Auden swung again, the motion effectively snapping me out of my daze. I brought up my sword to stop it, managing to meet his strike with my own. A jolt went through me with the force of the collision, sending me to the ground. I fell with a shout, my sword clattering out of my hand and across the floor once more. I lunged towards it, the stage scraping my knees as I threw my body over it—too slow. By the time my hand landed where the sword had been, it was gone, now in Auden's hand.

I cursed aloud, scurrying to my feet as Auden approached, both swords in hand. I backed up as far as I could until I was practically on the edge of the stage. There was no way to recover. *I've lost.*

For some reason, the thought didn't fill me with agony. If anything, I felt a hint of ... relief.

"Here," Auden said softly, smiling tightly as he extended my sword. "Take it."

I stared at him, scanning him carefully. "Why?"

"I don't want to win a skewed fight," he replied, a strange tone to his voice. "Now we're even."

And that was the difference between Auden and his father, when it came down to it. Auden was serious, competitive, and sometimes even intense. But at his base, he was also fair—something his father had never been. It was one of the things I admired most about him.

"Thanks," I breathed, and then he was on me again. He swung low at my feet, and I jumped over the sword with an agility I wasn't aware I possessed. I was only half aware of my actions as I landed, my body screaming in complaint at the motion. Mostly, I was in my thoughts, because something about Auden's words bothered me.

"We're even," he'd said—but it wasn't the truth. It wasn't fair that Auden could lose the Pathway despite the years he'd spent practicing his swordplay, just because he had the honor to hand me a sword. It wasn't fair that I was up here at all, when I'd skated by in this assessment on luck alone. It wasn't fair that he was going into this with as little sleep as I was because I'd kept him up all night with my screaming. None of it was fair. Yet he handled it so *well*, the eternal calm to my storm.

"I really am sorry," Auden said quietly, bringing me back to the present. "More than you know."

He had his wrist held back, sword prepped for a strike I would be hard pressed to deflect. My back was to the audience, my feet teetering at the very edge of the stage. The sword in my hand would do little good, considering I had no clue how to use it. I could likely dodge it again, but what was the point? Was I really going to be able to win this fight? If so, was that really what I wanted? My head was pounding, my legs were shaking, and my stomach was laden with acid. I didn't want to roll, or dodge, or fight. I certainly didn't want to hurt Auden. And, if I were honest with myself, I didn't really want to be Sovereign.

I didn't want to lie to my people all the time, didn't want to relive that damn battle every day, didn't want to choose between bad and worse for the rest of my life. For once, I wanted someone else to take the burden. *Take the pressure.* And so, as Auden swung, as the blade crossed towards my shoulders, just high enough to duck under, I made a hard decision—hopefully, the last of the sort I would ever need to make. A decision to end all decisions.

I stepped back, one foot following the other.

I stepped back, off the stage.

I stepped back—and just like that, Auden Bonavich was the next Sovereign of Atvas.

25

THE MOMENT AFTER

I wish I could say I didn't regret it, after. I wish I could say there was never a moment of doubt, that I knew the whole time that I had made the right decision—but that would be a lie. I regretted it the moment my feet hit the cold ground, the minute the crowd recovered from their shock enough to cheer. But there was a hint of relief, too, buried deep beneath the layers of exhaustion and disappointment, and that was enough. Enough to force myself off the ground, to let the smile come to my face as Auden's face lit up. If anyone deserved to be Sovereign, it was him.

Of course, it still hurt. It hurt when the cheers sounded, the crowd rushing towards him. It hurt when they brushed by me with their half-hearted condolences, pushing past me to congratulate him on his finesse, on fighting the odds and managing to beat me after all. I had half a mind to scream the truth, to tell them that I *chose* this—but it wouldn't have helped. If anything, it would make everything worse. I was watching Amaris congratulate him, the sight leaving a bitter taste on my tongue, when a voice sounded from beside me.

"Huh," Emmaline said, arms crossed. "I always figured it'd be you."

I glanced over at her, noting the expression on her face with no small amount of surprise. She actually seemed ... sincere.

"Really? Always thought you figured it'd be yourself," I murmured, but with none of the usual bite. I didn't have the energy.

"Yeah, right," she replied, tone implying that was the dumbest thing she'd ever heard. "As if any of us had a chance."

"Why, then?" I pressed, tearing my eyes from Auden at least. "What was the point of the pettiness, the cheating? To make Auden win?"

"I didn't cheat, Willow." She sounded exhausted, an annoyed edge to her voice that implied she was done with the topic. "And don't lecture me about pettiness, as if you're any better." I bit my lip; she had a point there. I supposed we were both immature—children, really. The whole spat seemed like ages ago now. A different life. "Trust me, we all wanted you to win."

I raised my brows, inclining my head to the line of people waiting to speak with him. "Really?" I said pointedly, "is that so?"

"Leeches," she scoffed, "the whole lot of them." I quirked a brow in question, and she sighed. "They were rooting for you. We all were."

"Well, that didn't happen." I kicked awkwardly at the ground, suddenly feeling worse than I already had. Nothing like finding out you let everyone down to lower your spirits. "I lost."

"You gave up." My head shot up at the words; how did she know? Emmaline rolled her eyes. "I was in the audience, Willow. I'm not blind."

"Did everyone see?" If everyone knew, I would have created an even bigger mess than I knew. Atvas would be torn, half believing I should be Sovereign, and half supporting Auden. They wouldn't trust his leadership, and they certainly wouldn't respect me. There would be no good solution.

"Doubt it. Luckily for you, they *are* blind," Emmaline confirmed, and I breathed out a sigh of relief. "Still a dumb move, though."

My cheeks heated. "You have no clue what I've been through—"

"Yes, I know," Emmaline cut in, tone exasperated. "Parents dead, not sleeping, bad best friend… I heard the whole sob story in the Charisma room, remember?" I frowned at her summary of my anguish. "Still," she continued, "doesn't mean you should give up."

I laughed aloud. This was insane—absolutely *insane.* "Am I hallucinating right now?"

"No." Emmaline patted my shoulder, leaning in close as if sharing a piece of very important information. "You're just dramatic."

"You hate me," I reminded her. "You should be happy."

"Like I said: dramatic." Emmaline rolled her eyes again, and I wondered vaguely if it were possible for a person's eyes to get stuck like that. If anyone's could, it would be Emmaline's. "I've never hated you, Willow. *You* hated *me*. It's not my fault I'm not willing to lay down and take it."

Perhaps it was due to the aching in my head, but absolutely none of this made sense to me. "You seemed happy enough to agitate me," I contended. "You insulted me constantly."

"Well, that was just some good old verbal sparring." She flashed a bright smile at me, cheeky yet endearing. "Everyone knows sparring with the best makes you better."

I couldn't help the laughter that bubbled out of my chest. It was sort of flattering, if I didn't think about it too hard. "You're not too bad yourself," I admitted truthfully. "A worthy contender."

"Oh, I know."

We watched the crowd in silence for a few moments, the events effectively sobering our expressions.

"Listen, Willow," Emmaline spoke softly, glancing around carefully. "I don't know who rescheduled this, but it's unfair. That never should have been decided without your input. Maybe if you bring that up, you can fight for a redo."

"What, hoping for another chance to beat me?" I joked, attempting a grin, but falling flat. Emmaline just sent a sharp look in my direction, one suggesting that she knew exactly what I was doing and would take no part. I sighed. "I'll think about it."

"Good," Emmaline stated. "You may be dramatic, but I'll take that over him any day." And then she was gone, disappearing into the crowd. I watched her go, frowning as I thought over her words. I'd thought Emmaline had no issues with Auden—or at least, less than she had with me. In fact, it had been Emmaline who I'd always resented Auden for defending. And what she'd said, about the others—*"everyone was rooting for you."* But that couldn't be right. Everyone always loved Auden, adored him even when he was stuck in number two. If anything, people supported me for my heritage alone.

"Hey."

I jumped, too deep in my thoughts to have noticed Auden's approach. He stood awkwardly in front of me, shifting guiltily from foot to foot.

"Hi," I replied softly, mustering up as much fake excitement as possible. "Congratulations." I could tell from the pity on Auden's face that it wasn't convincing. "You deserve it." That, at least, was the truth.

"I'm so sorry." Auden's voice was heavy, apologetic. "I honestly didn't know that last swing would knock you over the edge. I didn't even realize it did until ... after."

I tensed. I'd just assumed Auden, at least, had seen what happened. A part of me had hoped he would—hoped that he, at least, would know the truth.

"It's fine." I shrugged, pushing a half-smile to my face. "Only one of us could win, right?"

Auden watched me carefully for a moment before nodding, face solemn. "Only one of us could win, but I meant what I said before. I can't do this without you."

The proclamation did make me feel a little better. I didn't need all the attention—not as long as I was still a part of the decisions.

"I already have so many ideas!" Auden grinned excitedly, eyes growing lighter now that he knew I wasn't angry with him. "Like, what if instead of…"

And so it went, all evening long. I listened more than I spoke, letting Auden's excitement soothe my worries. I had to admit, it felt nice to have the pressure off of me. When the Council members banged on the door, Auden was the one who had to reply. When they had questions, he was the one who had to answer them. It was exactly what I needed to relax after the horrors of the day, settling my stomach and easing my headache slightly. By the time I drifted off to sleep, Auden's arm around my shoulders and my mind finally calmed, any thoughts of Emmaline's suggestion were out of my mind completely.

***

Saturday morning brought a strange tension, despite the peaceful feeling of Auden's arms around me. I shoved the unease down as I pushed myself up, staring deep into my own eyes in the mirror that stood by the bed.

My reflection seemed to glare back at me, as if I had performed a terrible betrayal. *"Of course you're nervous,"* it sneered in my head, *"you're throwing away everything we've worked for."* Somehow, the voice sounded a lot like my mother's.

The thought sent chills running down my body, and I stared at my mirror-self, transfixed. I hardly noticed as a heavy arm wrapped around my shoulders, and blue eyes appeared behind my reflection.

"Are you alright?" Auden asked, voice rumbling against the quiet of the morning.

"Don't do this," my mirror-self begged.

"Of course," I said, mentally pushing the mirror-self aside.

"Then let's do this." The voice was powerful, regal—the voice of a true Sovereign. "Together." I smiled at the addition, at the security implied, at the knowledge that no matter what, I would never be alone.

"Just like we always have," I amended, and he smiled so bright that it seemed to clear all unease from the room.

"And just like we always will." The vow simmered in the air, far more powerful than those we were to swear at the ceremony. There was a binding weight to the words as they settled around us, as if finally confirming something I'd always known. The feeling comforted me throughout the morning, chasing away the thoughts that threatened to unseat me.

Risa appeared once again to assist me, although I already had my ceremony dress selected; I'd had it for months now, actually. It was traditional to wear white, so that the Court pins we would be given might shine even brighter. I had once heard it also had to do with ancient rituals of marriage, but I'd always assumed that was a rumor.

We were quiet as I dressed, the merry atmosphere of the past mornings painfully absent as she arranged my hair into an elegant updo. My thoughts filled the silence, oddly melancholy despite the excitement of the day.

"Two months more," I'd once reminded Auden, the day this insane competition began—as if today would be the end, the clue to finally solve some eternal puzzle. Today was supposed to mark the end of childhood,

the end of the innocence I knew I'd already lost the moment my parents' bodies were lowered into the ground. It was only a few days early, but somehow the difference seemed felt like a lifetime.

"Brighten up," Risa said, smiling gently as she pushed a final pin into my hair. "This is supposed to be *exciting*."

I blinked suddenly, refocusing my eyes on the image in the mirror. "I am excited," I murmured. Risa didn't dignify that with an answer, merely raising an eyebrow in doubt.

She was done in what seemed like minutes, leaving me alone with my awful thoughts. I leaned into the mirror, resting my forehead against it. The moisture of my breath lingered on the glass, warping my image until it resembled the mess that lay inside. More than anything else, I couldn't stop thinking how disappointed my mother would be. After all her hard work...

But what did it matter, really? The purpose was still being fulfilled: Auden was still stopping the murders.

The thought propelled me into movement, leading me through the motions of the day. By the time I met Auden by the front door, my nerves were fully under control and my mask fully in place—just in time to face the public.

We took the car to the ceremony, an ancient but fascinating thing. The experience was just as entertaining as I remembered, and I couldn't stop myself from staring out the window the entire time. The world seemed to fly by, staring faces appearing only to fade from view moments later. Auden didn't speak, simply watching me with an amused expression.

"You act as if this is the greatest invention ever made," he chuckled, eyes tracking my hands as they ran over the old leather of the seats.

I glared lightly back at him. "It is! This walk usually takes us triple the time," I rested my head against the cool glass, admiring the feel of it on my skin. "It's practically a miracle that they still work after all these years."

"Yes," Auden mumbled, "a miracle, indeed."

I frowned at the tang of bitterness in his tone, opening my mouth to ask about it as the car rolled to a stop outside the Cathe. Auden flung open his door suddenly, moving out of the car before I was able to do so much as blink. I frowned but followed suit, taking in the scene around us as I stood upright.

People streamed in from every direction, moving around us in an ever-steady flow. Some stopped to look at the car we emerged from, mainly children. One child in particular caught my eye, a little girl of six or seven. She peeked out shyly from behind her mother's body, eyes focused on me. I smiled at her, and her large brown eyes widened before disappearing back behind her mother.

"Shall we?"

I turned towards the steady hand that Auden extended towards me. I hesitated, staring at the hand as if transfixed. It was only a hand—the same hand I had held dozens of times throughout my life. And yet, it felt like so much more. To hold his hand here, in front of everyone... It sent a message that I had accepted the results of the Pathway, that I was ready to ascend to my expected place in society at Auden's side.

"For my soon-to-be wife," Auden said, a certain tone to his voice that urged me forward. I grasped his hand at last, my skin settling comfortably inside the coolness of his. We emerged in front of the platform as one, the pair we were always destined to become.

26

— · —

FRONT AND CENTER

We strode to our seats in a quiet sort of strength. We were to be seated in order of the most recently updated ranks, with the incoming Court at the front of the block, and those who would be cast out in the very back. I avoided looking towards them at all costs. As badly as I wanted to glance at Vi, I refused to see Leo until I absolutely had to. I knew he must see us, though. Some small, vicious part of me smiled at that small piece of revenge, the only repayment I had to offer.

It wasn't unusual to have a large crowd at a Pathway Ceremony, gathered to watch the eldest class emerge into adulthood, but this wasn't just any ceremony; it was a Coronation Ceremony. Everyone, it appeared, had come to see the new Sovereign sworn into office. An immense crowd was gathered, some sitting on blankets while others stood. A few people had even brought chairs, dragged from the nearest community facility or perhaps from their own homes. I caught Emmaline's eyes as I made my way to my seat, passing her number six chair with a cordial nod. She nodded back, but her eyes seemed to bore into my soul, judging it.

It's none of her business, I reminded myself. *You said you would think on it, and you did. Sort of.*

"Congratulations," Amaris said softly, nodding at me from her number three seat beside mine. "And I'm sorry about your parents. They were good people."

I didn't have the energy to deal with the emotions that statement brought up, to recall the long days playing with Amaris in the gardens and the times she'd stay for dinner. My mother had always liked her, had been especially sympathetic when the friendship ended. So I just smiled in return and muttered out a tired "Thank you."

The ceremony started at last, beginning with a long period of speeches. Meaningless words spewed from the mouths of meaningless people—people who knew nothing of what they discussed. The first-ranked participant from last year spoke, as well as some high-ranked members of the Court. My father would have given a speech, too, if he were alive. Instead, the man from yesterday gave a short speech of remembrance for those lost in the rebel attack. If I had been more careful in looking over the plans, I would have insisted they remove it, and for good reason.

"...the unfortunate events of the past week, and for them retribution will be sought," the man was saying, face blank and unmotivated. "It is our priority to ensure that justice is maintained in Atvas."

The crowd grew increasingly riled as he spoke, murmurs breaking out. Many glared at Leo, the weight of their grief shifted to their shoulders. I was painfully aware of the knowledge that I did that. It was our speech at the funeral that condemned him to this hatred. I sat in silence and tried not to watch, frozen in my seat as the crowd grew increasingly aggressive.

"You've got to stop this," I muttered to Auden, so quietly that no one but us could hear. "It's getting out of hand."

Auden glanced back then, surprise dawning on his face as if he hadn't even noticed the conflict. "I'm not in charge, Willow. Until the Coronation is performed, I have no power."

I bit my lip. He was right, and I hated it—hated this responsibility, this weight upon me for these last couple of minutes. For I wasn't in charge, either, but something had to be done.

Despite the thought, I couldn't bring myself to stand, frozen as the scene played out before me. No one was listening to the announcer, their attention turned instead towards the back. Vi had begun to intervene, hair whipping wildly as she tugged at her restraints. Both she and Leo had them, binding them to their chairs, as well as being surrounded by Legality guards that were doing nothing at the moment. Something curled in my stomach, a sharp stab of betrayal at her defense of Leo. I'd *told* her what he'd done. How could she still defend him?

A jolt of electricity struck my stomach as my eyes moved, latching on to the gaze of the one person I didn't want to see. Leo didn't pay the crowd any attention, sitting limply in his restraints with his eyes straight forward—on me. There was something so pained, so *bright* in his stare. For the first time in days, I felt a seed of doubt in my stomach. This was *Leo,* and I knew him. At least, I thought I did.

Suddenly his eyes disappeared, blocked from view as Oakley jumped in front of Leo. I spotted a head of blonde to his left, clinging to his leg with wide eyes. A muscle in my heart pulled at the sight, just as Oakley attempted to push a particularly angry man back. A sharp gasp echoed through the crowd as the man pushed Oakley aside and he fell into the dirt. The man on stage stopped speaking at last, as if finally realizing that something far more interesting was occurring. The people around me began to stand as well, peering around each other to see.

I jumped up at once and wove through the crowd, careful to stay far from the jumble of limbs and yells as I strode towards the guards.

"Stop this," I cried, "stop it now!"

The guards complied at the first sound of my voice, interfering at last. I couldn't help but breathe a sigh of relief as things calmed down, the crowd forced to relent. My hand was moving before I even realized it, extending to help Oakley up. He knocked it aside, glaring viciously at me as he did so. My heart ached at the expression, and it was all I could do to stay composed as I returned to my seat. In all of my internal debates about Leo's future, I'd nearly forgotten that it wasn't just him who would be punished. I was casting out the Hayes' primary caregiver.

"Almost done," Auden murmured, laying an arm across my shoulders as I sat. "Just a bit longer."

At that very moment, I didn't envy Auden in the slightest. Most Coronation Ceremonies were peaceful, if a bit sad. But this one was shaping up to be the worst one in eight years.

The worst since that day, when the sky was so beautiful, and the screams were so loud...

I shivered despite the warmth of the air. Indeed, it was a bad ceremony, and a worse omen for the future. I couldn't remember a time when Atvas had been more unbalanced, more on the edge.

The man finished his speech quickly, clearly uncomfortable, and the calling of the ranks began in earnest. It started with the individual disciplines, beginning with Service and proceeding through the rest. The whole row was to stand, walking in a line to the side of the stage. Those not called by the end, after the first of each rank was announced, would be announced as cast out and line up to go to the boats. The whole thing was fairly efficient, borrowed from an old custom used to integrate adolescents into adulthood. Before I knew it, they had reached the Pathway participants, and then it was us being ushered to stand. I followed Auden, second to last in the line as they called the Pathway results. The names seem to go slower than with any other group, time stretching on impossibly long.

"Number three: Amaris Hewberry."

Amaris moved forward at last, faint clapping echoing in my ears as she received a pin and took her Court seat on the stage.

"And finally," the announcer continued, "number two..." My heart beat in my ears, blood rushing furiously as I waited. "Willow Aldridge."

I forced my feet forward, across the stage to the center. The clapping seemed a bit subdued, but perhaps that was merely my imagination. I shook the hand of the man who stood there, the monotone announcer from yesterday.

"Congratulations," he said flatly, pressing an envelope and pin into my hand. "May you live in the beauty of perfection."

I pressed my pin onto my dress quickly as I took a seat, marking me as an official member of the Atvasian Court. I'd always assumed this moment would feel like success, but really it felt like nothing.

"And now," the announcer boomed, "for the announcement of a generation."

I wondered vaguely why he bothered with so much suspense now. Clearly, Auden was the only one left. Indeed, dramatics was one of the things we had preserved from the Olden World.

"The winner of the Pathway to Perfection and the new Sovereign of Atvas is ... Auden Bonavich!"

The applause that followed was like salt in a wound, the sound pounding viciously into the uncertainty in my chest.

Still, I couldn't help but smile as Auden strode across the stage, face bright as the sun. He took in the crowd's reaction giddily, grinning like a child given candy, and I knew then that he had been hiding the depth of this desire for our entire lives. Auden Bonavich was built to charm, to shine, to *lead*.

"Do you, Auden Bonavich, swear to serve Atvas with dignity and honor?"

"I do." The words seemed to flow out of his mouth, without so much as a moment of trepidation. I wondered briefly if they would have come so easily to me, though I already knew the answer. It was the very reason I wasn't the one standing there now.

"Do you swear to protect each citizen as you would protect yourself?"

"I do."

"Do you accept the full responsibility of the Sovereignty, never to be broken until the next generation is named?"

Auden turned then, glancing to where I sat. I wondered briefly if it was for reassurance, but that wasn't uncertainty in his eyes. No, it was something much stronger than that.

"I do," he said, his eyes still on mine, and I stared blankly into the abyss of blue.

"I hereby name you Sovereign of the great Atvas, protector and defender of all its values. May you live in the beauty of perfection."

"May you live in the beauty of perfection," the crowd echoed back, a large chorus of voices that sounded strangely eerie to my disconcerted mind. Auden just stood there, arms wide as if soaking it all in.

The announcer spoke once more, voice echoing across the square. "Now, we will proceed with the Pairing ceremony. New members, please find the name listed in your Pairing envelope and stand directly facing each other."

I didn't need to open my envelope, but I did anyway, just to have something to do with my hands.

Auden Bonavich

I read the slip of paper quickly and emotionlessly before closing my palm around it. I had little need for it; I'd known what it would say my entire life. I smiled anyway, moving towards the center of the stage where Auden stood. He beamed at me, grabbing both my hands in his.

"We've done it!" His voice was exuberant, eyes wide with some sort of crazy adrenaline. "Look around, Willow. Paired, ruling Atvas together... it's exactly who we've always been destined to become."

It was precisely the same thought I'd had earlier that day, yet I resented it all the same. This may have been my choice, but I knew deep down it was not my destiny.

"I guess." The statement was terse, the type of passive-aggressive thing I might have once said to my mother.

Auden frowned, taking in my statement with a solemn sort of understanding. "I'm sorry if I'm being too much, I'm just..." His voice trailed off, and he gazed upon the crowd with a far-off look. He kissed both of my hands, staring me deep in the eyes. "Can't you see? That life of ours is starting at last."

My annoyance faded slowly, and I felt sillier by the moment. *What a whiny child I am, to get exactly what I asked for and pout all the same.*

"I suppose we'd better get the fire started," I replied, a small smile making its way to my face. It still felt foreign, but I forced it to stay anyhow. "For our questionably overheated house."

Auden grinned. "Don't worry, love. It's already burning."

Indeed, my chest was simmering from his steady warmth. *Love.* The name was a line drawn in the sand, a stark divide between the friends we'd been and the couple we were to become.

"Now, take your partners' hands," the announcer called, "and hold them in your own."

Auden extended his hands to me, brow raised in question. I took a deep breath and took them, effectively stepping over the line.

"May this be a bridge between you, through which you shall be bound for life," the announcer read. I glanced at Auden and couldn't help but smile at his eye roll. We had always made fun of this speech as children, and it appeared today would be no different.

"Now ladies, repeat after me: I—say your name—vow to bring children of the greatest quality into this world, and raise them in the beauty of perfection."

There was a high-pitched echo of voices, including my own, as we repeated his words.

"I swear to bring perfection into the position corresponding with my rank, and to ensure that my family brings value to Atvas."

We repeated these lines as well, giving a cordial nod at the finish.

"Now for the men, repeat the following: I—say your name—vow to protect and defend the honor and health of the children, so that they may be raised in the beauty of perfection."

Auden's deep voice rippled down my spine, and I realized then that this was really, truly *happening*.

"I swear to bring perfection into the position corresponding with my rank, and to ensure that my family brings value to Atvas."

The men repeated it once again, finishing with a nod as well.

"With these vows between you, I now pronounce you a Pair, from now until the end of this life. You will forever take on the family name of the highest-ranking member in the Pair."

A moment passed, and then it was done.

27

DOWN, DOWN, DOWN

"Mrs. Bonavich," Audèn murmured, bending to kiss my hand. I tried not to think of the crowd, of the Flawed who sat silently and watched these moments of intimacy. Of Leo, who stared from afar. I moved to brush my hair away from my face, but a gentle hand stopped me.

"Wait," Auden said, eyes roaming over my face. "Just ... stay still for a second."

I frowned. "Why?"

He just smiled, rubbing my hand with his thumb, and I grew suspicious.

"What are you doing?" I pressed, a faint blush growing on my cheeks.

"Just ... committing your face to memory." He gazed at me in a way that suggested he was doing just that. "There's nothing I wouldn't do to have you and me, just like this. I want to remember this moment for the rest of our lives."

"I think we can remember this without staring at each other." My voice was teasing, despite the swelling of my heart at his words. Today, yesterday... this whole week had been weird, some sort of strange nightmare that never seemed to end. Yet here I was, at the end of it all, with that horrid pressure gone and a husband who wanted to remember my face. I was grateful for that as I tugged Auden toward our chairs. I'd need that strength for what was to come.

"If you are to be cast out, stand."

They stood in silence, Leo and Vi among them. I wondered vaguely if the two had talked, if Vi had told Leo that he wasn't about to die. A few of the others were crying, but most stood still as stone. They had surely expected this, had prepared themselves beforehand.

"You are hereby marked as Flawed and will be immediately cast out to a separate location. There, you will have the opportunity to remake yourself into a successful member of society. You may take a brief moment to say your goodbyes, then proceed into a single-file line in front of the stage."

Some simply proceeded forward to the stage, either with no one to say goodbye to or with nothing left to say. Leo, guards guiding him, made his way to where his siblings stood. A wetness gathered in my eyes as I watched Eden—small, sweet, shy Eden, who had taken so long to approach even me—throw herself at the guard who held Leo's arm in his grasp. Tears streamed down her face, a different sort of tears than I had seen her cry. These were angry tears, frustrated tears. Desperate tears. She was yelling something, grabbing at the restraints on Leo's hands. I realized suddenly that he could hardly move his arms, and certainly couldn't move to hug her. She attempted to wriggle under the restraints and into his arms to no avail, and she emerged more frustrated than before. Leo seemed to be reassuring her, a forced sort of smile upon his face as he bent down to her level.

"Take off the restraints," I said softly. "They need to take them off."

Auden looked at me strangely. "What?" I didn't respond, staring as if in a trance. He waved a hand in front of my face. "Willow? Hello?"

I snapped back to myself, wiping away the stray tear that formed in the corner of my eye. "They can't even hug their families. We need to remove them."

Auden's eyes were soft, but his jaw clenched slightly. "You know we can't do that." His tone was soft, but there was a sharp finality to the words. "The people are already riled up. Do that, and there will be a riot."

I bit my lip. Once again, he was right—and once again, I hated it. I watched Eden for a few moments more.

"Do it anyways," I blurted out at last, unable to watch any longer. "We'll deal with the aftermath."

He looked at me a moment longer, and I hated the pity I saw there. "No."

"What do you mean, no?" I hissed. "They just want to say goodbye, for goodness's sake! They're not going to hurt anyone."

Auden placed his hand on mine, but I snatched it away immediately. "You're emotional right now," he said carefully, "and that's understandable. But I've been trusted with the responsibility to take care of Atvas, and I can't do that if I'm giving in to every emotional whim. Just... look away."

I shook my head, gaze transfixed as Oakley pulled Eden away at last. I watched as she cried, and the twins' faces twisted in pain, and Leo gave Oakley a look so heavy that I thought I might never breathe again. It was the look of one's burden being passed to another, the transference of something precious.

"It's all you now," he seemed to say. *"Take care of them."*

Suddenly it was too much to handle, and I looked away.

"It'll get easier," Auden said softly, and I wondered vaguely how he could possibly know that. I didn't dare to push it. It wasn't often that

Auden took a stand like this, but when he did... there would be no changing his mind.

So I just nodded, opting to look at my feet until the cast out lined up in front of the stage. They moved slowly down the line, climbing onto the transport that would take them Beyond. I had been to every ceremony since I was eight, and this was always my least favorite part. The whole process seemed awfully slow to me, and a solemn mood rested over the crowd. No one, it seemed, liked to say goodbye.

I spotted Vi near the back of the line, meeting her eyes as she passed me. Staring at each other, eyes burning, I tried to convey everything I should have said in person: *"You're the best friend I've ever had, and I'll miss you as long as I live."*

Her eyes were vibrant, too, a sense of desperation there, and I wondered what thoughts she was trying to send my way. There was a sense of caution, as if she meant to say, *"Be careful."* The thought was absurd; if anything, I should've been saying that to her.

Only one person remained at the end of that line as they moved past, one more familiar face to say goodbye to. I wished it didn't hurt so much when he met my gaze, gray eyes shining with pain.

"Willow!" Leo called, and I hated the way my heart clenched at the sound of his voice. It was so familiar, so comforting—and yet, it had been that same voice that suggested my parents be murdered, the same warm hands bound behind his back that had taken their lives. "Don't forget!"

My mind flashed back to that beautiful day eight years ago, when I had stood on this same stage and watched a woman be dragged to her death—although it's not as if I had known that at the ripe age of ten. Yet still, an eerie feeling came over me, as if I were being haunted by that moment. *"Remember me,"* she'd said—no, she'd *screamed* it, writhing in panic and pain. Leo wasn't screaming, though. He was downright calm as he walked, the storm in his eyes the only sign of his withering composure. Someone must have told him our plan, that he was not going to die. Either that, or he trusted me enough to keep him alive. I hoped it was the first, considering the way the latter made my chest twist.

"Willow!" Leo repeated, as if urging me on with his voice.

I lost sight of him as Auden appeared before me, the clenched stance of his jaw cutting off Leo's burning stare. "It's okay," Auden soothed, gripping my face between his palms. "We'll get him out of here. Just focus on my face."

It was a welcome break, a pleasant pause from both Leo and the eyes of the crowd. Murmuring had spread amongst them, their stares both judging and pitiful. I nodded slowly, staring resolutely at Auden's blue eyes as a scuffle sounded.

"Willow!" Leo said once more, and it took all of my willpower not to find him once more. The sound of his voice was practically magnetic, drawing me into his web of delusions as surely as he had drawn me into his arms. "You *know* who you are, Willow!"

I couldn't help but turn my head at that, giving into temptation at last. I wished I could say he glared, or spat, or even begged; it would have made all this easier somehow. Instead he just stared into my soul, that damned gaze that always seemed to see through every layer.

"Don't forget," he said, and his voice carried despite his soft tone. "Don't let them make you forget."

I wondered if he wished someone had told him the same, wondered if he realized how much the Defiant had made him forget who he was. I had no doubt that Leo was an innocent soul, corrupted by years of unrest and hardened influences.

"Remember," Leo repeated as the guards barked out an order to move, nudging him forward. His voice grew more frantic—not panicked screeches, but rather the hurry of one who knows time is almost up. "Remember yourself. Remember what I told you."

The guards pushed him the final step towards the transport, a long train-like vehicle that would take them to the ships. Leo stumbled up the steps, gripping the side of the door as if he could stop it from closing.

"Remember *me.*"

The words sent cold shivers down my spine. Leo knew what he was saying, knew exactly what emotions it would elicit. I swallowed down the uncertainty, the regret. It was just another manipulation, another move in the game.

A salty tear fell down my face as the transport drove away. I didn't wipe it away, didn't try to hide it. It wasn't as if anyone was watching me now, anyway. The attention was, and would always be, on Auden. People fawned over Auden as the ceremony ended, surrounding him in the way they used to surround me as we descended the stairs. A few people offer me a halfhearted congratulations, or perhaps a nod in my direction, but not much more.

"Just like her mother," I heard someone whisper as we passed, an unidentifiable voice, and my cheeks heated. I wished once more to scream, to yell that I had given it away, but I restrained myself. Discounting Auden's credibility could topple our entire political structure. It was certainly fragile enough to fall right now, balancing on a careful edge between unstable and nonexistent. So, I smiled, and nodded, and waved to small children, until we got back to the car. I collapsed into my seat almost instantly, too worn out to even marvel at the wonders of traveling by car. Auden didn't speak, head laid back on the seat as if he were contemplating a great deal of things. Surely, there were many things for a Sovereign to consider; I wouldn't know.

***

When we arrived at the manor we separated almost immediately, both lost in our thoughts. Where Auden went, I didn't know or care. I wandered to my bedroom aimlessly, in a sort of trance. For all my life, all of the planning between my mother and I, it always ended here. We never talked about the after, the future beyond the Pathway. For the first time in my life, I felt utterly unprepared. I lay on my bed, staring at the ceiling above as if it held all the answers.

Risa arrived sometime later, appearing above my vision. "Willow?" Her voice was timid, cautious. "Are you alright?"

"Fine," I sighed, pulling myself upright. "Just unsure of what to do now."

Risa smiled. "Well, you could start with getting ready for the ball."

She yanked open my closet doors, and I shot to my feet. I'd completely forgotten about the Coronation Ball—which was ironic, considering I'd been dreaming about it for years. It only occurred on Coronation years, so this was to be the first since my father's. My mother had planned this year's event months ago.

"Come on, just tell me one thing," I'd begged.

My mother shot me that look of hers—the one that clearly suggested I mind my own business. I crossed my arms. "Just one hint, and I'll leave you alone. I promise."

"Alright, here's something," she said, smiling tightly. "It's for the Coronation."

I groaned, flopping into the lounge chair beside the desk. It was one of those days I'd come to cherish, where I would see for a moment the woman my mother once was.

"How am I supposed to daydream about it if I don't know anything about it?" I whined, every bit the spoiled child I was later accused of being.

My mother glanced at me, amusement shining through her eyes, and for a moment I thought she might laugh. "Daydream too much, and you won't be invited at all."

I rolled my eyes. The idea was ridiculous. I likely wouldn't even know anyone who was cast out, much less face that future myself.

"Go do your schoolwork," my mother said at last, voice fading back to the commanding monotone I knew so well. "You'll see the ball when it comes."

My eyes teared up at the memory. The Coronation Ball—the last hurrah of my mother, ever the fastidious planner. Risa smiled softly, but didn't comment on the wetness of my eyes. Instead, she pulled a gown I'd never seen before from my closet.

"I asked the seamstress to make this for you," she said softly, "just in case you were too busy to be thinking about dresses."

"Thank you," I whispered, lost in awe as I looked it over, again and again. It was better than beautiful—it was the most incredible dress I had ever seen.

"Well, put it on then!" Her voice was enthusiastic, and I complied immediately. She styled my hair quickly and touched up my makeup slightly before pulling me in front of my mirror.

I stared at myself, emotions flooding through me. When I looked in the mirror, I didn't see a Pathway participant, or a Sovereign's wife, or even perfection; I saw a princess.

A princess, just like Leo always said.

I shook the thought from my head.

A princess, just like in the stories my mother once told me. I would've liked to think she'd be proud of me, but if I were honest with myself,

I knew she wouldn't be—not when I'd given up everything she ever worked for on a mere whim. Still, even she would have had to admit I looked lovely. The dress was simply exquisite, with a bodice of emerald flowers twisting into skirts of forest-green tulle that draped off my figure like the bloom of an upside-down flower. The sleeves began just below the shoulder, a transparent mesh with flowers of gems winding around them. My hair was left in loose curls, only a portion drawn into intricate braids on either side, coming to rest in a bun-like structure on the back of my head. Upon investigation, I realized that it was in the shape of a flower, made by pulling and pinning parts of my hair.

"It's..." My voice trailed off, and I realized I didn't have the words. "Perfect" didn't seem good enough for the beauty of this moment that Risa had given me.

She just smiled and pushed one final pin into my hair, patting my shoulder. "All good to go," she declared, checking the clock upon my wall.

"Thank you." I smiled, gripping her hands tight in my own.

"I'll be here all night," she smiled in reply. "Just to make sure everything goes alright."

I thought about declining the offer. After all, what could possibly go wrong? But a lingering sense of foreboding stopped me short. Despite being in my own home, I felt like I was in a strange forest, surrounded by vultures.

"Thank you," I said instead.

"No problem, dear." Her voice was almost motherly. "You just give me a shout if anything goes awry, alright?"

"I will," I told her, rolling my eyes at her fussing. Then, more seriously, "I.. I really appreciate it. It's nice to know someone has my back."

Risa gave me a sad smile, squeezing my shoulder reassuringly. "Well, the only thing I'm going to do with your back right now is push it," she responded, doing just that as she urged me into the hallway, "because you're going to be late for your big entrance."

"Alright, alright," I laughed. "I'm going."

I made my way to the stairwell, unsure where to find Auden. We were to enter together, to make our official entrance into society as Sovereign and wife. I moved down the hall as rapidly as I could, glancing at each clock I could find along the way. Risa was right: soon enough, we would be late to our entrance, and what a great reputation *that* would give us. Cursing, I removed my heels to move more swiftly. It was quite unlike Auden to be late for anything, much less something this important.

I heard voices as I passed my father's study, and I skidded to an abrupt stop. Unable to help myself, I pressed my ear to a familiar spot of mahogany—my typical eavesdropping strategy. If I thought I felt juvenile the last time I'd done this, it was nothing compared to now. In a gown, heels in my hand, I was a full adult playing a child's game. Yet I couldn't pull away—especially not when I heard the deep timbre of Auden's voice.

"...the Defiant?" he rumbled, voice far more serious than I would have expected. I frowned. A discussion about the Defiant, held without me there?

"No update," a voice replied apologetically. I didn't recognize it, but the deep tone suggested it was male.

"But they're staying quiet?" Auden asked.

I pressed closer to the door, my casual intrigue growing into concern. This seemed like a serious Atvasian matter, and yet I was excluded. But Auden had promised we would rule together...

"Not exactly, sir." There was a moment of silence, as if the owner of the voice was wincing. "It's all been very secretive, but rumors are spreading."

A beat of silence. "And what are the rumors saying?"

"That the Defiant didn't do it," the voice answered slowly. "That it was an... inside job."

There was silence for a moment, before a loud bang erupted. It was the sound of a palm hitting a table, frustration oozing from the noise. Auden cursed, voice losing all semblance of composure as desperation leaked through.

I flinched automatically at the eruption, mind whirring furiously. I'd never heard Auden so frazzled, not in the Pathway and not in the long days since. For him to be so upset about a stupid rumor was odd, to say the least. Of course the Defiant would deny their involvement in the massacre, would absolve themselves of guilt.

"It seems that the Defiant, wherever they are, took the painted slogan as a sign to speak up," the other voice added, growing judgmental.

"It was a necessary risk," Auden gritted out.

"Just like the first trial, right?" the voice retorted bitterly. "Would have thought you could win the Pathway without cheating, for all the bragging your father did about your skills."

No. It was Emmaline who had cheated at the first trial. It had to have been, because she was so smug and annoying about it. It couldn't have been... It was almost too absurd to think. Auden had won, fair and square. He'd handed me my sword, for goodness sake.

"Now we're even." The memory of his words sent a cold drip of dread down my spine.

How could I be so foolish? Emmaline wasn't the type to hide her schemes. If she had cheated, she would have admitted it, if only for the satisfaction of seeing my face. Besides, wasn't it Auden who'd discouraged reporting the cheating? Wasn't it Auden who had made me feel bad for listening to Leo?

I shoved my panic down, forcing myself to tune back into the conversation. I was beginning to get the sense that missing anything said in that room would be detrimental.

"That's none of your business," Auden was replying sharply. His voice was so very cold, callous in a way that reminded me distinctly of Ruben, but I could sense the underlying pain. The pain, and the guilt. More than anything else, it was that wretched guilt that confirmed the thoughts swirling in my head.

The voice let out a scoffing laugh. "Isn't it? You took a dumb risk with that slogan, and it may very well doom us all. My men are crippled with guilt, and they're afraid. They fear that they have bet on the wrong horse."

Doom them all for what? What piece of the puzzle was I missing?

"Do you speak on behalf of your men, or merely yourself?" Auden cut in. "Wrong horse or not, there's no turning back now. You did only what was ordered of you, and you will continue to do so as the crest on your chest demands."

The man (who I could only assume was a guard) paused for a moment, before emitting a soft, "yes, sir."

"Remind your men of that," Auden added, voice a bit softer. "I gave the order, and they followed it. Any guilt they may feel is entirely unnecessary."

The voice remained silent for several moments before answering. "Necessary or not, the weight of blood is heavy. My men are burdened by it."

"The blood is on my hands. Not theirs, and not yours."

"I could see how you'd think that, sir," the guard answered solemnly, "but you're not the one who shot the crossbow."

No, no, no, no, no...

My mind scrambled desperately, trying to find any explanation, any way around what was growing increasingly clear. My gut clenched violently as I came up empty, no other explanations possible.

The guard and his men shot the crossbows. The guard and his men killed my parents and the rest of the Council. The guard and his men were instructed to do so by Auden.

Pure, undiluted desperation was the only thing that kept my ear glued to the door as shock set into my body, invading my nerves one by one until nothing but a disconcerting numbness remained. Surely there was more to the story, a final puzzle piece that would reveal what a huge misunderstanding this all was.

"... she doesn't know anything," Auden rumbled, voice growing fainter. He must have moved further from the door, leaving his words almost inaudible. It left only a confusing jumble of words to decipher. "And as long as she still...need to keep it that way. She can't handle it, trust me. Perhaps eventually she'll see... once things have settled down."

"Sir, she's your wife. Don't you think she'll realize that..."

I pressed my body even further into the door, hoping desperately that it wouldn't creak open.

"...very hard to hide," the guard finished.

"Indeed," Auden answered grimly, voice suddenly *very* close to the door. "Luckily, I'm a superb liar." He paused briefly. "That's taken care of as well, then?"

"Yes, sir." The voice was closer as well, clear yet more grim. "Just as ordered."

Then, I fled. I ran as fast as I could, as fast as the bile that raced up my throat. Despite the excuses I wished to make, I wasn't stupid. I knew exactly what I had just heard in that room, but... how could it be? I ran without looking back and without stopping, safety the first thought on my mind. Without thinking, I ran to Risa, the only person I had left in Atvas.

I collapsed on the floor of my room, shaking, and she jumped up.

"Willow, are you—"

"Lock the door!" I rasped. Risa moved to do just that, staring at me as if I were a mad woman. Perhaps I was. Perhaps this was all a hallucination, a bad dream from which I would wake. Because if not, if this was reality...

"Willow, what's wrong?"

I vaguely heard the question, as if Risa were a million worlds away. It was as if I were in a different dimension, watching the pieces of a complex puzzle fall into place. Only, the image formed didn't even make *sense*. Why would Auden, of all people, want the Council dead? He'd killed his own father, not to mention my mother. He'd always loved my mother, sometimes even more than I did. He always joked that she was his second mother, perhaps because his own generally neglected him. Yet he murdered them all, and for what? There was no benefit of the massacre for him, nothing besides...

Oh. Oh, it was my fault.

I let out a sharp breath at the realization, somewhere between a gasp and a sob. It was all so clear then, a hundred warning signs leading to the edge of a cliff. When I first started working with Leo, that day in the woods, his horror when I told him that I was planning to run away... *"I can't do it without you."*

Perhaps it was insane to even consider that he would commit such horrendous acts for me, for a friendship based on lies and a future clouded with betrayal. But despite it all, despite my inability to predict this disaster, I *did* know Auden. I knew that he was kind to most everyone, but truly cared for very few. I knew that when he did care for someone, he was almost too loyal. I knew he was incredibly protective, to the point where it could be stifling. I knew his father raised him in a world of extremity, praising brutality over sympathy and indifference over vulnerability. I'd always known these toxins existed in his life, but I'd never thought to consider the dangerous concoction they would create. I hadn't noticed as they mingled together, burying the kind child he'd been beneath mountains of pain and fear and delusion. Auden had been spiraling, for perhaps longer than I could imagine—and there was nowhere left to go but down.

Now, it was too late. All I could do was shrivel up on the floor and hope the antidote would arrive before the poison withered my soul to nothing.

"Willow?" Risa prodded again, gentle yet insistent. "I need you to tell me what's wrong."

How could I explain that Auden was a walking paradox? He cheated his way into taking the Sovereignty with hardly a care for me, and yet he killed half a dozen people so that I wouldn't leave. In a way, he was little more than a spoiled child who wanted to play with two toys at the same time. And, like a spoiled child, he'd gotten his way.

If it wasn't so unbearably abhorrent, I might have been impressed.

"Is this about the boy?" Risa pressed, crouching down beside me. She placed a gentle hand on mine. "Leo?"

The name sent a wave of agony through me. Because if Auden killed them, then Leo... he was innocent. But hadn't he confessed? Hadn't he been holding the crossbow, found by the rafters?

I wracked my brain, desperately attempting to recall Leo's confession—only to realize that he'd never confessed at all. He'd apologized profusely, but he *had* lied to me about the raid being canceled. Perhaps he was merely confessing that. I didn't get to ask specifics, because he'd been taken away by a guard. A guard who very well could have been under Auden's control. Besides... Auden had been there at the meeting when Leo said he would take a crossbow. It couldn't have been a coincidence that a crossbow, of all things, was used for the murders.

Leo was framed.

"No," I croaked out. Risa had begun to panic, and the last thing I wanted was for her to call a medic and open that door. "It's not... Leo's innocent."

Risa frowned. "I thought he was cast out."

"He was," I whispered, heart clenching painfully. "He was. But I'll get him back."

How I'd explain that to Auden, I couldn't be sure. All I knew was that I had to find him. For as long as Leo was alive, alive and *innocent*, there was still hope. He was out there somewhere right at this moment, probably struggling to make do with meager supplies. I realized with a heavy heart that I'd never bothered to check over the plans for the Beyond. Who knew where they were sent, or if they had enough food.

Ever so slowly, a snake of unease began to slither in my stomach. Because there was one part of the conversation I overheard that I had yet to consider, partly because I could hardly hear it. But what I had heard...

"... she doesn't know anything."

"She can't handle it, trust me."

"...very hard to hide."

For all I knew, it could all be a reference to the truth behind the Council murders. Yet the last words that Auden had said... *"That's taken care of as well, then?"*

"No," I whispered aloud, the word swallowed by a harsh sob. I must have started crying at some point, because drops of salty pain assaulted my tongue as I wailed.

There was no proof. Nothing blatant enough to confirm my suspicions. But I *knew*.

When I was a child, old enough to read Intellect books but naïve enough to see good in everything, I was obsessed with animals. Cows, birds, fish, insects—I loved them all. Only, there weren't very many animals left in the world. Those that remained were kept on farms in the Service district, and my father refused to bring me to see them. But one day, as I sat in the gardens, I saw a rare ladybug. It was bright and beautiful, and I was intent on keeping it forever. I ran to fetch my mother, hoping she would help me capture it as a pet, but by the time I returned to the spot, the ladybug had disappeared. I sobbed for hours, in full mourning despite my mother's insistence that it probably just crawled somewhere else. But somehow, deep in my gut, I *knew* it was dead. Sure enough, I found its corpse curled under a bench the following day.

"He's dead," I gasped. "They're all dead."

I only caught a glimpse of Risa's shocked face before I threw up.

28

— · —

HAPPILY EVER AFTER

Auden Bonavich was a monster. It was the only explanation, the only conclusion possible for his transgressions. To deceive me in order to take the Sovereignty was one thing—a competitor's move, however hurtful it may have been. Murdering the Council was entirely despicable, in more ways than once. Yet somehow, this was worse.

Perhaps it was because the Flawed murders were the whole reason this mess had started in the first place, the very thing we were fighting to stop. Even worse, it was what my mother had devoted her life to fix. And though the Council massacre was a horrendous event that never should have happened, the one good thing that resulted was the opportunity to change things. To do better than those that came before us, to escape the curse placed on Atvas by Sovereign Coldwell so many years ago. Yet Auden had taken that and cast it aside, like it was nothing.

It was a stabbing betrayal that ached deep down, tearing into that vulnerable part of my heart that still believed in the good of the world and leaving it in tatters. But for all it hurt, it was the only tragedy for which I didn't need to question his motivations. Auden had told me them himself, only days ago.

"Sovereign Coldwell started the murders because it was easier than dealing with an actual population existing beyond Atvas," he'd said. *"But what if we took the harder path?"*

I should have known. Auden never took the harder path, not if he could avoid it. Efficient, sly Auden would never even consider the scenic route if a dark tunnel could take him where he wanted to go faster. Besides, I knew he wanted Leo gone. He'd said it himself: *"That's why he has to go."*

"I hate him." The words were dark, anger sharpening the edges of my melancholic tone even as I continued to sob. "I-I hate him so much."

I'd felt many things for Auden Bonavich throughout the years. Annoyance, appreciation, anger, care, even love. But not hate. Never hate. Yet now it burned within me, the warm fire in my chest morphed into a scalding flame that burned, burned, burned with no regard for my heart. I hated him for the things he did, and I hated him for lying about all of it. I hated him for showing me a glimpse of our future, for letting me see the best parts of him while shielding the worst. But what bothered me the most was the fact that it was all so *obvious*. The signs were all there, bright as the sun in one's eyes. He made me an unwilling accomplice in his crimes, and for that I hated him the most.

Sometime while I was busy spiraling, Auden knocked on the door. Risa, surely unbearably confused, glanced at me.

I had thought I was broken that day I found out about the murder of dozens of people. When my parents were killed, I knew I was. But now... a crack had spread in my heart, the betrayal shattering my soul the way a fist shatters glass, breaking it into pieces too small to be worth anything at all. It was a different sort of pain, one so intense and so very *raw* that it felt almost numb, like running a finger under boiling water, only to find it startlingly cold.

The path before me was uncertain, a battlefield with no happy end in sight. Almost every part of me wanted nothing more than to give up, to confess what I'd learned and accept whatever consequences came. They couldn't possibly be worse than my reality, than the nightmare in which I was living. Yet deep down, buried under layers of tears and broken glass, an ember still burned. It was an ember of not love but hate, not peace but war. It was an ember of life, and I refused to let it flicker into oblivion.

I held up five fingers, and Risa nodded, closing the bathroom door behind her as she left.

"She's ill," I could hear her say. I pushed myself off the floor and over to the mirror, bracing myself against the marble of the sink as a plan began to form in my mind.

"Can I see her?" he asked. "It's already ten minutes past our entrance time."

Glancing in the mirror, I knew instantly that I'd need more time than I'd requested for this. I was a complete and utter mess. Mascara was streaked down my face, which was shiny with sweat. My hair had fallen out of its styling almost completely, and some strands were moist—from tears or vomit, I didn't know.

"She'll just need ten more minutes," Risa replied, voice allowing no room for argument.

"Risa, come on," Auden sighed. "Let me in."

So, he did remember her, then.

"Ten minutes," Risa said again. The door closed quickly after her words, and she rushed in.

"I said five minutes." My voice was hoarse, raspy from both the vomiting and the tears.

Risa just shook her head. "Any fool could see you're not going any-where in five minutes." I grimaced at that, and her face fell. "Are you alright?"

"No."

A beat of silence passed between us, and I had the sudden urge to find a hole and curl up in it for all time. Yet there was nowhere to run, nowhere to hide. The only way out was through.

"How fast can you fix this?" I asked finally, gesturing to the mess that was my face. She glanced at the wall clock behind me and cursed softly.

"Hopefully, seven minutes," she muttered, and then she was on me. In a sudden whirlwind of beauty and pain, the minutes passed in chaos. Yet by the end of the promised ten minutes, I looked nearly as good as I had the first time—if you could look past the redness of my lids and emptiness of my eyes. I wished I could say I felt better, too, but that would have been a lie. I was shaking where I stood.

"It'll have to do," she murmured, ushering me into my heels.

I forced a smile at that—the first of many forced smiles I would give tonight.

In many ways, Auden had all the power. He'd made sure of it. He controlled Atvas, which meant he controlled everything; the Court, the guards, the children. At least in his mind, he controlled me as well. He played life like a game of chess, always two steps ahead with well-con-cealed plans. But what he didn't know was that he had inadvertently shown his hand, destroying both the Council and his invincibility at once. For now I knew his weakness, knew what he would kill for—me.

As long as I played along with his imagined future, I could not only survive but also attack. Perhaps I could discover the truth about Leo and Vi, could convince him not to hunt down the Defiant, could stop the Flawed murders for good. Perhaps I could change Atvas for the better. A glimmer caught the corner of my eye at the thought, something large and gold. It was that horribly heavy necklace from the gala so many nights ago. I moved towards it as if in a dream, fastening it around my neck with hardly a second thought.

"Are you sure you want that one?" Risa asked, scrunching her nose as she took it in. "It looks rather heavy."

"Oh, yes," I said, voice shaking, "it is."

Heavy, indeed. Heavy with guilt, with the weight of the lives lost thanks to my decisions. Heavy with loss, with the emotions bottled up too deep to feel. Heavy with responsibility, with the need for revenge. It was heavy, but I would bear it—for my mother and father, and Leo, and Vi. For Eden, and Oakley, and for all the innocent Council members slaughtered that night. For all who were hurting, I would bear the weight. For the Auden I thought I knew.

For myself.

Here we go, I thought to myself. *Deep breaths.*

"Willow?" Risa called from behind me.

"Yes?"

"You're not ... in danger or anything, right?"

I almost laughed aloud. I may have been in less danger the night that swords swung past my head. "Of course not."

And then I was out the door and onto the chessboard.

Auden stood at the end of the hall, terrifyingly exquisite. He grinned as I neared, eyes examining me carefully.

"You look ... wow." He gave me that look—the same one that had convinced me to hand over our entire civilization to him. For a moment, I wanted nothing more than to go back in time and stay away from that door, wanted to pretend nothing had ever even happened. Wanted to hug him like I would have, collapse into the arms that had always felt like safety. But then he extended that eerily steady hand, not a single tremor in sight despite his actions, and the urge was gone.

There was no safety left here—not with everything I knew. There was only sadness and fear, so heavy I could barely breathe. Perhaps it was that terror that drove me, the knowledge that my husband was the most dangerous man in all of Atvas.

I smiled softly, forcing a modest blush to my cheeks, and took his outstretched hand. Suddenly I was abundantly glad for the gloves I wore, for they prevented my hand from touching the coldness of his skin.

"Wow to you, too," I said carefully, making sure to scan him up and down. "Not bad, Mr. Sovereign."

He ducked his head, bowing to kiss my gloved hand. "Are you alright?" he asked softly. "Risa said you were sick."

I smiled, ever the appreciative damsel. *No, I'm not alright. I'm not alright at all.*

"Just some nerves," I answered. "Threw up a bit." *A lot.*

He smiled softly at me, rubbing a thumb over my hand. "Don't be nervous, Lo."

His voice was so soft, so gentle compared to the violence of his actions. I wondered vaguely which version of himself was the real one—wondered if even he knew the answer.

"Just follow me, and you'll be great," he finished.

"Exactly who we've always been destined to become," he'd said this morning. As if I were always destined to be second to his greatness. Perhaps in his mind, I was. The thought was enough to fuel me, to force the next words from my mouth.

"Together?" I asked softly, gesturing towards the staircase and the awaiting crowd.

He brushed a hair out of my face, hand lingering on my cheek. I shivered despite myself, wishing on every star that this weren't the truth, that the real Auden were hiding somewhere far from here. "As we always have," he answered, just like I knew he would.

I forced myself to grin, as if this were the happiest moment of my life.

It should have been the happiest moment of my life.

"And as we always will."

"We must pity those who are unable to see the truth, for they live in a dream world."

I had lived in a dream world for too long, but no longer. I had awoken to a nightmare, a world of betrayal and terror that smiled at my pain. And though it hurt, though it took every ounce of courage I had, I smiled back. There was no escape, no way out. There was only Auden, and me, and this wretched game we had to play. And if there was anything I was sure of, it was that I had to win. If I lost, if Auden realized how much I knew... I wasn't sure I'd survive the fallout.

"Presenting Mr. and Mrs. Sovereign Bonavich, the future of Atvas!"

We descended the staircase hand in hand, a happy couple ready for their entrance into the world of beautiful deceit and perfect lies.

Just like that, we were little more than two kids playing a game of pretend,

just like we always had—

and just like we always will.

ACKNOWLEDGEMENTS

Ironically, the first thank you for this book goes to the Coronavirus pandemic, during which this story began. I am a firm believer that there are silver linings to every situation—even global pandemics. Had it not been for the monotony of quarantine, my love for writing may have never come to the forefront of my life.

More than that, though, this book belongs to my support system. To my parents, Marcia and Bob, who never for a moment made me doubt my capability. None of this would be possible without your love, generosity, and wisdom. To my lovely sisters, Alyson and Julia, who cultivated my love for reading in the first place and continue to drive my passion with love and encouragement. To Kyle and Collin, my brothers-in-law, for supporting me both in writing and life. Thank you also to my friends, the many 'Vis' of my life who never failed to pick me up after a hard day. The most difficult part of writing is the mental game, and without your constant encouragement I fear I may have lost that challenge.

These acknowledgements couldn't possibly be complete without recognizing the other side of my support team. Thank you to Robin Fuller for your meticulous copy edits, and for showing kindness to a new author. Thank you also to my fantastic beta readers: Sofia Morrison, Emilee Viduna, Lizzy Messerschmidt, Emily Fletcher, Hannah LaFary, Olivia Zetty, Emily Graham, Jenni Sanders, and Brooke Teacher. I appreciate your thoroughness, enthusiasm, and willingness to work with me as we trialed the process together. I also extend a huge thanks to Sarah Messerschmidt, my creative partner and biggest cheerleader. No matter how busy or stressed you are, you never fail to make my writing a priority; sometimes, even more than I do myself. Thank you also to Mckenzie Galbraith, Emmi Owens, Maiah Deogracias, Mary Emma Zimmerman and Quinlan Scott for helping with my launch committees. Without your quick assistance in the direst of times, this launch simply would not have been possible.

Finally, thank you to my small army of constant supporters. To name you all would be a book in itself, and for that fact I am incredibly grateful. Thank you to the Zeta Psi chapter of Kappa Delta Sorority, who instilled in me the confidence necessary to take the step of sharing my work with the world. To those from my youth who continue to encourage me today, even from states away. To all the mentors who taught me the determination, persistence, and pure stubbornness that pushed me through the days of self-doubt. Last but not least, thank *you*. A book is little more than words on paper without readers to enjoy it. I may have written this book, but it is you all who truly bring the story to life, and for that I cannot thank you enough.

ABOUT THE AUTHOR

Danielle was raised in Lithia, Florida and educated at Valparaiso University in Valparaiso, Indiana. When not writing, she enjoys studying psychology, painting, dancing, and reading. She began writing Eminence at only eighteen years of age, during the initial quarantine of the Coronavirus pandemic. Eminence was inspired by a dream she had one night, from which Danielle worked to create a story that reflected the perfectionistic tendencies she saw in the world around her.

THE STORY CONTINUES...

KEEP READING FOR A SNEAK PEEK AT IRREVERENCE, THE NEXT CHAPTER IN WILLOW'S STORY.

IRREVERENCE

THE NIGHT OF THE CORONATION CEREMONY

The day Auden Bonavich was named Sovereign was certainly one to remember. Not just for the dramatic riot at the Coronation Ceremony or the disappointing performance of Willow Aldridge in the final trial, and not even for the bloody massacre just days prior, resulting in the death of the previous Sovereign and his Council. No, the day Auden Bonavich was named Sovereign was remembered for the absolutely marvelous Coronation Ball.

The party went on late into the night, a flurry of lovely dancing and vivacious laughter. It was immaculately planned by the late Sovereign's wife, luxury and wealth and opulence rolled into one night. All eyes were on the Sovereign and his wife, both dressed impeccably. If there was anything remembered from the ball, it was that the new ruling couple was perfect. They were beauty and grace, power and prestige.

No one noted the absence of the esteemed DeLoughery family, whose daughter had been cast out despite their prestigious standings in the community. No one commented on the unease thrumming beneath the crowd, the merry partygoers that still startled at the slightest noise. No one bothered to address the obvious divide in the Court members throughout the room, some falling at the Sovereign's feet while others threw glares at his back. No one questioned the strange stiffness between the newly named Sovereign and his wife, or the confused glances he gave her in response. And if they both downed a few more glasses of wine than propriety recommended, no one remarked on it.

Who could ever notice something so trivial at a ball so grand?

It was still early when two women slipped out of the ballroom, fanning themselves and giggling giddily. Make no mistake—they were proper women, true Court darlings, but even the most rigid of women could let go on an evening like this.

"Oh, he's just as dreamy as I thought," the younger of the two sighed dazedly. At only nineteen years of age, the raven-haired woman was still adjusting to the glamorous life of the Court. "And did you see the way he smiled at me?"

The other woman, who was a year older and therefore infinitely wiser, gasped around her giggles. "Shh! He has a wife now, you know."

"Oh, I *know*," the younger complained with a sour face. "Practically attached at the hip, aren't they?"

"Always have been, but they do seem closer than ever. I hear she'd been clinging to him like a moth to flame these past weeks," the other woman mused, her face growing more serious. "But can you blame her? After the horror of that night ..."

There was a moment of mournful silence, broken only by the younger woman's ignorant disregard. She hadn't been at the ball where the previous Council had been massacred, and she was growing rather bored of everyone discussing it all of the time.

"Oh, trust me," she grinned conspiratorially, "I do *not* blame her."

The two friends collapsed into a fit of giggles, so loud and rambunctious that they didn't notice the footsteps down the hall. In fact, they didn't notice anything at all until a woman brushed past them rather rudely, not even stopping to apologize.

"Hey!" The younger yelled, emboldened by the liquid courage she'd ingested only minutes before. "Watch where you're going!"

But the intruder didn't turn around, didn't so much as slow down. If they'd bothered to pay attention, perhaps the women would have heard the gasps of her short breaths. Perhaps they would have noticed the smudges of makeup beneath her eyes, the strands falling out of her eloquent updo, the hands that tore viciously at the heavy necklace around her neck. Perhaps, if they took even a moment to consider it, they would have realized that it was Willow Aldridge, wife to the Sovereign, who stormed past them in a fit of bereaved grief.

As it was, the women did nothing of the sort. They merely rolled their eyes, comforted each other, and slipped back to the party with hardly a second thought. Yet, they did notice as the Sovereign slipped past them, exiting the way they had just come and looking very confused.

"Why, that must have been the new Mrs. Bonavich who passed us so briskly," the older woman wondered. "Wonder what that's all about."

The younger smirked. "Maybe they're not as inseparable as you thought, and they've had an argument."

"Or," the older woman mused with far more empathy, "she's merely still upset about her parents' deaths."

"Hardly! His father died, too, you know," the jealous woman pointed out. "I bet she's throwing a fit because he beat her. I hear her mother did the same, when she lost."

"Yes, I suppose you're right," the older agreed reluctantly. "That must be it."

But they could not ignore the glassy tint in his eyes when he returned several minutes later, looking rather flustered. Even as he spoke, giving the expected address to the crowd, the Sovereign's hands shook just slightly behind his back.

Meanwhile, out the doors and up several sets of stairs, the Sovereign's wife lay huddled on the floor of a bedroom. It was a well-decorated room, but any illusion of beauty was tainted by the state of its contents. The sheets hung off the bed as if ripped, a priceless painting laid chipped on the floor, and the glossy wood flooring glittered with shards of glass that floated in puddles of spilled water. It was in the middle of this that she sat—as if she herself was the storm, and the calm had come at last. All that remained was the slow trickling of tears and a gentle breeze of despair, mingling with the destruction to create a distinct sense of hopelessness.

But she didn't seem to mind the devastation; in fact, she hardly seemed to notice it. The young woman's eyes were elsewhere as she tremored on the floor, hands clenched tightly around the wilted remnants of a purple flower. There was no one else in the room with her, but still she spoke.

"I'm trapped," she gasped around quick breaths. "There's no way out."

It wasn't true, of course; there were several exits to the room, a doorway and windows and even a balcony. But this was no ordinary woman, and for her no ordinary exit to do.

For Willow Aldridge, there really was no way out.